BY MICAIAH JOHNSON

Those Beyond the Wall
The Space Between Worlds

THOSE BEYOND THE WALL

THOSE BEYOND THE WALL

MICAIAH JOHNSON

NEW YORK

Those Beyond the Wall is a work of fiction.
Names, places, characters, and incidents either are
the product of the author's imagination or are used fictitiously.
Any resemblance to actual persons, living or dead, events,
or locales is entirely coincidental.

Published in the United States by Del Rey,
an imprint of Random House, a division of
Penguin Random House LLC, New York.

DEL REY and the HOUSE colophon are registered trademarks of
Penguin Random House LLC.

ISBN 978-0-593-49750-0
Ebook ISBN 978-0-593-49751-7

Printed in the United States of America on acid-free paper

randomhousebooks.com

2 4 6 8 9 7 5 3 1

First Edition

Title and part-title page art: ©kichigin19-stock.adobe.com (texture)

Book design by Edwin A. Vazquez

To the flawed but brave, ephemeral but essential,
passionate but irrational freedom fighters of
The People's Plaza at Ida B. Wells Plaza

June 12, 2020–August 13, 2020

And to anyone who has stood against injustice
in the face of an opponent larger and more powerful
than themselves, whether it be in Nashville, Cop City, Iran,
or your stepfather's living room.

AUTHOR'S NOTE FROM MICAIAH JOHNSON

When my agent (the incredible Cameron McClure at Donald Maass, without whom you wouldn't be reading these words) read the first draft of this manuscript, she said—accurately—"I didn't realize how angry you were."

Yes, this novel was largely conceived during the sixty-two-day sit-in at Nashville's Tennessee State Capitol. And yes, this protest produced hundreds of arrests under frivolous charges that dissolved shortly thereafter, and far more instances of brutalization, which proved harder to erase and linger with many of us still. If any faith in institutional justice remained in me—after living in America as a Black person with the misfortune to both study, and live through, historical moments of spectacular racialized violence—my time at The People's Plaza would have killed it.

So if you also sense an undercurrent of rage in this novel, you are not wrong. But it is not bitterness. Bitterness is anger with nowhere to go. Bitterness and resignation are close and tempting cousins. Anger with a target is Rage, and Rage is sister to Hope alone. We rage because we do believe things can be better, by fire if necessary.

Science fiction is an expression born from dissatisfaction with where the world is versus where the world could be. The same is true for protest. Science fiction is fueled by dreams of a different, but possible, future. The same is true for Rage. While bitterness is an isolator, a repellent to community, Rage is a beacon calling out to others. It is as much a communal invitation as any bonfire.

Come join me, Rage says, *at this spark that is lit by the distance between what the world is, and what we could make it.*

If you read this novel, which is like but also very unlike my own experience, and feel that fiery undercurrent, please know it for the call it is.

The night is long and dark, Rage says, *but I will keep us warm.*

PART ONE

i did not come to preach of peace
for that's not the hunted's duty.

—Danez Smith

CHAPTER ONE

THEY CALL ME MR. SCALES BECAUSE I'M A SNAKE.

Or because I'm real balanced.

Or because my father lent metal.

Depends who you ask, and they're mostly wrong. Doesn't matter. Wrong and right are moods in Ash. Not values. We tell one another stories we know aren't true, and we're glad to hear them as long as they stretch. No one cares if the endings are happy; we only care that they eat up time.

I like hearing stories. I'm not great at telling them, and I don't like doing things I'm not good at, but I don't have a choice. Too many of the other tellers are dead, and they're waiting for me to say their part.

We don't like witnesses in Ashtown, but I guess that's what I am now.

—

WHEN IT HAPPENED I WAS ON DROP-OFF. I WAS NOT SUPPOSED TO BE ON DROP-OFF. I'M THE MECHANIC. I fix things. I'm supposed to work back at the row downtown unless I get bored enough to beg Mr. Silk for a week's alt duty. But Mr. Cheeks'd been flaking, and he's covered my ass before, so I was covering his by doing his drop-off. You don't need to know any of this to understand what happened next, but I told you—I'm bad at stories.

Exlee was waiting for me when I came in. Exlee is always waiting for me, or maybe their face just looks that way because it's the face they wear to greet clients. I don't mind if it's just for show or just for me. It looks like they're happy to see me, like their life is brighter because I've walked through the House's door, and that's all I need.

"Hey, Pretty Girl."

No one is more careful about gender than the proprietor. Exlee doesn't even strictly believe girls and boys exist separately, but they still call me *Pretty Girl* because I like being called a girl as much as I like being covered in grime from other runners' rides. *Girl,* I don't mind. *Pretty*'s a lie, but even a lie sounds good coming out in Exlee's silk-smoke voice.

"Hey, Boss."

I call Exlee *Boss* because I used to, and because they're the only person in the wastes the emperor won't get salty at if he finds out.

I slid the package along the bar, deliberately stopping it just shy of Exlee's grasp because I wanted to steal the simple pleasure of watching those long, gold-dusted fingers tipped with glittering nails reach for its edge like the uncurling legs of a glamorous spider. They tucked the package behind their fan so delicately it was like someone tucking away a love letter from an admirer, or a raptor tucking away a chick. It looked like anything but a drop-off. I'm not sure what's in the brown bundle, but it comes from the emperor and goes to the House so we runners are all sure it's payment. What the two most powerful people in the wastes could consider valuable enough to trade's a mystery to me, but I don't really think in terms of value. I like to watch pretty things move. I like to make broken things fixed. I'm simple.

I remember that Helene X was dancing on the femme stage. We've been friends since even before I used to dance in the slot right before hers, so on my way out I stopped to watch her because I always do and always have. I always would have, too, if the world hadn't forgotten itself right then.

Helene's Wiley City all over—true pale, not that chalk-wash new providers use—with golden hair. That's the part I want to tell you. I want to tell you how she looked golden right before, twirling with her back too straight to have ever really been from here. I want to tell you how her eyes and mouth were that almost-but-not-quite-shut she'd perfected, an invitation the way a half-closed door can make you want to come inside more than one flung wide open. I wish I could describe the way her skin was pale but didn't look like a corpse.

Until it did.

It began at her neck. The tight ridge of it pulsing, at first strange enough to be erotic and then too much to be anything but grotesque. By the time the bones at the back of her neck had pushed through the skin of the front it was too late for her to scream, though her mouth made the shape. Her eyes were wide open by then, too. The front of her torso cracked in, then back out like her ribs were wings pushing through the wrong side. Finally, the bones broke through her chest cavity like something being born, the accompanying blood an arc of spray that painted the crowd.

The hot splatter hitting their skin gave them permission to panic. Everyone screamed. Everyone ran. I walked toward her. I don't know why. I fix things, I guess. It's what I do. I climbed onto the stage I'd last stepped foot on over a decade ago and gathered her fracturing torso into my lap. I held her together. She insisted on breaking apart. I held her harder. But then I was just breaking her too. Sometimes when you want to fix something too bad, you break it. The way you can shatter metal if you get it too hot, even if all you're trying to do is mend a crack. This was something I should already have known.

In the end, I don't know if I held her together more than I tore her apart, but I know that's how they found me: like a real runner, bloodied up and still trying.

"MR. SCALES, REPORT."

I've been cradling a glass of fuck-yourself-up juice from Exlee's secret stash since they pulled me away. The House calls it tar—it isn't, but it's thick as gum paste and it numbs your whole mouth on its way to numb everything else, so it might as well be—and I'm wondering where I can find a vat of it to dive into when the voice comes again.

"Back from the edge, Scales," he says, this time a whisper that comes with a hand squeezing my wrist.

I look up at my commanding officer.

"Huh?"

"I said report," Mr. Cheeks says.

We both know he didn't, but there're two other leathers checking out the scene and it wouldn't do to act too casual.

"Yes, sir." I slide the glass away. "Body looks like it's been lead-piped from every direction, but there's no assailant. Everyone saw the kill. No one saw a killer."

He nods, flexing the sea of tattoos he calls a neck, the only bare spots his pretty face and the column of his throat—left deliberately empty in case he ever considers being a colossal moron and falling in love. Usually I spend too long staring at that three-inch strip of uninked brown, but not tonight. Tonight his Adam's apple is too prominent to remind me of anything but Helene X's bones coming from the back to break out the front.

The two runners move out of earshot, and Cheeks leans in.

"You gonna puke?"

"You gonna fuck off?"

He holds up his palms—also tattooed, though they fade so fast the design changes from year to year. "Wouldn't blame you. It's a bad one, and you knew her better than the rest of us."

"I'm solid," I say, and it's not just talk.

I went through all the corpse exposure training the emperor could throw at me when I joined, and that was back when I was still a teenager in boot camp with lieutenants who assumed I'd never seen a dead body. Before I'd been pulled away, I'd forced myself to stare at what was left of Helene X. I took in the damage; not just what I'd seen happen, but what I'd missed. While I'd been trying to force her ribs back together like she was an oil pan that'd bottomed out in the off-roads, the tremors had continued down, shattering her hips, inverting her legs. I stared long and hard, trying to fit the pieces back where they were supposed to go, trying to find a pattern in the damage. And there is a pattern. I can't quite see it, but I know it's there. This can't just be chaos.

Cheeks lets out one of his long-suffering sighs. "I'm sorry about this. You were covering for me, if I'd . . ."

"No sweat. You couldn't have known. No one could have." The smile I force hurts, but I'm desperate to ease his guilt. "You can make it up to me Wednesday."

"Wednesday?"

I fake an appalled face. "Full moon? Midnight buggying? I outride you? You weep at your lack of skill?"

"Not how I remember it."

"That's all right. Denial is a fine coping mechanism."

"We'll see," he says, straightening back into *superior officer formality* as another runner approaches.

I can tell from my periphery who it is. Too tall and pale to be anyone else. Fucking Cross. Upside is, Cross walking in means I've got an acceptable target for all my impotent rage. I don't telegraph, but because he knows me as well as anyone ever will, Cheeks says, "Play nice, Scales," before I can even open my mouth.

It wasn't an order though. His mistake.

I'm still making eye contact with him when I shout, "Who let Ruralite trash into the House?"

Instead of stepping up to me, Mr. Cross lowers his eyes. He remembers, at least this time, that I outrank him. Anybody with a tattoo higher than his is allowed to haze him for life. He's smart, and mechanics can't get higher than major, so he'll make officer and pass me soon enough. But until then I have a collarbone star and he's still filling in his arms, so I get to make his life dogshit at every available opportunity.

"He's escorting the body to Viet's once the preparers get here," Mr. Cheeks says.

He's protective of the holy runner in a way I don't like. The way he used to only be protective of me.

"Sending the holy son to the deathkeeper? Aren't they competition?" I say.

"I'm not holy," Mr. Cross says.

"Did someone fucking ask you?"

He doesn't respond, which is the only right response.

I'm not holy. It's all he ever says when I come at him. Always with his voice and head low, not like a kicked puppy, but like an animal on a leash. Waiting. He says, *I'm not holy,* but he doesn't say *anymore*. He calls himself a sinner like it's always been true. As far as I'm concerned, it has. Runners wear an honest leather 'cause we know we're going to get dirty. Cross comes from the hyper-religious Rurals, where they wrap themselves in self-righteousness and call it purity. Out in the Rurals they pretend even aprons are just for show.

I want to go back to the row. I want to work on something I know how to fix and take the longest shower of my whole damn life. But I know how Helene felt about Ruralites, and I don't want him carrying her home.

"I'll escort. We don't need you," I say.

"You can't," Mr. Cheeks says. "You have orders."

"*Bah* orders. I'm not even on tonight."

Mr. Cheeks dismisses Cross with a nod, which means he knows how messy this is about to get and doesn't want me setting a bad example.

"You're being ordered back to the palace. I'll drive you."

"Why the fuck wouldn't I drive myself?"

"Because, *as you know,* it's protocol to be escorted after witnessing a traumatic event involving a loved one or relative."

"You saying I don't know procedure now?"

He looks a little sorry, but not enough to matter.

"Cross will bring your ride back to the row. Now's not the time."

"You're goddamn right it's not."

"Be. A. Good. Runner," he says, quietly, begging. It's in that stilted desperation that I finally understand: He's trying to protect me.

I used to be able to read him like the tracks of a fat snake, but he's been drifting from me for over a year. Ten years ago, I would have gotten it from the second sentence. Five years ago, I would have spotted the warning in his eyebrows before he said a word, but now I don't understand we're standing in a trap until this layered whisper. I should have known there was something behind all his talk of policy and the palace. We don't let bureaucracy tell us not to feel. Only one person is allowed to do that.

"He's here?"

"And watching you," Mr. Cheeks says.

Suddenly, the runner whose face always carries a pinch of charm looks nothing but tired. He nods over my shoulder. When I turn I see the shadow in the corner, the dull shine of well-but-not-too-well-oiled leather catching light. The shadow knows it's been spotted, probably knew from my body language the instant I understood he was there. A single hand reaches out into the light. Its long nail curves, a finger beckoning me. I swallow and take a breath, but I'm just buying time. Letting Cheeks see that I don't obey instantly, like it will matter so long as all I can do is obey. So long as all I *want* to do is obey. I try to look scared, but I'm not. I feel utterly safe as I walk into the corner with the man that is everyone's worst fear . . . everyone except me.

It's not that the emperor tries to be every Ashtowner's vision of danger; it's that they modeled all their nightmares after his father and the blood carried too true. I wasn't bred with the same fear of him as everyone else. I'm not from Downtown Ash. Everyone knows I'm a deepwaster. I didn't interact with the emperor, or even a single runner, until I came here as a young teen for work.

"Sir?" I say, because everyone also knows the emperor rarely deigns to speak first.

Nik Nik nods and I see he's not dressed for authority. He's not even wearing his rings. If he wanted to kill tonight, it'd have to be with his bare hands, unless he was in the mood to confirm the rumors about his having a gun.

The emperor lifts two fingers and holds them to the side of my throat. Anyone watching would think he was stroking my neck, instead of threatening my artery with the point of his longest nail.

"You knew her," he says. "You were friends."

It takes me no time to understand his implication. Unlike my bond with Cheeks, my tie to the emperor will never so much as fray.

"I didn't kill her," I say, answering the question that is more in the press of his fingers than in his words.

He drops the hand he was using to check my pulse. Heart rate mastery isn't one of my skills, so now he knows I wasn't lying.

"You going to blame me for every unexplained body until I retire?" I ask.

"Only the bloody ones."

At the mention of my worst crimes he squeezes my hand, because my monstrosity doesn't strain our relationship; it cements it. The blood on my hands matches the blood on his teeth. *Me too,* they say to each other, *I know.*

"Stop fighting Cross," he says. "I'll see you back at home."

"Cross is a dick, and it's not my home."

"It is," he says. "And it's waiting for you."

He walks away, giving me his back with the carelessness of a man who could kill me without much effort. It's a lie. People think the big secret between Nik Nik and me is that we're sleeping together. They're wrong. The thing unspoken between us is much more dangerous than that: The emperor is afraid of me.

I walk back to the others, the conversation making me feel exactly as helpless as witnessing Helene X's death.

"I'll come," I say.

"Figured," Cheeks says. He nods to Mr. Cross and then to the door. It's time to hand off my fob and follow in the emperor's tracks.

"Crash her and it's your skin," I say to the Ruralite. I look back toward Helene X. "And if I find out you prayed over her, I'm snipping out your tongue. You called her a sinner while she was alive, you don't get to violate her afterlife."

"I was a child," he says.

"So were we," I say, and turn away.

He never matches my venom, never makes a grand play at explaining himself. You'd think it'd make it harder to sustain my hatred, but then you'd be underestimating my stubbornness. The older the fuel, the longer it burns, which means I've got stores to hate the boy he was—and the man he became—forever.

—

MR. CHEEKS AND I COULD HAVE TAKEN MY CYCLE. A FEW YEARS BACK, HE'D HAVE THOUGHT NOTHING OF hopping on behind me for a ride through town. And I'd think nothing of taking the turns a little fast, just to hear him laugh at my back and call me wild. But at some point we both began to *notice* our closeness, to look around and realize we were the only friends who slept in the same bed, whose laughs were beginning to sound like each other's. When he noticed it, he did exactly what you'd expect if you knew a guy like Cheeks. He pulled away, kindly. No more too-closeness. No more late-night chats that ended in one of us—never both—crying. It felt like growing up, all over again. You hate it, but there's no point in fighting. Now he's started disappearing enough for me to have to cover drop-offs for him, and I've started getting called to the emperor's office for private meets, and neither of us knows everything about the other anymore.

Sometimes I want to call him back close again. Tell him there's no need to worry. Tell him there's no danger of us being more than friends. Tell him I only miss when we'd touch for the warmth. Tell him he's just a brother to me, and I'd rather have him as a friend than a lover anyhow. But he probably wouldn't buy it. Just 'cause it's a lie and all.

When the urge to ruin his peace gets too tempting, I remind myself not to be selfish; I remind myself that wanting to shift someone else's boundaries is a burden and a threat, not a gift or a compliment. Then I head down to the nightfire and find someone to clear his scent out of my head.

When Cheeks and I pull up, the palace is *alight*. Instead of the postdusk sleepiness the building usually falls into, all the lights are on and the number of runners on hand is doubled. The emperor takes the deaths of his citizens seriously, but this is too much for one murder, no matter how mysterious. Something else is going on. This suspicion is confirmed when Cheeks and I get to the emperor's office and the doors are closed. One death doesn't call for an emergency planning meeting. Alone, I'd never have the authority to open closed doors, but Mr. Cheeks is a left hand, so he walks in without flinching. I flinch. Every time I cross the threshold of the office I flinch: once remembering Nik Senior dying at the desk and once again remembering that it's Nik Nik's now.

The sound of important people talking turns me into furniture real quick. A two-second glance tells me I'm the only person in the room who isn't at least a lieutenant, so I cross my arms and lean against a bookcase—a way of turning invisible that doesn't look too much like hiding. The emperor is standing behind his father's desk. It's his usual post, though he'll never sit in the chair. He didn't pull on his ceremonial robe on his way to the meeting, but he did manage to grab his killing rings, so he looks less naked now.

". . . at least five, they say. But the city doesn't know about ours."

"So it's five *more* bodies? Six total?"

Cheeks asks the question like he's just clarifying, like he just wants to be sure of the number for his fucking notes or something. This is why he's the emperor's hand and I'm not. My mouth would shake to ask. My voice would crack in half. And it wouldn't be a question; it'd be a denial. I'd say, *Can't be five*. I'd say, *Stop your fucking lying*.

"Five more *reported,*" says another officer, which isn't a comfort. Five's plenty. One's plenty, the way it was done.

"If the bodies are as bad as they say, doubt they could be missed . . . even by the trash that passes for enforcement in the city," Mr. Tatik says, which, oddly, does make me feel better. Then she adds, "It's not a death that lets you go quiet," and I'm down low again.

Tatik is the oldest runner, one of the few from Senior's reign that was allowed to stay. She usually keeps to the outskirts, reporting on what happens in the deepwastes, but I've met her a dozen times before. She sought me out, the way she does with all femme runners, so we know we can go to her with problems we don't trust to our superiors. She didn't want me to go the mechanic route. She wanted me to end up an officer with ink up to my fucking ears like her. But I like fixing things. I like puzzles. And I like my fucking ears. I've got vices in spades but ambition's not one of them.

"You see the bodies? Looks like the Ripper all over again," says an older runner, and the others grunt in agreement.

If you hadn't been around for over a decade, you'd think we'd once had a serial killer named the Ripper and that he left bodies that looked like Helene X. But that's not true. We had a man named Ripper and he was a bastard. One day he was found at the House killed like hate, his body ravaged to shit. No one knew who killed him, but everyone figured he deserved it, so the death was answered with a shrug instead of a team. Rumors alternate between whether the emperor killed Ripper and Exlee helped cover it up, or Exlee killed him for hurting one of the Housecats and the emperor helped them cover it up. Neither version is strictly true . . . but neither is strictly untrue.

The particular gait of a booted runner who never had offense training—less because he lost his leg as a child and more because his brain was too bright to risk in the field—means the last person I want to see has arrived. It's not that I don't like Mr. Splice, usually we're close as cousins, it's just that he's our hack in the city and there's only one kind of footage he could be bringing on a night like this. If I blink for too long Helene X is behind my eyes breaking open again and again, so I really don't need to see the others. But no one asks me, and Splice projects the footage on the wall as soon as Nik gives him the nod.

He shows four feeds at once: two people walking, one at a restaurant, another sitting in a park. The park and restaurant are official surveillance. The others are personal cuffs. One moment the subjects are perfect and useless like all Wileyites, and in the next they begin to break. When the images replay it's the moments before the horror that get me. The victims share a blank-faced obliviousness, the kind of people who wouldn't flinch when someone walks behind them. It's like nothing bad's ever happened to them. Like they didn't believe in nightmares until they became one. I want to look away, but wouldn't dare with all these dipped teeth around me. I force myself to watch without blinking. I keep my arms crossed, even as other officers cover their mouths.

"Simultaneous," the emperor says, which draws my attention to the time stamps in the corners. If they're right, and I know they are, they happened the same moment as Helene X.

Mr. Splice nods, though it wasn't a question. "To the millisecond."

My back goes straight. If it's synced, that means any dream I had of this being some natural, random phenomenon is dead. I wait for someone else to make that observation, but when I read the room, the emperor is staring at me like he can smell my brain working. Still, I won't say it. I don't need the favor, and I don't want the attention.

"Wait, does that mean it's man-made?" Cheeks asks, only a minute behind me.

"That means it's murder," Nik Nik says, but he's still looking at me.

"I don't care if it's blood-hungry sand cats. I don't care about Wiley trash getting bent back," says Mr. Tatik, showing her silver front teeth. She has one jet-black incisor, and is still the only runner to have earned an emperor dip. "I care about *our* one. Did they create some problem that's spilling into our land?"

Mr. Tatik was around when the factories were still up, so I can't blame her for the chip on her shoulder. I'm not so fond of the city of shine myself, so when another lieutenant adds, "Don't they always?" I grunt in agreement.

Everyone starts discussing the deaths like they might be contagious, wondering if they should pull up records from border patrol about recent Wileyites who've come over. That's when I realize: They don't know. I wait for Cheeks to tell them, but this time he isn't just a few steps behind me.

I uncross my arms, about to open my mouth, then think better of it in a room full of my superiors. Mr. Tatik notices and holds up her hand for silence.

"Scales?"

"The victim at the House," I say. "It was Helene X."

Their expressions don't change. They don't know her, or, at least, they don't know the very first thing that anyone who has ever seen her knows.

"She's a Wileyite," I say. "Used to be anyway."

"Oh . . . so this may not be our problem at all," Tatik says, tapping her chin. For some reason she's still talking to me, probably trying to give me that hit of feeling important that she hopes will get me hooked. "If it's just Wiley City breaking, what should we do?"

Before I respond, I am pulled into a memory. It's an old one, which means it can't be trusted—but it's potent, which means it can't be denied.

A wasteland girl runs with her parents across the desert, trying to outpace the sun. It is sunrise, but the sun that is rising makes it seem like half the earth is darkness and the other half a laser. The trio make it to the city just ahead of the killing light of the bright day. The door in the wall doesn't slide open. They beg to be allowed in. They are asked for their day pass. They ask to be allowed to stay in the doorway, just inside, just tucked under that wide ledge. They are asked for the name of the citizen who is sponsoring them. In the end, only the girl is found alive, protected by the still-smoldering bodies of her parents. When the earth finally cools enough to walk, she peels herself out and returns to the wasteland as a newly minted orphan with a hatred for glass walls that will never go away.

Anyone with five minutes to kill will tell you I was the girl. It's one of Ash's favorite stories, filled with sun, death, a miracle, and an excuse to trash-talk the city. It's a story that's been repeated so many times since I came to Ashtown for work that it's not even mine anymore. It's air. It's dust. It's atmosphere. It's not even really a story about anyone's parents dying anymore. For most of Ashtown, it's a story about a door that never opens.

That door is why it's easy to answer Tatik. What do we do if Wiley needs help?

"Let them break," I say.

CHAPTER TWO

A LOW GROWL COMES FROM THE DESK. THE EMPEROR ISN'T HAPPY. I KNEW HE WOULDN'T BE BEFORE I answered. His displeasure, and the risk attached to it, brings me back into the present and clears my vision of decades-old images of star-charred flesh.

"Is that what *you* think we should do?" he says and it is completely, absolutely, one hundred percent a goddamn trap. "Proposing missions now, mechanic?"

I lower my head so far and so fast it's like I'm trying to shove my chin straight through my sternum.

"No, Sir. Just a preference."

"You directing? Jumping to a leadership track?"

"No, Sir."

"Expressing *preferences* about our direction is a right earned through promotion. Unless you decide to stop wasting everyone's time and get serious about leadership, keep your ideas to yourself."

It's one of his longer speeches. I keep my head down and don't say a word. I don't pout. I don't point out that Tatik had, in fact, asked my opinion. I also don't point out that he, and Tatik, and Cheeks have all had their turn begging me to move up and they'd be goddamn thrilled if I did jump track to leadership. I stand full runner—feet apart, arms ready—in total silence.

The true test of a runner isn't how much violence you can stomach, or how you react to a dead body. The true test of a runner is how expertly you can shut the fuck up. The emperor is like one of the reptiles outside of town—the ones whose names start with useless information like *red-eyed* or *striped yellow belly* but end with *dragon* or *monster,* which is what you actually need to know. They're scary, yes, but they have shit focus. If you stand still long enough they'll lick the air a few times and forget you.

Nik Nik stares me down a little longer before he moves on, turning his head to drag his heavy glare over the rest of the room.

"Do we have the name of the fifth in the city?" he asks, and I finally raise my eyes.

It's Splice's turn under the roving spotlight of rage the emperor's gaze becomes when one of his people has died. Unfortunately for Mr. Splice he's been asked a question, which means he doesn't have the luxury of standing silent until he disappears.

The runner breaks out in a fresh sweat. "No. Not yet, I mean. Rumor is it's some scientist. I'll get confirmation though."

The attempt to quell the emperor's rage only increases it.

When he says, "You should have it already," the words are nearly subaudible.

Splice lowers his head. I hold my breath. We're both waiting to see if his mistake is worthy of punishment. When Nik Nik's hand moves it's a wave of dismissal, not a backhand, and Mr. Splice exits without wearing failure on his skin.

Nik Nik begins to dismiss the others, but his gaze is pinned on me and I know I'm not getting out of this without another one-on-one. Mr. Tatik is one of the last to go.

"I'll keep my eye on the deep. Summon me if there's a real threat to us," she says as she goes. She's the only one who tells Nik what she'll be doing, rather than being told. I look down to hide my smile. Putting the emperor in his place one day is the only appealing thing about promotion.

"Scales."

"Sir?"

He motions for me to approach. Mr. Cheeks turns half away, which is as far away as he can respectfully turn on duty, but which also means we are firmly in his periphery when the emperor wraps his arms around my shoulders. I can feel slight pressure where his wrists meet over my spine. It's more hold than embrace, but it won't look like that to anyone watching. And someone is watching.

"Leave," Nik Nik says, a command no less irritating for its predictability.

The emperor is looking dead into my eyes when he says the word, but Mr. Cheeks knows it's for him. Cheeks stiffens, as always.

"On standby or off duty?" he asks, even though we're all on standby by default on a night like this.

"Stay in the hall," Nik Nik says, which Cheeks could have guessed, but he's my friend. He thinks I'm in danger, so he wants to buy time before leaving me in the arms of the bloodiest man in the wastes.

The emperor stares long into my face, only it's not my face he's looking for.

"You done?" I ask, my tone all kinds of disrespectful now that Cheeks is gone.

He smirks. Actually smirks. It's a little thing, but wide enough for the façade of the emperor to crack and the man only I get to know to step through. This is a miracle—not in that it's divine, but in that the world would call me sun-mad if I told. Everyone thinks deepwasters are one turn from delusion on their best day; if I run around spouting that the emperor can be playful, downright fucking *silly,* they'd have me sent to a quiet place.

"Don't begrudge me my fun," he says.

Fun is not a word his face should use.

"Fun for you is ruining my dating life?"

His eyebrows come together. "What's Cheeks got to do with your dating life?"

"Nothing, obviously," I say, too quickly. "But the rumors spread far. It's not just your enemies who think I'm yours. Pretty soon people are going to be dodging me at the nightfire."

He shrugs it away, as if ashing every one of my romantic prospects is a small thing. "Would you want a coward?"

"Do I have orders, or you just bring me to play?"

I do have orders, and when he gives them his voice is the low pitch of a eulogy.

"I need you in the city. They're calling these attacks, so security will be high. You're all I've got that can pass a citizenship scan since the new mayor's crackdown."

"In," I say, like there was ever any doubt. "What's the job?"

"I need you to see a scientist. I'll cuff you the address."

"Backup?"

He shakes his head. "You'll enter the city alone. No one else can know the location."

"You want him roughed up? Or just ask if he knows what's happening?"

The look on his face tells me we've misunderstood each other.

"Neither," he says. "This is a check-in. If he has info, get it, but your assignment is to make sure he's not the fifth. He's also a hermit, and he lives on the same floor where the unidentified body was reported."

I blink. Then blink again. Why send your highest combat-rated foot soldier for a wellness check? Jax has been in the city since before I earned my first tattoo; they could easily go knock on some Wileyite's door. Fuck, one of Splice's mechanical spiders could do it. I've done wellness checks before, but always in the deepest desert where Ashtown's most vulnerable live. No one in the Wiles needs me to make sure they're okay. But the emperor's eyes are bright with worry. On the surface this is just intelligence gathering, but there's a plea underneath it. Not just *See if he's the fifth,* but also, *Please, please don't let him be.*

Maybe he does need it to be me that does the job, because he needs it to be me that delivers the news if it's bad. I'm privy to his silliness, but I'm also the only one living who's ever seen him cry.

I nod, acknowledging the order like it's the most ordinary job in the world. Right before he shatters my nonchalance with a single sentence.

"If he's dead, I'm pulling you up."

"Fuck off," I say, stepping away from him as my concern from a second ago dries all the way up.

"If he is dead, I'm pulling you up," he says again, giving me an opportunity to respond correctly.

I lower my head, and nod.

I want to say, *You can't.* I want to say, *You promised.* Instead I say, "Understood."

He rewards my obedience with a courtesy he rarely bestows: an explanation.

"These are dangerous times," he says. "You will need to be more protected than ever before."

"Going public won't protect me. It'll paint a target on my back."

"You've had a target since you took up leather. This just adds power."

"I don't want power. I never did."

We're at a stalemate. He breaks first.

"Then let's hope the mark is still alive. For your sake."

This is how I know I am not young anymore. When I was young, I would have seen red. His disregard of my wishes would have mingled with my anger at losing Helene X to plant a black seed in my chest that would bloom big as a mushroom cloud and twice as deadly. I wouldn't have been able to keep my hands down. Worse, I wouldn't have been able to stop hitting him until someone stronger stopped me. And since Nik's the only one combat-rated higher than I am, there would have been no one who could stop me.

After all these years it's easy, almost natural, to swallow down what could lead to violence. To ground myself the way I learned when I first joined up. This is something people who've never worn leather can't understand. Places where violence isn't tolerated will never teach you how to deal with it, when it is avoidable, or how to execute it cleanly when you must. You have to accept violence as a part of life to know it, to tame it like a pet, to keep it in your pocket and understand when to let it out. There's nothing you can tell me about the right way to bruise flesh if your only rule is *don't.*

Nik Nik, still watching my face for a hint of disobedience, eventually looks away. He calls for Cheeks, but by the time the runner enters the emperor has his back turned to us both.

—

WE'RE ABOUT HALFWAY TO THE WALL WHEN CHEEKS TURNS OFF THE ROAD, LETTING THE ENGINE IDLE.

"You good?" he asks.

"It's not that kind of mission. Nothing wet, just info gathering."

"I don't mean about the mission. Himself . . . he's been taking alone time with you."

I shake my head. "It's not—"

Cheeks cuts off what I'm sure he thinks is a lie. "I don't care. You can get it with whoever you want, but I know he's got a lot of power . . ."

"You think the emperor decided to break his rule on coercive relationships and he started with me?"

Cheeks shrugs, but I can see he's relieved. He's given his whole life in support of this man. I can't imagine the courage it must have taken him to even ask such a question. What would he do if I said yes? Help me escape? Buy me passage through the desert? Hide me in the Rurals?

I decide I want him relieved more than I want to find out.

"Flattered, but it's not like that. We just . . . we understand each other. But it's . . . tied to something classified."

Cheeks flinches. His rank is higher than mine in every single way. If it was something on the books he would know before I did. Being left out on an off-books mission means the emperor doesn't trust him as much as he thought.

But he does trust him. He trusts him with his life, so I add, "It's personal, for me. It's from the old days."

Cheeks nods, pulling back onto a road that only runners would be able to make out in the terrain. He's not hiding his relief. "Oh, that makes sense. I know House business can be sensitive."

We drive carelessly fast until we get to a low area of vegetation that exists for about a mile in a full radius around the city. From a distance, in the moonlight, the pale plants look like a silver oasis. Only when you get closer do you realize the truth: It's all dead. Every stalk a long-ago withered corpse, too petrified to even burn on a bright day.

I, and everyone under forty, call it the carpet because it looks like an odd fuzzy rug made of dead plants. When Wiley first installed their artificial atmosphere to tame the sun, it was a wonder. Even before it was as powerful as they've made it now, it outperformed, and soon enough even the desert surrounding the city began to bloom with things decades-gone. It was a generosity the city couldn't stomach, so they installed an inhibitor to run along the top of the wall to catch and return the atmosphere back to Wiley. Like I said, most of us call it the carpet. But the oldheads? They call it the garden, with a mourning in their eyes like it's the name of a murdered childhood friend.

By the time Wiley's east wall is in sight, Mr. Em is already waiting on the ridge for us to be in range of the drones. In the glow from the city I can barely make out her long, dark ponytail and the backpack–fanny pack combo she's forever rocking. I remember from training that her favorite phrase to new runners was *Stay critical,* but it should have been *Stay prepared,* because there's nothing she's not carrying on her person at any given moment.

Once the drones are activated by our proximity, she takes off and rides straight toward them. She moves dangerously, weaving in and out among the dirt mounds, until the drones are forced to fall back and speed up as they try—and fail—to predict her path. She won't be able to get them confused enough to crash into each other, which is her favorite pastime, but she'll keep them busy while Cheeks drops me off. Any other runner would be laughing like only runners do—a throaty, uneven pitch loud and distinct enough to be heard over even the old engines. But Em has never been one to draw attention to herself. She's so quiet you'd never know she outranks Cheeks and carries more knowledge of our protocol and procedure than anyone save the emperor himself.

The drones screech off after her, leaving the wall unprotected, but for the stationary cameras with gaps in coverage so wide a boulder could find them. Wileyites are real touchy about surveillance in their walls. They've voted down facial scanning, total coverage cameras, even audio surveillance designed to hear the escalated yells of a fight or screams of distress when they were proposed for inside the city. They choose privacy over security every time. The citizens say privacy is a right they won't have violated, but apparently rights are only for people on one side of the wall, because their perimeter is crawling with surveillance drones armed with facial scanning and nonlethal—but not non-damaging—projectiles.

A decade ago some prominent citizen's body was found in the desert between Wiley and Ash, prompting the city to write a blank check to their enforcement. It didn't matter that we didn't kill the man they found outside. It didn't matter that Wileyites are more likely to kill one another than to be killed by an Ashtowner. They like fixing imaginary problems, and the vote to increase enforcement's presence at the border was unanimous. Unanimous because, of course, they didn't ask us.

Right now some uniform is watching the drone feed and wishing they could stun Em in the back just for existing. I like to picture them: huffy, licking their teeth, bad dogs brought to heel by tight collars, hands poised over the button to activate weapons they aren't actually allowed to use. Once, they would have. They would have stunned her for *looking* at the wall too long, and when we filed a grievance about the excessive force they would say her crime was trespassing despite this being open land.

Right after Senior's death, when they thought his new-ruling son would be softer, they went rabid. The city's enforcement wanted to use all the power-drunk violence they don't use on their citizens on us in the desert. In the city they were still nice. *Polite.* Clean-pressed uniforms who'd call you *Sir* or *Ma'am*. In the desert they armed themselves like militia and acted like hyenas . . . which I'd respect if they were honest about it. If I walk around geared up and punch someone in the face, I expect them to fight back. I'm not looking to lock them up for the most sensible of reactions. They wanted to beat us bloody, and then arrest for "assault" anyone who kicked dirt in their direction. They wanted to look like, be armed like, and act like a gang, but get treated with respect by the very people they terrorized. You don't get to have your bloodthirst and your city key, too.

The officers' turn in the desert ended the way all stories do when two gangs occupy the same space: blood on both sides, glory on one.

The mistake they made was an old one, but one they'll undoubtedly make again: forgetting we outnumber them, forgetting we are just as comfortable with bloody hands as they are and that we don't have delusions of being called a hero holding us back.

The last straw had a name, and it was Wills. His first name was Travin. Afterward, we called him Mr. out of respect, but he wasn't actually a runner. Just a boy who wore enough black to convince enforcement he was fair game. He didn't even rock leather—it was cloth—but in those days even a hoodie put a scent on enforcement's tongue.

Mr. Wills was almost certainly not the first of us killed in the desert by a pack of uniforms who wanted to play at hunting. But his death became a story. It had been seen and heard and shared by so many of us that we began to whisper his name across the sand. Every mouth changed the story's shape a little: He was crying. No, he was stoic. No, he begged for mercy. No, he said, *Do your worst.* He fought to the end. Or his hands were tied. They came at him from behind and he never saw it coming. They came at him from the front and he stood his ground. With his last breath he called for his mother. With his last breath he called for god. With his last breath he called for vengeance. Or he called for nothing with his last breath, because he didn't have one. He couldn't breathe, and his last words were just one more thing stolen from him.

It didn't matter which version was true. They were all *real.* Stories should never be believed, but they should always be trusted.

Still, we were diplomatic. We gave them time to deliver the officer up for justice in Ashtown. They didn't. We paraded through their streets, acid-etching their unbreakable glass with his name as we went. They still didn't give him up. See, the killing wasn't ambiguous. It was recorded. Ashtown and Wiley agreed the officer killed him. When they didn't deliver the killer up for charges they weren't saying, *He didn't do it.* They were saying, *He was allowed to.*

A week of no charges later, the runners went into the city. Not to parade. To work. They were quiet like a dark mist. No laughing, no howling, not one single revving engine. It was a procession for two funerals: one that had already happened and one that was yet to come. When the sun came up, the officer who killed Wills had been made a blood scarecrow in the desert facing the city's main entrance.

The city wailed.

He didn't get a trial, they said.

Neither did ours, we said.

But trials are a right, they said.

Then maybe you should have charged him, we said.

The next officer who overstepped delivered himself up for charges. He wanted to keep his skin, I guess.

It could have gone bad. When one city feels threatened they can appeal to the council of all the others to have weapons of mass destruction sent in. And if the threat is to the system that allows cities to exist as a whole, they usually oblige. We could have been firebombed into nothing, shot from the sky while we ran screaming. But by then the story had spread far enough that even the council understood. We weren't threatening the system; it was a simple retaliation. Their inaction meant we, too, were *allowed.*

This story hangs over me every time I cross Wiley's walls, the way it should hang over us all. But Ash residents have too many other things to remember, and Wiley would sooner forget. It's left to us runners to remember the time we won. They hate our violent parades and our bloodthirsty leader. They've forgotten that we're just the honest version of what licks its lips in wait on the other side of the wall.

As Em drags the drones into the desert, Cheeks parks to drop me off.

"Walk small. Be shadow," he says, the opposite instruction of a parade; the only instruction when you're running alone. He holds out his hand.

"Small as the sand, shadow as the cave," I say, taking his hand and meeting the half embrace. Then I pull up my hood, and step away.

The look Cheeks gives the wall before he leaves me is not different from the look he gave Nik Nik—a looming thing he can't fight, threatening to swallow me whole. His ride pelts me with dirt as he leaves, and I take it, eyes open to the dust, just to watch him go.

Once he's gone, I slide backward through the hologram of what looks like finished steel and slip into the dark the city doesn't know is under its skin.

—

I ALWAYS THOUGHT SCIENTISTS WERE RICH? LIKE, STREETS NAMED AFTER THEM AND PUBLIC PARKS AS backyards rich? But this one is on a low floor, down in the shadows, thirty floors from the dirt but it might as well be a gutter by city standards. It's still clean, there's still food growing along the walls, but I wonder how long it's been since he's seen the real sun or stars. Maybe he doesn't care about them. Maybe he's the kind of scientist that studies darkness and being this far down in the muck of higher floors is the closest he can get to it in a city with this many fucking security lights.

When I knock on the door there's a whole lot of shuffling before he answers, so I'm not surprised when I hear the high-pitched whir of a scanner. Unfortunately for him I keep my gear under a temp-safe pouch, so his scan won't show any metal but the studs in my clothes and the silver of my bottom incisors. I smile wide to give his camera a good look, but then I feel the rattle against the back of my thigh. Temperature scanners I can fool, but this paranoid bastard has a magnet sensor. He'll know I'm armed.

"I'm not here for trouble," I say. It's true tonight, though it isn't always and I'd say it even if it weren't.

When the door finally opens, the person that stands before me doesn't look like any scientist I've ever pictured. His left arm is bionic. The stained, stretched-out tank top lets me see he's lost all the bone and muscle as high as his shoulder and as far in as the start of his collarbone. It's a dingy metal—durable, but not pretty. In his flesh hand is a cane, which makes me notice the leg. Because he's wearing pants, I can't see what all is missing, just that one foot is metallic. Still, it's nothing compared to his face. The top left quarter of his face and skull are gone, replaced with mechanical parts. The blue lens where an eye should be catches the light flatly, like dull glass, and there are shocks of white hair immediately surrounding the metal plate on his head, though the rest of his hair is black.

I've seen a lot in my time, but I still swallow once before speaking to make sure I don't sound too shocked. I check the name I'd noted down on my cuff.

"You Adam Bosch?"

His nod is shaky, but affirmative, like he hasn't heard that name in years but knows it anyhow. Eventually, he takes a step backward, the sound distinctly hydraulic.

"I was," he says, and motions me inside.

CHAPTER THREE

ADAM BOSCH IS WATCHING THE FEED ON HIS WALL. I'M NOT ONE FOR TECH—I'M MORE GEARHEAD than circuitfreak—but I know the screen is expensive by how invisible it was before it turned on. In my town money buys you notice. It buys you shine, and flash, and the too-loud rumble of a too-big ride. In Wiley money can get you subtlety. Invisibility. Screens that look like walls, appliances that look like cabinets, and projecting cuffs that look like bracelets of the thinnest chain.

The tech feels too nice for this floor with its darkened windows and dust so thick you know it's at least partially the accumulated dead skin of the people on all the floors above. But what do I know? I haven't kept tabs on Wiley tech since I was young and things exclusive then could have become common since. Or maybe the truth is darker than that.

Shoved into the corner of his shelves like broken toys are old trophies and vidscreen certificates with his name on them. Maybe this low-level floor wasn't always the scientist's life. Maybe Adam Bosch used to be important.

The screen shows two women. The older one, chin like an axe, is speaking.

"She's cute," I say.

He's only been irritated at my presence, but now when he regards me his smile is cruel.

"That's the mayor. She ran on a campaign that promised to crack down on Ashtown elements in the city. She called runners every word for animal available to her. I somehow don't think you're her type."

I shrug like I don't care, but now that I know who she is I hate her. Her "Keep Wiley City Clean" campaign was xenophobic and dangerous for us, but worse, it was so fucking corny. I don't have a ton of give-a-shit for the city's politics, but I'm a little shocked to hear she won.

The white-haired woman beside her is keeping her eyes down while the mayor speaks.

"Her assistant can't stand her."

"That's not her assistant. That's the lieutenant mayor."

I scrunch my face. "Two mayors for a place this boring?"

He looks away from the feed at me. "There are six political parties here. Whoever gets the most votes gets to be mayor, second place gets lieutenant."

It'd be a recipe for assassination back home, but I guess Wiley doesn't have a taste for that.

"Is that why she's so nervous?" I ask.

"She's not . . ." Adam looks up. ". . . Huh, she does seem nervous. Maybe it's the bodies."

Right. Now that I'm paying attention, she could just be shaken. I guess most Wileyites need a few blinks to process brutal death. They profited off it for centuries, but god forbid they have to *see* it. It was the scientist's casualness that made me forget. When the newsvids showed the incidents—though they're calling them *attacks*—he didn't break into the standard *Oh God, why* or *No, no, no!* at the unexplained loss of life. He just tilted his head and watched like a curious bird.

The mystery of the lieutenant mayor doesn't captivate him, and he changes the feed away from the politicians until he finds yet another image of death. For a place that calls us savage they sure are maximizing the replayability of seeing bodies turned inside out. I guess it's hard to keep cruelty neatly packaged; it always spills its way back home.

Adam mutters something under his breath for the someteenth time since he turned the TV on. He hadn't heard about the attacks before I showed up, which seems impossible, but having seen inside his apartment I'm less surprised. The trash heaped next to a perfectly organized workplace hints at a singular focus that shuts out things deemed unimportant—which, for him, seems to include the news, the state of his home, and basic hygiene.

Eventually, he says, "It's bad math."

"You know what this is?"

"Isn't that why the emperor sent you?"

"Sure," I say, partially because it's good for a runner to lie sometimes, just to keep in the habit, and partially because it's no business of his if my emperor was worried sick about him. No business of mine, either, but I still find myself sizing him up and down, wondering why this Wileyite of all of them matters to the ruler of the wastes.

"Do you have other videos?"

I check the television. The surveillance clips are there, but only one of the private vids has been sent to the news.

"One more," I say.

I download the vid from my cuff to a fob and hand it to him. The tech must seem ancient compared to what he's used to, which is why he looks at me like I've handed him a fat worm.

"It's just a fob. My cuff doesn't project so good, but this will. You can also download it into your screen . . . or you can ram it into your fucking head, I guess," I say as he does just that.

His biological and mechanical eyes both move like he's watching something, and Bosch begins to mutter yet again.

"Dop backlash? Must be. But how would the displacement work?" he says, entirely and completely to himself.

I get the feeling he could hold a whole conversation like this, asking and answering questions himself on a closed loop, so I interrupt.

"Dop what?"

"Dop backlash. What happens when a multiversal entity encounters itself," he says, casually, and when the word *multiverse* hits my ear I recognize him.

A long time ago, Wiley City had the ability to travel to other universes, and Adam Bosch sat on top of the whole operation. I never knew his crime, but I know that Ashtown is the one who made him pay for it by taking his empire. We rode in, blew his life up literally, and rode back out again. I think back to those awards, those certificates. I'd wondered what had changed. Us. We changed his life.

Someone else would probably feel remorse, or pity, at seeing how low we've brought him even so many years later. I just feel a fierce pride. I want to yell, *That's right. It doesn't matter if you're the smartest city scum there is, when Ashtown marks you, you stay marked.*

"Oh yeah! You're the guy! You're the one whose . . ." Here I stop before I say *shit we blew up.* ". . . company used to do that. So this is related?"

"I need to see the bodies."

"If you see a body, you'll know for sure?"

He's staring at nothing with a clarity reserved for the very smart. Geniuses look at things they don't understand the way the rest of us look at things we want: all intensity, hunger, and desire. Or maybe that's just me. In his stare I can see that he is younger than I'd assumed from the half-white hair and body mods. He's not yet old for a Wileyite.

"Doesn't matter. All the runner tricks in the world won't get a body from enforcement on an investigation this important."

Shows what he knows about runner tricks, but I don't say that.

"Won't be necessary," I say, already messaging central to see if he has palace clearance. I'm not entirely surprised to find he does. "You in the mood for a road trip, Scientist?"

I'm not asking if he's in the mood to leave. I'm asking if he'd rather a road trip or a kidnapping. I tug at my gloves as I ask, so he doesn't misunderstand his options. To his credit, he doesn't look afraid. In fact, he hasn't looked afraid since I got here, even when his well-dressed mayor politely implied Ashtown had something to do with the deaths. Maybe Wileyites don't fear Ash anymore. Or maybe he's got nothing left to lose.

He doesn't say, *I'll need to take your picture with my cuff,* or *I'll be missed if I don't come back.*

All he says is "I'll need my tools," and he says it to himself.

—

I WAS WORRIED ABOUT BOSCH ON THE SCAFFOLDING BUT HE USES HIS CANE LIKE ANY OTHER LIMB and negotiates the terrain as well as I do. He sweats a lot and complains very little, which is all I could have hoped for. It's a Wiley mistake, to assume what someone can and can't do by looking, and I'm kicking myself for it even before we get to the sand.

"We can go slower here," I say. When he raises his eyebrow I nod toward his cane and add, "It's soft."

I'm picturing the tool that's been helping him go step-for-step with me in the city turning into a liability as it gets stuck in the soft earth, but he turns the body of the cane against the handle and two metal discs pop out from the end. One disc lays flat on the ground while the other hovers above, and I can tell before he demonstrates that the magnets are strong enough for the repulsion to hold his weight.

"Oh . . ." I say, eyeing the cane again. "It's like your ride?"

I think the look on his face is confusion, so I try to clarify. "It's what we call our vehicles. Like an extension of you. You can trick it out however you want."

"I'm aware of the name for runner toys. But my work is nothing so pedestrian as that."

Shows me for talking to a Wileyite like he's a person.

When we make it to the meetup, Mr. Cheeks is waiting for us. He doesn't hear us right off, so he's just standing, arms crossed, face lovely as a lake turned up to the moon. I don't realize I've stopped walking at the sight of him until Bosch runs into me. It's an unusual feeling, his breath hot against the back of my skull. I'm the tallest runner, unless you're counting Nik, but Adam Bosch is a Wileyite. I can't tell from here, but he'd probably be just under the emperor.

Cheeks looks at me, and his face and body language turn violent so rapidly I want to step back. But his rage isn't for me.

"You following her? What do you want?"

Cheeks widens his stance. I see him make quick fists and I

know, because I know his gear as well as I know his face, that he's pushed out the spikes in his knuckles.

Adam, with all the self-preservation instinct of an infant, doesn't step back or lower his head. He's studying Cheeks like a curiosity, and it's going to get him hit.

"He's my mark, Cheeks. He thinks he knows what's going on with the bodies." Neither man moves. Adam is smiling. "I radioed the palace. He's got clearance."

Cheeks relaxes, flexing his hands out to put the spikes away and finally moving toward the driver's side door. "I got the message that we might be escorting a witness back. Didn't think it'd be you."

"Do we know each other?" Adam asks. "I'm afraid most of you are quite beneath my notice."

The look Cheeks gives him at that comment should have him scrambling away, but instead Adam claims the front passenger seat, leaving me the back. Which is fine. Riding in the front would just be sitting next to Cheeks with the backs of our knuckles six inches apart and me having to hide that I'm aware that our knuckles are six inches apart and will never be any closer.

"You don't know me. But I know you've got reason to hate runners," Cheeks says as he starts the vehicle, finally answering the question but ignoring the insult.

That's what Cheeks *says,* but he spoke like he was the one with reason to hate, and if he recognized Bosch that quickly he must have been keeping tabs on him in the years since we set his irreplaceable equipment to explode.

"And I suppose most people welcome your rabid packs with open arms?"

Another insult for Cheeks, and me, to ignore.

I lean back, cross my arms, and check out. Cheeks outranks me, so if anything needs to be said to the scientist, he'll say it. Which suits me just fine. I've got a low tolerance for talking to important people, and between the meeting in the emperor's office and grabbing a Wiley brain, I've had my fill. I stare out the window, quiet like the grunt I am, a simple mechanic with no business being this far from the row.

I assumed we were heading back to the palace, but then Cheeks turns off the easy path. I lean forward, but bite my lip. Because he outranks me, I'm not *technically* allowed to question where he's going. I'd do it if we were alone, but we're supposed to obey rules and shit when other people are around. Eventually he takes pity on me.

"Scientist's wanted at the body. We're destined for the Keeper tonight."

"Always were," I say, which is what you say when someone mentions death . . . or life.

Far as I know, Viet is not a bad person, but that patch of dirt outside of town where ends and beginnings collide will always give me the creeps. Cheeks and I spit out the window as we cross onto the Keeper's plot. Adam stares at us at that, but less in Wiley disgust and more in that same persistent, unsettling interest.

Elitist Wileyites? I know them well. They don't scare me. But this, this weirdly intense studying creature, makes my skin crawl. He doesn't look at us like he hates us or pities us or is disgusted by us. He doesn't look at us like we're human at all. I wonder if it's because we're Ash, or if he looks at every single thing like a test subject, other Wileyites included.

When we get to Viet's place the torches are lit. Tradition dictates the land be divided between life and death, to accommodate Viet's dual roles. The north and east are all about life, dawn, and birth. Here are the birthing pools, but also the blessing sands where children delivered elsewhere can come to let the land know them. The south and west are death and sunset. It's here the dead are prepared for burial.

In the *south* of the south, a cut of land in a ridge so deep it sees the sun only a few times a year, is Akeldama, the field of blood. This is where people—almost exclusively from the city—come to request their own death. There is a runner stationed there to provide the service, but even other runners aren't told who holds the scythe. It's dangerous to be an Ashtowner killing Wileyites, so anybody serving is called Jack Ketch, and only Viet sees their face unmasked. There was a rumor that Nik Nik himself served a tour under the hood, but like all the other rumors, he probably invented it himself. The old rumor was that Nik Senior served, but I can testify that one is as true as blood.

When we get out of the car the emperor is waiting in front of Viet's place. He walks up to the car to lay eyes on our cargo, and the scientist *moves*. Cheeks and I have barely left our seats when Adam Bosch launches himself at the emperor, throwing a spinning piece of metal at Nik Nik's neck. I've got Adam's arm twisted behind his back in the next second, but he makes a fist with his mechanical hand and activates a magnet, and the thin, curved slab of metal reverses direction like a boomerang, taking Nik Nik's neck with it and pins him to the metal hood of Cheeks's ride.

I panic. My vision goes rage-white and before I've had a conference with my hands they have positioned themselves—one on Adam's chin and the other on his shoulder—to snap his neck.

"Stand down, Scales," Nik says just before it's too late. I see his chest rise, and realize he's being held down, but not choked. Only then am I able to pull myself back from the killing edge.

Adam seems unbothered by the danger he's in. He keeps his eyes trained on Nik.

"When you were young your father made you fight another boy. To start the fight he said one word. What was it?"

Nik Nik's eyes only cloud for a moment in confusion before understanding dawns. Which must be nice, because I still have no idea what's going on. The emperor raises a sharp-nailed hand to his neck, wrapping his fingers around the metal. Then, still keeping eye contact with Adam, he pulls the magnetized collar off. It takes strength, his forearm shakes with the effort, but strength he's got and he lifts the metal enough to slip out before letting it slam back down on the hood.

He walks slowly toward the scientist who is now my prisoner.

" 'Excel,' " he says, and I don't realize he's answering the scientist's question until I feel Adam relax. He looks over Adam's shoulder to me. "Release him."

"Boss . . ." It's as far as I get before the look in the emperor's eyes shuts down my objections.

Before I let Adam go, I flex my knuckles up and back, activating the quick charge on my gloves, then I squeeze my palm into his shoulder.

"Ow," Adam says, more indignant than actually hurt, placing a hand over his new burn.

"Oops," I say, stepping away to take my post against the car.

The emperor looks at me, but it's pride, not censure, so I shrug. He retrains his gaze on the scientist.

"I take it you believe we've been infiltrated?" Nik says.

"It's the bodies," Adam says. "It's what happens when you send people from one universe to another. If you're going to start an invasion, you'll want leadership. But it seems it's still in the testing phase."

"And you test on pawns, not kings," Nik Nik says.

Adam nods. "I had to know. The phrase your father used came from a poem his father read to him. The poet didn't survive to write in many worlds. I imagine whatever he said on other earths was equally uninventive."

I wait for Nik Nik to backhand him for his insolence about Senior, but instead every ounce of rage is out of his body despite just being attacked.

"I'm returning to the palace. The Keeper left on an errand. Wait outside until he returns," Nik Nik says to us, then focuses on the scientist. "I look forward to hearing your findings."

Definitely not a request, that.

As he takes long strides back to his ride, I'm wondering why he stayed after Viet left. Then I realize—he'd wanted to see Adam.

When Viet comes up the hill from the south of the property he is out of breath and leaning on his staff, the bottom of his long robes stained permanently red with what I am only partially certain is red clay from the area. We know better than to ask where he's been. He can be the Keeper of life or death, but right now it's most certainly the latter. If a child was born on the same night the air itself brutalized Helene X, it would carry the stain for life. Better to think he was tending to a corpse. You can't curse the dead.

"We need to see the body," Cheeks says.

"Whose body?" Viet says, face so placid he must be full of shit.

"Fucking guess," I say, spitting on the ground, this time for insult, not superstition.

Viet looks askance at Adam. He won't know everything about Adam like the children he brought into the world, though he's old enough to have done the job, but the Keeper must figure him for a scientist right off.

"You can't cut her up," he says to Adam. "She's seen too much already and I've promised her rest."

"I need to take samples . . ."

Viet jams his stick into the ground, and Bosch sighs.

". . . They'll only be from the surface. I won't open her up any more than she already is."

Viet takes a moment to size us up. In the end it's Cheeks's tattoos, signifying his relationship to the emperor, that convince him. Viet finally nods and leads us inside.

Helene's preparation room smells like flowers, and I'm sure when someone from the Rurals comes to inter her it will be no later than midday and have only the finest oils. The House takes care of their own in death as well as they do in life, and Exlee has never let one of their chicks go into the dark with anything but the absolute best.

Adam moves toward the table and motions to take the tarp, but Cheeks stills his hand.

"Stand guard," he says to me.

"I was there. I've already seen it."

The prospect of watching the scientist harvest from the body of my friend is as appealing as chewing spikes, but Cheeks thinking I can't do my duty is worse.

"Guard," he says again.

I can't deny a command the second time, even if I know it's just a friend trying to protect me, so I turn on my heel and walk outside.

Viet's place is on a hill, so I "stand guard" by sitting, staring up at the stars. Eventually I close my eyes and focus on every sound. There's the biting howl echoing through the many valleys that open up to the south of his property, wind tracing gashes in the earth formed by long-gone water. There's the soft cries of the desert creatures Viet's rumored to feed, fewer birds than there used to be, but just as many reptiles. But mostly, there is a hush so profound it's noticeable. These are the oldest rocks, and they're sitting on ground so still it used to be ocean floor and hasn't yet realized it's not anymore.

I'm straining to hear that long-extinct ocean in the rocks around me when I hear footsteps instead. The steps are in a runner's march, someone taller than Mr. Cheeks, but the same weight.

"Mr. Cross," I say, but I don't open my eyes. "You're back?"

When he doesn't speak, I slit my eyes up to glare at him. His eyes are a little more haunted than usual. I'd assumed the life of a runner would weigh heavy on a prince, but I'd also assumed he'd last no more than six months. I've lost track of how many years it's been now. Five? No. It must be ten, or close to it. Doesn't matter, he has no reason to be here. I'd bet the memory of Helene X's body is breathing on the back of his neck, and Viet's is the closest to a holy place he's allowed in anymore. He must be seeking solace, but a runner has no business needing it.

"Scales," he says. "I'm sorry."

I tilt my head at him. "For what?"

He looks down. "For sneaking up on you."

"*Psh,* as if you could. You walk heavier than a dillo, Cross," I say. "What are you doing up here anyway?"

"Thought I should take night, since you've already been on shift all day and I'm rested up."

"Got it covered, thanks," I say, tilting my head back up to the stars in dismissal.

I'm listening to the sound of him walking back down the hill to wherever he parked when I realize something's wrong. Mr. Cross isn't the same weight as Mr. Cheeks. He's taller, sure, but still a pale waif compared to Cheeks's solid bulk. He's just walking heavy.

What are you carrying, Holy Man?

I look back inside the hovel. Cross came here armored and armed. Was he looking to try fists? Does he hate the scientist as much as Cheeks does? Or is he stupid enough to think he can take me on the side, when he can't even take Em at practice and I'm twice as rated? Or maybe he always wears body armor. That would make him the worst kind of runner, the kind that's afraid to die.

It's not my business. I'm not an officer or a rat so there's fuck all for me to do with this bit of intel. Just means if I ever fight Cross for real, I'll go for the throat instead of breaking my hand against body plates.

I push thoughts of Cross away so I can focus, *really* focus, on the stars. We don't talk about it enough out here. Every year runners escort a new crop of scholarships—kids who've proven themselves smart enough to get boarded into Wiley's schools—into the city and everyone talks about what they'll gain, how high up they'll be, how much more money they'll make in the end. We never say the truth. We never say, *You're giving up this wide horizon, you're losing every one of these stars, you're losing the salt of ash on your tongue and you'll never taste anything like it again.* I guess that's because everyone from here can't see it. They don't leave, so they never know what they won't have once they go. And the ones that do leave never come back. They settle for a lower-to-mid-level Wiley City living, and the letters they send come slower and slower every year.

I know, though. I know what it's like to be somewhere else long enough to see Ashtown as special. Long enough to know there are far darker places than even the town in the city's shadow.

—

THE IMAGE MOST PEOPLE HOLD OF HELENE X IS HER OLDER, POLISHED, ELEGANT. THEY THINK OF HER AS that worker so well-booked she only danced because she liked it, long past the need to intrigue clients. But I remember when she still bit her lip before she spoke. Exlee had her train me when I came into the House, but she'd been there barely a year, so it was like a toddler training a baby: We both just kind of stumbled along together. What she did teach me—how to enjoy but also understand sex as an interaction, not a source of fear or shame—she taught me by accident. She taught me through example. She was always nervous, always aware of how much she stuck out in a world of Ashtowners, but in bed, on her back looking up or on her knees looking down, she was so at peace in her body you could never doubt she was an expert at precisely this.

I know her regulars will say dumb shit about her appeal. They'll say her nipples tasted like peaches, say it smelled like roses between her legs. It's not true, soft colors just confuse the senses. What they should talk about is her utter joy. The way her hands only stopped shaking once she was naked, the way she smiled just as big and bright after she made you come as she did after you made her.

After the Ripper was murdered at the House, Exlee let everyone take whatever time off they needed. Helene X was the first to ask to be put back in rotation. Exlee said, *You need to heal.* And Helene X said, *That's what I'm doing.*

While I was working, hers was the style I most tried to emulate. I know what people say, that I wasn't suited for sex so I chose violence. But the truth is I am equally good at both, but sex is less messy, and I'd still be providing at the House if Exlee would let me. But I'm banned for life as a worker, welcome only as a customer now. Exlee said it was for my own good, but we both knew that was only half the story. After I packed up, Helene came out and pressed a gemstone into my hand. At first I thought it was a necklace, but it was a purple crystal on a chain like a pendulum.

What is it for? I asked her. We all knew she had an odd collection of shiny bits from her old life, but she only brought them out like this, as gifts when you least expected it, mementos showing up when you were well and truly down.

It helps you find your way, she said.

I don't know if she meant literally, like a compass, or mystically, but I kept the crystal on the chain, and I did find my place. That a lost soul like me, who should have been dead thrice over, could find a life that suits me so well . . . there must have been some kind of spell at work, and why not hers? If anyone asks, I'll say her crystal was magic.

Helene X? I'll say at her funeral. *That girl worked miracles.*

CHAPTER FOUR

FROM THE MOMENT I GOT UP TO MY ELBOWS IN A BEAUTIFUL GIRL'S BLOOD I'VE BEEN BREATHING LIKE prey. Shallow, quick. Breath like uncertainty. Breath like panic. But when I walk into the runners' hall the next day I'm greeted by a sea of leather and I breathe right for the first time since I couldn't keep Helene X together.

This is what it's supposed to look like when the world tilts wrong: a gaggle of runners, moving in concentric circles, ready to unfuck the earth's very axis. I'm groggy and late to the action—Mr. Cross was right about me being too tired for watch, though I'd lick a spiked lizard before I'd admit it—but the speaking hasn't started yet, just the moving. A gap opens in the bodies and I slide in, a runner on each side as we sway in unison. It's our own surf, left to right with our arms over one another's backs, moving how we live every single day. When I first came I was too tall, the runners around me couldn't reach to cover my back. So I learned to hunch low and they learned to strain high, and within our compromises I found somewhere I fit. That's the lesson: As long as someone is stretching to reach you, you'd better bend to reach them. This is how a runner always has coverage.

The circles move around one another getting smaller toward the center like a clockwork target, and in the eye of the human hurricane is the emperor. He runs his hands over our backs, passing between the lines of our bodies no matter how hard we try to keep him out, always stronger, always faster.

We never let him win.

We always want him to win.

He always wins.

I am eager and afraid for the coming touch of his palm. There is a thrill there, too. Let this man you've watched kill run those same nails over the back of your neck. If you're in good standing, you'll just get a touch. If you're fucking up, you'll get the nail. But whatever pronouncement you get, you won't be alone when it comes. Your kin will hold you up even if the emperor sees fit to push you down.

When Nik Nik comes to me I'm a little afraid he's being enough of an asshole to let his hand linger on my neck, indicating special favor. But he's not in the mood for play, and he passes his hand over me with neither judgment nor affection. Once I'm cleared, I don't expect him to linger over anyone, but he stays on Cheeks . . . because, of course. Love Cheeks, but he will never not be a kiss ass, and I've accepted that he'll always be a better runner than me because he cares way more than anyone should. But when the circle disperses for the meeting to begin, Cheeks touches the back of his neck. His fingers come away red.

He and the emperor share a look, and then Cheeks turns to look at me. I shake my head, denying what I don't know, but his face shifts into a glare. He's looking at me like he hates me. He's never looked at me like that before. I'd do anything to make that look stop. I'd go to my knees at his feet begging him. I'd use my given name and his too so he'd know I meant it. But I don't get the chance. In the next second, Cheeks becomes the least important thing in the room.

I know the gasps of the other runners must happen after the raw sound of knuckles smashing into flesh, but they seem to arrive at the same second. I don't have to ask who took the hit: Mr. Kat is bent over, vomiting between the emperor's feet. Getting a cut on your neck is a warning, getting beat during the meeting is a judgment.

The emperor's eyes were dancing as he moved through the circles, and I thought he was feeling the same relief I was to be back among my people. But his eyes weren't dancing—they were scanning. I was excited like a puppy getting to play with other puppies. He was a shark catching a scent.

Mr. Kat is gagging now, and I can tell from the whimpers in between that the abdominal contractions are their own agony. No one moves to stop Nik. No one moves to help Kat. We are frozen . . . until the second blow lands. It's sharp, quick, and from beneath: knuckles bashing a chin so hard and sure that the sound of teeth shoved together is as loud as a slammed door. It relaxes us all even though it sends Kat to the ground. Today will break bones, and tear flesh, and batter organs, and loosen teeth, but it will not take a life. Nik Nik doesn't beat those he intends to kill.

Unlike his father.

Unlike me.

Nik Nik finishes by calmly grinding Kat's hand beneath his boot until the fingers bend wrong. Then he turns to us with his hands raised, as if he's just given a successful speech instead of maiming one of our own. His knuckles are red, but after years of this I know they're so calloused the color is just someone else's iron, not irritation from impact. Spray from Kat's broken nose has painted droplets on his face. He raises his chin, giving us a flat look. Waiting.

I am the first to applaud. The runners on either side of me join in quick. Mr. Cheeks used to begin the cheers, grunting loud with each blood drop, hyena-laughing at each broken bone. Not because he loved violence, but because he loved the emperor and there is no getting closer to Nik Nik than watching him perform his art. These days, Cheeks joins the punishment cheers later and later. Today he joins in just before the end.

After we quiet, the emperor says, "The city is aware of Helene X's death."

He doesn't offer it as an excuse for Kat's beating, but it is. Kat must not have told for profit, and must not have told anyone like enforcement, or instead of turning to the sound of fists on flesh we would have turned to the sound of Kat hitting the ground, bleeding, chemically paralyzed, and waiting for the poison-hastened end.

Nik Nik nods to Mr. Cheeks to begin the meeting, and he does.

He hosts smoothly, no hesitation, like we can't hear the wheezing breath of a broken runner in the back of the room. You'd think with the way Cheeks has been getting skittish with the punishments that he's moving away from the emperor. But that's not it. He's still knuckles-first anytime someone says a cross word about Himself. It's not distaste that has him clapping slow and quiet. It's fear. Or guilt, maybe. I'm not sure, but he's been looking at punishments like they're fires that could catch. He's been looking at beatings like he's next.

The meeting is a short one, Cheeks telling us things I already know about the bodies that fell into our laps last night, and that the funeral arrangements for Helene won't be announced until the body is released back to the House. He tells us the code—1895—we'll be using to radio in if we see anything related to the new phenomenon. He tells us, though we already know, that if we see something, radioing in is all we can do.

A few people steal glances at me at the last comment, which means stories of my failed and desperate attempt to keep Helene alive have crawled across the desert while I slept. Most everyone knows I've got history with the House, that it was the first place I landed in Ash, working a few years before I took up running, so I'm sure the filthy gossips have made the story twice as dramatic. Runners love sentimentality, so they've probably called us sisters, or lovers. They'll say I screamed *I love you* while she died, or vowed vengeance or something. As if I could do anything when it happened, as if I could even speak.

The only person in the room who doesn't look at me is Cheeks. He hasn't looked at me all meeting, even though we usually share a few side-eyes while he presents. I don't know why Cheeks thinks his cut is because of me. I intend to run up on him right after the meeting ends, but once he's finished with the last of the formalities, he calls the names listed for additional mission assignments and I'm one.

I walk up with a half dozen others who are being pulled from regular duty for an exemption. This means I can't ask him *What the fuck?* My irritation only grows when Cheeks motions me and Cross forward together as a team.

"His office," he says, instead of giving us the assignment. "Both of you."

"Serious?" I say, looking from the face of my best friend to the one I wouldn't save from a fire for a prize.

Cheeks looks into my eyes. "As hate."

I don't want to fight, not at all and especially not in front of Cross.

"Later," I say, letting it be a goodbye, a threat, and a promise.

THE DOOR TO THE EMPEROR'S OFFICE—HIS ACTUAL OFFICE, NOT HIS FATHER'S THAT HE ONLY OCCUPIES on ceremony—is closed and neither Cross nor I have lieutenant status, so we have to wait until the current guest leaves. It's Tatik, and judging from the way she slams open the door, Nik Nik has indeed decided to waste his resources on a "Wiley City problem." He motions us inside without lifting his gaze from the desk, and I'm a little, but not a lot, surprised to see the scientist with him, smirking at Tatik's disrespect. He's leaning on—*on!*—the emperor's desk and I'm shocked at his ease despite being in the presence of a man Wiley only knows as the most prolific killer walking.

"Sir?" I ask, giving a low nod.

"We need a team in the city," he says, then nods at Bosch. "Show her."

Adam sighs. "Demanding."

"If you don't—"

Adam presses the plate beside his eye and a projection begins. Once I recognize the footage I want to look away, but I force myself to watch the four . . . no, five now . . . Wileyites get torn apart by nothing all over again.

"Wiley's fifth body was identified this morning, along with another batch of footage. The security footage we can account for, but these two"—he waves his hand, leaving only the two feeds from civilian cuffs—"we can't."

He's not going to tell me what he sees, and I sense the test in the air.

"Play it again," I say.

He does, and at first I don't get it. Mr. Cross straightens, so I know he does, which makes me even angrier. But I'm no longer one of those people who loses focus with rage. I've learned to get mad like a laser instead of a brush fire, and my refusal to lose to the Ruralite makes me pay attention like never before.

The recording resets to the happy before, when the victims were just oblivious civilians.

"Wait . . . Why were they filming? Nothing's happened yet."

Adam smiles wide. "You passed."

Nik Nik crosses his arms. "No, she didn't."

I look from one to the other. "Why not? I'm right, aren't I? That's what's wrong with them."

"You're right, but he knew it first," Nik Nik says, nodding at Mr. Cross.

I look at the runner, and I know my face is giving him all the unwarranted hatred Cheeks showed me earlier, but I can't stop for my weight in metal.

"So it was a race?"

"No, but he got it first, and you *knew* he got it and instead of asking him you wasted time figuring it out yourself. A good leader doesn't know everything. What a good leader knows is how to trust those who do. Learn to use your resources, Beloved."

Beloved. He says it sharp enough to raise his upper lip and show his onyx teeth. I close my eyes to keep them from rolling. I wonder how many hours it will take before Mr. Cross tells the whole regiment that Nik Nik is grooming me to lead. Half of Ashtown will be checking my finger for a bonding scar by sunrise.

"What's the mission?" I ask low, through teeth that don't part. Not that I'd ever hiss at the emperor. That would be disrespectful.

"Intel gathering. Figure out why they began to film. See if they had a tip-off, or if they're involved. Trust your gut," he says.

"I don't need him for that."

"You need backup."

"Give me Cheeks," I say.

"The one from before? He would stand out like an unattended chain saw," Bosch says.

Nik ignores the interruption. "The city has decided we're to blame for their murders."

That stumps me. I mean, I'm not surprised they would, but even they must know that doesn't make sense. It's like they think we've got quarter over ghosts.

"I know you can pass a citizenship scan, but I'm not sending anyone alone while they're looking for a scapegoat so you'll need backup. With his"—the emperor waves a hand at Mr. Cross's pale skin, blue eyes, Wiley height, or some combination of the three—"looks, they won't even scan him."

"Can't believe they're putting this at our feet when they've got five and we've got one," I say.

"They're Wileyites. They would eagerly blame you for a fire while they were still holding the match," Adam says, in a Wiley-perfect accent that makes all of us look at him. Either oblivious to the irony or finding it beneath him, he ignores our stares and picks up one of Nik Nik's metal nail files.

Nik Nik grabs the file out of the scientist's hand. "When are you heading back to the city?"

"When I get bored of mystery and air that tastes like shit," Adam says, activating what must be the same targeted palm magnet from last night to yank the nail file back. "At the moment both are sufficiently novel."

Nik Nik turns his attention back to someone he can control, which means he turns his attention back to me.

"Mr. Splice has the cuff IDs of the uploaders for you to speak to. Jaxon is standing by to outfit. They've been ordered to host you for as long as it takes."

"I'm sure Jax *loves* that," I say, as my cuff vibrates with the new intel. "And what if it isn't an enemy sent for us? What do we do if it's a Wiley City problem?"

"Solve it, and shame them with what fucking heroes we are," he says.

I don't shrug, but I do give a look that says, *Sure, fine, whatever you want.* The city and its shame are worthless to me. I'd be buzzed if they never thought about us again as long as they let us forget about them, too.

But then the emperor finishes: ". . . And remind them that no one but Ash gets to do bloodwork like that."

Now my nod is emphatic and genuine. That's what the real stakes are. Used to be when people wanted to picture a mangled corpse, a bloody unimaginable horror, they'd have to call up a runner kill. Now this fucker's diluting our effect. It's bad for business. We runners don't want to parade ever again, so we need the old kills to stick. Because we'll do it. We'll ride our vehicles through the streets, eyes closed and howling mad. We'll crush the innocent, and our own hearts in the doing. We'll try not to cry as we clean the blood and bone and tissue of adult and child alike from our treads. But we'll still run, because Ashtown needs us to.

There is a story from before the walls of a woman who escaped her captors and took her four children with her. When they finally caught up to her, she looked them in the eye and sawed through the throat of the nearest child. It scared the captors so bad they left her alone with the other three. Seeing what she would do to her own made them too afraid to test what she would do to them. Do you see it? The emperor is the woman, Ashtown the children, and Wiley City the captors. Runners? We're the saw.

I cross my arm over my chest and bow. But when I rise again the emperor has a hand on my shoulder. For a moment, time collapses. This isn't the office his father died in, but it feels like it. When I look at him, using black-tipped nails to grip my shoulder and his eyes a plea as he looks down at me, I'm a scared little girl again, and he's barely an adult who's just gained a whole kingdom, and we're making each other the kind of promises we're only hoping we can keep.

I haven't fallen alone into this gap in time. I can tell by the hurt and hope in his eyes that Nik Nik is thinking of the day his father died, too.

He leans forward, whispering low so I alone can hear.

"Keep yourself safe, little sister."

I stare into his eyes as I nod this time. When he calls me sister it sows the sun's own warmth into my chest, and I am fiercely proud to be claimed by my big brother, even if just in whispers.

—

THE FIRST TIME I SAW MY BROTHER I WASN'T STANDING IN FRONT OF THE EMPEROR'S DESK. I WAS hiding under it. He bent down and in his eyes I could see rage and hurt and helplessness and it was all my fault. I was sorry, but I knew I wouldn't be in a moment. In a moment, he would obliterate me. Those large hands with their sharp ends would unmake me and I could finally, finally rest. Men who were supposed to keep me safe had hurt me. This one owed me nothing, had every reason to kill me, but he didn't. I had only just learned that we shared a father, shared blood, but he'd known much longer than that.

He told me not to be afraid.

I told him I didn't know how.

He told me to learn.

He made me want to be someone else, someone who knew how to be brave. But I couldn't lead the life I'd lived and know anything but fear. So I shed it. On my knees, I decided I had clawed my way out of the red clay of Ash fully formed that day. I pretended every scar I had was just a birthmark. I pretended I had never been hurt.

It wouldn't work. You don't overcome pain by ignoring it. In a few years, I would let my brother down. He'd protect me and cover up my failure, and I would have to leave the House forever. But in that moment, under that desk, I believed. I believed I was born right then. Not when Senior brought me into his office. Not when I won the first fight of my life. Not even when I was discovered, my hands covered in an important man's blood, and looking up into my older brother's eyes for the first time. No, the first moment of my life was this one, because it was the first moment anyone had ever shown me mercy, so I could believe that was all people ever did.

It was the moment when Nik Nik reached out with no weapon in his hand and a promise in his mouth. I took his hand. And I was born.

—

CROSS AND I ARE GIVEN TWENTY MINUTES TO PREPARE FOR TRANSPORT, BUT NEITHER OF US NEEDS IT. It's no use bringing supplies into the city when Jax is just going to outfit us and toss anything visibly Ashtown that we bring. I swing by Splice's workshop in the courtyard and bang twice hard on the door.

"Jesus!" Splice says, odd spectacles wrapped around his face, giving his black eyes an insectine multiplicity. "Always knocking like tribute's due. Shit."

I don't know how many feeds he's watching right now, so I make it quick.

"My gear?"

He nods, and motions me in. Cross moves to follow, so I slam the door in his face.

"Hate that kid," I say, walking over to Splice's bench. I pick up a soldering iron. He slaps it out of my hand.

"Yes, he's polite, clean, and minds his own business. I can see why you don't get along."

I hiss at him. He shoves a box at me.

"Oh, beauty," I say, pulling the new gloves out and tossing the box over my shoulder just to heighten the irritation on Splice's face. "Did you get the—"

"Heating circuits dialed up? Yes."

"What about the—"

"Razors? Of course. Deployment's tricky, 'cause I didn't want it to happen when you didn't want it. You'll need to tuck your thumb and make a fist to trigger it."

"Smart," I say, sliding them on and squeezing them. Only an idiot jonesing for a fucked-up hand would punch with their thumb tucked.

"Did we fix the—"

"Backlash on the stun? Yeah, sorry about the last batch," he says, rubbing the back of his neck where his locks meet his shoulders.

These new gloves are a dream. Metal in the knuckles, stun-capability palms. These are the best gloves I've ever had. Shit, these may be the best I've ever seen.

Still . . .

". . . I had an idea."

He looks about as irritated as he is unsurprised. "I can only imagine. You want acid deployment? Some kind of tiny palm engine that lets you fly?"

"No, I . . . wait . . . can you do that?"

He glares at me, so I begin outlining what I am actually thinking. As I talk Splice gets that intense look that happens whenever he sees a new puzzle. So close to meeting Adam Bosch, I can't help but notice the similarities, down to the missing foot. Except that Splice is a bleeding heart, and if he could give up his genius tomorrow to end the suffering of others, he'd do it, no question. Adam? Doubtful.

"Magnetic recall?" he says, then smiles wide. "You've been around the scientist."

". . . Maybe."

His smile widens and lightning fast he puts me in a headlock to rub my short hair with his knuckles. "Little snake's jealous someone else's got tricks."

"Maybe! Ow. Cut it out!" I say, breaking his hold with a spin, though we're both laughing. "You don't have to do it, I was just curious."

"I'll look into it. Himself said I can use all the materials I want for your toys and it's fun to play." His face shutters, and I know he's about to fake a casual tone just before he does. "Any idea why?"

He does me the courtesy of not looking at my finger or my throat when he asks, like there's an invisible tattoo there. Splice and I go so far back, I don't know if he'd feel betrayed or relieved to know the truth.

I hold a finger up to my lips. "Nothing I'm gonna risk my teeth to tell," I say, hoping he'll think I'm on something classified, rather than deducing, accurately, that the emperor is just in the mood to spoil me.

I put my hand on Splice's shoulder and squeeze once. "You're the best, Splice."

"Yeah, yeah," he says, but then his visor beeps, and he looks sideways, his eyes tracking something that makes him flinch.

I was going for a quick goodbye, but instead I put my other hand on his other shoulder, a soldier's hold forcing him to look me in the eye.

"You good? The shit you're seeing . . ."

"It's fine," he says, lowering his head, then meeting my eyes again. This time he's paused his feeds. "It's rough, but it's fine. Himself's sending me off for care once we wrap. Says I can have three whole weeks."

I nod. Three weeks off work with care at the House? I've only been on full care once, and it was only for a week. But what a week. Care at the House is someone cooking for you, massaging you, leading you in quiet moments of reflection with the gentlest hum. I'm happy Splice will get that, and I'm happy my brother could see he'd need it.

Cross doesn't ask questions as I leave Splice's, but he does look down at the gloves like he notices the difference. Hell if I know how, because these look exactly like the ones I went into Splice's wearing, just the black's a little less faded. As we head toward transport, I see Mr. Cheeks in the hall, but his eyes narrow and he turns at the sight of me.

"Wait here," I say to Cross, and run after him.

I grab Cheeks by the arm. "It's not me," I say, "whoever served you up for censure, it was anybody but me."

He takes a moment, holding on to the rage he's had since this morning, and then he exhales.

"Swear?"

"On oil and blood."

He touches the line on the back of his neck, though the emperor's cuts are so fine he probably can't feel it anymore.

"Wouldn't have blamed you. I've been a bad friend."

He wants me to disagree, to spare his feelings. I shrug. The memory of his hate from earlier, how he jumped to it before even talking to me, keeps me from reassuring him. He continues.

"Truth is . . . I thought you were jealous."

I barely contain a confused headshake. "Jealous? Of what? You know I care fuck all about promotions. And you've always been more favored than me."

"Not that kind of jealous," he says, but my stare stays blank. "You know, like . . . Never mind. I thought you had feelings for me and since I've been seeing someone seriously you acted out."

Seeing someone? *Seriously?* It takes the floor out from under me. I feel like I could puke, and I wonder if that's what happens when you feel the death of your oldest wish.

"Doesn't sound like me," I say, the words surprising even me, considering my mouth is dry with grit and my world's tilted wrong.

But his smile is weightless now, shining like dawn. "Yeah, I know. Looking back . . . it's mad."

"The maddest." I punch him in the arm, and it feels like gnawing my own off. "You're dreaming wild, Cheeks."

"I know, I know, row mechanic in love. That'll be the day. I just"—he steps forward, closing in for a secret—"Splice let it slip that the emperor had him put an echo in my gear."

I step back. An echo means all of Cheeks's communications are being copied to someone else and monitored. His location is probably being logged too. Only one reason that would ever happen.

"You've got a wolf on you," I say, and if people weren't being torn apart by air, it'd be the most unbelievable thing I'd ever heard.

Cheeks? Emperor's favorite? The man who loves my brother so much he would get cited for having a religion if it wasn't the emperor he worshipped, has a wolf? See, we don't have anyone set to sniff out our own runners. No designated internal investigators. If we did they'd be a constant target, everyone'd hate them. Instead we have people made wolf for a bit and then released from duty once the investigation is over. If we find out someone was wolf, it's no real harm, 'cause we all know you're not allowed to say no and we all know it's temporary. A wolf's only a wolf while they're appointed, and you can trust them again once they're through playing dog. Emperor says it prevents division, but the truth is you'll get more from a temporary spy than a known and permanent stooge.

Cheeks nods. "I'm not sure who it is. Figured you'd be a pretty smart get. I saw you got a new gear allowance, and you said you were working on something classified, and I thought maybe it was you."

Me? Everyone's little sister? Wolf?

I don't ask Mr. Cheeks if he's been fucking up. The presence of a wolf means he has been. I just nod.

"It'll pass. We've all had our turn under the eye," I say, even though I never have as far as I know. "You've got a witness, if you want me."

A witness can counteract a wolf, if they like you enough and the emperor believes their testimony. I'd eat teeth to protect Cheeks, and he knows it. That's probably why he thought Nik Nik made me wolf; put his closest friend on his tail and rob him of his best witness at the same time.

"Thanks, sorry I . . . sorry I assumed," he says, and gives me a half-hug that I accept.

I wish I could be self-righteous, be mad at him for accusing me without asking. But I *have* been lying to him. I have hidden myself from him for longer than he knows, and I'm not about to tempt fate by throwing stones about trust from my puddle of lies.

"It's fine. We're good," I say.

"We're good," he repeats on a nod, squeezing my shoulders.

We're good . . . and it's all we'll ever be.

"Oh, right, and about buggying. I'm not gonna be able to swing it."

I keep my smile tight. "No problem. With everything that went down last night, I doubt we'd have been able to spare the time."

"Next moon?"

"'Course," I say.

And the smile I give him feels just like a noose.

CHAPTER FIVE

WHEN I WALK BACK UP TO CROSS, HE'S WATCHING CHEEKS OVER MY SHOULDER, BUT HE DOESN'T ASK. I spend all day, every day with Cheeks for years, and not one rumor of us being together ever crops up. Emperor looks too long at me a couple of times and everyone's measuring me for dipped braids. I know why. I can pretend I don't, but I do. Cheeks got his name because no one's got a face like his. Those cheekbones? Those eyes? He's beautiful. I'm . . . the ogre of the row. Him taking up with me strains belief when he's always had a taste for delicate, beautiful things. But the emperor's always liked a rough one, so people were ready to start that rumor and run with it.

That's the thing. I *always* knew. I knew it'd never be me for Cheeks. I've seen his exes. I've had crushes on his exes. But we got on so well, I thought one day being someone he liked talking to, someone he trusted, might evolve into something more. It's stupid. I know. That's not how people work. I've got no right to cry over this. But I really want to cry over this. Caring about losing a crush is childish, but that must make me a wailing infant because I want to hit red-hot metal until it flattens and then put it into an ice bath just to hear it shatter. I'll get over it. I will. I'm just gonna wallow a bit till it stops stinging.

As we head to transport, Mr. Cross walks two steps behind me and doesn't talk at all. Which is annoying. I mean, yeah, sure, I bite his head off every time he does speak, and more than once I've said, *Speak to me again and I'll take your tongue,* but now I need a distraction from my own idiotic disappointment. I decide it's on me to break the ice once we're loaded into a vehicle.

I melt against the curved metal wall at my back. It means I'll get jostled more, but I like feeling the purr of the ground mix with the vibrations of the engine in my chest. These rides are meant to transport whole teams, and it's just us two, so I sit wide as I revel in it.

"Hate going into Wiley. Concentration of shit with a wall around it."

He shrugs. If he's surprised I'm talking to him, he doesn't show it.

"Haven't been much. I haven't liked the Wileyites I've met though, so stands to reason I won't like the city." He tilts his head at me. "How come you can pass a citizenship scan? I thought we couldn't fake them anymore."

I smile. "Jealous? You worried Splice is playing favorites?"

"No, just didn't know if we had a new contact in the city or something."

"God forbid," I say. "My papers are good because I got them right before the crackdown, so they're grandfathered in under the lesser security application that was easier to fake. Once they expire, I won't be able to get new."

"Too bad."

"No skin off my neck. Not going to miss interacting with more like that fucking scientist."

"Adam Bosch?" he says, but they were never introduced.

"You know him?"

"We blew up his property, few years back."

Why does everyone else from that mission recognize Adam right off? Maybe it's me. I never care which Wileyite we do dirty. I'm always just there for the fun of the doing.

"It was my first run," he says, which also explains why he knew the mark by name and face. He hadn't stopped caring yet.

"Well, I'm glad we made him hurt. That guy's an asshole. I don't know why Himself puts up with him."

He's staring at me. "You really don't know?"

"They fucking?"

I know the emperor's seeing someone, but despite all these rumors swirling about us no one's ever jumped me as a warning to back off. Makes sense if the person he's seeing is a Wileyite, though the idea of our emperor going in the walls for strange sits wrong.

"I'm surprised he never told you."

"I'm not exactly in the emperor's confidence, despite what everyone thinks," I say, and it's half hiss, the venom of a snake to match my name.

"I meant Mr. Cheeks."

"Cheeks knows?" I lean forward, invading the runner's space. "*You* know?"

"I'll tell you," he says, matching my posture to bring our faces into conspiracy range.

It's awkward. My feet are too big for an Ashtowner. So are his. Sitting across from each other in the transport we have to lace our boots between each other's or risk touching.

"Price?" I say, because his tone tells me he's got one.

When he looks up his eyes are a wide blue. They hold me in place, not because they are exceptional but because it's too rare a color. In the city blue and silver are so common they're boring. Out here it's the color of the sky and nothing else. I wonder if that's why the missionaries came to the desert in the first place; they'd already made their world white and Christian and they wanted somewhere brown and pagan to stand out against. I guess having all that power doesn't hit right if you don't get to feel special on top of it.

Cross is still looking at me as he calculates his ask. His pause is dramatic enough that I wonder if his price will be physical, my mouth or hand, but what he says is worse.

"Stop hating me."

I rear away from him, craning my head all the way back to show my shiny bottom teeth. I'd have been less disgusted if he had asked to fuck.

"No dice, Holy Man."

He leans away, and this time his silence suits me perfect.

—

WHEN I FIRST GOT TO THE HOUSE I WAS TOO YOUNG TO DO SKINWORK, SO I SPENT YEARS LEARNING THE trade and running errands. I was coming back from dropping supplies off to a former Housecat that was still favored enough to get care packages, when I saw a boy who looked like light. He was leaning against the wall beside the door, too young to be a client and at the wrong entrance for counseling or healing. Unlike every person in the House his eyes were the color of barely tinted water, even lighter than Helene X's, and unlike every other person in the House, he looked broken on the inside. I thought his parents must have sent him for counseling, because no one could see anyone that unhappy and not try to fix it.

I walked up eagerly. I was so brand-new I was excited to see someone more lost than I was.

"It's around the corner," I said.

"What?"

"Counseling. You're depressed, right? Counseling's at the other entrance."

And yeah, I'd learn better about my approach later, but I hadn't taken the full care unit yet and I was just trying to help.

He turned on me full of rage, but it wasn't the bright, hissing Ashtown rage I'd come to know. It was cold and threatening, and reminded me of the darkest days of my childhood that I'd promised to forget.

"I don't need help. You do. You're a sinner."

I didn't notice the pamphlets in his hands until he shoved one at me. Still in shock, I almost took it automatically, but then the door opened and Exlee was between us.

"Your people know the rules. Get back on the sidewalk."

He glared as he went, first at Exlee, then at me. "You're cheapening yourself. You'll never know glory. You don't deserve it."

I gasped as the words hit, but Exlee turned me toward the door and walked me inside. I know they knew about my temper and worried I'd attack the miserable boy with the evil tongue. But no,

I didn't feel an ounce of rage. I felt . . . like he was right. Not about any god. But about me being unworthy and covered in sin.

I saw the boy and his family dozens of times after that, and each time they shouted at me I'd return it with twice the venom. But deep down, I was afraid those near-white eyes saw through me. I'd always had a voice in my head saying I wasn't good enough. After that day, the sound of it changed.

That's what makes it so easy to hate Cross even now. When I heard a voice telling me I was worthless through my most insecure years, it was him.

—

EVEN IF I WEREN'T SENIOR ON THIS MISSION, I'D BE TAKING POINT. I SPEND MOST OF MY TIME ON THE row, sure, but I'm almost always the emperor's choice for courier in the city. Cross moves slow, taking in even the interior tunnels like they're points of interest. I wonder if he's been back since we used him for the hot job on Bosch. Or if he'd ever been here before that.

Jax lives on the sixtieth floor, not low enough to feel invisible and not high enough to attract attention. They've been in the city for long enough that they've got citizenship—though whether it's real or manufactured I don't know and it's rude to ask. When they open the door, I brace for their reaction. Sure enough, Jax lets their lids half fall at the sight of me.

"Here we are."

I nod.

Jax left the House for Wiley a little less than twenty years ago, which means Jax was preparing to leave right when I was getting promoted to full service, and we fundamentally don't understand each other. We got into a fight one night. Okay, it wasn't *one* night. It was the night of Jax's going away party, and it wasn't so much a fight as me ruining said party. Everyone was so cheerful about them going to the city, but I was full of acid. I finally said the city is trash, and the people who go there end up being trash too. And yes, yes, I was young, and abrasive, and I probably had the *tiniest* crush on Jax and was mostly raw about them going, but I still stand by every word, even if I am old enough now to know why it was cruel to say it during their celebration.

Our staring is interrupted by Mr. Cross.

"We've got city work. We need outfitting and housing."

The reigning champion of not reading the fucking room, this guy.

It is endlessly gratifying that Jax looks irritated at his interruption. They might not recognize him as precisely as I do, but they can tell he's not a runner from downtown. When they look back at me we get to share a moment of *This asshole, am I right?* camaraderie that reminds me of when I was new to the House and they were teaching me how to dress and move.

"Yes, the emperor's lieutenant cuffed me the instructions, *obviously*," they say at Cross. "Now come in before the whole neighborhood spots you."

Their voice has taken on a touch of the city, but they dress very much how they always have: T-shirt, gray vest, close-cropped hair, with long, natural-looking but artificially enhanced lashes the only concession to vanity. Exlee—who aggressively exhibits all of the gender spectrum at once—always called Jax a Wiley enby, all androgyny and muted colors. I never thought much about the difference, except that I desperately wanted to unbutton Jax's vests to feel their buzzed hair against my palm as I cupped the back of their head.

Jax instructs Cross and me to shower and put on robes while they ready our new clothes. They were a costumer back in the House, now a fashion designer in the city. I'd comment on the lateral movement, but in Ash I let an important man bark orders at me under threat of physical violence, and before I got to Ash, I did just the same.

When Jax dresses me, I'm surprised to find the crush of my teen years gone, or, at least, tepid. Jax is still attractive, but I no longer salivate at the sight of them like I'm smelling good food. I wonder if it's because I associate Jax with the city now, and so I could never really want them again. Or maybe I can only balance being attracted to one person who will never want me at a time.

For me, they've chosen clothes in an expensive but durable material. I pull my hair back to complete the image of someone important, but practical. I could pass for project supervisor on the newest round of construction, or a city employee inspecting a site. Jax hands me a pair of glasses—thick and wide, the kind used by people afraid of debris rather than people who need to see—to complete the look. Staring in the mirror I allow myself to imagine another life where I'm a landscape architect or engineer in this city of glass. I shudder.

I expected Cross to be outfitted the same as I was, but when he enters the room he's in a button-down shirt, nonsensically showy pants, and these odd cloth shoes that only the rich think pass for casual. I know the type he's meant to be instantly, and seeing it makes my mouth go dry.

"A financier?" I say, and Jax nods. "Why?"

"You're too rough to ever pull off inherited money, but I barely had to outfit this one at all. Dressed like this, they'll think his Ash traits are eccentricities." Jax straightens Cross's collar. "Does he not seem authentic?"

"I hate it," I say. "So it's perfect. Let's go."

—

OUR MISSION IS SIMPLE ENOUGH: TALK TO THE PEOPLE WHO UPLOADED THOSE TWO VIDEOS AND FIGURE out why they started recording. If the answer isn't satisfactory, if they smell dirty, act accordingly. And here's me, years of training to keep my violent half at bay, hoping to god that at least one of them is guilty. Not just because I want to wear the blood of anyone who had a hand in Helene X's end, but because having a face to pin all this on is the only way I'll ever feel good again.

The first uploader we're meant to interview is on the same floor as Jax, but there's no answer. We head to the second, which is on the seventieth floor. It's a new-money floor. Greatness adjacent.

When the address is in sight I tap every pouch on this khaki-ass vest that should, and does, contain a weapon.

"Going into an interrogation with all my best gear trapped in some bullshit pocket," I say, walking just a little faster in my irritation. "Brilliant."

"It's not an interrogation. We're just asking questions."

I turn to him like he might suddenly look as useless as he is. "That's the same thing."

He sighs. "Do you really think that's how this is going to go? An invisible force kills half a dozen people, and you think we're going to knock on a door and see the villain? You think this is going to be something you can punch to solve?"

"No . . . maybe . . . fuck off." I take a few more steps before turning to him again, and the fact that I have to tilt my head up to look at him just makes me rage all over again. "So what? You think it's God? Some divine force? Your Jesus going piñata on mortals?"

"He isn't mine. The Christian bible wasn't even one of my texts."

"Not the way I remember it."

"I was a *child*."

Here we go again.

"And so was I. I wasn't even working full service when you and your stepmom threw pamphlets at me. You called me a whore for learning pressure points and aromatherapy."

The silence stretches awkwardly between us, distinctly different from the usual kind, which is just my hatred and his apathy.

"No," he says, finally. "I don't think this was God's work. I just don't think we're going to find it was some kind of petty criminal."

I snort. He and I have precisely one thing in common: At our rank, no one's paying us to think.

He opens his mouth to say some more stupid shit, probably, but we're at the address and in range of their doorcam.

The woman who answers is a real Wiley City special. Her white hair is perfectly styled to "effortless." Her outfit is in the same cool, synthetic silver that swirls a little but mostly compliments her ice eyes. This floor doesn't have a lot of people with Wiley blood as far back as hers obviously goes, so she must have married someone newer.

"Are you"—I act like I'm consulting the vidscreen cradled in my arm—"Charlotte Andrews?"

I look up, touch the bridge of my glasses, try to seem a little nervous to be out with the boss.

She smiles kindly at me and nods.

"Oh good! You're listed as a direct witness to the events last night, and we're trying to get a clearer picture of what went wrong and if it could be . . . well . . . if it could have been environmentally related."

"Rather, that it could *not* have," Mr. Cross says, playing the callous financier perfectly.

"Right, yes, that it could *not* have been environmentally related," I say. "Can you tell us what you saw?"

It's easier than it should be. Wileyites talk like nothing bad can come from it, and she recounts her story like she's been dying to be asked. I don't know this victim. Charlotte Andrews isn't talking about my Helene X, but her self-important glee in the wake of such horror gets to me. Cross elbows me to fix my face. I hadn't growled, but I could have, so I lower my eyes and tap pretend notes onto the screen. I'm just writing stray lines I remember from old songs, but Cross is staring at my work over my shoulder. Right, the Ruralites teach all of theirs to read. I stop typing.

"And what happened before?" I say, hoping she's talked enough now that we can ask the real question.

"Before?" she asks, finally wary and at the worst possible time.

"Yes, you were recording early in the event. I didn't know if you noticed something off, or maybe observed an anomaly before anyone else could?"

"Oh," she says. "You mean the double?"

"The double?"

"Yes, there was a double of the woman standing right behind her. It stopped by the time I got my cuff recording, but I figured something was going to happen. It was . . . whispy?"

"Whispy?" I ask.

"Yes," she says, surer now that I've challenged her. "Like a ghost. I thought it was one of those new projections—you know, the ones you can send out while you're still sitting at home—and it was malfunctioning or something. Letting us see the user behind the sim. I thought that the whole time, that it was an avatar glitch, or maybe a new holographic art installation? Have you seen the one that happens on Eightieth? With the carnivorous flowers? You should go! Anyway . . . then I saw the blood."

Her ability to bounce between the blood of a victim and some fucking play is unnerving, so I'm eager to nod, take a step back, and give a cursory, "Thank you for your time."

Cross isn't done, though.

"What was the second image doing?" he asks. "Was it moving just like her, like a shadow but a step behind?"

"No, that's why I thought it was just the real her controlling the bot," she says. "It was standing still. Watching. Smiling, maybe? Yes, definitely smiling. She was excited."

—

AFTER WE LEAVE, I HEAD STRAIGHT FOR THE PARK WHERE IT HAPPENED AND SCAN THE ROAD. I HAVE TO verify it's the right park by the surrounding businesses, because there are too many parks in this shit city and every one of them looks exactly the same: too-green rectangles filled with waxy-leaved plants that have no business in this climate, and "natural" walking paths that take more maintenance than a cat at the House. The city wants its parks to show it cares about nature. But it killed an ecosystem when it was built, and endangers another by casting its constant light and unnatural shadow across a once untamed desert.

If Wiley City cares about nature, they must only care about the right kind. They must only care if the nature is pretty, or serves them. They must only care if the nature makes them feel good about themselves, or if caring makes them look good to others. And they must only care if the nature got here the way they wanted it, by them planting it, not by it coming naturally or preexisting them in this space. Basically, if Wiley City cares about nature, it's in the same conditional way it cares about us.

I get to the spot where the death took place, but then my memory fails me. I can't remember the victim's journey. Cross will know. The lesson my brother taught me just a few hours ago floats across my mind . . . where it promptly begins warring with my pride. Eventually I sigh, and look over my shoulder at him.

"Do you remember where the vic was walking? Which direction?"

He tilts his head, less like he needs time to remember and more like he's surprised I'm asking him at all. After a moment he raises his arm, and points to a corner.

"She came from there, the video started while she was walking past that window."

I walk in that direction, pulling up her data on my cuff as I move. Mr. Splice would have reviewed all the camera footage from the square, but our witness said the doubling had already stopped, so he might not have seen it.

I look at my cuff, then point down the street. "She lived that way. Probably came from there."

He nods, but I can tell he's still not sure what I'm doing. I'm relieved he's not better at every part of the job than I am. He would stop now, call in the info, and wait for next steps. He was raised in a culture that normalized memorizing twenty-page-long passages to save their souls, so of course he's got a better memory than I do. But he was also raised in a culture that accepted whatever a man in an apron told them was true, so his instincts are trash.

I get the name and address of the business in the center of the next block, and call up Splice.

"Can you pull surveillance from these locations?" I give him the information of the business with the best vantage of the street, and add a few of the surrounding ones just to be safe.

". . . These are just around the corner from the third victim."

"Yep, so you already know what I'm looking for."

"I'll find her," he says, and cuts off.

We go back to Jax's to eat. When my cuff beeps next, the message is from the man Himself and it's in all caps.

"Footage must have been interesting," I say. "We got orders. We're being called back."

Mr. Cross looks up from his plate, but knows better than to request info that might be above his clearance.

"We're staying here until the wee hours. An escort will be waiting by the wall at four in the morning. Himself says sleep early. Gonna be a long day."

"What about the other witnesses?"

I shrug. "I guess they've got all they need."

He's studying the table. "The footage must have showed the anomaly, and it must be undeniable. That's why we can let the other witnesses slide. It's something so obvious anyone would have recorded it so they're not suspicious."

"Hey." I snap my fingers at him. "We'll know what's on the footage once they want us to, and we'll think exactly what they want us to think about it. It's good to think through our jobs, and anticipate next moves without needing a handhold. But if you go further into trying to decipher the motives of our superiors, you're just begging to donate blood to the dirt."

"Does it make you mad?" he asks, blue eyes staring into mine like he's discovered something interesting.

"What?"

"That we can't question our superiors?"

"Are you fucking *un*well? You got a problem taking orders, go back to the pulpit where your kind play God."

"Right," he says, head hanging down like I'd swatted him. "That was out of line, I'm sorry. I'm not used to working with others."

He was testing me, I realize. I wonder if he's going to be one of those runners who tries to climb by outing others as not good enough instead of proving themselves on their own merit. But something else he said distracts me from the appealing vision of Cross learning what happens to snitches.

I'm not used to working with others.

"You're on a solo assignment?"

Runners are nothing if not pack animals, and our few solo

shifts are usually reserved for those of us who can't stand people or those who people can't stand.

I'd never really troubled myself to know what post the Ruralite held. He always seems to be free when we need coverage, so I assumed he was floating. But of course, floating was for newbies and as much as I hate to admit it, he hasn't been that for a very long time.

"Yeah. It's a distant one."

A distant assignment and he doesn't have a partner? I wonder if it's a post I don't know about . . . or, more likely, if he was supposed to have a partner but no one wants to work with the Ruralite.

"Eat up and turn in," I say.

He nods. "You told me. Long day."

It's a miracle we've gotten through a whole assignment without killing each other, and neither of us speaks for the rest of dinner like we don't want to risk it.

"You want next?" he asks, coming out of the shower.

I'm lying on the bed—he's got the cot beside me—and I keep my eyes trained on the wall at the end of my boots. He's wearing too little clothes and it's been too long since I got laid. If I don't pay a visit to the House or the nightfire soon I'll be humping a rock in the desert.

"I'll shower at home."

"What if you get put back on your post?"

"Then I'll shower at post."

The shop has not just a shower, but a kitchen and a deceptively comfortable hammock.

"Huh. Must be nice."

I lose the war against looking at him. "You're in the deep and your post doesn't have a shower?"

Deep posts aren't nine-to-fives. They're usually days on, days off. It's not like border patrol or range work.

"I meant to have a home and a post. That they're separate."

"You're full time?"

He nods.

No wonder he's always volunteering when we need a hand. Wonder he doesn't go crazy, out there in the wastes unpartnered. His honesty makes me feel just a little guilty for the lie I told earlier. Really, he's been around long enough he should know better than to believe the emperor gives a single shit when we go to sleep, so long as we show up on time. But he's gullible like those in the Rurals always are and always have been.

Jax is out going to whatever kind of party people who dress others go to at night, so I just have to wait for Cross's breathing to calm before I sneak away.

CHAPTER SIX

I'VE GOT TO GO HIGH IN THE CITY, HIGHER EVEN THAN CHARLOTTE ANDREWS LIVED, BUT I COULD MAKE the trip with my eyes closed I've done it so often. It's still early evening, but the sun is down, so I hadn't expected to actually see her except maybe through a glimpse in the window. I'm unprepared for the vision of her standing in her garden. I've seen her a few times in the last couple of years, but it's only been in the dim light from inside the house. Or in the shadow of her husband, who always demanded she keep her face turned toward the ground. Now caressing the soft petals of flowers that have been her only joy since I left, she looks . . . happy. Seeing her happy makes me realize I've never seen her like that before.

Her husband must be out of town. I wonder if he's away on prescheduled business or if the cowardly sack of shit hit the skies the second the first body started breaking. He would be one to leave his wife behind.

I try to enjoy the fact that she looks free and happy and whole for the first time in my memory, but as always the cloud of him shadows any affection I could feel for her. Why choose him? Why watch him break me and still choose him?

"A bit old for you, isn't she?"

I turn around and shove back before I'm even sure it's Cross. But of course it is. Who else remains such a persistent pain in my ass?

"This is none of your fucking business."

"I could just ask her how she knows you," he says, and makes like he's going to walk over.

The punch, when it connects, catches him off guard. But he doesn't look surprised until I take the dagger from my pouch and drag the tip across his newly-reddened cheekbone. He thought I was just punching him to punch him like anyone on the street wants to punch him. But when I mark him, it's like signing my name on a write-up. Anyone who sees him will know it was a punishment.

"Insubordination," I say, giving him his crime in case he wants to bring it to the emperor for protest. "Remember your place. And mine."

"What is your place, exactly?"

"Master Chief. Which puts me rungs above you."

"That all?" he asks, eyes darting to my finger. Still unmarked, not that that matters to the gossips. He's asking if he's just been sanctioned by the future empress. Maybe, but not the way he's thinking.

"I've never been the emperor's girl and I'm getting real tired of hearing myself have to say it."

"You've never said it. Not to me."

"That's because up until now you've at least been good at staying out of my fucking business. So much for that."

I turn and walk back toward Jax's in a mood to end all moods. I'll need to catch some sleep before we head out, though like all runners I can operate on precious little. Mr. Cross, obeying a command I didn't have to give, follows me.

When we get back to our room, Mr. Cross lays down in his cot and I get in bed. This time, instead of lying on his back with his arms crossed, he takes off his jacket and moves onto his side, curling up a little bit the way animals sleep in the cold.

"You weren't sleeping earlier," I say. It's clear now that I compare it to the real thing.

He opens his eyes. "I wasn't."

"But your breathing . . ." It's so obvious it should have been my first thought. If I'm going to be this sloppy, I deserve to get followed. "You were meditating. You still meditate."

"No . . ." he says, but he's lying. And he has every reason to lie.

The House offers something very similar to meditation, but it's not attached to any god. A *Ruralite* meditating means he hasn't sworn off his faith. It means he hasn't done the first thing it would take to be worthy of running.

"You're still communing. You've taken an oath, Cross. Jesus. You're the one should have a wolf after him, not Cheeks."

He sits up on his cot. "It's not like that. I'm not communing with my congregation. I don't have a congregation. I *am* cut off. I don't even do it at the prescribed times." He sounds good and panicked. "Please, please don't tell anyone."

It's the most he's spoken to me this whole trip, and possibly ever.

"You're not allowed to hold two traditions. A runner and a runner only, through this life and the next. You took the vow."

"It just helps keep me level, the meditating. It's not prayer."

"You sure?"

"I had a bad time when I was young. The runners helped me get control, but the meditating helped first. It helps me focus when I'm stressed. It keeps me from doing . . . anything else."

The *anything else* hangs between us, invisible but impenetrable like a dust cloud you can technically see through, but only if you're willing to lose your eyes.

He's looking at me, desperate, scared, and begging for me of all people to protect him.

Cross's family aren't just Ruralites; they are the head family of all the Rurals. The first time I saw him, passing pamphlets and judgment downtown with his stepmother, his face was flat and unwavering and certain. When he walked into the row the first time, it looked exactly the same—a prince who'd never had a doubt in his life. I've never seen him unsure . . . until now.

This is the part where I'm supposed to say that, despite having wanted it for so long, seeing him scared is unpalatable to me and I can be the bigger person. Nah. His fear hits like warm honey. I'd spread his misery on dry toast to send it down easy. But it's not as good as it could be. It's close. I do want to see him scared. And humbled. And half broken. But I want it to be because of my own power, not because he's afraid I'll rat. Fear of me isn't bringing him to his knees; it's just the emperor's shadow.

I ask a question I never thought I'd be directing at the Ruralite prince.

"Addiction or depression?"

Asking him about depression reminds me too much of our first meeting, and I half expect him to respond with the same judgment and rage. Instead, his posture softens like he's tired of holding up his own bones.

"Both, but in the opposite order."

I nod, because that makes sense.

"Only my sister knew. My twin," he says, and that makes sense, too. He does mope around like half to a whole most of the time.

And me, I don't say, but it's true. I knew he needed help the moment I saw him, I just stopped caring somewhere along the way.

"Are you going to report me?" he asks.

I look at the insubordination mark on his face like I'm considering giving him a second. I won't, of course. My mouth was a vault the moment he told me why he needed it. But no need for him to know that.

"Don't give me a reason to. I'm not wolf, and I don't report over harmless shit."

"Thank you, De—Scales. Thank you, Mr. Scales."

"Just call me Sir if the name comes so hard," I say.

It's as close as I want to get to addressing that he almost dropped my old name from his mouth like a goddamn first mark. I hate that he knows the name. I hate that he ever saw me as a teenager, ever saw me cry as he called me and everyone I cared about unredeemable. I still know his name too, but I won't say it. Real names are for lovers and children. They have no place between us.

—

NOT SHARING TRUE NAMES IS MY FAVORITE THING ABOUT BEING A RUNNER. I LIKE THE IDEA OF STORIES and I hate the idea of truth. Names—real names, fixed names, *government* names—are too concrete to be made into a story properly. You say, *A man named Diamond Jones died trying to eat a mountain and that's why there's a crater in the wastes.* And someone says, *Actually, I checked, and there's never been a man named Diamond Jones* or *According to his obituary Diamond Jones died from cancer, not mountain-eating.*

But if you say, *Once—once* and only *once,* because dates are as bad as names for stories—*a man loved the ground so much he ate a mountain and it killed him but it killed the mountain too,* people will learn from the story without truth getting in the way. They'll learn that to love something is to open wide and hope what you love is digestible. They'll learn that if you love so much you consume the thing you love whole, neither of you will survive and neither will your love. They'll learn not to eat fucking rocks.

I know I said real names are for lovers and children, but that's not strictly true. I know Mr. Cheeks's birth name. I figured it out the same way I figured out everything about him—I asked. I asked him about his life every day, all day. I asked him questions when we were partnered and when he was at the shop and that stretch when I was out at his place more than my own. I've seen the shack where he was born. I know what his childhood home smelled like. I've even read the angsty digijournal he kept from so long ago I wasn't even in Ash yet, so I know that he honors his mother's husband, but has never stopped wondering about the man who left him behind.

I know what you're thinking. You're seeing someone in love and you want it to become a love story. Stop. Being in love with someone doesn't entitle you to them; wanting someone doesn't obligate them to want you back. I know that better than most. Like I said, no rumors of Cheeks and me ever surfaced because some stories are too weighed down with disbelief to carry on the wind. Even before this confirmation of him seeing someone else—*seriously*—I never thought it'd be him and me. Last year I even helped him write messages to someone he wanted so badly it froze him solid. And I did my best writing in those messages, because I want him to be happy more than I want him to be mine.

I know how it sounds. Like I'm shoving a knife in my own chest so I won't risk cutting him. Maybe I am. But if I'm going to choke on poison by my own hand, you can at least let me congratulate myself on how well I take it. It's a cold consolation, but that's the only kind I'm likely to get.

—

WHEN TRANSPORT DROPS CROSS AND ME OFF AT THE PALACE, IT'S STILL EARLY ENOUGH THAT THE SUN is nothing but a dream the sky is having just along its edges. We're summoned into the emperor's office, but only after we enter do I realize it's been turned into Adam Bosch's makeshift lab. There are computers running some kind of program lined up against one wall, and the man himself is looking down at what I assume is a magnification screen and what I hope are not Helene X's tissue samples.

Adam and Nik Nik are talking, and there is something so strange in their closeness that I stand for a moment watching them, not at all eager to be addressed. Is it just that Adam isn't one of his citizens, isn't a rival or follower, so Nik Nik can be himself in the scientist's presence? Something about the other man being here has made the emperor seem young for the first time in my knowing him. I wonder again if they're fucking, but I know it's not that. They are close like two people comfortable being close, not close like two people dying to touch.

Cross has walked to the screens on the desk. The problem with being raised a prince, being raised by a father who looped his children in on leadership decisions, is he only acts subordinate when he reminds himself to. He turns a vidscreen on the desk to study it, then rears back. I'm guessing from how quickly he looks away that it's an image of a body. Serves him right. Nosy.

"You gonna puke, Prodigal?"

He shakes his head, either at me or to clear the image from his brain. "Is it true what they're saying? That the body looks just like the Ripper's, and it was found in the same place?"

"You'll have to ask Scales," Nik Nik says, finally addressing us. "She was there for both."

"You were at the House for the Ripper?" Cross asks, and I glare at the emperor.

"Yeah, and if that's what they're saying they're wrong. Ripper was botched, sure, but you could tell he died from a mangled throat. Helene . . . there's no telling."

"There's telling," Adam says. "I can tell you."

There's a flash of something evil behind his eyes, like he'd love nothing more than to detail my friend's cause of death just to watch my reaction. Like even the tears of another person are valuable data.

"Tempting, but I'll pass," I say. I don't let him see how much he shakes me.

I turn to Nik Nik like Adam doesn't interest me. "That what you called us back for? To hear the autopsy?"

"The footage you had Splice pull was fruitful," Nik Nik says.

He gestures to Adam, but the scientist was already beginning to project the video over the desk. I lean forward, prepared to take in every minor detail in case this is a test. But the anomaly is so clear, the only test is whether I can watch without fainting.

"What . . . how . . . ?"

The video shows the woman walking as expected, but this time there is a specter standing at her back. The image is linked to her. The shapes aren't following her by moving. They're standing still but perpetually being dragged a few feet behind. The shadow figure looks almost like a projection. It's made entirely of blue to white light and absent any other colors, but it's still easy to tell that it looks exactly like the woman who is about to die. She's watching herself just before her body is torn apart.

"She doesn't look scared," I say, because this is the part threatening to take my feet out from under me. "The witness was right. She looks excited."

"They both do," Nik Nik says.

"Both?"

"Show the enhanced image," Nik Nik says, as if Adam wasn't going to do it without permission anyway.

The screen shifts away from the video feed to a still image. The ghost of the woman is clearer now, so I can tell they aren't wearing the same clothes, just similar ones. Like it's her from a different day, but pulling from the same wardrobe. Over her shoulder is a second, shorter shape. Another woman perched on a desk like a gremlin as she watches on. I squint and lean forward, then it hits me.

"The traverser."

Caramenta isn't quite a legend in Ashtown, but she's not far off. We all know about her. I told you Adam Bosch used to be in charge of traveling the multiverse, but you have to know he'd never do anything dangerous or dirty himself. Cara was one of us, an Ashtown girl sent to the city to walk between worlds. But every time she came back, she was a little less ours and a little more theirs. The last time, when she came back with haunted eyes and permanent dark stripes in her skin, it became clear that she wasn't theirs either. She belonged to something else entirely.

No one's seen her in years. I heard once she went rabid, mind rattled because Adam Bosch sent her walking through too many worlds, and once the industry died her mind couldn't take being in one world for the rest of her life. There are rumors she killed the hero Jean Sanogo with her bare hands, held on a few more weeks, then disappeared into the desert forever, seeking the sun's justice. There are other rumors that she wasn't mad at all, but in love. She killed Jean Sanogo crying, then went to the south of the south, and let Jack Ketch take her.

It doesn't matter what's true. She stopped being a person years ago and became a story. On her best day, she's still a puzzle, people doing her the courtesy of acting like it isn't all figured out. But mostly, we talk about her like a finished tale. Like someone in a Ruralite book, or wasteland graffiti. A ghost.

I feel a little bad about that, honestly. I remember those few months she hid out here before she disappeared, fixing what she could with what was left of her money. But she never really belonged, so most people pretend it never happened. She had that strange look in her eyes the whole time, like she was never seeing just one of you. The last story of her is only told by kids. They say she didn't go into the deepwastes, or to the executioner. They say she worldwalked one last time right off the planet. But everyone knows the traverser died even before she disappeared.

The screen shifts again and I see an even fainter image, a ghost of a man standing next to her. He's city-dressed, though I can't quite make out his features. There's something familiar about him. It would be easy for him to be good-looking, if his eyes weren't so intense in that *I might dissect you and play with the parts* kind of way. There's something about the hard set of his jaw . . .

I gasp and step back, trying with all the force of my neck not to look at Adam, not to compare him to himself.

"That's you."

"That's barely me, and it's definitely not her," Adam says, his voice tight. "This version of Cara is unmarked. Traveling marks, I mean. She tends to pick up a few scars no matter what universe she's from."

His eyes dart to Nik Nik when he says this, so mine do too, but I'm not sure why.

"Do you think she's involved in this?" I ask.

"You can't honestly expect to have this conversation in front of *him,* can you?" Adam says.

Cross's face as he looks at Adam is a knife. He may hate me, but he is raging at Adam, as clear and dangerous as when he was a boy.

"Surprised you remember," he says to Adam, his voice an ice that matches his eyes.

"You were one of my best employee's beneficiaries. How could I forget?"

It takes me a minute, but then I remember, too. Cara isn't just important because she was the world walker. Before she was hand-picked by Wiley to do a job that sounded like a miracle, she was the Ruralite ruling family's eldest daughter.

"You're her brother," I say to Cross.

"No," Nik Nik says quickly. "He's yours. He's mine." He looks at Adam. "We have one family. Family is what we choose, not what leaves us behind."

He's censuring me, but it's Adam who looks away.

"Regardless, it's both cruel and stupid to discuss her in front of him. Even those who leave can't help but feel for their past," Adam says.

He and Nik Nik stare at each other for a moment, exchanging something I don't know enough to understand, before Nik Nik finally nods.

"We can discuss it on the ride, as long as we leave the boy here," Adam says.

"The ride? We going somewhere?" I ask.

"We'll discuss it on the ride," Nik Nik says.

I take the hint, and turn to open the door.

When Cross moves to follow, Nik Nik stops him.

Cross shakes his head. "Protection detail wouldn't like this, you going out with so little cover. I'm coming too."

When the emperor turns—slowly, so slowly—toward Cross, I do not wait for him to act. I look away. Still, when Nik Nik backhands Cross I hear it. The sound is metal on flesh, so I'm guessing he led with the edges of his rings.

I look up to see Nik caressing Cross's newly reddening face.

"I'd worried that mark on your cheek was Scales letting old prejudices show. I see now you've earned it," Nik Nik says. He's cupped his fingers along Cross's chin, but he lets the nail of his thumb slide along the new injury, another insubordination mark. "Don't earn a third."

Cross should have known better than to tell the emperor what he should do, but I still feel bad for him. Nik Nik and I have a different relationship, as do Nik Nik and Adam for some fucking reason. Cross followed our informal lead right into a bloody mouth.

I don't like the look in Adam Bosch's eyes at the violence. He likes seeing people lowered. Or maybe he just likes displays of power, the weak bowing to the strong. Or maybe all this, and Cross's blood, too, is just data to him, a bruised face just as good as a fun fact.

"You're released to your post until morning," Nik Nik says and, just when I want to gloat over Cross getting backhanded, the emperor grips his shoulder. "You have always served well. Don't stumble."

I don't make a gagging sound, but it's a near thing. His eyes will be gleaming off that compliment long after his facial swelling goes down. I can't handle the smirk on Cross's lips or the adoration beaming out of his eyes. But I don't have to. I sucker punch him right in the solar plexus, grateful I watched him get ready this morning so I don't have to worry about body armor. He doubles over and I catch him against my shoulder.

"See you later, *Brother.*"

I pat his already darkening cheek before I turn away.

He'd committed two insubordinations in a day, so I was technically allowed to punish him. But that's not why I did it. Cross is an asshole, but sometimes he looks so much like an innocent child you've got to kick him just to prove you don't believe it.

When we leave the room, Adam looks back at the door.

"We should lock him in."

"Don't," I say, too quickly, too demanding, and to the emperor.

When Nik Nik first turns, it's in reaction to my daring to give him a command, even if only we and a Wileyite heard it. Then he must see my reasons on my face, because he raises his eyelids again, opening the narrowed slits that could have been the last thing I saw.

"I can't see you do it. I can't know you would do it," I say.

I'm looking down, not because I am showing respect but because I can't meet his eyes. I wish I could, so I'd stop feeling so young and so stupid. There's nothing for it. There is a part of me that is an adult, and a part of me that will never be older than thirteen.

Adam is openly staring at us, but he doesn't ask questions. After a moment Nik Nik turns away, leaving the door unlocked and my weakness unaddressed, which is all the pity I can take.

THIS IS SOMETHING I SHOULD TELL YOU OUTRIGHT: I CAN WORK FOR A MURDERER, BECAUSE I AM A murderer. But I cannot work for a man who would lock someone in a room for days in their own filth, because I was that too.

I said that like a riddle, didn't I?

Was I the man who locked someone in a filthy room for days?

Or was I the person locked in?

I'll tell you for free that I was not the man who did the locking. But I wasn't always the person who'd been locked in either. Some days, I was the room. Others, the filth.

—

WE MAKE OUR WAY OUTSIDE WHERE MR. SILK IS JUST CHECKING IN. IN SILK'S SHADOW, PERPETUALLY, is Sai, a recruit so new and so young Em's given them leathers just a little too big so they have room to grow. Sai's all dimples and light, and I revel in it, even as I know it won't last.

I wink at Sai behind the emperor's back, and Sai breaks out in a wide grin before catching themselves and setting their face to runner stone.

"I'm traveling," Nik Nik says.

"Deepwaste or in town?" Mr. Silk asks.

"Rurals, and not covert," Nik Nik says, and Mr. Silk nods before turning to order the appropriate ride.

"Rurals?" I say once the others turn away. It's not *technically* a question.

"Someone has a trace on Adam, we're going to flush them out to see if they're involved."

"Why do we think they are involved?" I ask.

"Because I wasn't being tracked until after bodies started dropping. They've tried hacking my files remotely, but now I've received a ping that someone has tried breaking into my apartment."

"Did you check your doorcam?"

Adam sighs. "I said *someone* is tracking me. Not *a total and complete idiot* is tracking me. Of course they've left no trace . . . Oh, absolutely not."

I turn to see that Adam is reacting to the gold off-roader being brought to the front of the palace. I don't travel with Nik Nik. I've never had escort duty even on the rare occasion he does listen to his security detail enough to take protection. But I remember the procedure well enough from training, so I move to open the emperor's door.

"I wouldn't get into that gaudy monstrosity even if my leg would let me," Adam says.

Nik Nik bares his teeth. "It was my father's."

"I know, obviously. Why do you think I refuse to ride in it?"

Obviously? The word hitches my interest, but I keep my face level as I hold open the door, waiting like a good, oblivious soldier.

I expect a violent reaction, but instead Nik Nik looks down at Bosch's metal foot.

"I can lift you."

The quiet sentence takes the air out of me. Of course he *can* carry the weight; he spends most of his time picking up heavy things for no practical reason other than to be able to lift even heavier things later. It's the idea that he *would* help the scientist. He's offering to bend. Runners and citizens hold others up. The emperor only holds others down.

Adam must recognize the rareness of the offer, because he drops the condescension that has veiled every word I've ever heard him say.

"Thank you," he says. "But I can't."

Nik Nik nods and motions to summon his day ride—a long vehicle in white that is about half as tall as the one in front of us.

"Let's hope we don't encounter any wildlife," Nik Nik says, as if the new ride isn't still higher and twice as long as most of the vehicles I service.

Granted, neither of these is even close to the biggest of the rides he's inherited from Senior. That distinction goes to Beast—Senior's parade ride. A square flatbed with duraglass walls and tires nearly as tall as two men. Since the parades ended before I made mechanic, I never had to work on Beast. Thank Christ. That tank is barely a ride. It's half construction equipment and half bad magic. There isn't even a chair or steering wheel; you stand while operating its levers and it doesn't drive so much as crawl forward like a creature without a predator or a care in the world. It didn't just liquefy bodies during the parades—it was a home eater.

Still, the all-white cruiser won't have a problem crushing anything we encounter, even if it is Senior's "smallest." Wildlife is the one thing I'm not worried about. I hate to say it, but Cross was right. This is next-level reckless and there should be at least one other runner with us. Nik and me against the whole wide desert? With a cyborg Wileyite I don't trust riding in the passenger seat?

"Yes, god forbid you have to swerve around the creatures instead of running them right over."

The puzzle of their relationship has distracted me, and I've neglected the protocol I remembered so prettily the first time. Luckily Nik Nik doesn't notice and opens his own door as Adam takes the front seat. By the time I follow and get in the back, Bosch has the cover of Nik's radio off and they're arguing about something new.

"I'm not bugged," Nik Nik's saying as he begins driving away from the palace. "Mr. Splice does a weekly sweep."

Adam doesn't stop, or look up. His mechanical eye is rotating, which I'm guessing is how he focuses. We don't have many prosthetic eyes out here in the Ash. They're pricey, and get permanently scratched during sandstorms. Mostly, we just rock patches. I always assumed I would too, if I ever lost an eye. I'm not sure how I'd react to losing the same part twice. But credit where credit's due, Adam's enhancements make a strong case for cybernetics. I wonder if it could let me see through doors before answering them. I wonder what fun little tricks Splice could rig into one. Though, come to think of it, Splice has always kept his foot as simple wood, despite being more than qualified to trick it out. Maybe he's most comfortable with the invisibility of his prosthetic, while Adam is comforted by optimization.

"Of course you named your pet hacker *Splice*. Is that so everyone knows exactly whom to bribe so they can bug you?"

"Runners don't go for bribes," I say, professional pride pushing the words out before I can consider if getting between these two is worth the trouble it borrows.

Bosch pauses in his destruction of the radio to look at me, glass-lens eye spinning while the other just squints. But it's Nik Nik he addresses, still. He seems to love nothing more than poking the most dangerous man in the wastes.

"And don't even get me started on this one. This"—he motions to me—"is your dumbest move yet."

"Oi!" I say, thinking he is referring to the rumor of our relationship, so well spread it has apparently reached Wiley. But what he says next undoes me.

Thing is, they want you to admire smart people, but they don't tell you it's because they're dangerous. Adam never looked at me, just straight through me. He takes the quiet thing I am not allowed to say and says it loud.

"Your own sister, Nik? Out running around in a leather vest with the rest of your rabid pups?"

CHAPTER SEVEN

NIK NIK SPEAKS BEFORE I CAN. "DON'T SAY ANYTHING."

But the look on my face has already confirmed it for him.

I lower my head. Stupid. Stupid. I'm the easiest way to get at the emperor, his most vulnerable part, and I've just confirmed my identity to this Wileyite stranger who at *best* is unnervingly cunning and at worst is a power-mad sociopath.

"I don't need her to confirm it. I've got eyes," Adam says, snapping the cover to the radio back into place. "Well . . . *eye* and something better."

He looks back at me, the light catching on the silver scars radiating out from around his metal plate. He's leaning forward, closing the distance to me as much as possible with the seats between us. I think he's trying to shock me with his appearance, so I refuse to look away.

"How did you know?" I ask, because no one has ever known. I spent years nowhere near the emperor. Never angling for a promotion. Never wanting to be assigned a cush spot at the palace. I wanted to be near my brother but I knew it was for the best. It all seems wasted now.

"How could I not?" he asks. "We used to look a lot alike, you and I."

It takes time for his meaning to set in, but once it does I sit forward, excited.

"You? You're one of us?"

He shakes his head. "You're a bastard. I'm the heir."

Bastard isn't an insult with any real teeth, and it's not technically true anyway so I move right past it.

"Firstborn?" I breathe the words out more than say them. "You're dead."

"Only pieces." When it snaps into place it's so obvious, I'm sure if I'd been Adam I'd have figured it out right away. What had Nik said earlier? *Family is what we choose, not what leaves us behind.* I thought he was talking through Adam to shame me, but he wasn't. And what had Adam said back? *Even those who leave can't help but feel for their past.*

I throw my head back at my own stupidity. "That's how you knew what Senior said! You were the boy he made Nik fight. You're Adra."

If Cara's a bedtime story, Adranik's a fable, and the lesson for children to learn is *Don't be weak.* He was Nik Senior's firstborn son, too physically unimpressive to satisfy his cruel father, too intelligent to want to change. He was murdered as a boy to clear the path to the throne for his stronger, more violent, younger brother.

Or, at least, that's the story.

"My *name* is Adam," he says. It's a snap, as if I've mispronounced his name, rather than said his true one.

"And that's why you're heir to nothing. Too cowardly to own your place," Nik Nik says, then eyes me in the rearview mirror. "Both of you."

If he's dead, I'm pulling you up.

Now it makes sense. If Adam had been dead, I would have been his only sibling. Funny, I thought I already was.

"*That's* why you were so panicked when you ordered the wellness check. You knew he was your brother."

The words, still said in the barely-thinking shock between my discovery and the revelation of Adam, just slip out. Bosch turns to Nik Nik. For the first time the look on his face isn't smug certainty. It's utter confusion, and it sits on his face wrong.

"Would you care if something happened to me? No. Of course not. Right? Why?"

The questions are rapid and half-whispered. He's only asking himself.

"He doesn't have an heir," I say, offering a reason other than love, other than the truth. Nik Nik's affection for his older brother feels like a precious thing, now that I've discovered it, and I want to protect the secret.

"Oh . . . yes, of course," Adam says, looking back out the window.

"We shouldn't all be here. This *is* too great a risk," I say.

I'm just trying to change the subject, but it's true. The windows of the vehicle suddenly feel too big, and the desert beyond too impossibly long to catalogue every threat. The only three pieces of Senior on this earth and we're all in one place. Nik would never arrange such a reunion, it would be too risky if the plan got out. But he's taking advantage of this spontaneous trip. He's wanted this, his big brother and little sister breathing the same air, even if we didn't know we were.

"No one knows who we are. If we start acting like heirs it will give the game away," Adam says. "Besides, I've survived worse."

I eye his scars again. "Senior do all that to you?"

"If only. No, I was tricked, and by a garbage git of all things."

The way he says it makes it seem like being tricked is worse than losing an eye, a leg, and an arm. He says it with real venom, but it's not haughty or bratty like you'd expect from a Wileyite. There's something almost scary in the emptiness of his face when he's angry.

"You put my cover on crooked," Nik Nik says, pulling Adam back.

"Your cover is warped. I put it on the way I found it."

Nik Nik grins with just the left side of his mouth. "Told you I'd be clean."

"Only because your runners are too stupid for tech."

"Sure," Nik Nik says.

"They're probably poisoning your food."

If I close my eyes we could be siblings on a road trip. I catch Adam's reflection in the mirror.

"You lied," I say.

"Probably. When?"

"You said you used to look like me. But you look like your mother, and I look like mine."

He turns to study me again, and Nik Nik shakes his head.

"He was bluffing. He assumed it was our mother who cheated and had you in secret."

Adam's face falls. "She was the one with a reason to go elsewhere. He played at love."

"It wasn't—"

"Hush, Scales," Nik Nik says.

Adam knows something is being kept from him, but won't lower himself to ask. He thinks I'm older than I am, that's all. Everyone does. Since I was old enough to tell people my age they've been quick to tell me I looked old for it. Adam thinks I'm from an affair, not the time after his mother's death. I'm not sure why it's worth hiding, but if I owe loyalty to any of my blood it's Nik, so I keep quiet.

When we pull to a stop, I get out first and open Nik Nik's door. Adam clears his throat from the passenger side.

"He's not serious," I say.

"He takes power where he can these days," the emperor says, which is not exactly a command, until he adds, "they'll need to see him to believe the threat is credible."

He's not telling me who we're flushing out, so I'm not asking, but if they need to believe in a threat, it's true that Nik alone won't cut it. The emperor has no more interest in a war with the holy than he has an interest in a war with the House. The current head of the Rurals is new, but even she will know he's muzzled.

I open the door for my newly decided least favorite brother, and then move to stand next to Nik Nik.

"Are we going to knock?" I ask.

"No," says Adam. He pushes himself back to sit on the hood of Nik Nik's car, which dips under the weight of his mods.

I look at Nik Nik for an order or an explanation. He gives the latter.

"We're testing a theory about the person tracking him. If he stands there long enough, they'll come. If no one comes, we're wrong."

I nod. I'm prepared to settle in—runners excel at nothing if not standing around without looking bored—but something in the dirt catches my eye. At first it's just an off pattern in the ground, but once it pops out it hits me like the blow I gave Cross earlier. I lose my air and fight not to show it.

You've gotta be shitting me.

"Gonna take a leak," I say, and walk toward my own broken heart like the idiot I am.

—

I MARCH TOWARD THE CORNER OF THE COMPOUND LIKE I'M GOING TO USE THE BUILDING FOR COVERAGE. And I do use it for coverage, but instead of taking a piss I follow the tracks in the dirt that I know as well as I know my own hands.

Around the side of the house is a runner's ride. Not just any ride, but one armored enough to belong to a ranking officer that Nik Nik might ride along with, yet fast enough for someone who still runs border patrol sometimes. It's tight work. Every seam flawless. So much armor you'd think it'd be obvious the person putting it on was in love with the person it was meant to protect, but fit so tightly you don't hear shifting or straining even on the bumpiest stretches, because the person who put it on also knows the value of hiding in plain sight. It's the kind of work you get when your mechanic spends as long as possible fitting seams into each other because it's the only way she'll ever get to touch you.

I catch the movement of a curtain being pulled over a window, so I bang my fist against it.

"You want me coming in there? Better yet, Himself?"

Cheeks opens the window and in the next second I grab him by the shoulders and yank him through the frame. He finds his feet quickly and shoves away from me.

"Did you follow me? I thought you weren't the wolf?"

"If I was wolf, you'd be skinned. Himself and the scientist are out front, I'm escorting."

"The emperor is out here with just you? That's not enough coverage." He's already checking his vest to see what weapons he has on him. "I should—"

"*You* should get the fuck out of here before anyone knows you came. If you wanted to do protection detail you should have been more careful where you spent your off-hours."

He looks a little shamed, because he knows I'm right, then he shakes his head. "I can't leave now if Adam Bosch is here. Anything could happen. Do you know his plan?"

I open my mouth to tell him, but then something stops me. Should I tell him there's no real threat? That we're just making scary noises to flush out someone else? But if I do, and he tells someone . . . But who would he tell? He's probably just up in it with some random Ruralite or deepwaster who stays here. Can't be he's really rolling around with someone high ranking? Not like he's screwing the princess, right?

Right?

Nah. Of course he is. It wouldn't be my luck if the one I wanted was hooking up with anything less than fucking royalty.

I shrug. "Who knows? Wileyites, man. Twice as crazy as us on a bad day."

"You don't know the half with that one." He looks over his shoulder into the house, like squinting will let him see through walls to Bosch. "I shouldn't even have come. I just had a bad dream, one of those ones that feel real? Like a warning? I needed to see her."

"Well you've seen her. Now get gone. Roll your ride back behind those hangers and leave from there. We're in the emperor's day ride, so you can beat us back to the palace easy, especially if you cut through the river."

And you can *cut through the river, because I bled my hands to make sure you'd be light enough to.*

The prospect of leaving with two dogs braying at the door doesn't seem to appeal to him, and I'm beginning to wonder if

Cheeks has known all along that Adam has the same feral blood as Nik. As me.

"I'm here. Things shouldn't get too . . . out of hand," I say.

He nods, either because my promise puts him at ease or because he's remembered he doesn't have a choice.

"Gotta get back. Told them I was taking a piss."

I turn quickly away, feeling guilty for not telling him more, and guilty for telling him anything at all instead of serving him up.

"Scales," he says, and I turn back, eager, quick, like the trained dog I guess I'm always going to be when he says my name. "You won't tell anyone, right? With the wolf out . . . you won't report this, will you?"

I pretend to think. "Depends," I say, but the anguish on his face makes me cut the play short. "Tell me you love me?"

A smile cracks his face. It's an old joke between us, and it's all the promise I can give.

"I love you, Scales."

"Tell me you're madly in love with me and I'm the smartest runner and the best mechanic ever."

"I'm madly in love with you and you're the smartest runner and the best mechanic ever," he says, half laughing.

"Okay, I *guess* I'll cover you."

"Thanks. You really are the best."

"Yeah, yeah. Just clear out before you get caught. Hate to stick my neck out for nothing."

I walk back around the house to join my brothers, thinking I can't feel any lower than I already do. That is, until about forty-five minutes later, when then the front door opens and the leader of the Rurals walks out.

—

FUCK, SHE'S BEAUTIFUL. I COULDN'T QUITE REMEMBER WHAT THE LEADER OF THE RURALS LOOKED LIKE so I've basically been picturing her as Cross in a dress. I couldn't have been more wrong. She is all soft light and golden hair and tiny feet that would probably shatter if you so much as thought of putting them in metal-tipped boots. Of course, I've seen her before. She never preached hate at the House, but she used to offer aid around the city proper. That made her my favorite of the whole hypocritical family, but beyond that I never paid her much mind. She was just a girl, eager and smiling, with nothing at all to do with me. But I guess I've never been good at spotting the threats that will destroy me.

Every step she takes toward us slaps me with our differences. Every part of her is smaller than every part of me. Her limbs are so delicate, like vines instead of branches. Her hands are small. Her nails are clean. I cross my arms, like I'm trying to be intimidating, but I'm just hiding the dirt and grease forever sitting in my nail beds.

This sounds like romantic jealousy, but I swear it's not. I don't really get jealous. I've always enjoyed being with multiple people, and I wouldn't begrudge anyone I'm with that same joy. But Cheeks is my best friend, and I'm meeting someone who will, one day probably soon, matter more to him than even I do. So no, I don't love that our meeting is happening when I'm days from my last shower and dressed in yesterday's leather. She's not even as short as I want her to be, the Wiley blood of her missionary grandfather giving her inches to go with that hair and those eyes. Eyes I've seen before, and often.

Only my sister knew. My twin.

I wouldn't have guessed they were twins at first, but as she gets closer I see him in her face. No wonder Cheeks is so protective of Cross; looking at him is like looking at the woman who holds his heart. Probably calls him *Brother* when I'm not around. Now *this* is jealousy, and there's nothing romantic about it. I don't like Cheeks having a real sibling, instead of having to pretend that's what I am.

When she finally reaches us, she nods in deference to Nik—not quite a bow, but as much as she can do to a terrestrial being without violating her faith—and then turns her attention to Adam. Me? She doesn't even register. I want to say, *I know what your man looks like when he cries. I've nursed him when he was sick. And no, I've never fucked him, but I've stitched his worst splits and that's kind of like letting someone inside of you, isn't it?*

But it's not. And I know it.

She's so pretty, even looking at her is humiliating. When she speaks her voice doesn't have a hint of acid.

"Are you lost, Traveler?" she asks Adam.

It's a standard Ruralite greeting that probably could have been a genuine offer in another time or another mouth, but the context has shifted it into an expression of irritation regardless of the actual words. Like how *Can I help you?* translates to *Fuck you want?* if you wander into shopper's alley right when they want to close down for the day.

Adam, who was sitting on the hood of Nik's precious ride, is now fully reclined on his elbows, a man casually visiting from Wiley sunbathing in the middle of the Rurals. *Retired:* The word hits me at once. It's a Wiley thing, retirement, unless it's a euphemism for being killed. I wonder if that's why Bosch has this odd mix of intensity and laziness, of genius and carelessness.

"Me? Lost? No, not yet anyway. Thank you, Esther."

Esther. I didn't need to know that. Didn't need to know that my name makes people think of reptiles and hers makes the sound of a secret being whispered.

Her serene helpfulness drops, revealing a steel core.

"What do you want with my people, Bosch? There's nothing here for a man like you but religious counsel. If it's conversion you seek, I'll need to clear my schedule. I anticipate the confession portion will take . . . a good while."

I so desperately didn't want to like her, but Adam's such a pain in the ass it's hard not to want to smile at that.

"I'm afraid flesh-to-metal is the only conversion I have the energy for at the moment."

If she came out here for a straight answer, she's going to be disappointed. I could have told her that.

"Whatever you've come for, don't dally. We harbor deepwasters in this region. They don't like strangers. Shame to lose such an important man to a mishap in the desert."

The elegant threat is delivered looking him directly in the eyes, and I'm sweating for her. She thinks he's some scientist—one she and her sister have history with, apparently—she doesn't know she's threatening the emperor's kin. She doesn't know Nik loves him, and Nik doesn't know his favorite runner loves her. A lot of hearts will break today if this goes sideways.

Her eyes shift toward the horizon. A car is approaching. I should have seen it farther off, but I was distracted by their exchange and I can't shake the feeling that was deliberate. Esther was a spectacle to pull our gaze while the real threat drove up.

"Please let one of my people know if you need water or lemonade. The desert is ruthless when the winds are high."

She turns away, her long dress and hair blowing sideways.

The car approaching looks to have one occupant. We can see the driver's side, which doesn't have any artillery or assassins strapped to it for a quick attack. I wish I'd been watching before the car made its last turn so I could have checked out the passenger side too, but their distraction worked, if that's what Esther was. The car stops at an awkward distance. I have to move up slightly so I can follow protocol and position myself between the driver and the emperor, but it still feels like I'm leaving a lot of space around him unprotected.

I pull my gloves down tight as I approach the driver.

She has her hands on the wheel and her eyes forward, the way tourists are told to do to keep safe during one of our patrol stops. Her black hair is long and covering her face, but I can see she's Asian and Wiley as fuck.

I rap against the window with the metal of my knuckles, and I like the sharp sound. I may be three categories below a spider mite compared to Esther, but I can at least shrink a scared Wileyite down to size. And this one *is* scared. Her face is still, but her hands are shaking. Granted, she's not looking at me. She's looking at the passenger side . . .

Oh, for chrissakes.

Realization hits me just as the person hidden on the other side of the car unstraps and launches at Adam.

CHAPTER EIGHT

I DON'T HAVE MY BROTHERS' LONG-GAME INSTINCTS. MORE OF A REACTOR THAN A PLANNER, ME. SO it's not until I slide across the car to intercept the would-be assassin that I understand who's been tracking Adam, and why coming here would draw her. We connect before she's gotten good enough footing to run, and when our tumble ends she's beneath me with one side of her face smashed into the ground. I only need to see one side, though; I'd know those stripes anywhere. Her skin's nothing like her brother and sister, but the cool resistance in the eye glaring up at me comes from the same well.

"You're awfully small to be causing all this trouble," I say.

"You roll up on my family and call *me* causing trouble?" she says.

She's garbage git through and through: scrappy, dark, with a bad attitude and the kind of fearlessness that could have easily made her one of us.

"Fair enough," I say, and pull her to her feet with her arms behind her back. "You gonna be good?"

She's glaring hot knives at Adam, so I know it's a lie when she answers, "Fucking angelic."

I keep my hold on her.

Adam's face has gone empty. I'd thought he'd be gleeful. He's been so flippant this whole time, but whatever she represents has put him low. He was watching her, but his eyes flick over the top of her head. I think he's looking at me, but then he sighs.

"I wouldn't do that, Ikari. You know how impolite Ashtowners can be. This one is especially ill-mannered. She might kill you."

Just as he says it I feel the plastic touch the base of my neck. Great. Letting a Wileyite get the drop on me in front of my boss was exactly how this day was always going to go. Bet the love of my life's hot-ass girlfriend saw it happen, too.

Nik Nik seems amused at the irritation in my face.

"I trust you don't need help," he says.

I nod. I'm irritated, but not worried. I'm a mechanic by choice. If performance scores dictated roles, I would never have been anything but a fighter.

I drag my thumbs along my palms, sliding the batteries in my gloves into place. I kick the traverser's knees in as I turn, keeping my heel on her spine so I can grab the barrel of her friend's stunner. The Wileyite is strong, which I didn't expect, but when you hit someone in the throat that isn't used to being hit in the throat they all react the same: strong or not, they put both hands over their neck. As she does, I keep my hold on the stunner and twist it out of her grip. She makes to grab for it again, but I grip her wrists with one of my gloves now that the metal piping of my palms is good and heated. She screams at the burn and steps away.

When all's said and done, I've got her friend under my foot and her weapon in my hand. Her face is all stone, so I don't see the rewarding disappointment of an opponent out of options.

"Are *you* gonna be good?" I say to the Wileyite.

"That depends on what you intend to let him do to her," she says evenly, and I know it's the gods' honest truth.

I squint at Bosch. Was this just some revenge mission? Was this the Ashtowner who outsmarted him and he's just using his brother's resources to trap her?

"Rest easy, Dell. Your wife is the one tracking me," Adam says, before shifting his gaze to Cara. "I would like to know why."

I feel the tension go out of the woman beneath me. She's moved past *Kill him now, kill him fast,* so I step off her. She gets up, brushing dirt off clothes that look like a more expensive version of Ashtown. Her eyes tell me *Kill him* is still the plan, but it's less urgent.

Cara's face gives away less than nothing. "Just keeping tabs on the shittiest person I know."

"Sure. And I suppose the fact that you began tracking me the night six people turned inside out is a coincidence."

"Six?" Cara says.

"You knew the whole time? How?" the wife asks simultaneously.

The look Adam gives her is boredly exasperated. He gestures to himself as if to say, *Because I'm me,* before turning back to Cara.

Despite the intensity of his glare, Cara doesn't flinch. It's her wife who breaks.

"Cara wasn't tracking you."

"Dell . . ."

"I was."

Only then does Adam stop his staring contest with the world walker. "You? Why?"

"Because my father went out golfing the day those people died. And when he came back, he called me the wrong name. The next day, he'd taken his stuff and fled to another city. He hasn't contacted us since."

"You risked my wrath because your idiot father is more idiot than usual?"

Dell must know him from before, because she's neither affected nor surprised by his particular brand of arrogant insult.

"Standing up to my father and demanding he call me by the name I chose was one of the hardest things I have ever done. I imagine there are a lot of worlds in which I was not that brave."

Adam doesn't quite look impressed, but he looks like he's trying not to look impressed, which is basically the same thing.

"Then you already know what's happening."

"Someone is trying to bring people over, but it's killing the ones here instead of the ones sent," Dell says.

"And you?" he says, shifting to Cara. "You miss the father-in-law who, as I recall, worked hard to cut you out of the Ikari family assets? Or do you just still follow her around like a faithful dog after all these years?"

"If there's fuckery afoot I know you're the one behind it," Cara says, then deliberately looks him up and down. "Maybe I'm just itching for an excuse to finish the job."

It's the first time I've ever seen anything at all truly affect Adam. I'd already suspected she was the one who'd gotten the best of him, but the way his hands curl into fists even as his face remains so very, very still cements it for me.

"He isn't behind this," Nik Nik says. "We'll pool our resources to figure out who else might be involved, and how to stop it."

"And why would I ever consent to working side by side with someone like him?" Cara says, as rough and direct as Dell is elegant and calm.

"Because you destroyed him for killing others, so I doubt you'll let your prejudices cost more lives," Nik Nik says, then grins. "But also because *he* isn't the one asking."

The sound of Nik Nik playing with his rings feels as loud as a crash.

The traverser does the only thing any Ashtowner who came up in the reign of Senior can do in the face of the emperor. She lowers her eyes, and nods.

"Yes, Sir."

WHEN CIVILIANS TELL THE STORY OF MY COMBAT QUALIFICATION, THEY TALK ABOUT HOW A BARELY adult girl beat all twenty competitors, two soldiers per rank, leaving them in a twitching heap of broken bones without sweating one drop and while laughing the whole time.

When other runners tell the story, I was stone-faced and unafraid, systematically rolling through my opponents with measured hits, careful not to disqualify myself by breaking their bones. Runners say I fought like a machine, like something inhumanly efficient.

Both stories say I was fearless.

Civilians are wrong about the laughing, runners are wrong about my stone face. Truth is: I *was* smiling. Truth is: I was sweating. A lot. And the truth is: I was fucking terrified.

You've got to understand, I've spent my whole life not being good enough. I was a burden and a disappointment for my entire childhood. I did my best at the House, but I know what I look like, and I was the least requested on roster.

When the first two runners stepped into the ring, they weren't fellow runners executing a formality, they were my obstacle to finally being loved. Each person that came in was the thing standing between me and belonging.

Of course, I had unfair advantages of strength, height, and wingspan. Most of those in the runners ranks were older than me, coming up through malnourished childhoods that ensured their bones would never be as dense, their bulk never coming as easily, as mine would.

But I didn't care if it was fair; I cared that it was mine. Until that moment I had rage issues. I had an explosive killing temper. But even though the temptation in the ring would be to red-out and go berserk, I held myself in check, because everyone knows if you can't control your violence, if you break those around you or yourself, you earn the lowest rank. You get marked as the worst soldier. I didn't want to be the worst. I wanted to be the best. I wanted to make my brother proud.

So when I wanted to wrap my hands around a throat, I pulled an arm into submission instead. When I wanted to snap that arm, I put someone on the ground instead. And when I wanted to kill, I let myself get hit instead. In the end, every opponent agreed I was in control, and I earned the third-highest rank ever given, making me the highest ranking still serving, not counting Himself.

It was the emperor who came to me afterward, bringing a cloud to all my glory, to tell me he wouldn't approve me for combat work. It broke my heart, but in the end I understood. I was his sister, but if I did lose control as I had in the past, only this time killing another runner or, god forbid, unjustly killing a civilian, he would have to kill me. Worse, he would have to hate me, and he wanted that even less.

In the end, I became the best mechanic I could be, but I still keep that day, and my ranking, as my own private bright day. The day when I was tested and succeeded, the day when everyone knew

I was valuable, when not even Cross and his shitty family could say I wasn't good enough.

It was the day I knew a runner was what I'd been meant to be all along.

I'D THOUGHT THE BICKERING BETWEEN ADAM AND NIK NIK WAS BAD, BUT THE ICE THAT SETTLES BE-tween Adam and the traverser is suffocating. She can't quite look at him. He won't stop staring at her. Since she's in the back with me and he's in the front with Nik, his dramatic turns to regard her are unmissable. But she keeps her gaze fixed on the world passing by the window. The vibe isn't quite ex-lovers, but something undeniable. Like a father being forced to sit next to the son he abandoned. The opposite of casual. The opposite of resolved.

Eventually Adam gets tired of being ignored—big surprise, I imagine he's used to holding the attention of others.

"Too squeamish to view your own handiwork? I'd thought better of you, Caralee."

I want to correct him, because that's not her name. But I learned my lesson this morning about getting between hissing sand cats, so I hold my tongue.

"I'm not squeamish," she says to the window, then turns to him. "And I'm not sorry. Live by the sword, die by the sword, Bosch."

"A sword would have been a mercy. But you chose this for me. A prolonged, rotting death. This twisted agony."

This is the first time I've ever noticed him mention his appearance, and of course he's only doing so to guilt her. He sounds hurt and disgusted, but he also sounds full of shit.

Cara leans forward and I tap her knee to remind her to behave. But she's not going to attack, unless you count words as poison.

"This isn't the death I would have chosen for you. If I'd had my way, you would have been beaten to death outside, in a park on the eightieth floor, surrounded by your colleagues. Your death would have been overseen by a man you'd been loyal to, so you would be forced to realize in the end that you'd never been valued, only used. Then you would have been dumped facedown in the dirt outside the city for enforcement to find you after the flies and carrion birds and god knows what else already had. That's what I would have chosen for you. That would have satisfied me . . . This rot is what I settled for."

I let out a low whistle at the verbal evisceration, and Adam turns his head to me. It's unsettling. I've gotten so used to his petulance, his spoiled-rotten arrogance, that when she ends her monologue I expect an eye roll or a pout. But his face is dead calm, calculating. This, I guess, is what he actually looks like when he feels something. Everything else is performance.

"Live by the sword," he says, tasting her words. "I guess you'll learn all about that, in time."

Cara had gone back to looking out the window, but this last bit jerks her head around.

"Save it. You already tried convincing me I was poisoned, remember? You lied. It's been a decade and I am no worse than the day you exiled me."

"Yes, nearly a decade and you are no worse. Not even a little. Years have passed and you haven't aged a day." He stops, just long enough for her face to shift from confusion to horror. "I never said I'd poisoned you. I simply asked how long you'd planned to live."

I'm close enough to her that I can feel her stiffen, but her striped face remains set. I've only heard bits and pieces about Adam experimenting on those who worked for him. It was never confirmed, but I believe it. Nik Senior razed the factories and mines that took his people's safety for granted; figures the same misstep would cause Nik Nik to blow Adam's shit to dust, brother or no.

"You're full of shit, Bosch," she says, and goes back to looking out the window, though I imagine now her reflection looking back is its own unwanted reminder.

"You should be thanking me. Given the disparate life expectancy between Ashtown and Wiley City, Ikari would have had to bury you in a matter of decades. This way, you'll live to watch her die. Isn't that nice?"

I tense, sure I'm going to have to pull her tiny hands from

around Adam Bosch's throat any second. But she doesn't react. Just keeps looking out the window.

Where did she learn to eat shit like such a pro? She hasn't been through training, but at some point she must have been so afraid of consequences that she learned not to punch someone who spat at her.

Nik's eyes meet mine in the mirror, and they hold the same question. If he doesn't know how a Ruralite daughter got like this, I sure as hell don't. My guess is only Adam knows for sure. What must it be like, to know the person you hate most in the world is the one who knows you best? I look back into Nik's eyes, grateful the person who knows the truest version of my story is the one I'd protect with my life.

I'm looking into his eyes, thinking about how I'd die for my big brother, when the world turns sideways as the universe calls my bluff.

—

IT STARTS UNDER THE FRONT PASSENGER SIDE, A BOOM THAT SENDS MY AND ADAM'S SIDE OF THE vehicle feet into the air, the wheels on the driver's side coasting forward alone for a few precious seconds. At first, I think it's an animal or rock. It's clear we've hit something too hard at too high a speed, and I'm already mentally calculating how fucked my week is going to be if we snap an axle on Nik Senior's pain in the ass ride, when the explosion hits.

I understand too late that what we hit wasn't a rock. It was the delivery device impacting hard enough to attach to the wheel, just like it was meant to. Going as fast as we were, getting hit as hard as we did should have sent us spinning. Any other vehicle in the fleet would have tumbled over and over again, spinning us like rag dolls until we fell apart. If we'd taken Senior's other ride we'd have been so tall we'd have flipped from a sneeze. But this behemoth is twice as heavy but half as high, so we only flip once and then skid. There's nothing to skid into, so it's just a matter of waiting until force is done with us.

As soon as we impacted, I'd taken a deep breath, focusing on the minutia of my body to keep my perception anchored in the moments when the mind wants to retreat into panic. Just like Em taught me. That's the only reason I have enough clarity to trigger the panic button in my cuff, even as I reach across to cover Cara. *Civilians, Emperor, Fellow runners, yourself*—the preservation order fires in my head fresh as the first day. The second the skidding stops, I pull out my knife and cut Cara loose, then myself. I kick and kick, forcing my door to scrape open across the dirt. Any other ride, I could kick out the windows. But nooo, we had to take one of Senior's stupid fucking tanks. Cara's smaller and lighter than Adam, but Nik is stronger than me, and by the time I've pulled her clear, he's done the same for Adam.

Cara's awake, just stunned.

Adam is not.

Brand and Rust should have cleared the road just ahead of the emperor, and they're reckless on their cycles in ways only competing siblings can be, so I'm not surprised to already see the snakes of dirt climbing into the sky announcing their arrival.

Nik Nik isn't moving. He's staring at Adam's unconscious form like he's trying to decide how to feel. Did he pull him out so fast because he's a civilian and that's the preservation order? Or was it panic? Was it love?

I cuff Viet for medical, or worse, and then move back to the upside-down ride where Adam was sitting. The wheel weld is crushed in, but I know all the rides have emergency repair in the back so I grab a bar and pry the wheel back open. I take a picture of what's left of the device that attached itself to us, and send it to Splice.

Jesus fuck what happened? Is that Nik's ride?? he sends back, but because he's a runner first and a gossip second—narrowly—he immediately follows up with, Proximity detonator. Gotta be within half a mile.

I send the message to Brand and Rust before they can even make it all the way to us.

Prox det. Half a mile radius. Do a sweep. I look at Nik, his killing eyes. Bring who you find back to us.

"Oh good. You're alive," I say once Cara sits up.

"Usually am," she says, then immediately looks around.

I know just what she's looking for, and sure enough her eyes don't stop until she sees Adam lying in the dirt. You'd think the prospect of her nemesis being done in for her would put triumph on her face, but instead her brow furrows. Disappointment? Confusion? Like if he's dead she no longer knows what happens next.

Nik should be scanning the horizon with me, or at least displaying some sense and retreating in case the assassins try again, but he hasn't left Adam's side. He's staring down, his hand on Adam's neck, checking for a pulse in the same way he checks for a lie. His face is so closed off I don't know what he's feeling, but his eyes look lost so I'm not sure he knows what he's feeling either.

Adam's such a piece of shit, it's wild to me that there is one person in the world who can't cope with the idea of him being gone, much less two. It gives me hope. If you have to be more of a monster than Adam to be totally abandoned, it means I might not die alone either.

I'm pulled out of my thoughts by a low whirring sound. Nik should have heard it first, but he's too distracted looking for signs of life.

"Don't touch him! Move your hand!"

Nik obeys instantly, and I'm just hoping Cara will be too shaken to register I've given him an order and he's followed it. It's less than a second between Nik pulling his hand back and the wave of electricity surging through Adam's body.

Adam sits up on a gasp, his mechanical hand spasming open and closed.

"A *built-in defibrillator*? You've got to be absolutely shitting me," I say.

And even though he was just in an accident, even though he was just unconscious, even though he just had fuck knows how many volts of electricity coursing through his body, he takes a moment to look proud of himself. Then the part of his brow that can furrow does and he scans the area. I think he's scanning for danger—*finally* someone other than me is—but he just relaxes once he's seen Cara. I guess neither one knows what they would do without the other.

Brand and Rust pull up with three prisoners—two on Brand's cycle and one on Rust's. I can't tell the twins apart, but I know their bikes on sight. Brand brings his ride in clean and on time for every scheduled maintenance. Rust runs through tires like they're disposable. He also habitually waits to bring his personal ride in until the rotors have to be shaved, like he just loves the sound of bad brakes.

"Almost too easy. They were hiding behind a rock. Literally," Rust says.

"Think they're a trap?" Brand asks.

Then the one on the back of his cycle slides off and runs for it with her hands cuffed behind her back. No one moves. It's not like she's gonna get away. I wait until she runs past me to reach out and grab her by the hair, yanking her back violently enough to curve her spine, then kicking her knees hard to bring her down onto them.

"Nope. Just Wileyites," I say, looking down at the white strands in my hand. I bend her neck back to see her face, and it's familiar. All at once I realize: I watched her fall apart. This is one of the victims of the attack. No, no, that woman is dead. This is the one who was watching it happen. The one who was *excited.*

I turn to look at Nik, expecting to hear an order for retrieval and interrogation. But he's turned away, staring at the place where Adam's heart stopped. Only I can see his face. He makes eye contact with me and holds it, then brings one sharpened nail up to his forehead and makes a slash down to his eyebrow. The cut is deep enough to bleed like a river, but it's still not too late. He could wipe it away, and no one would know. But he doesn't. He waits until the blood has traveled down his face, off his chin. With a jerk of his head, his blood hits the ground. *Now* it's too late.

The woman is on her knees with her back to me. I realize I've never heard her name. I'll have to learn it now. I put my hands more firmly on her shoulders. She's tense under my touch.

"Take a deep breath," I say.

For reasons only a Wileyite could know, she listens. I don't tell her to close her eyes, but she does. I wait until her spine softens with the relief of being given an order she knows how to execute, I wait until I feel her shoulders rise with the swelling of her chest, I wait until she's just about to let that breath go, and only then do I snap her neck.

Her body seizes with the suddenness of its own death—a disbelief occurring at the cellular level and moving through her nerves—but I expected this and keep my grip. Once it's done, I lay her on the ground. I move to put dirt on her forehead, but Ashtown wasn't her home and I don't know if she'd want to be guided back. I settle for crossing her arms over her chest. People always say the dead look peaceful even though they usually don't. But I swear to god she does. I doubt she even knew it happened. I bet she's sitting in the dark already, eyes still closed, still waiting to release that last held breath.

I turn to see Rust and Brand staring at me wide-eyed. I don't make eye contact with their prisoners.

"Emperor's blood!"

I yell the command only once, but I could have whispered it. I step sideways so they can see Nik's face, and that's all it takes. Within minutes, the other two are dead. Rust slits the throat of his prisoner, still bent over his bike. Brand's prisoner is standing so he pulls the man against his chest, his forearm an air-ending bar despite the struggles of a body not ready to die. He drops his man only after he's well and sure it's over. Rust's way is quicker, but Brand knows what I know: Take every chance you get to practice killing without a weapon, because you'll want to be good at it before you *need* to be good at it.

When Viet arrives Adam refuses medical help, which means Cara does too, which of course means I'd sooner chew off my own arm than get checked out. So there's nothing for him to do but take the bodies. There's a trill in the air and Cara rolls her eyes and hits a button on her cuff.

"I'm fine," she says, before *hello*. "My earpiece got busted in the wreck, so you're out loud."

"Sabotage?" comes Dell's voice.

"Looks like," Cara says, looking back at what used to be our ride. This motivates Adam, who stands to examine the wreck closer.

"Your wife keeps a high-altitude drone trained on you?" Adam says, clearly meaning to imply that Cara's untrustworthy or Dell's paranoid.

"Only when I'm out with psychopaths," Cara says, at the same time Dell's cool "Old habit," comes through the speaker, equally unbothered.

I walk away to give Cara at least the illusion of privacy, since Adam's messing with the wheel weld and so unlikely to kill, or be killed by, her.

I stand next to Nik, but I don't say anything. Emperor's blood is one of the most ironclad runner rules. You spill the emperor's blood—which includes harming his family—you die. Technically what they did to Adam counted, Nik just cut himself to tell Rust and Brand what he already knew and I am just finding out: Adam is a part of him, his blood is Nik's, and so are his injuries. I wonder if my brother realizes that means Adam's crimes are his too, but after seeing his face when Adam looked dead, I doubt he cares. God knows he took my sins onto his hands easy enough. Who knew? Yerjanik Nazarian—the sentimental sibling.

I see the dust cloud approaching and stand ready until I get a message from Cheeks.

New ride should be approaching, he says. You driving?

No. Himself.

Tell him hurry.

Haaaa. You're funny.

Serious. Need you back to ID.

I stare down at the screen wishing it said anything else. An ID means a body, and if Cheeks needs me, it's someone I know. I look away from my cuff, realizing this may not have been the only attack today.

CHAPTER NINE

I'VE JUST PROCESSED THE MESSAGE WHEN ADAM REQUESTS TIME TO LOOK AT THE TECH THAT ATtacked us. Which wouldn't be a problem, except so close to almost losing him Nik Nik doesn't look ready to leave his big brother's side. But Cheeks couldn't have been more serious, so I clear my throat and proceed to risk my neck.

"Mr. Cheeks has requested us back."

"Has he?" Nik asks, raising his uncut eyebrow.

I do *not* tell the emperor to hurry, because I'm not actually suicidal, but I do say, "I'm needed for an ID," which is just as good. That's all it takes for him to nod.

When transport comes he instructs two of the escorting runners to stay with the scientist.

Adam motions to Cara. "I could use a second pair of hands for my examination."

He says it casually, like a dog that steals food slowly hoping you won't notice it happening.

Cara looks at him like he's just asked her to fuck a cactus.

"I will never—never—work for you again." She spits on the ground to seal her vow, then turns back to me. "I'm riding back with you, yeah?"

I shrug and hold my hand out to transport like I'm presenting a prize. Adam's face was comically insulted when she spoke, but as she turns her back to him his expression falls into one of sad disappointment that is far more subtle and undoubtedly real.

Cheeks is waiting out front when we pull up. He half runs to pull open the emperor's door.

"You're okay," he says with real relief, then he sees my brother's cut and his eyes go ten kinds of feral. He turns to me.

"He's bleeding. Did you—"

"It's handled. They're dead," I say, and he relaxes. "Where's the body?"

"There's a body?" Nik Nik asks calmly, clarification not hysteria.

"Not a body, but we need Scales to ID. Others would know better, but we're trying to keep this under wraps."

His voice drops when he finally registers Cara with us.

"World walker," he says, smiling. "Finally joining up?"

"And run around smelling like oily hides and sweat all the goddamn time? Not on your life, Cheeks."

Cheeks summons a runner on palace duty to escort her inside.

"Ready quarters for her on the opposite side of the compound from our current guest," Nik says once she's out of hearing. "Place a detail between them."

Cheeks's eyebrows knit. "Is she meant to be kept here against her will?"

It sounds like he's checking Nik's preference, not questioning his orders.

Nik shakes his head. "I'd rather not start a war with the Rurals just yet. The detail is to keep her from killing him."

"Or the other way around," I say, because one of us has to remember that Adam is kind of a piece of shit.

Cheeks nods and cuffs the order to whomever he thinks is best.

"Her wife and sister will be along shortly. They'll need to be accommodated," I say, hoping he'll be better able to conceal his response if he hears it from me instead of the emperor.

His eyes only widen a fraction of a second before he nods, delegating from his cuff, then begins walking toward the aboveground dungeons. Cheeks opens the door—he'd have to, I don't have dungeon access and Nik doesn't open his own doors—and leads us in.

I'd assumed injury. When Cheeks said there wasn't a body, but an ID was needed, I'd assumed they were unconscious. But the single figure in the cell is unharmed. More than uninjured, they're Wileyite. They've probably never been harmed in their life. I take in their clothes, but I don't recognize them. I am about to tell Cheeks I can't identify a Wileyite because I don't know any, but then they look up, glaring with eyes pale blue . . . and familiar.

"More filth to gawk at me?" they say.

There you go, Dexi, just like that.

I take a breath.

"It's her. That's Helene X."

—

"WHO ELSE KNOWS?" ASKS NIK NIK.

"Just me and Black Dragon," Cheeks says. "He thought it was a city trespasser and radioed me. I thought it was Helene, but I couldn't be sure. Scales saw her last, and I knew I could trust her, so I cuffed."

Nik Nik listens, looking every so often at Helene-Not-Helene from the corner of his eyes, but doesn't ever face them directly. It's bad luck, to bare your face to a ghost. Anyone raised in Ashtown would have the same hesitation. But I didn't come to Ashtown until I was a teen, so I can't take my eyes off the phantom. Phantom? Zombie? I haven't decided. I am practically pressing my face through the bars trying to figure it out when they turn, rolling their eyes at me.

"Must you?" they ask.

I want to tell them yes, of course I must. I cared for you, and you were gone. I tasted your mouth with mine, and then I heard that mouth scream your last. Instead, Cheeks's words finally process, so I ask, "Your feet hurt?"

The figure tilts their head. "Isn't my discomfort your aim? I'm a hostage, aren't I?"

"You're not a hostage. You're a ghost."

Mr. Dragon thinks himself a nomad. If he encountered this person on his route then they must have been walking far out into the desert, and all in Wiley City dress shoes.

I walk back to Nik and Cheeks, who are still trying to solve the problem of the walking dead.

"If this gets out there will be a panic," Cheeks says, which is true.

"If we don't tell the House and Lee finds out, there will be a war," Nik Nik says, which is also true.

"We're gonna need some slippers for Hel . . . whoever that is," I say.

"I'm running a hotel now?" Nik Nik says.

"No, but Exlee's not gonna whistle when they see you've kept one of theirs standing in their own blood and blisters," I say.

"*That* isn't one of theirs," Nik Nik says, but he nods to Cheeks to summon some footwear anyway.

Cheeks and Nik Nik craft the message to Exlee, instructing doorstaff to bring them down when they arrive. A referential tap tells me the slippers are at the door, and I get them, careful not to let the first mark delivering them see who is being held.

"Here," I say, holding up the slippers.

When the figure looks up, I toss them onto the cot so they won't have to walk for them. After a moment of uncertainty, they begin switching shoes. As I thought, their feet are ragged. If this were Helene X, she'd be livid. Footwork was one of her most profitable and least time-consuming hustles, and these toes wouldn't be sellworthy again for at least a month. I look away, remembering touching those feet, or feet just like them, years ago.

"Why do they keep calling me that?" they ask, putting on the last slipper.

"Helene? It's your name. Or . . . the name of someone with your face."

They pause. "It's not *my* name, obviously."

"Why is it obvious?" I ask.

"Well, because I'm . . ." They gesture to their body, once-dark gray slacks and sweater coated in the sand from the high winds of the outskirts.

"You're what?" I ask.

Of course I know what they're getting at, but I'd never say it. I'd swallow my tongue before I did.

"A man," the figure says. "Clearly."

I close my eyes at this proclamation. I was afraid of that. Few people who hadn't slept with Helene even knew the city had once called her "male." She worked hard to leave that label behind. I tell myself this isn't her, and this person has every right to claim any gender. But it still feels like desecration.

"Helene was her grandmother's name," I say. "Her grandmother was always kind to her, so when she died when Helene was fourteen, she took her name and came here."

They—no, *he,* I think, forcing myself to honor how he's chosen to identify, the way Exlee taught me, no matter how ill it sits—nods, processing, then looks at the wall. He's rubbing at his wrist. Helene used to do that, back when we were both still new, and seeing it makes her feel even more gone somehow.

"My grandmother was named Helene, and she was always kind to me . . . but she died when I was seven, not fourteen."

I look at Nik to see if he's listening. Of course, the emperor always is.

The next person to come to the dungeon door doesn't knock, which is how I know who it is.

"It's not what it looks like," I say, trying to keep Exlee from getting their hopes up, but they're already running up to the bars, tears forming in their eyes.

The captive moves farther back onto the cot, pressing against the wall.

"Don't touch me."

Exlee processes the look on Not-Helene X's face—the fear, the disgust. His eyes take in Exlee's beard and breasts and pronounce them a *freak* even if his mouth is too afraid to form the word. The tears of hope and reunion dry up. I see them understand. This isn't Helene. If it is, they've lost her twice.

I am watching Exlee's heart break. They let out a long stream of air soundlessly, not quite a sigh, more like a deflation, hope leaving the body. Then, as quickly as they broke, they rise. Exlee raises their chin, looking down their nose at the figure in the cell like they are not just a stranger, but trash. It is the look of elitism usually reserved for visitors they don't trust. The face from a moment before, the raw love of a friend and parent, that was a face only those of us who have ever been under their care get to see. This look is withering and cold.

By the time they turn back toward the rest of us, the tears in their eyes have been replaced with magma. Thankfully they never punch down, so the only place they can unload all that rage is at Nik.

"Is this some kind of joke? Did you brainwash her? Who dressed her like that? I will kill you."

Because it's Exlee, Nik Nik doesn't take the threat personally.

"I don't play those sorts of games. If we knew what was going on, I would tell you, but I don't."

"If you don't, who does?" they ask.

Nik Nik meets my eyes, because we both know the answer and what happens next.

"I'll see how much longer he'll be at the site and ready a briefing room," I say, grateful to walk away from Exlee's pain and Helene X's ghost.

—

I'M SURE ADAM THINKS HE'S EXPLAINING SOMETHING TO US, BUT ALL I'M TAKING FROM HIS TALKY-TALK is a massive headache. At least Exlee looks lost too. Cara seems to have understood before we got here, even seems a little excited by the intrigue. I don't know if I've ever met anyone as curious as the traverser, but I guess you don't get to be a world walker by shying away from new experiences.

"The device used to attack us was old-fashioned—combustion and shrapnel. No electronic pulsing, nothing like the brand-new mini-atomics."

Mini-atomics makes us all shudder. Mini-atomics and everburn incendiaries are the weapons only the council of cities use, and they only ever use them on the people outside the walls. Because inside would be a human rights violation. No telling what that makes us in their minds. I'd say dogs, but they're quite manic in their protection of dogs, so we must be less.

"So you're saying they're broke?" I ask.

"No," Cara says. "That's the only kind of device that could survive the jump. The more sophisticated the technology, the more shorted out it gets. He's saying they're traversers and they brought the device with them."

"So that isn't my Helene down there? She's just another traverser?"

"He," I say, though it makes me sick to do it.

Exlee's showing teeth when they turn to me, so I hold up my hands.

"Oi! This version of Helene identifies as a man. You're the one who taught me that's what we go by."

There's a moment of stillness on their face while they process, their moral code warring with their heart.

Eventually, Exlee exhales. "So I did." They turn to Nik. "Was he involved in whatever marked your face? Will you kill him?"

Nik Nik is studying Exlee. "Would you have this one spared?" he asks.

"Not if this Helene drew your blood. I know the rules and I am not a traitor," Exlee says, too savvy for such an obvious trap.

"And if he didn't? Would you have me eliminate this anomaly for you?"

"I would never tell you what to do with one of your citizens. I know my place well enough," they say.

We must all be holding our breath, because the sound of my brother's leather creaking as he leans forward is as loud as a good knife on glass.

"But if you could, and I would listen . . ."

Exlee swallows. No winning here. Refuse to answer a third time and you've insulted the emperor. Answer and you've told the emperor what to do. I look down, because there are too many ways for this to go bad and either way someone I care about gets hurt.

"Yes, if it were my place to ask, I would ask you to spare . . ." another bracing swallow ". . . him."

Unblinking, but still not taking his eyes off Exlee, Nik Nik slowly leans back in his chair, waving his hand to free Exlee from questioning, and we all finally exhale.

"I see this does not concern me, and I'm needed at the House."

Exlee rises and moves across the room. They pause at the door, looking at Nik. "I apologize for thinking the worst."

It's beneath the emperor to accept an apology, or even to be apologized to really, but he nods anyway.

Once they're gone, Cara's nose wrinkles. "Really? He? Helene would hate that."

I glare at her. "How would you know, Ruralite?"

She's not wrong—Helene would absolutely spit to have a version walking around like she'd never made herself—but between her presumptions, Cross's existence, and Esther's refusal to be anything but perfect I've had it to the neck with Ruralite mouths.

I hit her with the full force of my glare, but she just glares right back. Her eyes are too dark, not dark brown like everyone else's, but like the empty black of a place light can't live. Too late, I realize it's a trap. Those eyes are tar, and I'm sure even if I tried to look away I would be held in them. Maybe it's just the stripes on her face. They make her appear otherworldly so my eyes are playing tricks. Just a trick . . . but I still can't look away.

"You would be surprised," Esther says, making Cara look at her, which frees me.

I look around, but no one else seems to have noticed that Cara is clearly a fucking witch.

"What does the fact that they are all traversers tell us?" Nik asks.

"That someone is better at this than he was," Cara says, throwing a thumb in Adam's direction.

"Hardly," Adam says, indignant as ever. "Though, yes, this is an advancement. Typically when someone traverses they must ensure their alternate self is already dead or risk the kind of death and mutilation the Housecat suffered. This other world has figured out how to off-load the backlash onto the version of themselves already occupying the world they seek to enter. They kill the dop, then send the new one safely over."

"Oh wow. Killing a bunch of innocent dops so that some rich assholes can come over? What kind of sadistic monster would do that?" Cara says, leveling a glare at Adam that tells stories.

"My way was one human killing another. That is as natural as the sun rising. I never planned to weaponize the backlash."

"Only because you didn't figure out how," Cara says. Her tone leaves room for zero doubt, and Adam's *Well, true* shrug confirms it.

"Three are dead, Helene's downstairs . . . so where are the other two? Did they not come over with the rest?" Cheeks asks the room, ending the fight with Cara in the lead.

Adam tilts his head. "It's possible the ones who attacked us had to earn part of their passage by doing a job. The other three may have just paid to get over and used their dop's resources to slip away. Dell Ikari says it happened with her father."

"Splice is monitoring chatter in the city, but nothing like that is being discussed," Cheeks says.

"Might not be reported. Houses and banks use facial scanning. Death reports are delayed due to the investigation. Hell, there might even be more deaths than we know. They could have slipped in and hid their own bodies," I say.

"You think someone from another world could just slip into ours assuming a previous identity, and no one would notice?" Cheeks asks.

Adam's chuckle is low, dark, and entirely out of place in the conversation.

"I don't know, Cara, do you think such a *wild* thing could even be possible? 'What kind of sadistic monster would do that?' "

"Fuck off," she says, then turns to Nik Nik. "You may want to send a team."

"So it is possible," Cheeks says.

"It is. In the city, it is," she says, a desert creature who must have learned how to put ice in her voice from her Wileyite partner. "Wileyites don't pay attention like we do."

"They've got soft eyes, you mean," I say. "They don't spend their lives scanning for danger."

"Soft everything," Cheeks says, spitting toward, but not directly at, Adam's feet.

It's the first time I see Adam's eyes move independently from each other. His biological one stays straight ahead, while his mechanical one moves diagonal and down, staring at Cheeks's spit.

"You go," Nik Nik says, turning to me. "Check around the addresses of the dead in the city for any sign of imposters. They must have prepared to blend in upon arrival, so you'll need to be inconspicuous. Soft feet. Wide eyes. Flush them out."

I nod. I wasn't going to give the order, but I knew the second I saw who was in the cell that I was bound for the city again.

"Cuff Cross as backup."

I open my mouth to whine but then I see the look Nik and Cheeks give me. There are too many people in this room. The heads of the House and the Rurals are involved in this now. If I challenge Nik Nik in this room, he'll have to shut me down with blood to save face. Or worse, reveal that I'm family so it doesn't look like a foot soldier's getting mouthy.

I nod deeply, accepting the order.

"Cuff him now. I released him to his post in the south, so it will take time to get back."

I nod again, the portrait of procedure and obedience, even as I type, Hey Fucker. Got orders, into my cuff and send it.

"I still have old files from most of the worlds archived," Cara says. "I can find worlds where Helene never transitioned. Figure out which world is coming over."

"No, you can't," Adam says. "You appeared on the projection behind one of the other victims. You're still alive in their world. You won't have the file."

"I'm alive there?" she asks. It's a happy kind of disbelief, like she'd forgotten she was alive anywhere else.

"Yes, and we seem . . . close. So narrowing it down won't be a problem."

Her eyes catch his at that revelation. "You said once there were only three . . ."

"Yes," Adam says, but then his smile turns toxic as wasteland sludge. "It may only be Wileyites dropping now, but be patient. I may get to give you a traversers' death yet."

"How many pieces do you have to lose before you stop threatening me?"

"I'm not threatening you. I'm not the *me* who will kill you. You saw to that. This is an Adam totally outside of my control. Which makes this little mess your fault."

"Like hell! I know people like you don't face real consequences, but you could at least take a drop of responsibility," she says.

"Had my operation been allowed to continue, this Adam would be dead by now instead of killing our citizens," he says. "You took out the centipede, and now we're all being plagued by spiders."

What he doesn't say, but probably means, is if he'd never had his shit blown up he would be the one who figured out how to mangle people to death from across the universe. After all, if this Adam is the centipede, and all other Adams are spiders, the rest of us can't be much higher than flies.

"We haven't discussed the most important question," Cheeks says, which surprises me because I was already looking at the door.

"What's that?" Cara asks.

"Was the attack the other world's Adam trying to kill ours? Or does Nik Nik in their world ride on the passenger side?"

Leave it to Cheeks to remember the attack despite the invasion. I'd seen how sick he'd looked when we pulled up, how bright the relief on his face was when he saw the emperor was fine. But there's no way for us to know which version is true, and I can already tell Cheeks and my brother are gearing up for one of their long debates about increasing Nik's personal security.

I turn to the emperor. "It will take time to cross the desert and get outfitted," I say, because there are too many people in this room for *This is boring as shit and I don't need to be here.*

He nods. "You're dismissed. But don't leave until Cross gets here."

I place my arm over my chest in a perfect form salute before heading out of the room. As I go I stick my tongue out at Cheeks, stuck in the meeting hell we both hate. He smiles a little before returning his face to regulation stoic.

I SMELL HER BEFORE I SEE HER, BUT I KNEW SHE'D FOLLOWED ME OUT EVEN BEFORE THAT. YOU DON'T have to have Ruralite gifts to know when you're being tailed, and I felt her eyes on me as I left the meeting room.

I'm standing out front waiting for Cross to pull up when she finally decides to approach me. It's not fear that has her stalling—wish it were—it's just curiosity.

"Which is it?"

"Pardon?" Esther asks, all light and politeness.

"Which of your men's been running on about me? Cross or Cheeks? You clearly think you know something about me, and they're the only way you could have learned."

"What makes you think either of those men are mine?" she asks, but she doesn't deny she's heard stories.

I spit between us. An insult in Ashtown, but meaningless in the Rurals so it shouldn't get me in trouble.

"I don't know if you don't."

She's been staring at me like she could see through me since the start of the meeting. She's still doing it, too. Those eerie light eyes so different from her sister's, but no less unsettling.

"What is your name, soldier?"

I cut my eyes toward her. I'd bet my best teeth she already knows, and I want her to know I know that before I answer.

"Scales," I say, rubbing my nose with the back of my hand to disguise that I'm looking for signs of Cross on the horizon.

She nods, but won't tell me what the name means to her.

Does she know me from talking with Cheeks? Did he say, *There's this girl I work with. She's my best friend! I value her!* Or was it *There's this girl who follows me around at work. I let her think we're friends, but she's honestly so thirsty.* Or maybe he never mentioned me at all. Maybe it was Cross who gave her my name, breaking his oath to complain about me to the only person who would never tell.

Finally, blessedly, I see the dust rise as Cross rolls up.

Beside me, Esther turns to go inside.

I wasn't raised with a sibling, but I can imagine she'll want to see her once-brother. Want to reassure herself of his well-being, even if they're not allowed to be true "siblings" anymore.

"He'll be here in a few seconds," I say, after she begins walking away.

She doesn't even fully look back. I see the barest glimpse of her side profile as she says, "I know."

And then she's gone, just as Cross's rough entry pelts me with dirt.

"What are you looking at?" he asks.

I turn, but there's no sign of the princess. I wonder how often she's done this. Ducked just around the corner so he'd never know she was around. Maybe the leader of the Rurals knows something, after all, about loving someone she can't touch. Maybe, impossibly, that porcelain angel and I have something in common. I think about telling him she was here, that she's still around and loves him so much she can't even look at him. I wonder if reminding him of what he's lost will hurt him enough to satisfy me.

Doubtful.

"We're headed to the city."

"Yes, Sir. Has something happened?"

"Long story," I say, and wave to tell transport we're ready.

"EMPTY," CROSS SAYS, UNPLUGGING THE SCANNER FROM THE SECURITY PANEL OF THE BUILDING.

We override it and enter the apartment. It's empty now, but someone has been here. Clothes are missing, and there's an open safe in the bedroom.

I barely contain the urge to throw my clipboard. We came as fast as we could. Jax even reused the same outfits as before, narrowing their eyes with a brusque, *I haven't had a chance to wash them, but something tells me you won't notice.* Their insult was just play, cubs catching each other's ears in their teeth but not biting down. That they care enough to tease me means they're on their way to forgiving me.

Standing at the dead person's newly ransacked house, out of breath and in yesterday's clothes, we're still too late. It's another empty home. If the city's dismembered are reappearing, they've regrouped and moved on already.

My cuff beeps and I jump a little, thinking that somehow the emperor was made aware of our failure through telepathy. But it's not Himself; it's Splice.

Disturbance. Three blocks north. Intel?

Whenever there are runners in the city, Splice watches the feeds around us like a raptor watching its young. If he's pinging me about a disturbance, it must have him worried. I look north. I can see a few people gathered, but not the cause.

I start walking instinctively, then turn around to motion for Cross, but he's already stepping beside me.

"I know," he says. "There's a disturbance at that house."

"Your Ruralite gifts manifesting?" I ask.

"Just my special gift of having eyes and being taller than you."

"Whatever," I say. "And you're not taller than me."

"Am too."

"Dream on."

My cuff beeps again, which means Splice can see we're on the move. He's sent me an address, the exact house Cross is already directing us toward, and a profile. The source of the excitement is apparently the home of a widower named Alden Woods. I look at his picture: Good shape. Midforties. I can take him.

I fill Cross in as we walk. He's still dressed like a bored rich man, so I elbow through the crowd like I'm both his assistant and his muscle.

"Make way. Clear the way," he says, the nasally whine of irritated authority.

I make like I'm checking my digital screen as I shove toward the front. We're not in any official uniform, so I half expect it to fail. It wouldn't have worked in Ashtown. They'd want to know why. If I tried bossing a crowd out of leather, they'd ask who died and made me emperor. But this is Wiley. Cross looks like a property owner and I look like security, so they're happy to obey and step aside. The city can bray all they want calling Nik a dictator, but he just uses force to make people bow to one man. He doesn't change the way they think, just how they behave if he's in earshot. The city uses education, and vidshows, and goddamn etiquette to train people into bowing to anyone who seems more successful than they are. They don't even know they're doing it. Everyone in Ashtown knows Nik's name and what they hate about him, even though they pay their dues. These people moved for a stranger with a clipboard without even knowing why. It's the Wiley City way. Don't disturb the process. Don't make a scene. Don't break the rules. Even if you don't understand them. Even if they are unjust. Even if there is a family of three, running from a burning death, and the rule is stupid protocol about not opening the doors. Even then. Smile over charred flesh and a brand-new orphan while the city congratulates you on a job well done.

A wasteland girl runs with her parents across the desert, trying to outpace the sun.

"Mr. Woods, we're entering the premises," Cross says, snapping me back.

Cross shifts to block me from the crowd and gives a nod, so I slide four round magnets out of my pocket and place them in a cluster around the door's e-lock. Once they're in position I activate them, causing a quick flash of electricity to arc between the four points, overriding the electronic security. Then I just use the magnets to manually pull the latch back, and we're in.

Time has been the battleground of our day, and we've only lost. We were too late getting into the city, too late getting to the houses where the others might have been, and now we're too late again.

Mr. Alden Woods has already become a story.

CHAPTER TEN

THE STORY THAT USED TO BE ALDEN WOODS WILL HAVE MANY VERSIONS, DEPENDING ON THE AGE OF THE teller, the personality, and the language they were born speaking. The story that stretches through the city, the story that began with the crowd gathering outside but will be told for years, goes like this:

Once upon a time there was a man who lost his wife. She'd been gone for years, but one day he walked into his living room and there she was, her white hair catching the light like an angel, but her eyes shining and so, so alive. He ran to her, gripping her hands, then shoulders, then her waist. Crying, but so overwhelmed—equal parts shaken and elated—that he hadn't even registered his own tears.

"I lost you," he said. "Where have you been?"

"Looking for you," she said, holding his face in hers, bringing him close. "I was afraid you didn't make it."

He looked up at her, the hitch of uncertainty tripping up the machine of his joy. "Make it?"

Some will say this is when it happened. Others will say it was after they kissed, and she sensed the stumbling uncertainty of a man who had not kissed her in five years. It doesn't matter. The stories will agree that once his uncertainty became obvious to her, she changed. She began to hiss like a creature with cool blood. Her mouth stretched wide, teeth bared, hands becoming claws. She ripped out his eyes and his tongue and then ate his organs . . .

. . . No, sorry, that last part's not right. That's the version children will tell—edgy ones, the ones trying to prove to their friends they are brave by pretending to relish violence. The ones who have not yet learned the difference between being brave and being cruel.

Among adults and neighbors, it will be told like this: She didn't hiss, she wailed. She cried, *No, no, no,* and backed away from him. It was then she reached for the statue.

The stories will all agree that before she was finished the walls were covered in blood and tissue. The stories will all agree that he didn't, not for one second, fight back.

It's the last part that gets me as Cross and I look over the body. Alden's forearms should be a bruise collection. His knuckles should be red with trying. But he took it all without defending himself. Was it disbelief? Or something . . . worse? Deeper? I'm not sure what adjective to grab, or why a small part of me feels jealous.

The only sign he was conscious at all during the attack is the blood on the thumb and two fingers of his right hand. I lift his wrist and look closer.

Cross has been taking pictures, video, and samples. This might not have anything to do with us, but once the city takes hold we won't have access, so it's best to take what we might need, just in case.

He sees me staring at the hand and saves a photo to his cuff.

"Can you see it?" he asks.

"See what?"

"How it happened," he says. I've been crouched down by the body. He copies my posture so we're level. "He got hit the first time, and it must have shocked them both, because there was a lull. He touched the wound on his head, kneaded the blood between his fingers in disbelief . . ."

". . . and before he could process what was happening, the killer found their bearings and finished the job."

"Maybe, or . . ." He lets his sentence drift off and resumes recording the room.

"Or what?" I ask, rising to my feet because he did. He's turned his back to me and is taking screen recordings of the images on the mantel.

He looks over his shoulder at me. "Someone's coming."

I turn toward the entrance, but I don't hear or see anything. "No one's coming. What do you mean 'or'?" I say, turning back, but he's gone.

I open my mouth to call for him, but then I hear the click of the door opening behind me. Have I mentioned that I hate the Ruralite most when he's right? I fix my face so that when I turn around I'm not visibly pissed off in the middle of a murder scene.

It's two enforcement officers. I start to square up then remember I'm not dressed like a runner. They don't know we're rivals.

"Oh, thank god," I say, my voice high and proper, sounding nothing like myself and everything like a woman ten floors up who gardens at dusk. "I told them to call you, I wasn't sure if they listened. I didn't know what to do, it's just . . ." I pause, like the sight of my thirtysomethingth dead body is going to undo me. ". . . I didn't know what to do but those are his neighbors, they knew him, so I thought it was best I kept them out. Did I do okay? You probably don't want to look. It's bad. It's—"

I cover my mouth with my hand. One enforcement officer looks genuinely concerned. The other just takes a step back in case I puke. While I'm looking away something on the counter of the kitchen catches my eye. It's out of place in the neat, modern space, its colors too warm for a place like this: a jar of honey, the label handwritten.

"You can go back down to your home now. We've got it from here."

This is from the "nice" one, but he still says *down* to your home, of course, because I certainly couldn't live on this floor, not with this skin tone. I must be one of those lucky adoptees, or a scholarship kid.

"Wait. We need to do a citizenship check. In case we have questions," says the asshole.

The nice one looks at him. "Come on, John. She's had quite a shock," he says, throwing me a pitying smile.

"You know the rules," the other one says, stepping up with the scanner.

This is what every feel-good story about these fucks misses.

Yeah, there are nice people in enforcement, but it's not about numbers, it's about policy and *policy* always sides with the assholes. The ones they call *bad* are the ones who actually follow orders and department culture. Every nice thing the other guy does is an aberration that people use as an example of why they should exist. I remember the city getting all smiles over a story of an enforcement officer who found an Ashtowner—not a runner, just an exiled civilian—in the city and gave them a blanket and some hot cocoa. People *praised* the uniform for doing something that wasn't policy, wasn't even common. But policy never changed, so the kid was kicked back out into the desert to starve. Kind officers are just the exceptions that ensure the rule goes on.

It's the clipboard problem in Wiley, the way the crowd moved for Cross and me despite being no one because Cross looked rich. They know enforcement only serves the superrich, but they're so hell-bent on pretending being rich is a virtue they respect their private gang too.

Yeah, I know I'm ranting, but you try watching an incompetent uniform fail at taking the same citizen scan three times in a row. It's enough to put anyone over the edge. Scans are supposed to be quick—Wiley would only allow such an intrusion if it was convenient—but he's having issues with his device. My face hurts from trying to answer questions politely while keeping my mouth tight enough to ensure my bottom lip never dips to reveal my teeth.

"Is this going to take much longer? I'm just on an internship and my boss . . ."

"Stop talking," says the officer, fiddling with his scanner.

The Ashtown in me wants to say, *Maybe if your lot spent half as much money on tech as you do drones, your scanners wouldn't be shit.* But that would bring attention. This man has never once looked at me, just through me, dismissing me as insignificant as easily as one swats a bogfly, and my life depends on keeping it that way.

Scanner problem fixed, the officer lifts his device to my face. I open my eyes and lift my chin as the light passes over me. My heart sits in my throat as the image processes, but then the device *tings* its affirmative chime.

He looks at the screen then back at me.

"You're unemployed?"

"Internship," I say. "I told you. And if I don't get back soon, I won't even have that."

He looks at the screen again, clearly bothered by something even though my citizenship scan should come back clean.

"You can go," he says, and then adds the part he's clearly been thinking. "And . . . I'm sorry to hear about your father."

My mouth goes to sand, my tongue a dead stone. "My father?"

"Jeffery Ackerman was a good man."

I swallow twice but still can't answer.

That name in the mouth of enforcement unlocks a memory. No, *unlocks* isn't the right word. It's not like I have forgotten. Not like I could.

—

I WASN'T CLUMSY.

I wasn't.

They told people I was clumsy, and told me I was clumsy, but really they were just unwilling to make room for a child that acted like anything but an adult. But this was back when I still believed I was clumsy. I told you. Stories are powerful, and none are more powerful than the ones you let others tell you about yourself.

The day I'm remembering was a busy one. I was walking too slow, and he was mad, but we were in public so I would have to wait until we made it home to see how mad. I sped up, trying to solve the problem, and I stepped on the back of his shoe. Again, not because I was clumsy but because I was scared. But it was a bad step. I didn't just graze the back of his heel, I full-on stomped it, yanking him back midstep and even tugging at the hem of his perfect pants. When he turned on me his eyes were all ice and fury. This, like all my mistakes, he took for a deliberate act of malice. It wasn't. Later I would absolutely learn the kind of fire that trips a man who demands I walk faster, but it would be years before I became the monster he always assumed I was.

Anyway, I was so small then that I couldn't have hurt him, but people on the street had seen him trip, had looked over at him. I hadn't hurt him, but I had embarrassed him, and that was unforgivable. He whipped around, grabbing me by the hair and yanking my head up so that it could properly meet the open hand he brought down across my mouth. It was a bad hit. A flustered, sloppy thing. When elegant people slap each other in movies, it's always so neat and crisp. But using your body to do harm to another is always a little awkward. Because of his hand in my hair we were standing too close. His palm smooshed across my mouth instead of cleanly smacking my cheek, and his fingers bent backward because of it.

"Sir!"

The enforcement officer was outraged, seeing only a larger shape assaulting a smaller shape, but when he got close enough to see us clearly confusion corrupted his righteousness.

"Sir?" Same word, but as a question now.

The hand released my hair, and then hit a button on his cuff to project his ID. His usually neat palms were shiny, and I knew he couldn't stand it. I'd left a trail of drool on his hand. He'd left a bit of blood in my mouth.

"Sorry you had to see that. She's being especially unruly today."

He said "she" like the officer knew me, or should, even though we'd never met.

The officer looked from the ID to me to him to the ID again. I was not surprised when he nodded.

"Try to be more careful," he said. "Have a good day, Mr. Ackerman."

—

WHAT DOES IT MEAN TO TELL A MAN WHO STRUCK A CHILD TO BE CAREFUL? CARE IS FOR PROTECTION. What are you asking the man to protect?

You're going to call me a liar, I know. You think I lied when I said my irritation at enforcement was just because they were keeping me for a citizenship scan, and now you can see I have many reasons. But lies are just stories, and now you have another. Maybe my hate stems from an old wound. But all good passions do. Isn't that what they teach in the Rurals? That spilled blood brings clarity, and splits the world in two? A man stabs another man in the side with a spear, and the water and blood hits the earth creating sinners and saints, light and dark? Well, blood on a nine-year-old's teeth can do the same thing. Every drop of child's blood I lost taught me what a demon was, and I can't unlearn that gospel any more than Esther could unlearn her religion.

But now . . . Jeffery Ackerman is dead and enforcement is standing here calling him a good man.

Thank you are the words I should have said for the sake of my cover, but I can't quite make them come out when I want to scream their opposite. I want to say, *Take it back*. I want to say, *I don't want this*. I heard cats used to have this habit, where they would bring a fresh kill to their masters and pretend it was a gift. That's what the officer has done. He's opened his mouth and the corpse of my father has fallen out.

I leave abruptly, hoping the officers will mistake my panic for grief and that Cross will find his way to Jax's when he's done hiding. Hearing the name again is a reminder of what this city is, and who it praises. I want nothing more than to get back to my desert, where I won't have to breathe filtered air or walk under a fake sun or see shiny buildings or speak to people who worship cruel, stupid men as long as they are rich enough. Describing a person as *rich* in Ashtown implies the words *greedy* and *selfish*. The wealthy in Wiley get respected for hoarding. They get thought of as *good* and *wise* and, most laughably, *hardworking*. Just like enforcement. Wiley is full of people wanting blue ribbons for doing bad shit.

If I had Cross's skills with explosive powder, I would have leveled the city years ago. Let the rubble become shelter for animals that fancy burrowing. Let the broken pipes make an oasis of bubbling water. Let this gridded patch of earth become something useful for once.

—

"WHAT'S WRONG?" JAX ASKS, FOLDING UP THE LAST OF THE BORROWED CLOTHES.

I tighten my vest in the mirror, then begin sliding on my gloves. "Nothing."

"Bullshit nothing."

"Found out someone I knew died today."

"Someone you liked?"

"Someone I hate."

Jax slides the glasses I'd forgotten I was wearing off my face. "You used to have a problem with hate, back when you came to the House."

"Not hate. Anger. But I'm better now."

The *I swear!* is silent, but Jax hears my defensiveness all the same and grants me one of their rare, sly smiles, so lovely and calming it could soothe a lightning strike.

"I know. Exlee and I, we talk."

The revelation that Jax still checks in with the House, and that Exlee sees fit to pass on kind words about me of all people, quells my shakiness. It makes me desperate to go home, where I am suffered, and loved, and understood.

"What you're experiencing now is grief," Jax says.

"No. I wouldn't—"

"Not for the person. For the feeling of having someone to hate. You had a burning core keeping you going, and the first thing you feel when it goes out is cold."

I nod, wondering how they could have known about the creeks of dry ice my veins had become since I began processing the news.

"But that fire was killing you, Scales. Its absence opens up potential. It's a hole that you can fill with anything in the world now. Choose wisely."

Jax didn't do full service work at the House. Their specialty was exactly this, letting people in crisis air their confusion then offering a piece of clarity in a room filled with smoke and gentle music. They are using their old skills again, and they are using them for me. I know now that I am well and truly forgiven, even though I haven't earned it yet.

"I'm sorry," I say, "for how I acted when you were leaving. I don't know why I did that."

"You did it because you were a kid with a crush."

Well, yeah, but . . .

"You knew?"

"Of course I knew. Subtlety was never among your strong suits." The smile drops from their mouth when they look at me again. "I hope somewhere in the last decade you've overcome the instinct to punish the thing you love just because you aren't allowed to have it."

Shame blooms in my stomach and I hope I've caught it before it shows on my face. I think about Cheeks. Have I ever wanted to punish him for not wanting me? Even a little? I didn't turn him in to Nik at the Ruralite compound. I want that to count for something, but I was a spoiled child once, and maybe I still am.

"I hope so too," I say, but I'm only talking to myself. The proximity alert on Jax's door camera has beeped, and they've walked away to let Cross in.

"Where have you been?" I say when Cross enters.

His look is dark, and I can tell something is wrong in the brief moment his eyes land on mine before darting away.

"We have orders," he says.

"And?"

Cross swallows. "We're meant to be on standby until morning."

"Here?"

"No," he says. "Ash."

"Well, thank Christ for that. We still partnered?"

He nods once, sharply. Neither of us is particularly happy about that part. And why should he be? I've been ten shades of shit to him for years now, nursing a hatred of him that's almost as old as my hatred of Jeffery. Jax is right, it does feel good, but Jax is also right, it's not good for me.

"Cross," I say.

"Yeah?" he says. His eyes manage to stay on mine this time, the bright blue so intense I almost lose my nerve.

"This job . . ." I clear my throat, wipe at my face. I say the next part quick, like taking down bad medicine. ". . . you've been really solid. That's all. Glad to have you watching my back."

His brow furrows, and I can *feel* him overthinking it, so I go on before he can speak.

"Anyway, don't fuck around gathering your stuff. If he wants us on standby he must think he'll need us," I say, and leave the room to let Jax finish undressing him.

—

BEING ON STANDBY IN ASH MEANS BEING AT A JUMP HOUSE WHERE THE EMPEROR CAN GET YOU quickly. Given where our assignments have taken us, I choose the hideout halfway between the palace and the city's wall. It takes less than an hour to get us there and settled in for the wait.

"Goddamn it," I say, for probably the fourth time. "My cuff isn't transmitting."

I've been trying to send a message to Nik confirming our arrival since we got here, but I keep just getting the *in process* screen without completion.

"It's all right," Cross says, bringing me a glass of water. "I messaged."

I take a sip. The water tastes like licking the bottom of a pond, but I don't say anything. I don't want Cross to know that drinking that overly filtered cold shit in the city a few times is all it took to lose my desert tongue.

"It's just . . . weird. It's never happened before," I say.

It's like I've had my service shut off, but obviously cuffs aren't something you can make people pay to use. I wonder if someone has put me on limited contact through runner channels. But only the emperor could do that, and Nik Nik wouldn't. Not to me, anyway. I take another sip of water that tastes slightly more like shit than usual, and realization hits me.

The emperor isn't the only one who can limit cuffs. A wolf can do it, too.

I cuff Cheeks using our private connection, a thread we established so our most inane jokes wouldn't go through the palace relay.

Respond if you get this. Testing something.

If he doesn't respond my cuff is just broken and I'll have to take it in for repair. If he does respond it means I'm blocked out of the runner network. Worse, it means the wolf has its eye on me and I'm in danger.

My cuff beeps. I sigh, pieces falling into place too late to avoid what comes next. I've got the shape of it now. Enough to prepare for the reckoning, but not enough to avoid it.

It's gonna be a long night.

Testing what?

I'm wolf throttled. Tell Himself. Tell him I've just checked in to the Limbo jump house. Tell him hurry. Tell him alone.

My cuff dings again, but I can't check it because a vise has grabbed my lower intestine and is trying to pull it up through my chest. I barely make it to the toilet before vomiting up my last three hours. The water didn't taste off because I'd been spoiled on Wiley's. Cross served me swamp water.

I sit back on my haunches, feeling stupider than I have in a long time. I feel Cross standing behind me, waiting, even though he doesn't speak.

My cuff dings, reminding me of the waiting message, but I don't need to check it to know what it says.

"You gave me wasteland water," I say, not bothering to get off my knees or turn to face him.

"Those raised in the wastes can drink it without getting sick. All of them."

We both know the immunity never goes away, which means we both know now that my wasteland backstory is a lie. I wipe my mouth with the back of my hand, which draws attention to my cuff.

I open the message.

Why jump house? You're supposed to be off duty till noon tomorrow.

It's what I expected, and I add it into my neat little pile of Things It Would Have Been Nice to Know Thirty Minutes Ago.

"You're the wolf, yeah?"

I don't need to see Cross nodding to know that he is.

"Welcome to your interrogation," he says, his voice so close he must be right at my back.

Time's up. I go down in a bright, electric wave.

WHEN I WAKE UP I'M BOUND TO A CHAIR IN THE MIDDLE OF THE MAIN ROOM. CROSS HAS REMOVED ALL the furniture. He thinks things are going to get messy. He's not wrong. I clench my fists against the arms of the chair. My tongue feels fat and fuzzy, the telling aftereffects of electric shock, but my strength is already returning. When I tilt my head back I feel the contact burn at the back of my neck.

"Stunner?" I say. "You cheated."

"I d—"

When his mouth opens wide I spit strong and true, hitting him right in the back of the throat and making him choke.

While he's bent coughing, I tuck my thumbs in and make a fist so tight it's painful. I'm rewarded with the *click* of the razors being deployed. I'm glad Cross and I were never friends. My friends all know what my gloves can do.

When he looks at me again I'm sitting still like a good prisoner. He moves back to his pack and puts on a face guard. He places the circle of black plastic on top of his head like a crown.

"You're very good at that," he says, pressing a button on the side of the guard to deploy an electric shield over his face. It's a good call; my next loogie was going straight into his eye. I try for it anyway, hoping the shield hasn't warmed up yet, but it sizzles and evaporates on contact.

The face guard goes with the rest of his serious-business interrogation outfit. He's stripped down to a tank and his leathers, an outfit designed for movement and bloodstains, and he's gloved up. His gloves catch shine in the light; the leather across his knuckles is rigged for pain. I can see from here it's just a metallic underlayer, nothing too fancy, nothing like, say, the emperor's sister would get to wear.

"And I didn't cheat. Regulation says when there is a combat differential a wolf is authorized to use incapacitating techniques against a target. You're rated five levels higher than me."

"You're goddamn right I am." I pretend to strain against the ropes he's used, trying to subtly rub the razor blades against the restraints. "And you're going to feel every single one of those levels when I get out of here."

"Don't make this harder than it has to be. I was tapped to do a sweep for embedded traitors. And you were right, I did think Cheeks's missing time was incriminating, but it's nowhere near what I've got on you."

I start to press harder against the ropes, but the blade on the outside of my left hand is flipped the wrong way and slices into my wrist instead. I keep any reaction off my face as I focus on correcting it.

"Fuck you. You don't have shit on me. You're targeting me because I treat you like dirt and the wolf appointment's gone to your head. You know I'm loyal."

He'd been leaning back on the stool, but once I speak he snaps to attention. He stands to his full height, and uncrosses his arms so he can point at me. His blue eyes are all blaze and fury. It's the kind of righteousness that grows like a weed in the Rurals, always making its bearers very loud and very stupid.

"I thought you were! Fuck, Dex, you were the one thing I was sure of."

I glare at him through the top of my eyelids. "When I get out of this, I'm going to break one bone for every time you disrespect me. You dropped my old name. That's one."

He looks away. "I didn't mean to."

"Untie me if you're so fucking sorry."

He raises his hand to wipe at his face, and probably run his hands through his hair like I've seen him do a hundred times these last few days, but then he remembers he's got a shield on and stops.

"I wish I could. But you're a spy from Wiley, and I need to know who you report to."

There's a beat after he says the words where I just look at him, then I laugh. No, I bray, a real runner's laugh, all dead eyes and high pitches, exposing every inch of teeth and gum and tongue.

"I hope you're just setting me up for revenge. 'Cause if you're serious you've lost your goddamn mind."

He taps his cuff, and a family picture projects, bright blue and wide as the wall. It's a well-dressed man staring dead ahead, and a woman standing beside him who is too warm and beautiful to be there. It's a three-second loop, not a still, but you'd never guess that from his unmoving face. Between them, so small and dark you'd almost miss her, is a girl forced into a black dress with a white collar. Her hair is badly managed, but the barrettes in it are platinum. She's looking down in one frame, but then looking up in the next, never quite smiling. The image doesn't show the father gripping the base of her neck to make her look up, but that is what happened.

"Your name is Devon Ackerman. And you were raised a Wiley-ite."

PART TWO

How much can you change and get away with it, before you turn into someone else, before it's some kind of murder?

—Richard Siken,
War of the Foxes

CHAPTER ELEVEN

THEY CALL ME MR. SCALES BECAUSE I CAN CLIMB ANY DAMN THING.

Or because I turned my first wasteland kill into gloves, wearing the skin of its spine on my knuckles for years.

Or because I used to be real good at piano, but scales is all they've heard me play.

They call me Mr. Scales . . . but they didn't always.

—

A WASTELAND GIRL PULLED BETWEEN HER PARENTS. THE SUN RISING BEHIND THEM A GLOWING mouth that wants to eat them and was always going to. They run to a door that does not open and was never going to. I survived. I am the girl.

But that's just another story, a wasteland story and I was the first to tell it. I whispered it long before I came to the desert in need of a cover.

It's true that a girl's parents pulled her through the desert to save her life. It is true that they were turned away and the parents covered the girl as they died. I watched it happen from behind glass so thick and in an atmosphere so regulated that all I knew about bright days was the pretty way they made the sand shimmer. I was ten. The girl looked ten. I told myself the girl was ten and she became ten. Over her were the bodies of people who loved her. At my back was a man with his hand tight on my shoulder. He was my father and he hated me. I did not know then why. He'd brought us down to this low floor to watch the bright day take over the sand the way in Ashtown we climb the mountain to watch the stars fall. Looking back, I think he wanted precisely what happened, for me to have to watch people that look like me die. My father was always trying to make me grateful.

He said the people caught out deserved it because they hadn't made their own preparations. He said you can't expect everyone else to take care of you, you had to take care of yourself. He said no one owed them or their families anything. He said, it's sink or swim, the strong survive and the weak perish.

"Lazy," he said as they collapsed, his second-favorite word. "Worthless," he said next, his first-favorite.

In my pearls, lace collar, and chemically straightened hair, I looked down at the featureless mass that used to look like people but now just looked like love. And I wished. I wished I was the girl underneath. I wished I was loved, and protected. I wished my father didn't resent me and my mother wasn't such a coward she wouldn't even protect me from one man, much less the sun itself.

Years later, when my mother took me to Ashtown, I knew it was to kill me. She'd sat quietly by while her husband had proven again and again his dissatisfaction with me. Thirteen-year-olds trade nothing so eagerly as a dirty secret, so I'd heard about the south south of Ashtown. I didn't know the term *Akeldama* yet. In Wiley, they called it Suicide Valley. I knew what it was, but when we got there I didn't fight. I didn't refuse to get out of the car. I didn't run, even when the hulking man in a hooded robe stepped out from the shadows. He was the widest man I had ever seen, and his scythe was so dark it was either made of a different kind of metal than our knives back home, or he'd simply never cleaned it.

He looked through me like I was nothing, like my parents' friends had looked through me my whole life. Then he recognized my mother, and he looked back at me intensely, like I was suddenly the only thing in the world. The executioner took off his hood, and that was the first time I saw my father's face.

You gonna whine about me lying to you again? 'Cause I won't hear it. Just because something didn't happen doesn't mean it's not true. Would you like me to tell you the facts? How I didn't taste unfiltered air until I was thirteen? How, no matter how much we might wish it, bodies are not dense enough to protect from the rays of a bright day, and that little girl smoldered and cooked beneath her parents? I may not have run from the sun, but I spent my childhood scared of something infinitely more powerful than me and sure I was dead from one moment to the next. And that girl may have died in the sand that day, but I carried her with me, I invented her face, I dreamt of her. She whispers out of my mouth to remind others of her parents' sacrifice. If that's not alive, what is?

When Nik Nik told Exlee my backstory, an orphan raised in the wastes coming into Ash for work, it didn't even feel like a lie. It felt like a gift. He said the desert needs certain stories, and it was already full to the brim of dead children. It needed something else, and that's what we gave it. Saying I didn't have parents never felt wrong. Saying I came from a place that wanted me dead didn't feel like a lie either. The only thing that felt false was pretending anyone had ever cared about me deep enough to turn to ash. That's never been true, and it never will be.

A wasteland girl runs with her parents across the desert, trying to outpace the sun.

"Bullshit. Doesn't look a thing like me," I say, staring at what I know damn well is my own seven-year-old face.

What I say is technically true, because it's been nearly two decades since I let chemical straighteners near my hair or skin lightening lasers near my face and the effects of both have long since worn off.

"Ruralites really do think all other Ashtowners look alike, huh?" I say, knowing it will hit hard.

"I'm not a Ruralite," he says.

"And I'm not Wiley," I say. "This photo all you got? No other pictures?"

His mouth hardens. "You know it is. Your parents kept you out of the public eye. They wanted to pretend you were their biological child, but once this family photo leaked the tabloids all said the same thing: You were a stolen Ashtown child and Estelle's pregnancy was fake or ended in a miscarriage."

They had said that? I had no idea.

Against my usual nature, I stop being a pain in the ass and try a new tactic. I look him in the eye and let the rage leave my face.

"Come on, Cross. You can't *really* believe this."

He crouches down, looking up at me through his dark hair. "I don't. I can't. But I have to. The closest I have ever come to betraying the emperor is wanting to bury this and say nothing. You know I've watched you most of my life? You can hate me all you want to, but by my math I've known you longer than almost anyone you see on a regular basis. I'm only even a runner because of you. I still remember the day. I was waiting in the alley beside Blay's, and there you came. I'd known you for so long but this time . . . you were so happy and whole and I thought I could be too. You made me believe in all of this."

I know exactly the moment he's talking about. He thought he was watching me happy, and he was, but it wasn't pure because I knew he was there the whole time. I'd just kicked ass at my combat testing, and I was riding high. I never thought to question why the holy son was waiting in a buyer's alley. It never occurred to me he was there for anything but preaching. But I knew he was there, so I laughed my loudest. And when Dragon and Tear tried to lift me up between them, I let them. And I didn't hush Blay inside when he started a chant with my name.

I wanted their love for me to dissolve any judgment he could have. Worse, I wanted my joy to be a blade aimed straight at the heart of the boy I knew couldn't smile. I wanted to wound him. I didn't know he already was.

Crouched down, looking up at me, he could be that boy again. That's why I almost use his name. Why I almost—just almost—ask him to let me go. I think if I could do it, if I could say his name while looking him in the eyes, if I could ask him with heart, like I need him, he'd do it. Can everyone else see how much he wants to be loved? Or is it easy to miss because he doesn't have a partner? It feels like the decades have collapsed, and I am once again seeing something in him no one else can. But I'd wanted to help him then, and I learned my lesson.

I lunge at him, growling. I'm tied to the chair—though the movement does help weaken the ropes—but he still flails backward. He reaches back and catches himself before fully falling on the ground, then stands, his face guarded once again.

And I laugh. I laugh like he is the stupidest thing I've ever seen. Like I never saw his heart. Like I don't have one.

"So what were you?" he asks, like the pause in the interrogation never happened. "Spy? Assassin? Why would a man as famously cruel as Jeffery Ackerman adopt an Ashtown orphan, except to groom them. He made gear for security and military use. He did business with Senior. Was he hoping to take over? Were you the key to his plan?"

This last part is so utterly wrong, it eliminates all the shock and fear that rose inside me when I saw the photo. I'm not found out. I'm not ten. And this guy, this guy's a fucking moron. There's a shadow in the corner of the room that wasn't there when we first got here. I realize how much time has passed. Cross has already lost.

I lean back in my chair. "Ackerman? Oh! I know Ackerman. He's that smith out by Lou's. Does our rim repairs when I'm busy. Doesn't look like that though."

"You know that's not who I'm talking about."

"You sure he doesn't weld for us?"

"Certain."

"So, this isn't about a rim job?"

"It's—" he stops, goes to pinch the bridge of his nose, remembers the face shield, and drops his hand in frustration.

He looks up irritated.

I make a show of tilting my head back to see what he sees. "You looking for God, Cross? You still pray?"

"Of course not. That would be treason."

"Bet you do. Bet I can make you." I smile wide, hoping the light catches my silver and makes me look just like a knife.

"You're stalling," he says. "I was watching you in the house. I saw you pass the citizenship scan. I know that officer called you

Jeffery Ackerman's daughter and I know I caught you stalking his widow two days ago."

It isn't until he says this that I connect Jeffery's death with Estelle's lighter demeanor the other night. Hadn't I thought she looked happy? Hadn't I thought she looked free? If I wanted I could have walked right up to her and no one would have stopped me.

"Maybe I killed him," I say.

"And pretended to be his daughter?"

"Maybe I killed her, too. Used her digits for citizenship 'cause we're the same tone. Would've popped the widow to round it off, but you caught me."

"Stop it. You didn't kill him."

And there's something about how he says it, how hard he is working to keep his face dead, that tells me something unexpected.

"Did you . . . you killed Jeffery Ackerman?"

"He's a rich Wileyite. How would I have?" he says, and he's right, but that isn't an answer. His face gives away nothing, and I can't tell if I've hit true or if he just knows more about the death than he's saying.

"So one photo and curiosity about the father of my dummy identity's death. That's what you got?" I ask, drawing his attention to my face as I use the arm of the chair to turn the last backward razor. "I'm gonna beat the shit out of you."

"No . . ." he says, and finally uncertainty creeps into those zealous features.

"What is it? Don't get shy now."

He licks his lips. When he speaks, his eyes don't meet mine. "You left the House when you were nineteen."

"Yeah?"

"Same time Ripper was killed."

I let my face go cold. "That so?"

"You came to Ashtown when you were thirteen."

"Sounds right."

"Same time Senior was killed."

Fuck.

"Stop!" I yell, pressing the batteries in my palms to heat the razors in my gloves. I push off the ropes and jump to my feet just in time to stop the shadow racing to Cross's back.

I shove my hands into Nik Nik's chest, barely holding him. His eyes, trained on Cross over my shoulder, are a killing dark.

"I've got this," I say. "I can give just as good as you."

I look over my shoulder at Cross. "Back room. Now."

He doesn't look like he wants to go, and after a second I realize it's because he doesn't want to leave the emperor alone with me. Finally he leaves, giving me a final look that I imagine he intends as a threat. I turn back to Nik.

"You didn't see his face. He's grasping at straws."

"If he knows."

With the ice in the emperor's voice, that's a whole sentence.

"No one knows. Least of all an oblivious Ruralite."

His eyebrows knit together as he understands my tone. "You . . . you really expect me not to kill him. Does he mean something to you? Do you like him?"

Oh, for fucksake.

"No! I hate him. But he loves you. No one but Cheeks looks at you the way he does, and that kind of obedience is always good to keep in the chamber. I'll kill Cross myself if he missteps, but I'm not giving up that resource because he hurt my pride doing his job."

"Did he injure you?" he asks, which is the only question that matters. Anyone who draws the emperor's blood maliciously—regardless of whose body it's in at the time—gets put to dust.

"He didn't. A quick tase. Restraints weren't even tight." I hold up my wrists to show him, too late seeing the trickle of blood running down my arm. His eyes narrow. A cut is enough to get Cross mangled in the street.

"That's not him, that's me. I used my razor deploy to escape and . . . I don't think I loaded the spring right after last time." I squint at my gloves. "I might need Splice to install a guard that comes out with it. Or a Kevlar guide?"

My brother is exasperated at my tinkering now, which is a step back from murder.

"We'll tell him the part of the truth he is already certain of," he says. "It suits me to have someone else on fieldwork aware of your importance. All the same"—he looks at me—"he will need to suffer for this insult."

I smile my widest. "Not a fucking problem."

When we enter the back room Cross is standing at full runner attention. Anyone else, I would assume they straightened out once they heard the door opening, but I'd bet he's been standing like this the whole time.

"You were right. Jeffery Ackerman did spend time in Ashtown, and had deals with my father. But he didn't come alone." Nik Nik tilts his head toward me. "He brought his pretty wife."

Cross just looks confused. Dedicated runner but, like I said, not the greatest at making connections.

"Jeffery's daughter didn't look different from him because his wife miscarried and they adopted. Jeffery's daughter didn't look like him because she wasn't his. Estelle was unfaithful," Nik Nik says. "And Dad . . . never could resist touching anything delicate."

The truth rips Cross's air from him.

"No . . . you're . . ."

Remember how I said my smile at getting to give Cross correction was my widest? I lied, 'cause this one stretches so far my face hurts. I hope my mouth doesn't even look like a mouth anymore; I hope it looks like a trap, like one of those toothy plants that eat prey whole.

". . . emperor's blood?" I offer, real helpful like I like to be.

He always looks a little like a ghost, but the change that comes over his face turns him full corpse. Pale, like always, but a little sickly now. I like seeing the bright dawn of impending death break across his features. He knows as well as I the cost for harming the emperor's blood.

"You're authorized," Nik Nik says.

I'm Senior's git. I don't need permission to kill or maim. That he follows protocol means I'm acting, not as his sister, but as his soldier. I wonder if he thinks that will keep me from going too far.

"Close the shutters on your way out," I say to my brother, as I slowly circle behind Cross. "It's going to be loud."

Nik nods. That nod, that response to me asking a favor, is a stronger proof of my lineage than any other.

Before Nik Nik can get out of the room, Cross yells, "I claim the tribunal of truth!"

Fucking kiss ass.

"I don't go easier on truth tellers," I say.

"You don't go easy on anyone," he says, then looks back at the emperor. "I claim the tribunal of truth."

I roll my eyes, but look at Nik. "Do you have it on you?"

Nik Nik nods, which puts the smile back on my face. If Cross was asking just to stall, he won't get long.

"Knees," Nik Nik says, switching a thick ring from his thumb to his index. Every civilian knows his middle fingers carry rings that combine to kill, and that knowledge is so bright and heavy they never ask about the others. Even I don't know them all, but I know this one. This one is just for us.

Cross goes to his knees in front of the emperor, mouth already open even though Nik hasn't given the command yet. Do Ruralites still do sacrament like the old faiths? I don't know, but the way Cross waits on his knees, head back, mouth open, eyes closed, he can only be waiting for the flesh of something he'd die for—God's bread or lover's skin. When Nik Nik places the ring against his mouth, Cross widens then closes it slightly, no teeth, just enough that his bottom lip is forced slightly down around the shape of my brother's knuckle.

Sometimes, my brain reaches into the vast and wild infinite to send very unhelpful information right to the front. Right now, it does me the *un*favor of making me aware that seeing Cross like this makes me want to fuck him. No, no, I don't want to have sex with him. I want *him* to be fucked by *me*. I want to see how far this vulnerability, this devotion and willing helplessness can go. I bet he'd let me tie him up twice over. I bet he gives his lovers access to every single part of him.

Doesn't matter. I'll never know.

Wanting something is not a license to have it. An old lesson, but a good one.

The sound of the ring unlatching to drip liquid into Cross's mouth snaps me back into the moment, and I vow to head to the House or at least the nightfire before I do something well and truly stupid. The reminder goes double once I watch Cross swallow.

I remember the taste of the not-honey from that ring from my initiation over a decade ago now. It's thick as blood and sour as truth, which is what it brings. Everyone who takes the leather gets questioned under the influence of it. Once it hits your system it acts like a truth serum, only it doesn't compel you to tell the truth. It just makes a lie feel like razor wire's being dragged through your whole fucking body. So more like a truth serum's fucked up older cousin, I guess.

Nik Nik holds Cross's chin up so he can watch his pupils for the chemical's take. After what feels like an eternity that's got to be aching the holy runner's neck, the emperor nods.

"He's ready."

"Could be a false positive, better test it," I say walking over, finally getting my chance to play enforcer.

I stand next to the emperor, grabbing Cross's chin to strain his neck back up at me. "Tell a lie, Cross."

He swallows hard, a quick flash of panic in his eyes. Probably he's never felt the burn of lying during a truth tribunal before, but we've all heard the screams of someone who has.

Finally his eyes flash up to mine and he nods.

"I hate you," he says, licking his lips.

For a second, nothing happens, but then his neck bulges with the strain of holding back his scream. But the serum is just getting started. His skin reddens and he doubles over. Pain defeats his clenched jaw and his new scream is an agony so total he drools as he makes the sound. His body contorts and he tries to escape the thing within, wriggling hard against the ground but then bending back like it's hot to the touch. Veins emerge from his forehead down his neck beneath pale skin turned hot pink and trending to full red. Eventually the pain passes, and he's panting on the ground.

"Do you think another test will be necessary?" Nik Nik asks.

Cross panics as much as he can, which is about as much as a newly shot animal. His eyes go frantic and his nostrils flare. We both know every lie hurts worse than the last. We both know he'll lie anyway if I command it.

I crouch down. "We can move on. I'm betting that last answer wouldn't be a lie anymore."

"I don't," Cross says through a broken voice. "I don't hate you."

The pain doesn't come even when I'm sure it will.

"You should. You'd hate me if you had any sense."

This isn't real. He was raised in a faith that didn't let him hate anyone, and maybe he just never learned. It feels like something unconditional and blessed, but I'm sure it's just brainwashing.

"I'll leave you to administer the questions . . . and his punishment," Nik Nik says, though I'd almost forgotten I was supposed to cause this twitching creature even more pain.

"Anything specific you want me to ask? Or just the vow?"

"The vow will do. Report any surprises. I'll log the punishment as insubordination correction," Nik Nik says. Which means Cross will get tomorrow off to recover.

"Have you ever conspired to knowingly harm the emperor or his kin?" I say, pitching my voice back to the standard interrogator. The word *conspired* is important here, because it's the only reason I was able to pass my questioning. I haven't had to answer the questions since my first day, but I don't need to consult my cuff for the verbiage. I know the questions like I know every name I've ever had.

"No," he says. No pain, unsurprisingly. Slowly, as if afraid to be too near the light overhead, Cross makes his way back onto his knees.

"Do you swear your loyalty to the emperor—"

"Yes."

". . . and his kin," I say, finishing my sentence.

"Yes," he says. No pain, but I do notice it's quieter than the first.

"Do you understand you are one of a whole, and a failure to care for your fellow runners is a failure to care for the emperor?"

"Yes."

"Do you swear to care for all of your fellow runners?"

"Yes."

"Do you understand that you are a machine, and failure to care for yourself is a failure to care for the emperor?"

"Yes."

"Do you swear to care for yourself?"

"Yes."

We both realize he's lying too late. The pain passes through him like a killing current. He must bite his tongue to keep from screaming. It doesn't work. It just means that when he passes out, blood crawls out of the side of his mouth like a fat leech.

CHAPTER TWELVE

I MUST BE GOING MARSH SOFT, BECAUSE WHEN HE WAKES UP I'VE CLEANED THE BLOOD OFF HIS FACE and I'm still here making sure he doesn't choke on his newly cut tongue. Once I see that he's stirring I toe him in the ribs to bring him conscious. So maybe I'm not going *that* soft. He tries to sit up, but it's slow and strained. I've heard the day after failing a truth tribunal feels like waking up after working out your whole body for a month. He's bad off, but he'll be even worse tomorrow. He manages to sit up, using the wall as support.

"Did I get my punishment?" he asks, and of course it's his first question. He can't belong again until after he takes his stripes, and I'm beginning to understand how badly he wants to belong.

"Yeah, you're square," I say, which is a goddamn lie. I didn't even get to punch him in the face *one single time.* "But we're not partners anymore. Go back to your old assignment."

I know the disappointment in his eyes doesn't come from missing out on my sunny disposition. He must just hate his home post that much. I know it's remote, which may account for his unhappiness. Someone this desperate for approval would need an audience to please.

"You really don't like your post," I say. "I guess it's good you're probably due for a promotion, yeah?"

"I was," he says, shaking his head as if the weight of his mistake last night is just now hitting him. "Now I'll probably die with these marks."

"Himself isn't petty as all that. You were just doing the job he hired you for."

"Himself. Is that really what you call him?"

"What else would I call him?"

"I don't know. Brother, maybe?"

We were almost cool for a second there, but his mouth ruins the party once again.

"Thanks for reminding me, I almost forgot," I say, giving him time to see what's sitting on the ground between us: a fire blade and a mound of white powder.

He swallows and nods. "Can I choose where?"

"Sure," I say.

I'm not a monster. I was going to brand his thigh or back. I'd never insist on a memory mark being worn publicly.

That's why I'm so shocked when he says, "The front of my neck."

"What? No."

"No?"

"I mean, it's bad protocol," I say. "Can't tattoo over branded skin. It'll prevent marks from taking if you get promoted."

Or if you fall in love, but I don't say that. I wonder if that's why he wants the front of his neck done. He's had his heart broken and is using me to be dramatic.

"Fine," he says. "My face then. No marks required there."

Jesus, what is with this kid?

"I don't do faces," I say, inventing my position as I say it and then struggling to back it up. "Makes you too obvious a mark if the emperor's enemies want to torture someone for info."

"Runners don't talk," he says, but he doesn't need to. Everyone knows it's true. No amount of torture can compare to what we do to ourselves, so it's useless for outsiders to try.

"Best not to test it," I say, some more bullshit for my quickly accumulating pile.

Truth is, I've never had to do brand work before. It's usually a job for commanding officers or overseers. I'll burn people for pain or punishment, sure, but even that's rare and it's not burning someone you're going to keep around with a mark they're meant to see. I don't typically apply hot metal to anything but other hot metal.

"Listen, you may feel shitty enough that you want the world to stare at your shittiness right now, but it will pass. Don't make a permanent decision based off a temporary feeling."

Don't make a permanent decision based off a temporary feeling.

Anything smart I say is stolen, this time from Exlee. More specifically, Exlee cleaning blood out from under my nails while I sat in the bath, a few hours before I left the House for good.

"Thigh then," he says, finally having some goddamn sense.

"Back or front?"

"Front."

Naturally.

"All right," I say. "Strip."

He's still too weak to not shake as he stands to slide out from his leathers. Any other runner, I'd offer to hold him up. But he's not any other runner, and neither am I. I'm the one who hurt him. If I offered help, it'd just be an insult. He's already in a dark place, and it's risky to kick someone who's down lest they go right off a ledge.

I heat the metal while he gets into position.

"You're being given a memory mark. It's—"

"A burden but not a punishment. It's an assignment to carry a secret for the emperor until the day I die."

". . . right," I say, wondering if he knows the lecture because he's given the mark before, or because he's been given one.

I don't have to wonder long.

When I get into position in front of him I see the other memory mark on his opposite thigh. I don't ask, can't ask, but I do stare just long enough to see the cleanliness of the lines. This mark was made by my brother himself.

I look up at him, wanting to ask but knowing I can't, and he looks down, full of the answer but mouth sealed just as tight. He breaks the stalemate with a painful smile. For someone who works alone it must be just one more isolation, one more roadblock that was almost community. We're silent now, but it's unnatural. Constructed. The kind of protocol silence where the civilian parts of our brains have a thousand things to say, but our runner minds give just as many reasons to shut up. I'll half my tongue to keep from asking what secret the first mark represents. Which is just as well, because he'll give every inch of skin before he answers.

The whirring of the blade converting power into heat fills the room with just enough sound that I can't hear his breathing. It's the same tech my gloves use. The heating metal in my gloves is smaller, but they get just as hot and heat up in half the time.

Cross has decided to stand while he's burned. It's a bold move, but given how he took pain last night, I doubt it will be a problem. He won't collapse, or kick, or flinch. On my knees in front of him, I can't help but remember him in the same position last night. I'm on my knees in front of him while he's undressed, but there's nothing sexual here. I wouldn't let there be. Last night, I was an observer between a commander and servant so my mind wandered. Now that I'm temporarily in the position of power, sex can't enter into it. It would mean I didn't respect his role as a soldier more than his existence as a sex object. It would taint his position forever.

Runners are allowed to fuck one another; it's the whole reason we have the nightfires. But that's not sex creeping up on you while you're trying to work. Blurring the two isn't fair to either party. And if there's a rank difference? Or, god forbid, they didn't want it and you are their direct supervisor? Well, hope you aren't attached to your pinkies 'cause Tatik takes them for even a first offense. She says it helps you remember, the next time you want to touch something you shouldn't, if your hand is a little smaller than it should be.

"You know the secret you're meant to keep?" I ask, falling back into procedure.

"You are the emperor's sister. You are Nik Senior's daughter and . . ."

"And?" I ask.

". . . and you killed him."

It's best that we're sealing him now, before Nik Nik finds out that Cross knows. If the emperor was here, this heated blade would be going through Cross's heart, not against his skin.

"Very good," I say. I check the blade. It's a bright orange now. "Now say it again."

He does. And as he says it I turn a rectangle of his thigh into a window into his flesh, trying my best to mirror the position of my brother's, so his burdens at least look symmetrical. I was right; Cross doesn't flinch. So there's no doubling from having to reapply the brand. It's just one clean rectangle, strong and thick and true, like a locked door. If he tells the secret, it'll get a cross in the center . . . and it will be on the thigh of a corpse. The visual is a clumsy metaphor—it can be a locked door if you let it, but it can look like an old-fashioned coffin if you'd rather—but it's effective.

The logic—or what runners call logic that others might call superstition—is that telling the secret while being hurt this badly will associate breaking the emperor's confidence with this kind of pain, make it so their mouth fills with bile just to think of spilling the words. But I don't think Cross needs the extra incentive. He's loyal as a twice-kicked dog with a new master.

I press the powder into the new burn, and every muscle in his body tenses as he strains to keep his cries to himself. This time he succeeds. I guess a brand is a feather tickle compared to lying under the emperor's gaze.

I'm surprised he wraps the mark quickly with his own leather. Letting oxygen get to it will help it heal. He doesn't want that. He wants it to be recognizable as the emperor's mark. He wants everyone who sees it to know he holds a piece of my brother.

"See you around, Cross," I say as I gather up the powder and knife, but I'm hoping it's not true. Seeing him in the world, this idiot who gave up a dirt throne just to be put on shit detail, is like watching a tragedy that just keeps happening. I wonder if he thought he'd be granted officer status immediately because of his birthright. I bet he thought running would be easier than being a perpetual servant, then he got here and discovered serving is all we do. I wonder if he still would have done it, knowing he can't go back, can't ever leave without being hunted down.

I stand to go. I've already wasted too much time wondering

about the well-being of a blue-eyed boy who didn't know how good he had it.

—

STOP MAKING PERMANENT DECISIONS OFF TEMPORARY EMOTIONS.

You know that person who has seen so much of you? Who has seen you at your dogshit worst, seen you when you were toxic trash and—worst of all—too full of your own hurt to even know you were trash, but still somehow cares about you? That person for me is Exlee.

I know, me and half of Ashtown. But it doesn't matter that making people feel loved, comforted, and safe is just what Exlee does. It doesn't make it any less valuable. Some people say, *That's just smart business*. Okay? Does that make the memory of them feel any less like home? *They don't* actually *mean the kind things they say*. So fucking what? They said the words, and they were kind, and they had a positive effect on a scared child. Exlee's unconditional love for me might just be a story they are used to telling, but a story doesn't need to be true to help you fall asleep, and Exlee's love didn't need to be real for me to build a life around it.

The first day they brought me into the House, they bathed me to get the blood off my hands. The day I left the House, they did just the same. First, when I was thirteen, and Nik Nik dropped me off with some paper-thin story about being from the wastes and needing training to be a Housecat. It would be years before I could work, but Exlee's always been used to people using the House as an unconventional orphanage.

Exlee took me into the bath, rolling their eyes as they worked oil through my hair.

"Does that man think they rock it straight in the wastes?" they said, clucking their tongue. I had curly, curly roots, but even wet the length of my hair was stick straight and thirsty as dried straw.

"It'll have to go," Exlee said, as if I might be sad. As if I could feel anything at all, right then.

"I don't want it anyway," I said.

While Exlee got the scissors for what they called *the big chop,* I sat in the bath feeling worthless, despite soaking in water that felt like satin and smelled like pink blossoms and honey.

"Do you know what I'm cutting?" they asked.

I turned, surprised and reassured to encounter a question I could answer, to encounter something I could know in the dust storm of things I couldn't.

"My hair?"

"Wrong. Try again."

"The ends of my hair?" I said, trying again, like this was a classroom and the question was math.

"I am cutting you. I am taking off every piece of who you were before this bath. Here, I'm cutting off your feet." *Snip snip.* "There. Now your legs." *Snip.* "Thighs? Those'll have to go too." *Snip snip snip.*

Exlee continued the dismemberment and it was a stupid game, but I *felt* it. I believed I could be someone new. I believed I could leave the old me behind.

"Give me your hand," Exlee said, and I did. The moment they touched me, the shock broke, and I cried. I cried but I could *feel.* I could feel the warm water, smell its thick sweetness, feel Exlee's hand in mine, as soft as the milky water but as warm as a hearth. I'd have given them anything they asked for, I was so grateful.

They put the scissors into my hand. First, they held the last stringy strand in front of my face.

"This is the last piece of you," they said. "It's your old name. It's your old face. It's everything you ever hated. It's everything that has ever been done to you. If you cut this off you leave this bath as a new person. Brand-new. But . . . maybe you don't want that."

They tapped a throbbing place in my neck, scratching a little with the point of their nail so I'd be sure of the location.

"*This* is an artery. If you don't want to move on from who you are. If you want to wallow and hate and punish yourself forever, this'll do the job. We both know you know how," they said, acknowledging that my coming to their door the night of Nik Senior's murder was no coincidence.

It was easier under the desk, with Nik Nik reaching out to pull me up. My brother had decided on my survival without offering a choice or soliciting my input. All I had to do was accept it. Exlee was making me *decide*.

I stared at my reflection in the scissors. I hated myself, that much was so clear even Exlee could see it, but did I think that the self I hated was all I could ever be? If I did, I should turn the water red and end the lie. Or did I think I could move on, turn my old life into nothing more than a story I could just stop telling.

I grabbed the last piece of hair and sliced.

—

I'M ALREADY LYING AWAKE IN MY HAMMOCK AT THE ROW WHEN MY CUFF TELLS ME IT'S TIME TO GET UP and head to the palace. Usually, I have no trouble sleeping. If I'm sitting in my bed wide awake in the morning, it's because I'm hungover and trying to will the spins away. This morning I'm just . . . thinking. Lying awake during perfectly good sleeping hours thinking. Truth be told, I'd rather be yakking. I'm not what you'd call a *thinker.* I'm exactly as existential as a wasp. I eat, I fuck, I sting back what stings me. But here I am, not just thinking, but thinking about Cross. I can't shake this pit in my stomach. I've honest-to-gods killed fuckers before without so much as a flicker of guilt, so why does it feel like sending him back to his post is the worst crime I've ever committed? There was something in his eyes when I told him to go back, something hopeless. I can't shake the feeling that something bad and permanent is about to happen to him.

What was it he said about meditating?

It keeps me from doing . . . anything else.

But it's just his post. How bad could it be? If he's remote he can't be an enforcer like Cheeks. He can't be getting blood under his nails routinely enough to bother him. Maybe he's doing something else? Something worse? But what could be worse than breaking in civilians who don't properly respect the emperor? Everyone knows that's the worst detail. Only about five percent of us are on enforcer duty at any given time, even though civilians think that's all we ever are.

My cuff beeps again, telling me it's past time. I grunt when I get up, hoping to leave the dark cloud of my mood in the hammock, but it follows me.

Dispatch instructs me to see if Cheeks is ready, so when I get to the palace I head to the workrooms. Cheeks favors the third one, dead middle of the right side, and sure enough when I arrive it's the only one closed. I know Cheeks's work, so I wait until I hear a lull in the crying before I knock.

When he comes out I see the civilian he's breaking through the sliver of room that opens up as he slips out.

"Holy shit," I say. "That's a Wileyite."

"Not anymore. Far as they know she died years ago."

"That's a traveler?"

He nods. "She killed the guy whose body you found yesterday. He was her husband. You come to fetch me?"

"Just seeing if you're fetchable. Status check, but dispatch didn't want to rush you . . . Guess I can see why."

"I'll come," he says, almost too eagerly, pulling the runner bandana from his pocket to wrap his hand. He leans back into the room to address Tear. "Don't put her in the same cell as the other one. Himself doesn't want them talking. But walk her past to shake him up."

The other one is the person who is not Helene X. Cheeks may have bloodied up this intruder, but I don't think anyone has had the stomach to do it to the other. Not when we're still mourning that same face.

Cheeks is quick to close the door and turn away from the scene inside.

"You this excited for another bullshit meeting?"

"Nah, but she's ready to give," he says. "Tear can finish up."

It's not a lie, I guess. Mr. Tear is as good a breaker as any, but it feels like he's just grateful to be out of that room. I've seen Cheeks bloodcheck a hundred people, easy, and he's never flinched. Hell, more than once I've had to remind Cheeks to clean other people's blood off his hands before eating. His work fits him so well he doesn't notice it most of the time. But he definitely didn't enjoy it today. Today, he noticed every second of what he does. Not sure that's a great trait in an enforcer, but he's served the post so long, Himself would approve a transfer.

Transfers. Right. If Mr. Cross is so over his head in his post, he can always just transfer too. No skin off my back if he's too desperate for approval to do it. Right?

I look at Cheeks, who isn't looking at me, and wonder if everyone is losing their nerve all at once. I think back to what I saw in his workroom: the woman's pale skin making the bruises twice as dark as usual, the hair in front of her face almost completely pink, milk with a helping of blood mixed in. Pretty pale nails shining on the ends of broken fingers.

I focus on the violence as we walk, waiting to see if her pain makes me feel anything like empathy or disgust.

Nope, just hungry. Which is good. It means my judgment is impaired only when it comes to Cross, not the world in general.

"Sorry I didn't respond to your message yesterday," he says.

Honestly, I'd forgotten I'd cuffed him. I'd been so turned around—maybe just about Cross, but maybe also a little about Jeffery dying—I reached out to see if he was free. But I hadn't expected him to reply, and he hadn't. It's been that way for a while. Before I thought work was eating him whole, but now that I see what he has going on with Esther, I understand. I don't fault him for it. If they have to hide from both her people and his, the dead of night must be something precious for them.

"Ah, I was just bored. What's up with you today? You off-kilter just from giving a Wiley murderer half what's due?"

He shakes his head, but the tension in his jaw could crack rocks.

"Cheeeeeks."

He smiles at me, caught. "I guess this relationship has my head round. Can we hang out later? I could use an ear."

" 'Course."

He hugs me quick then steps far away and schools his face when we approach the doors.

When we go into the meeting room everyone is already assembled. Adam Bosch still hasn't figured out where home is, so he's standing beside Nik Nik at the front. Esther, Cara, and Dell are on the other side of the room, though I'm not sure which of the two men they are avoiding.

Esther looks at Cheeks, but he doesn't return it, keeping his head down like a bad dog. I wonder if that's why he's so shaken by working over the Wileyite: He's never had to lay hands on a pale blonde before. Is he looking down because he's ashamed? In front of *her*? She, who uses thousands of people's beliefs against them to continue her family's empire? No. 'Course not. That'd be mad.

I've heard stories of this from the past. The way men would rain blood to avenge a fair woman. Pale women were like queen bees. If a man the wrong color touched them, a crowd would spontaneously emerge to light him up, to set him on fire, to rend him to pieces. I didn't think we did that in Ash. We're runners. No skin is too precious for violence, regardless of age, gender, color. I don't like to think of Cheeks reviving old traditions. I want to believe he wants Esther because he wants Esther, not because he hates himself.

When we move farther into the room, I'm surprised to see Exlee in the interrogation seat in front of Nik. Surely this can't be that. Surely they just chose that seat to sit in. But then Nik Nik barks his next question and I see red.

I scan Exlee's face for a single mark that will justify punching even my brother, but Exlee smiles lightly, flicking a fan of acknowledgment as if there is nothing but pleasant memories between us. They seem so unbothered you'd never guess they were sitting in a place where civilians are allowed to die.

I position myself behind Exlee with my arms crossed to show public support. Rather than their night look of sequins and leather, Exlee has dressed today like the distant past. All light, gauzy, rose-colored lace in haphazard layers so that every step will produce the mesmerizing effect of something freshly bloomed dancing on the breeze. Exlee has a whole wardrobe like this, things more romantic than explicit. This one in particular has always reminded me of being in my mother's garden, watching fallen blossoms get swept up by the false breeze from Wiley's air recycling units. They look almost angelic, an effect heightened by the fact that the lace is so thin, their genitals and nipples are whispers of shadow underneath.

Exlee's mouth, a soft gold glitter over the nude that they always favor over black or red when they're dressed like this, curves slightly when they see my stance.

"Silly thing, I need no protection from these men," Exlee says, meaning Nik Nik and Adam, but somehow also any man who ever lived. Like anyone who still clings to the gender binary is automatically unworthy of being considered a threat.

Feeling a little embarrassed, but standing my ground, I look over Exlee's head to Nik Nik. If I was out as empress I'd have the authority to ask him what's going on, why the person dearest to me in the entire world is in an uncomfortable chair while Nik wears his mean face. But I'm not an empress, so I wait and hope he'll take pity instead of making this one of his many "teachable moments."

I'm looking at Nik Nik like a begging puppy, but it's Dell who sees the question on my face and addresses it.

"I have been having . . . conversations with those who knew Alden Woods," she says. "He apparently made a trip here the night of the attacks."

She's the first person in the palace to call them attacks, which makes sense. Dell doesn't want to call the thing that took her father away an accident.

Adam holds open his palm and a digital ledger appears. Everyone's done a turn on border patrol, so I recognize the form instantly. It's the entry records.

"Your fresh corpse passed through less than an hour before Helene died," Adam says.

His name is there, clear and even. Mr. Core took the intake, and I'd trust him to the end. But Woods's isn't the only name I recognize. I look at my brother, but he hasn't seen. Maybe it's best he doesn't. But why was my dead stepfather traveling to Ashtown?

"I told you already," Exlee says. "Alden didn't come to me. He wasn't one of mine. I don't have him on the House records at all except for once thirty years ago, probably on a dare like all Wiley-ite teens looking for a taste of Ash."

"Market's not for another two days. House is the only place he could have gone," Cheeks says, and I wonder if he knows he's lying.

I'm just now realizing that if it came down to it, I don't know if Cheeks would protect his new heart or his old one. I didn't think anyone could be as devoted to my brother as Cheeks is, but I've never seen him in love before.

"Not the only place," I say. I turn to Esther. Cheeks has been looking down since he entered the room, but she stands proud, swimming in lies with her head held high. "Your holy books don't say anything about letting someone else take the fall for you, Princess?"

Unless you were watching real close, you'd never have noticed her reaction. The momentary rage that narrows her eyes, the irritated tilt of her head disguised as moving her hair out of her face. Beyond that she doesn't deign to respond to my accusation.

I step toward her, but suddenly there's a hand on my arm, squeezing hard.

I turn, coming face-to-face with a raging Cheeks.

"Fuck you think you're doing, Scales?"

I'm in utter disbelief, but I do yank my arm out of his grasp. "Confronting a suspect."

"Do you know who you're talking to?" he says, sounding just this side of devotion. If he didn't twice outrank me, I could pull him for that alone.

"Obviously, otherwise I wouldn't be asking."

"That doesn't even make sense." His voice is near breaking. "You're just jealous. You're jealous of her and talking wild."

CHAPTER THIRTEEN

THE WORDS TAKE THE AIR OUT OF THE ROOM. I CAN'T BREATHE BUT NEITHER CAN ANYONE ELSE. I brought attention to myself to protect Exlee, but with a few words Cheeks has co-opted all that visibility to paint me not as a soldier, but as a hysterical woman.

I could fight with him. I could say he's wrong. But right now? I don't ever want to speak to Cheeks again. I use my four-inch height advantage, which I've always known he resents, to look clean over him at Adam.

"Do you have Cross's pictures from the scene?"

Adam nods. "He delivered them to end his tenure on the case. What happened with that one? I *liked* him."

He only says it because he knows I dislike Cross, and I'm trying to swallow down the red wave that wants me to skin Cheeks alive, so I ignore it and stay focused.

"Pull. Them. Up," I say through my teeth.

Either because he can't control the order of the photos, or because he's a sociopath, the first image is of the ravaged body. I think of the woman, the small blonde in our cells, and think *this* is what love turns us all into, in the end.

"The kitchen counter, zoom in."

He does, but not enough, because he doesn't know what he's looking at. He's so Wiley he doesn't even come to market, so the jar of honey with the handwritten note means nothing to him.

"A little more in the center," I say, and he adjusts the image. I am rewarded by a few good gasps. "That jar of Ruralite honey is unopened. If border patrol's records only show him coming in once, it must have come from that day."

"That could have been a gift from another Wileyite. One who went to the last market," Cheeks says, but the anger in his voice is already turning to confusion, which is halfway to acceptance.

I keep my eyes trained over his head like the only thing less significant than what he just said is whatever he's planned to say next. I look over him like I never loved him. Like my heart isn't still skipping beats from him ripping it out.

". . . It wasn't a gift from a Wileyite," Esther says, which causes me to turn around toward her. She nods at me once, conceding a point to an opponent.

Cheeks lets out a quick gasp that tells me he wasn't lying to protect her. He had no idea. He might be lost in love, unable to see her clearly through his feelings, but Esther . . . love or not, she's kept her edge. They're replaying Alden Woods's death before my very eyes: A beautiful woman doing what needs to be done. A devoted man paying the price. Maybe it's for the best I've always been ugly. I do quite enough damage without something that powerful in my arsenal.

"Does this mean the blonde gets to sit in your time-out chair?" Adam asks Nik.

Esther's glare is cooler and promises less violence than her sister's, but it communicates hatred for Adam exactly as effectively.

"That won't be necessary," she says, adjusting the grip on her staff. "Alden Woods was mine."

Cheeks is back to playing soldier, but his face is dark with hurt and embarrassment. Good.

"Lover?" asks Exlee, looking at Esther as if she is finally interesting.

"Congregant. His wife died several years ago. He'd been having difficulty adjusting. His church wasn't helpful, so he came to ours. For the last week, he'd been having intense nightmares of her reaching out to him, so that night he came to me."

Cheeks's head is hanging down. Hurt, self-loathing—no rage though, not like he had for me. She must be too pretty to get anything but disappointment. I'm being petty. I know. I'm bitter, and I know that too. But my arm *hurts* where he grabbed me. Hurts worse than any time we've dinged each other sparring, or crashed our bikes into each other, or gotten each other so drunk we turned daylight into a knife. He wanted to hurt me, out of anger, and so he did. It could make me cry if I let it. He had to know how fucked that was, but he didn't even hesitate.

Why didn't he hesitate?

There's a knock at the door, and I recognize Mr. Tear as she enters the room. She's wiry, darker than anyone but maybe Dragon, and keeps her hair near-shaved. They say her name is Tear because all leathered up she looks like a tear in the world, a line ripped through the desert that is letting in the dark of the void beyond. I think it's just because she's real good at cutting folks up. Sometimes people will mistake her name for *Tear* like the tears she makes people cry . . . and that's pretty accurate too.

"I've got the prisoner's report," she says, looking around the room, as surprised as I am to have so many non-Ashers in our fucking business.

Nik Nik holds up a hand to stop her, then scans the room. In the end, his gaze only skips on Dell. She notices, looks down at the fine bracelet that must be a cuff, and turns to Cara.

"You should go," Cara says. "It's getting on in the day anyway."

Dell nods, and I expect them to kiss goodbye, but instead Dell just stares into Cara's eyes. It might not be a physical touch, but the intensity in that gaze makes it feel like a tongue dragged along the side of a neck, and I have to look away. When Dell does kiss her, it's on the forehead on her way out.

She's clearly reluctant to go, and I wonder why she'd leave Cara alone with the rest of us. Maybe they have kids and childcare in the city is a pain in the ass? They don't just have communal grounds of kids, roaming like wild packs with retired Housecats paying half attention like we do here.

Once she's gone, Nik Nik raises two fingers, bidding Tear to continue with her report.

"The woman's named Anna Woods. Says she and her husband

paid fifteen million dollars a few years back to fund an ark. They both got a spot over here for their trouble."

"Ark?" Adam says. "Very original."

Mr. Tear looks at him. "Says it was built by a man named Adam Bosch."

"A *lesser* Adam Bosch," he says. "Obviously."

I rub my forehead. "You really can't help yourself, can you? You'd die if you had to shut the fuck up."

He turns to me, his smile sinister. "Oh, I can hold my peace when I must. I'm *great* at keeping secrets."

He rotates and closes his mechanical eye, a cyborg wink. I didn't need the gesture to get his point. Secrets, I've got them, he knows them, and I'm the only one who has to watch their mouth.

Mr. Tear is looking at Nik Nik for permission to teach the Wileyite some respect. When the order doesn't come, she continues her report.

"She and her husband came over the night of the event, but when she landed she couldn't find him. The address was different here too, so she had to track down the house she could enter. When she got there, she realized his alternate self was still here. She thought he was blocking her man from coming and . . . she handled it."

As Tear finishes, she sounds a little like she respects Anna. Maybe she does. Takes guts to handle your first kill with no training or prep. And for that first kill to have your husband's face? Takes even more than guts. Takes a lot of heart, or none at all.

Actually . . .

"We recruiting her?" I ask.

"Not your call," Nik Nik says.

I give my best *Aw shucks I was just asking* shrug.

"Might not be a bad idea," says Tear, whose marks, silver to catch the light instead of the black that would just get swallowed, go up high enough for her to get to say shit like that.

What are we going to do? Turn her in to the city so they can put her in a box forever for loving her husband too much? She wouldn't be the first who got recruited off a murder. Makes more sense to teach them how to control their rage, or hurt, in our ranks. They get to rebuild their lives and figure out what went wrong, and the mandatory partnership for runners is better surveillance than some fucking uniform throwing food at them three times a day.

Shit, I got recruited off a murder. Wearing the leather's done me nothing but good. I haven't killed anyone—out of anger, mind you—since.

"I'll consider it," Nik Nik says, and dismisses Tear, but as far as Adam is concerned Tear is already gone. We all are. He's moving toward Esther like a hound who's caught the scent.

"Did Allen—"

"Alden," I say, and I swear he's going back to his Ashtown roots enough to growl at me. But I have to correct him, just to show I can. When you discover a corpse you're responsible for it. Bad luck to forget the name, and I need all the good grace I can get.

"*Whatever.* Did he experience any distress while he was with you? Cramping? Spontaneous bruising? Any pain at all?"

Esther shakes her head. "No. We were doing a ritual cleansing. He felt extraordinary after. Light. Healed. I checked in the next day. He didn't have the dream again."

"Where is this cleansing?" Adam says, and it's barely human.

This is the moment tension enters her. She keeps it off her face, but she hasn't learned to control her telegraphing spine. This is the secret she would lie even to the man she's sleeping with to keep.

"Does it matter?"

Nik leans in. "Answer the question."

She takes a breath. "A cave. It's where we do all of our private rituals."

Adam takes this news like it's the best day of his fucking life, moving faster than I've ever seen him as he rushes her.

"This cave, it's dark, isn't it?"

"All caves are dark," I say, helpfully, though they both just glare at me for my trouble.

"Is it *dark*?" he asks again, and this time it means something more than a shadow. Something jet. Like a whole room full of whatever is in Cara's eyes and beneath the stripes of her skin.

"It's in the black hills," Esther says. "So yes, it is dark."

"I need to access the cave. I'll take samples to verify, but we should begin harvesting if the substance is viable."

I don't know who Adam is talking to. He's making a plan like he's in a room full of people who work for him. We all look around, wondering who is going to tell this man that he's a long way from his lab. More than that, I saw how he lives now, and I'm guessing he's a long *time* from whenever he thinks he is, from when he could say things into a room and trust someone would write it down or make it happen.

It doesn't help that he's thinking too far ahead of his question. He's already looking to the side, probably planning out studies and experiments. He has missed the part where he asks permission, where Esther gives her consent.

Eventually, it hits him that no one's moved. "What are the coordinates of the cave?"

"No," Esther says, has probably been waiting to say.

This snaps him back. "What?"

"I'm not telling you that. This place is sacred to us. We only allow guests during a ritual. I won't invite the kind of harm you bring to a place of healing."

"I . . . want access," he says, and the edge of rage in his voice tells me he's lived a life where *want* is merely the step before *have*.

I'd wondered how this bored and lazy trickster was ever the successful threat people painted him to be. But I'm seeing glimpses of that man now. This is what he's like when he cares. This is what he's like when he has something to do, something to lose. This is the version of him that keeps Esther and Cara and Dell scanning rooms for an exit whenever he's around.

Thank god he chose the city. I don't want to know what someone like that would do with the emperor's throne and the runners on command. Nik Nik doesn't have a curious bone in his body. He's uninventively cruel. He hunted for sport, but didn't hold glass over ants or anything. Curiosity and bloodlust are probably best kept separate.

"No," Esther says.

"I could make you," Adam says, and everyone in the room believes him.

Esther's hand tightens on her staff.

She says, "I doubt that very much," and somehow everyone in the room knows this, too, is true.

I thought I'd hate her for a good while off her lie, but with that strength and defiance? This is the kind of girl I'd let lie to me twice. Hell, someone who can keep a secret and stares down the threat of torture without sweating? That's a runner's wet dream. Cheeks doesn't seem to agree, beautiful face pointed at the ground in a pout.

I wait for Nik Nik to give me the sign to intervene—not let what looks like a Wileyite threaten our royal guest—but he doesn't. I expect Adam to hit her. To turn to Nik Nik and say *make her.* Instead, Adam tilts his head.

"You would let your people die? I did not think you so callous, Ruralite."

That throws Esther all the way off. "I'm protecting them. Which is why I am keeping you away from our sacred ground."

"The man was with you when his dop came through. It should have killed him the way it killed the others. But something about what you were doing or where you were doing it saved him. Since I doubt prayer and ignorant ritual holds the power to keep two hundred and six bones from turning into six hundred and eighteen, it must have something to do with *where.*"

"I won't—"

"Do you know how she got her job?" Adam says, pointing to Cara. "I had valuable people die on mission. So you know what I did? Do you know who I sent next?"

The words stop Esther, dissolve whatever firm denial was on her tongue. She doesn't want him to go on. He goes on.

"Something went wrong with Alden Woods. I'm guessing he wasn't able to cross over, and his mangled body stayed over there. That means the next wave won't be more Wileyites. I wouldn't risk that with paying customers, and neither will their Adam. It will be them." He gestures toward everyone else in the room. "It will be whatever poor and desperate volunteers he can get his hands on. He will do it. I *have* done it. The next people to be killed by dops will be Ashtowners and Ruralites."

Esther takes a breath. When she sets her jaw and looks out of the top of her eyes, I recognize the gesture instantly. It's Cheeks's unique brand of enraged helplessness playing across her more delicate face.

"Show me a map," she says.

Adam is too focused to even smile in victory. He touches the side of his eye and a blue-lit outline of Ashtown and Wiley comes to life in the center of the room. Esther looks uncertainly at Adam, and then walks forward, into the light map of the world. She raises her hand to point at the southern mountain range, which her people call Mount Tabor and my people call The Spine. Adam zooms in at her direction until the mountain that borders our town on one side is entirely in view.

It's the same mountain system Viet operates at the mouth of, but on the other end. The place Esther indicates is farther north, the tip of the mountain that exists in Ruralite territory. If you follow the foothills down to where they stretch into the wastelands—which no one ever does because the wind and sand make it hard for people to see but the predators have evolved to see just fine—you'll get to the Keeper's hut. If you keep south? You'll find the field of blood, and Jack Ketch. I haven't been to Akeldama since my mother brought me and my father was playing executioner. I don't even know who is acting as Jack Ketch now. Hell, most people think it's me, so it's one of the emperor's secrets kept tight.

"Here," she says, pointing to a dark patch. "This is the mouth of the cave. The opening is narrow and wedged between two ridges, so it's easily mistaken for a shadow by outsiders."

"Does this cave have any other odd characteristics?" Bosch asks. "What does it look like?"

Esther's fingers flex on her staff. "It's dark, like you said."

"Magnets?" he asks, and we all look to her for an answer.

She nods. "It's not uncommon though. Most mountains contain something that will mess with—"

"And time? Does it affect time?" he asks, and if I didn't know any better I'd swear he was interrupting out of excitement instead of his usual rudeness.

". . . Cuffs tend to be slow once you exit the cave, but they don't seem slow in it."

Adam moves to look at the depiction of the cave projected in light, like he can learn something from staring at it.

"Of course not, if you're in the cave you'll be subject to the same relativity. It's an astronomical element, but how can it recreate the conditions of space . . . ?" he says, making very little sense.

"It's a blessed place," offers Esther, making even less.

"Right," I say, sucking my teeth. "So we're headed to a magic cave today, yeah?"

Esther looks scared now that I've said the obvious out loud.

Nik Nik cuts off any possible objection by staring into her eyes. "Thirty minutes to prepare, and then you'll take us there."

It's not a request or a question. Esther nods, her jaw tense.

—

"SCALES, WAIT," CHEEKS SAYS, CATCHING ME IN THE HALL AFTER THE MEETING. "I'M SORRY. I thought—"

I turn around just long enough to punch him hard, digging my knuckles into his gut. He gasps and bends.

I grip him by the nape of his neck. "Don't. Talk. To. Me."

I throw him aside and walk away.

"You didn't have a choice," someone says just at my back.

I jump when I turn, unused to being snuck up on. The initial fear doesn't quite dissipate when I see it's Cara.

I don't know if my reverence for her comes from her legend—the world walker who stood in the void long enough to become it—or if it's just genuine respect for one of the few who left Ashtown and still saw fit to give back. The education center doesn't have her name on it, but the rumor that it was her doing has been running rampant since it broke ground. Granted, the rumor was that it was her last act before she killed herself, but Ashtowners do love adding a bit of drama.

"Yeah, well. He was asking for it."

"When people hurt us, we have to protect ourselves. We're

human. Even if it kills them. You were just trying to protect yourself."

"I've seen Cheeks walk away from three blades. Pretty sure he'll live," I say, but I know all this gibberish is not for me.

She's talking about Adam. Whatever she did to him must not be finished. Maybe it will kill him yet, and for some reason she wants me of all people to know how she sleeps at night.

She doesn't say anything else. Just stares at me with those eyes like we're in a play and the line is mine. But I've got nothing. So I walk outside. She follows, silently. I'm good at making out people. But once she gets out of my line of sight I can't even hear her footsteps. I only know she's there because when we go outside to take our spot in the caravan, Adam looks up to us both.

"Let's see . . . safe," he says, pointing to me. He looks back down at a piece of his wrist that is now a screen, and then points to Cara. "Unsafe."

"What's new," she says.

"What's this about?" I say.

"The earth that's coming over. I've got the files on it. You don't exist there. You can't be dop-killed."

"Sweet!" I say, holding my hand up for a high five.

I don't know if Adam or Cara is less impressed by my display, but neither slap my palm. Cara even looks at me like I've said something wrong. What? What is there to do when you learn you're not going to die but celebrate? Imagine being sad that you're not on the chopping block. *Oh, poor me, I can't die.* Fucking weird.

Adam turns away, maybe a little gleeful at telling people they get to die, and his mechanical foot makes an impressive whirring.

"I don't get it," Cara says. "I can see how the Lot's Wife took your hand, and your skull. But how did it travel to your leg? That wasn't me."

"My mechanical arm was more efficient than my original arm," he says, like it's obvious.

I'm not sure what that has to do with anything, but Cara gets it immediately. Like it or not, she clearly knows him better than I do.

"You got rid of your leg for efficiency?"

"I didn't get rid of it. I replaced it. That was my leg. This is my leg now. More efficient. Less prone to breakage . . . it doesn't . . . perfectly agree with the existing leg, but overall a net gain."

"Cool," I say, and Cara glares at me for it, but what else is there to say? Man's heart is a diseased potato but there's nothing wrong with his mind. The logic's sound.

On the caravan out, I was afraid Cara would want to ride with me. She doesn't. Adam and Esther do, though, so there's really no winning. With Esther navigating, I'm the point driver. Nik Nik and Cara and a few other runners are tailing me. Cheeks opted to sit this one out. I want to believe I've bruised his kidney, but I'm sure he's just neck-deep in fee-fees over Esther.

As we approach the mountain I can't keep my eyes from traveling down the foothill toward Akeldama at the other end. I park at the mouth of the cave and everyone lines up behind me. When Nik Nik walks up I move to stay in front of him, while Rust and Brand cover his back. The entrance of the cave is a whole ten feet away but we cross the space like a crew of half-assed explorers. Nik Nik, Adam, Esther, Cara, me, and four other runners on escort. Nine people marching into the unknown.

I'm glad I'm armed for an ambush, because this feels like there's someone with a shiny blade just waiting to take the emperor out when he squeezes into that hole in the mountain. I may one day have to be empress, but I'm not ready to ascend, not like that, not yet, and not alone. The ground we are standing on is the tan-gray of the Rurals meeting Ash proper, but the closer we get to the mountain the blacker the dirt becomes. I'm sure it's a natural warning, like the bright spots on a poisonous reptile. If we had half a brain between us, we'd stay put. But I'm the one taking point and I've got orders, so I don't have the luxury of having a brain, not even half. I take the first step.

When the screaming starts, it's not Nik Nik taking an assassin's blade. It's Cara.

The moment we stepped from gray earth to black, she'd stopped.

"Do you feel that?" she'd said, and then knelt to touch the

earth . . . and screamed bloody horror. She fell forward, caught herself with both hands in the earth, gasping for breath. But when she opened her mouth she only screamed again.

I only take a second to pivot from worrying about Nik Nik to saving her. She's so small, it's no work at all to carry her back to the gray. It was only a moment, but I know what I saw: The dark from the sand tried to trap her, and the longer her hands touched it the darker her marks got, like the black from the sand was feeding the dark in her.

When she opens her hands, white sand falls out of her palm.

"The dirt is clear. The darkness comes from the liquid beneath seeping up," Adam says, mechanical eye zooming in on what's left on her fingers.

I ignore him.

"You okay?" I ask, which should have been the first thing she heard. I keep my voice even, but I'm staring at the marks on her face. I swear they were barely darker than her skin before, but they're jet now. Her eyes can't get any darker, but the irises seem bigger.

"I'm fine. I'm the same as always," she says, which can't possibly be true. Unless I don't know what she means by *always*. "Thank you."

"No problem, now we're even," I say. Or, I must say it. Because the words come out of my mouth, even though I don't know what they mean.

"We are," she says, suffering from none of my confusion.

I turn back toward Adam. "Can this black dirt harm the rest of us? Or . . . cause hallucinations or something?"

He grabs a handful of black sand with his mechanical hand and squeezes. When he opens his palm again, the crystals in his hand are white too.

"It's just like hers," I say. "Is this what it does? It seeps out into whatever it can find?"

"No," he says. "When I held it in my hand it was stationary. I had to extract it to turn it white. It happened naturally with her. It's a sympathetic material. It seeks itself . . . even across the multiverse."

I realize he's sucked the liquid into his palm somehow just as the screen that is his wrist goes bright with data. He doesn't look down, but he does nod for no visible reason, so he must get the data it discovers simultaneously.

I want to overload my gloves to sparking. Show him I've got a fancy hand, too. Instead, I raise an eyebrow.

"So? Safe or nah?"

"Safe," he says, finally. "The liquid is dense, barely a liquid. It shouldn't make it to the air. It only poses a risk with contact. And even that won't be serious unless you're covered in it or . . ." his eye flicks toward Cara. "You've been exposed to it before."

Her face is still, but her hands are fists. She's just mad at him, but I'm newly put off the idea of this mission now that I know a semisentient, possibly deadly tar is what we're after.

"Though . . ." Adam trails off dramatically and I know he's got bad mischief planned for the end of the sentence. He turns toward Esther. ". . . Your dad spent a lot of time here. And he died young. Was it cancer?"

"Stop trying to spread fear," I say, because even I can tell he's being a dick for attention.

"A valiant effort," Esther says. "But most people know my father killed himself."

Adam shrugs.

"You should stay out here," I say to Cara, eager to separate Adam from his favorite prey. Then I turn to Nik Nik. "Will you be staying outside, Your Highness?"

I can't tell him what to do, but I hope he reads in my eyes that I'd like him to stay outside, where it's safe.

He can, he does, he doesn't care.

"I'll see this bit of my land for myself," he says, reminding Esther that this, and everything we allow the Ruralites to call theirs, belongs to the emperor at the end of the day.

"This way," Esther says, walking toward the mountain. She wants us in so she can get us gone, but she is also taking wary looks at Cara. She wants to be free to take care of her sister.

"Let's go," I say, because Esther telling us to come would roll right off the runners behind us. At my word, they begin walking forward. I take one last look at Cara standing in the sand, and walk into the cave.

And that's it.

That's the last moment I could be sure of anything at all in this whole world.

CHAPTER FOURTEEN

***BECAUSE MY FATHER LENT. BECAUSE I'M A SNAKE. BECAUSE I'M REAL BALANCED. BECAUSE I CAN** climb. Because I made gloves. Because I play. Because my tongue is forked.*

Because they don't

Because they don't love me enough to know my name.

They call me They call me They call me They call me They call me They call me They call me They call me They call me

metal. anything. out of my first wasteland kill, wore the skin of its spine on my knuckles. piano. I can climb. For years.

I can climb on my knuckles for years.

I am? No. They call me.

—

I'M ALREADY LYING AWAKE IN MY HAMMOCK AT THE ROW WHEN MY CUFF TELLS ME IT'S TIME TO GET UP and head to the palace. Usually, I have no trouble sleeping. If I'm sitting in my bed wide awake in the morning, it's because I'm hungover and trying to will the spins away. This morning I'm just . . . thinking. Lying awake during perfectly good sleeping hours thinking. Truth be told, I'd rather be yakking. I'm not what you'd call a *thinker.* I'm exactly as existential as a wasp. I eat, I fuck, I sting back what stings me. But here I am, not just thinking, but thinking about MR. SCALES. I can't shake this pit in my stomach. I've honest-to-gods killed fuckers before without so much as a flicker of guilt, so why does it feel like sending him back to his post is the worst crime I've ever committed? There was something in his eyes when I told him to go back, something hopeless. I can't shake the feeling that something bad and permanent is about to happen to ME.

My cuff beeps again, telling me it's past time. I grunt when I get up, hoping to leave the dark cloud of my mood in the hammock, but it follows me.

In the meeting room everyone is already assembled. Adam Bosch still hasn't figured out where home is—

"You're out of time," Cara says, looking dead at me.

"You threatening me?" I ask, and she doesn't roll her eyes, but exhales with enough irritation that she might as well.

"What are they about to say?" she asks.

"How should I know?"

She doesn't respond. I turn to look at Exlee, and I know. I know this is wrong. And I know I've been here before.

"'Silly thing, I need no protection from these men,'" I say, the same moment Exlee does.

"You are *out* of time," Cara says again, but this time I understand it.

I go to rub my temple, but my hands feel . . . false. And it's not new. It doesn't feel like my hands are fake, it feels like my whole body is fake, always has been, and the thing that's off is just that I'm noticing it.

"You're just jealous. You're jealous of her and talking wild."

It's not Cheeks's line, not yet, but he gives it early. Or maybe all the time between what Exlee said and what Cheeks said happened, and I was too busy thinking of my own hands to register it.

You know that feeling you get when you're about to throw up? Like something's rotten in your belly, and your body can't stand it, but that's okay because your body is about to expel everything it can't process? How you dread it, but it's also a relief because you know that whatever's in you will be gone soon? That's what it feels like, but in my brain and not my stomach. Like something is about to pour out of some part of me I didn't know I had.

There's a hand on mine, and when she touches me the world goes dark.

It's Cara, but Not-Cara. Her eyes are the same night-dark, but there is something bubbling in them. Something alive.

"Move forward," she says. "You know what comes next, find yourself where you belong."

Just move forward?

Easier said, and all that.

I start running. It makes sense, right? You know, catch back up with myself? I've taken several steps before I realize I haven't moved.

"What are you doing?"

"I was . . ." I clear my throat. The explanation sounds too stupid to say out loud. ". . . just processing."

I close my eyes. Focus. How do I feel? Like my brain needs to puke. What happens next? Maybe I need to envision myself moving forward? *Visualize.* I picture myself gliding forward instead. I picture flying. I picture wings sprouting out of my goddamn head flapping me to the present.

Doesn't work, but it's closer than running like a goddamn idiot. The sound of the wings I'd imagined beating lingers even after I've given up imagining them. The slow, comforting *whomp whomp* of them sounds familiar. And I realize the way back isn't physical motion, or visual imagining. It's sound. It's the humming heartbeat of the universe. Those wings are the sound of my heart beating wherever I'm supposed to be. I just have to be in the place that sounds right.

The first language I ever trusted, decades ago now, was music. Music didn't get me in trouble, didn't give me away. I hum chords, and they sound wrong. Low pitched and slow. I want to be somewhere with a higher tone. Somewhere faster? Is that what the past and future are? Just lower and higher music? Side by side? Or are they not even side by side? Are they totally collapsed, identical, and I can only hear a difference because I'm perceiving it from where I'm supposed to be?

I'm a survivor, not a theorist, so I leave the questions and go straight to practice.

It works . . . almost. I move, but in the wrong direction. I know this before I open my eyes, because the too-low tone is only lower now. When I open my eyes, it's even worse.

"Not here. Please."

I know this couch like a dead pet—something familiar, fraught, and hard to look at. I don't know when I've traveled to, but I know it's the past, back when I used to hang around Cheeks's living room like a bad smell. I don't do that anymore. Not since I got the feeling that he knew the thing we weren't supposed to talk about, not since I became aware that it was entirely possible for my best friend to be afraid of me.

In a moment the light changes and he's there, jumpsuit hanging around his waist, white undershirt stained with shades of tan: sweat, dirt, and blood, old and new, his and others. Now I know what day this is, because he's leaning forward with his elbows on his knees and he's staring at his own clenched hands. I know what day this is because when he looks at me, he looks concerned.

"Don't do this," I say, to the universe, to my brain, to whatever entity could stop the replay. It doesn't listen.

"I hate him!" I yell, gripping my hair at the roots. "I hate his fucking face."

"It's going to be okay," Cheeks says, standing up to match my pacing.

"What if he wants mechanic? What if I have to train him? Do you know what he used to call us? Call *me*?"

He comes up behind me, hugging me against him. I could break the hold if I wanted. He's shorter, weaker, the angle's awkward. But I don't want to. And after what he says next, I'll spend too long never wanting to.

"You think I'd let that happen?" he says. "Stay here tonight. We'll get drunk and talk shit about him till the sun comes up. In the morning, I'll go down to the palace and talk placement. I'll have him put somewhere he'll never bother you."

I nod, feeling instantly lighter because if Mr. Silk is going to listen to anyone, it's Cheeks. I want to stay. I want to have this night and the year that follows. I want to linger in that sweet, fragile place between realizing I want something and learning I'm never allowed to have it. The excitement of discovery before the disappointment.

But now that I am on the other side I can appreciate this moment for what it is, not what I mistook it for. Because this, this is a worried friend offering to make it better. Nothing more, but certainly nothing less. It was beautiful. I can see that now that I'm not distracted by what it wasn't.

"Thank you," I say. "You're a really good friend, Cheeks."

And it was true, wasn't it? I wasn't so stupid, so fooled, by someone who ended up being as loyal as a parasite in the end? I don't want to think about it, and I don't have to, because the world is slipping away again.

I can tell instantly that I'm closer than before.

". . . safe," Adam says, pointing to me. "Unsafe," he says pointing to a nothing that becomes Cara as he gestures.

We're outside now, but the world outside hasn't fully registered. Instead of the vast desert, there's only darkness just a few feet out from the patch of dirt where we are standing.

"What's new?" Cara asks. Which is what she said to Adam before, but I still answer like it's fresh, like she's here.

I look around. "There's darkness, everywhere. Everywhere but where we're standing."

"You're close," she says. "Don't go too far."

I'm half listening, half already leaning forward. I'm excited now, now that I know what I'm doing. Sound, music, the rightness of a note that's meant to follow—that's the kind of magic I used to be good at. It's like riding a bicycle to move through spaces where the sound isn't right, searching for the space where it is.

Just when I find it, just when I find the slip of the world where my heartbeat makes the right sound, I hear something else. It's another heartbeat, reaching out to mine. But this one . . . it's slowing down.

To follow it, I have to move beyond where I know I'm meant to be. But I can't head back to safety in fear. I'm a runner. Runners press on.

The space I've emerged in is dark. Not the darkness of being beyond time, just a room with shitty lighting. There's a high-pitched hum signaling the wrongness of this place, or time, and I know I won't be able to stand it for long.

I've never been here—a shock, that, considering I thought I was just retracing my steps back to myself—but I recognize the *type* of place all the same. It's a runner's hovel. A single, judging by the hammock. The hammock is empty, but the room isn't. There's a shape in the corner, something that used to be tall folded in on itself.

I crouch down, but part of me already knows, has known since I woke up this morning.

It's Cross. Or, it used to be. I can tell it was a poison death. I'd have to be Viet to know which plant did the job, but the job was done, that much is clear. His head is low, but his blue eyes have been open so long they look white. They look . . . dry. How long does it take eyes to dry? To look like the painted wood of an old doll? He's always looked like a doll to me, I realize. Like those too-pretty things my mother used to try to make me carry, the ones I tore apart and beheaded in a rage even though I knew acting out would only get me punished. And she would ask, *Why did you destroy it?* And I would never answer. She eventually assumed it was because the dolls didn't look like me, so I had to break them. But that wasn't the reason. I'm not the one who needs to crush anything different from me; that's Wiley logic. I just . . . they were so beautiful. They were so beautiful it made me feel ugly. I couldn't be them, so I tore them apart. It wasn't supremacy. It was jealousy.

I kneel at Cross's feet. Is that what I did to you? You were so beautiful I either had to have you or destroy you, so I ripped everything out of you and left you to deal with the mess?

"I'm so sorry."

"You didn't have a choice."

It's Cara. Or something that looks like her. Or my mind just showing me a form I respect enough to listen to when the world goes wonky.

"I sent him here. I sent him back even though I knew he hated this post. I was so mad . . ."

"When people hurt us, we have to protect ourselves. We're human. You were just trying to protect yourself. It's not a reaction you can control."

I'm already nodding when I realize it's what she said earlier when she was—or wasn't—talking about Cheeks.

"You can't linger here. You need to find your way back," she says, and I understand.

I know now that this is a wild dream. I close eyes that I'm sure aren't really open, and listen. It's odd, the sound. Because I'm sure I could hear it all the time if I'd really known about it. I try to find the source, try to focus, but then I realize . . . it's me.

I hold my own hands to my ears and listen to the sound of the universe, just like you can hear the desert wind in certain rocks, or like they say you could hear the ocean in seashells. The sound I make belongs to the me I am. The *when* that I am. The me I need to be again. I can hear the note I want humming, clear and true.

I could follow it right now if I wanted to . . . but instead, I slide forward, just a little bit more . . .

Blood. Fire. Screaming. Hundreds of enforcement officers marching out of the city's walls like ants. More blood. More fire. More screaming.

I snap back to Cross's hovel almost as quickly as I left. I wasn't long in the further future, but I can still hear the screaming. Still smell the bodies. That horror is precisely what I get for not knowing when to quit. I put my hands back over my ears, this time eager to be back where I belong. I hear the hum from my palms, the sound that is me. I follow it, and open my eyes.

—

THE FIRST THING I SEE IS CARA. THE FIRST THING I NOTICE IS THAT SHE IS DRIPPING WET. THE SECOND thing I notice is that I am too.

I roll onto my side and vomit up black water.

"That will help," she says. "Get it out of your system."

She sounds nothing like she did in my dream. Her voice isn't an odd echo of a thousand others. She's just one person, and it's just one voice. The other was just a trick my mind was playing.

We're in the cave, but not in the main part. In the center of the cave is water that looks clear, maybe a little thick, like something mineral my mother would pay extra to bathe in. But the black pool I've presumably been fished out of is at the edge of the cave. There's a little fence separating it from the rest. Seeing it, I begin to remember. We'd entered the cave. Adam had tested Esther's pool, the one she uses to perform ceremonies, but there was only the slightest trace of anything that wasn't water or salt. He'd sent me to the other pool to get a sample. I'd fallen in? No. I'm a runner, boots sure as sunrise. I don't trip.

Cara's shaking, and I'd mistake it for shivering if I hadn't seen what happened to her outside. This is pain, agony moving through her body that she won't give voice to. She's glaring hot fire at Adam, stopping only to shake her tightly curled hair, dispersing the not-water in a circle around us. Adam steps back, avoiding even the smallest droplet of spray. I look back at the dark pools, and I know the liquid in it is the same that stains the ground outside. The same that brought Cara to her knees.

I would have been extra cautious near the pool . . . and Adam would have been extra curious.

"You pushed me," I say.

Adam doesn't care enough to lie to me. Or maybe to anyone. What would he lie for? He's got nothing left to lose.

"After what happened outside, no one else was going to willingly touch it," he says.

Nik Nik looks at his brother as he says this, like he's just realizing this isn't a happy family reunion, and he can't trust him. I don't know why he ever thought he could. Nik Nik is his mother's son, like all the stories of the old country kingpins. Hard as nails but soft around family, brutal and superstitious, harsh and sentimental. Adam is very clearly Senior walking the earth all over again, cutthroat and pragmatic. And me? I've never thought about it much. Unlike my brother, I don't think about myself in terms of my father's shadow or my mother's expectation. Being a daughter doesn't interest me. I guess . . . I guess I've just always wanted to be a sister. Nik Nik is my brother. Adam has just proven he isn't.

"What happened while you were under? Did you hallucinate? What did you see?" he asks.

I don't need Cara's well-timed glare to tell me to keep my mouth shut. Mood I'm in, I wouldn't tell this fucker my name to claim a prize.

"Pink elephants," I say, spitting the last residue of the black sludge in my mouth at his feet. He steps back again, confirming that he knows exactly what this shit is. Or he knows at least enough to fear it. It's meant to be feared, I realize. Only Cara is wet. She alone went in.

"You saved me," I say.

"No one else was going to," she says, and I wonder if she knows how special she is. How many people would use *no one else is doing it* as an excuse *not* to act, rather than as motivation. Would've made a hell of a runner, I bet.

I remember carrying her back to safety earlier and before I can even process it, I'm saying, "Now we're even" just like I did before, only now it makes sense.

Why had I said it then? And had she talked to me about Cross before we even came into this cave? Could what have happened to me have leaked out even before the event? Is it possible that it doesn't matter what time I fell into the mind-fuck-sludge, because time became irrelevant once I did?

"Don't worry about it," she says, either talking about saving me, or reading my mind and talking about everything else.

I can't stop looking at her, half in wonder and half in fear. Jumping in to get me has made her marks larger and darker again. When she lived among us she had a face with marks slashed across it. Now her face is more mark than skin. Blur your eyes, and you'll lose track of which color was hers first. I feel woozy, that same brain-nausea from my dream, and I see her with no marks, and then I see her as she is now, and then she blinks into a version of her whose every inch is the black of ink. A version of her where even the whites of her eyes have gone obsidian, whose hair has grown large, wider than her shoulders and halfway down her back. This last one scares me even more than the others, who also scare me.

I close my eyes and put my head between my knees.

"Whatever you're experiencing, it's temporary," Cara says.

"She's right," Adam says, as if I needed his endorsement to trust the person who fished me out of hell. "You probably only got a mouthful. It'll pass through your system like a drug. It's not like you were, say, injecting it into your veins over the course of several years or anything."

He looks at Cara when he says this, and I know without being told, that he is detailing precisely what happened to her under him. Where could someone learn such arrogance? To harm someone and openly talk about it without fear of consequences? Who taught him that that was power? There's too much Senior in him; he can't tell the difference between power and cruelty anymore. I want to hit him for her, for whatever curves her life has taken because of him.

Adam comes forward and kneels down beside me. He reaches for me.

"Get away from her," Nik says, and it's so quiet he almost sounds sad. Maybe he is. Maybe his heart just broke.

"I was only going to take a sample from what's trapped in her hair. I need to test the pool if I'm going to use this to save others."

Nik Nik looks at me, and this time he's giving the rarest of looks. He's sorry. Maybe he's sorry I have to do this, or maybe he's sorry he ever brought Adam around at all. But I don't want him sorry, so I shrug and look at Adam.

"Get it over with."

He threads his mechanical fingers against my scalp. His motions are careless, and he yanks my head slightly back in the process. I glare at him, but he glares back.

If he thinks this is intimidation, he really should meet the man who raised me. Adam's scary in an unfeeling scientist way. But he probably wouldn't lock a child in a closet covered in her own filth because she threw a tantrum. Probably wouldn't wrap duct tape around a four-year-old's face for laughing too loud while he's trying to sleep.

Eventually, his wrist beeps, and he releases me. The bit of hair he grabbed is dry, and the sample he's taken through his palm is finished processing.

"This should work. It shares traits with the barsamin I experimented with before, it's just . . ." Adam turns to Cara. "When you felt it, did it feel like when you were readying for traversing?"

Cara takes a moment, then frowns. "Yes and no. Same type of feeling, slightly electric, but . . . bigger, if that makes sense. Like the formula I received put one line of light in my blood, but this one . . ."

"It felt like dozens?"

Cara nods. "At least."

Adam closes his hand. "When I first analyzed barsamin, I hypothesized that it behaved less like a liquid and more like a mycelium—an elaborate network that was connected to, and receiving messages from, the larger organism of itself, even across universal divides."

"Like . . . mushrooms?" Cara says. "Barsamin. That's what you injected me with all those years?"

"Not me, Dell, and yes," Adam says, before continuing with his story. "But when I returned to it I didn't see the hyphae that made me believe in its interconnected nature. Now I'm understanding that the threads withered in those samples, and these . . . are still connected."

"Is that . . . normal?" I ask.

"None of this is normal. Mycelium is how fungi stay connected. Barsamin is an astronomical element," Adam says.

I say, "Fuck does that mean?"

Cara says, "You mean like iron?"

"Yes," he says, ignoring me.

"It just means it's not a material that is made by earth. It comes from space," Nik Nik says, not caring if I understand, but clearly wanting to show he's at least as smart as the garbage git. "Like iron."

"Iron, iron, everybody knows iron," Adam says. "But *iron* is just the aftermath of large stars exploding, and is brought all over the earth by meteorites. Barsamin is made from the evaporation of black holes. Black holes! There is only one native deposit of iron on the entire planet. There are no native deposits of barsamin . . . at least, I thought there weren't."

"Cool," I say, like *boring*.

"Barsamin is the most significant discovery of the last hundred years."

"Dude, it's mud."

"It is no—" He takes a breath. "Before me no one even supposed the remnants of black holes would be tangible. They all thought it would be radiation. I'm the one who discovered its tangible form. I *named* it. I found its purpose."

Nik Nik's head tilts, but whatever he is thinking he saves for later.

"No, you didn't. Esther did. You called it science. She called it God and she's been using it to protect her flock," Cara says. Her smile is wry as she leans in toward him. "Don't you just hate it? When you think you're reading a story about science, and it turns out it's been a story about magic all along?"

He doesn't understand her, but I do. Perfectly.

I stand. I'm shaky on my feet, but I am on my feet.

"Did you gather what you need?" I ask.

"Not even close," he says. "If we can find a way to infuse this, we can make a protective shell to defend against incoming worlds. Like . . . like making a giant survival hatch."

It sure sounds like I'm done here. "So I can leave you with a protective detail and get the fuck out of this cave?"

"You aren't even remotely curious, are you?"

"Sometimes, but this doesn't sound like business that pays me," I say.

"And that is all that your little world is made up of, isn't it?" he says, like it's a diagnosis and not just good sense.

"My little world's got everything I need. Fuck I need to go reaching for?"

"No vision in the gutter," he says, and this time I know it's a dismissal.

"Vision or no, you're in the same gutter as me," I say, more to have the last word than anything.

Adam's already forgotten me as he looks around at the cave with the longing of a hungry pup. My body aches a little, and at first I think I dinged my arm in the fall, but then I remember what Cheeks did earlier. I walk outside still dripping wet and holding my bruised arm.

The runner on entrance duty—Rust or Brand, who can say?—looks me up and down, but I just shake my head.

"You and your partner keep watch over the scientist. He's an asshole. Try not to act on it." I look around. "Where is your partner?"

The soldier shrugs. "Went to take a leak. Haven't seen him since."

Only then do I see the tension in his shoulders.

"I'm on guard duty," he says, which means he's not allowed to leave the entrance of the cave. I already knew he was on guard duty, so him telling me means he's asking a favor without asking it.

I nod. "Which direction did he go?"

I'm *almost* sure now this is Mr. Brand, but trying to tell Brand from his twin brother is so impossible I'm sure Silk schedules them together so no one has to differentiate.

"That way," he says, visibly relieved when I walk in the direction he indicates.

I know there's a problem before I see the corpse.

The desert has seen more life than anywhere, but when it wants to, it can look completely untouched. It's not like a forest, wildlife and tree roots and moss and ivy constantly crawling through. The desert can look like it's never known a human foot if you leave it alone after one good rain. That's how the ground out here looks. Peace eternal. Peace like death. Until you get to the part where the soft tan surface is disturbed into a dark brown. The runner's tracks. Not bootprints, but wild and irregular marks like those made by a wounded animal. He fell to the ground, and began to drag himself. When I get to the body I realize two things: First, this one is Brand, not the other. Second, whatever happened, it started with his legs.

The lower half of his body is the most mangled. The body usually likes to fall apart at the joints, to say goodbye to its pieces where it's already falling apart. But not today. Mr. Brand's once-solid shinbones are both broken and pushed out so that his lower leg looks like a V. It's like he's some kind of insect—a cricket or mantis—that evolved new joints for jumping. I don't know it's Brand because I recognize him. I know it's Brand because he's older by three whole minutes and has always acted like it was a decade. I know it's Brand because once he realized what was happening, he dragged himself away so his brother wouldn't witness it. I know it's Brand because of the bloody dagger in his hand. Only an older brother would slit his own throat to keep his little brother from hearing his death scream.

"Goddamn it," I say, at the same moment I hear a low breath behind me.

I turn to see Nik Nik, my own older brother, standing behind me.

"Send Rust to get Viet," he says. "Don't let him see this."

I'm not surprised he can tell Rust from Brand on sight. They say he can identify each runner by the sound of their breathing alone, which I don't believe. They also say the reason he refuses to learn to read is because he was once told it would affect his exceptional memory, and he wants every bit of recall power to tell his runners apart, and that I do believe.

I nod. "Adam said . . ."

"I know," he says. "It won't just be one. Call it in."

I go to type a system-wide alert with a disaster code, but my cuff lights up with one already coming in: *1895*.

"They already know," I say.

Nik looks down at my cuff, and nods.

When we walk back to the cave, Mr. Rust is shaking. At first I think maybe he already connected the code coming through to his missing partner and knows his brother is dead, but then he points at the horizon.

"We have a problem."

I follow his finger, but I didn't need to. The signal is designed to be impossible to miss.

"Fuck."

There's a huge column of smoke coming from the palace. The smoke is white. It's not a house fire; it's a ceremony. Someone important has died. Not everyone gets smoke. In fact, only three people would qualify, and since Nik Nik and Esther are here with me, that leaves only one.

I turn to my brother, suddenly more desperate than I have ever been.

"Exlee," I whisper, but it's so choked I'm not sure anyone can hear.

"Focus," he says, like his hands aren't fists too. "Do you hear that?"

I do, but it's distant. I am so used to hearing the roar of wind through the hills to the south, I didn't recognize that this isn't that part of the mountain, and there isn't a breath of wind. The roar shouldn't be here, but it is. It takes me a moment to realize it's not coming from the mountain at my back, just bouncing off of it.

"Screaming," I say. Nik Nik nods.

CHAPTER FIFTEEN

WE HAVEN'T EVEN MADE IT TO ASHTOWN PROPER WHEN I BEGIN TO SEE THEM. AT FIRST, I THINK THE long dark shape is a mudcroc, out in the daytime and too close to people. I swerve before processing that what I mistook for the ridges of a reptile's spine is the exposed rib cage of a human, pushed up and out by the same mystifying force that took Helene X.

"Fuck," I grit out, swerving even farther away.

There are others when I look too far out toward the horizon, long patches of dark red catching shadows with the harsh sun behind them. Soon enough, I'm jumping at shadows, dodging harmless bushes. Normally I'd never drive this recklessly with two rulers of the wastes riding along, but I don't know what would happen if I drove through a body in that state, felt that crunch like the runners of old.

I think I might lose my mind.

I may have two rulers sitting near me, but all I can think about is the missing third. It doesn't help that when I look in the rearview mirror, Cara's always staring back, like some kind of wise nightbird or evil serpent. Some bad omen. Something that already knows it's too late. I know I didn't experience time travel. I didn't slip between worlds. I hallucinated and my brain just used what it already knew. That's why Cara was saying things I'd heard her say before. But it still feels like I'm living under the axe of fate. Like I'm running out of time.

I slide into the palace grounds so hot I stop sideways, a cloud of dust announcing our arrival to match the long stretch of agitated dirt I've already left in our wake. Despite the disruption we must have made no one comes out to greet us, or to see what's wrong. Everyone here already knows what's wrong. I'm the one about to find out.

I run toward the crowd gathered at the end of the yard, where the column of smoke is already a beacon to others who are lost, grieving, or just curious. I elbow through, prepared, but never really prepared, to see Exlee lying, forever silent, waiting for Viet.

But when I get through all I see is a tangle of what once was leather, flesh, and . . . braids.

I *know* Nik Nik is behind me, but I have to turn and reassure myself he's alive and whole. Only a decade of the hardest training in the desert keeps me from hugging him.

"It's . . . you," I say.

The crowd has noticed us now, and the reactions are a mix of cheers, from those who were here to mourn, and dismay, from those who thought the great dragon of Ash had finally gotten what was coming to him.

"Not me," he says, pointing to the shiny bits around what probably once was a head. "I haven't tipped my braids in years."

He sounds sure, but he must be shaken. What must it do, to see your own corpse? Even if you can barely recognize the body, how do you ever feel real after that?

Cara steps up beside us then.

"The cave," she says. "It worked."

I don't know how she can think about cause and effect at a time like this, but she's right. The cave protected my brother just like it protected Alden.

The crowd, who have been loud as static on a bad radio at the sight of us, begins to hush. The people around us part, revealing Exlee.

At least, I think it's Exlee. I've never seen them showing an emotion that wasn't, at least a little, manufactured. But what's on their face now is pure. A moment ago I was so sure I had lost them,

I was full of love and fear. But now, seeing Exlee's face glistening in tears and contorted in a real and undeniable grief, it's like I am seeing them for the very first time, and I love them all the more for it.

That's when I see the box they are carrying.

Black and sealed, I recognize it instantly, even though I haven't seen it since I was a young teen and my brother ascended: the inheritance box. It's the vessel they opened after Senior's murder. It was a formality, everyone knew Nik Nik was the heir Senior chose, but we still had to wait for Tatik to officially present and open the box. Tatik had my father's box, but I'd always assumed Viet had Nik's, the way Viet had the old ruler of the Rurals, the way I'm sure they have Exlee's.

Why is Exlee keeper of the next emperor?

I only have a second to wonder, because when Exlee looks up and sees Nik Nik, the light comes back into their eyes, the box slips from their hands, and I know: Exlee is in love with my brother. It's so pure and open it can only shame me, make me question if I've ever loved anyone in my whole rotten life.

Nik Nik moves forward, catching the box like a serpent striking prey. His face is such a mask there's no way of telling if he's staring at someone he cares about or a not terribly interesting rock. He believes in nothing more than hiding your heart, so much so I'm sure I'm the only one even aware that my brother has one. He holds the box out to Exlee.

"A bit premature, but I appreciate you following protocol so swiftly."

Exlee hasn't caught up to the moment, hasn't processed enough to put the mask back on.

"You're alive."

"The emperor is eternal," I say, providing cover.

That does it. Reminding Exlee who Nik is reminds Exlee who *they* are.

"Of course," Exlee says, turning. "I'll return this to its place."

"Return once you do. I'll have need of you," Nik Nik says, too sharply, and Exlee's back stiffens.

"Does the emperor seek to run the House? Shall I step aside?"

It's exactly the kind of layered, indignant reply I would expect from Exlee, and I'm guessing Nik Nik deliberately barked at them to get this response, to let the crowd *hear* that response, and let the scandal of the House and Throne fighting wash away any other whispers.

"You keep your place, and I'll keep mine," Nik Nik says, a threat and a promise. "But we will need the House's voice today as we decide how to proceed."

That unexpected compliment, that rare admission of *need* from Nik, will wash away the sting of his performative demand. Was it performative? Was my brother provoking Exlee to help hide their relationship? Or is my brother indifferent to Exlee and genuinely irritated at their display of affection? His face is stone as ever.

The crowd is already buzzing with the stories they will carry back across the desert. They will say how Exlee threw themselves over the body, weeping until Nik Nik was revealed to be alive. They will tell stories of how Exlee came to spit on the body, and then to kick dirt over the spit to drive the insult home, and then tell about the awkwardness when Nik Nik caught them. And they will, of course, tell stories of me. They will say I glared daggers at the one I love the most, because, of course, I'm the emperor's piece and I felt threatened by Exlee's presence and beauty and confidence. And every story will be true, because they will be heard.

Exlee turns away, and Nik Nik lets them, and the formality of their parting makes me question the affection I was so sure of a moment ago. What must it cost to turn your back when you want to touch someone so bad it wrecks you? This, this is the kind of devotion to duty my brother thinks I am capable of. This moment makes me sure I'm not half as fit to lead as Exlee. Because if I cared that much about someone, someone I thought was dead, nothing would keep me from licking every inch of them clean when I found them again, public or no.

And of course, of course, of course, a thought like that sends me looking around. Doesn't take long—I can pick Cheeks out of a crowd the way a raptor spots a fat rat. At first, seeing him alive and whole among all the dismembered bodies sends my heart soaring. I'm too close to the vision the tar showed me, of us on his couch, happy. But then I remember how we actually parted, with him accusing me of letting jealousy—*Jealousy!* When he knows I don't even ask monogamy from my partners—get in the way of doing my job. My smile drops into a glare that I struggle to keep once I see his eyes are wet and his hands shaking. I put a hand over the bruise he left on my arm, press it gently to let the pain remind me not to comfort him.

I step aside, letting him see Nik Nik alive. It's wild, to watch yourself fading out of someone's vision. But that's what happens. The moment I step aside, revealing Nik Nik and Esther, Cheeks looks like he's had a prayer answered.

He closes the distance quickly, his hands opening and closing like he's never wanted to touch something so bad in his whole life. I'm as shocked as Esther when he moves past her and falls to the emperor's feet. Nik Nik looks confused.

"No prostration. Today must be greeted upright," Nik Nik says, pulling Cheeks up to stand. Cheeks barely, just barely, manages to keep himself from hugging the closest thing to a dad he's ever let himself have. Nik Nik must see his devotion, his hurt, because he reaches out and grabs Cheeks by the shoulders. In the tension and uncertainty of bodies littering the street, my brother kisses Cheeks's face, bestowing high favor on him—not at his most worthy, but at his most wounded.

I meet Esther's eyes, but they're a pair of locked doors, showing nothing. I clear my throat and turn away from a whole heap of not-my-business.

"Hey, Silk," I say, spotting the runner out of the corner of my eye. "I need quick leave."

Silk looks uncomfortable. "Himself wants all hands on deck. There's going to be more bodies."

"That's what I'm afraid of," I say, then step closer. "Silk, please. I just need to make sure someone's in one piece."

The dramatic sigh means I've already won. Silk, like damn near everyone who signed up before me, treats me like a slightly annoying sibling.

"Tatik and I are doing head count and arranging duties. We'll be handing out assignments in an hour. Be back here to get yours."

I pat Silk's arm. "You're a gem. I ever tell you that? A goddamn diamond."

"You've only got an hour. You can suck up to me when you get back."

I turn back to blow a kiss as I walk to my ride, almost knocking someone else over.

"Where are we going?"

I yelp out a shocked *goddamn it* and turn. It's Cara. Of course it's Cara. It's always Cara.

"Don't you have anywhere else to be? Does fucking a Wileyite pay so good you can afford to be a pain in my ass all day long?"

"Sure, after the exchange rate."

Shows me for trying to shame a garbage git. They're trained on shame. Fed it as babies until they're immune to it. It only makes them stronger.

"I'm going for a drive," I say, walking past her.

"Great. Love a road trip."

Boy do I miss the days when the traverser was just a rumor and shadow, not the bane of my personal fucking existence.

She's already beside my ride. I've stopped walking.

"What?" she asks. "You want me to drive?"

I recoil with full indignation before I get that she's joking, that someone with eyes like that is even capable of joking.

"*Psh,* just you try to touch her," I say, getting in the driver's seat.

"Bet she'd love it."

"Bet she'd choke," I say, starting her up.

As we take off, I wish we were on my bike, where the wind and roar would make conversation impossible. Luckily, Cara seems no more inclined to talk than I am and I suspend my irritation about her long enough to be grateful for her silence. I couldn't fake lightheartedness, I couldn't fake the runner's infamous and expected rough humor. I'm too focused, too desperate, trying not to say, *I think I made a mistake.* Trying not to say, *I think I killed a man I didn't mean to kill.*

—

I DON'T MIND KILLING, LONG AS I MEAN IT. AND MY FIRST KILL? MY VERY FIRST? WELL . . . THAT WAS the kill I meant the most. When anyone sees someone like me being brought up, they see a quiet child, a victim turned doll by a lack of options. I think even my not-father got bored when I stopped reacting to the cruelty. I can't imagine how unnerving it must be to backhand an eight-year-old for staring at you just to have her go on staring after you've hit her.

I think my mother knew. She could tell that I wasn't a spirit broken into obedience, I was a spring held tight and losing, a monster being born but holding its breath. Often when she'd care for me afterward, she'd tell me how he wasn't a bad man, how he'd been brought up rough, how his mother didn't love him right. The last time, the very last time, she was icing my back and opened her mouth and I looked at her over my shoulders, eyes so much darker than hers she didn't know how to see humanity in them, and something in my gaze silenced her. Looking back, I think she knew that if she'd said one word of excuse, I would have snapped her neck.

It took awhile, but eventually I realized that she didn't take me out to Senior to keep her husband from hurting me. She did it to keep me from killing him. It was just in time, too.

I knew my biological father for three hours. He tucked me behind a rock while he finished his turn as Jack Ketch, then hid me in the back of his ride when he drove home. No one saw him bring me in. I think, maybe, he was considering killing me and didn't want whispers of a dead daughter to bring back rumors of Adra. When he brought me to his office he had not spoken one word to me, and I had not spoken one word to him.

It was then that Nik Nik entered and I knew, because I understood that this man was my father, and this younger version of him must have been my brother. I have never wanted a parent; until that morning I thought I'd had both of mine. But I had spent long days and longer nights dreaming of an older brother, someone who would come save me, someone who would lay my father low and rescue me. I was so struck by him that I didn't even notice how the fight started. I began really paying attention only when I heard the too-familiar sound of an angry man.

"She's just a girl."

"She's an inheritance complication at best, and a targetable weakness at worst. I want you to do it."

"No. You can't really think—"

When Senior hit Nik across the mouth I felt the blow as my own, because I had felt the same sting a dozen times.

"On your knees," Senior said.

"Dad, please," Nik said. His head was as low as his voice. I would learn only later how rare this sight was, how seeing a pleading, scared Nik Nik was like seeing a flying dragon: Tell all you want, no one will believe you.

"Knees," Senior repeated, walking over to the back wall of his office. He pressed a button on the wall to reveal all manner of pain: whips, belts, heat sticks, restraints. One long whip seemed to have pieces of sharp metal or black glass throughout, so that it could cut while it bruised. That wasn't the one Senior picked. He chose a wide brown hide, no thicker than a belt.

Nik Nik went to his knees. He removed his coat and lowered his head, and I knew then that there were no heroes in the world, no strangers riding in to save me. But I could be one.

Senior didn't hold back for the sake of his own blood. If anything, he put too much into it, rearing back until he was almost off balance, and bringing so much power into the strike he pitched forward. I could feel those blows too, could remember too easily how a man could hit you so hard in the back you feel it to the front of your lungs, how the force can stutter your heart. He was so into it he lost track of me, the small, silent girl whose name he hadn't even asked.

He didn't like the whip with glass in it . . . but I did. Nik Nik took two blows without a sound, but I made sure he never had to take a third. I've wondered so many times what it must have looked like to him, to turn around after an interruption in agony and look up to see his father, purple-faced and struggling, his new sister a spider monkey on the old man's back, pulling pulling pulling the glass-ladened whip around his neck so hard it would take a coroner to tell if it was strangulation or blood loss that got him. Senior was strong, and I was small, but instincts are powerful, and he wasted the time he should have used shoving me off to grab fruitlessly at the whip, earning nothing but mangled fingertips as he met the barbs. It was over so fast. Senior went to his knees, and then facedown, and I spent the whole time on his back, riding him down like a giant beast. It wasn't until a pair of boots showed up in my vision and I looked up to see Nik Nik standing over me that I released the whip and skittered sideways to hide under the desk.

I didn't even notice my hands were as mangled as the old man's throat until much later, even though the damage was so deep random bouts of pain would keep me in gloves even as an adult.

I don't dream about Senior's murder anymore, but back when I did I was never killing him. It's always myself I sneak up on, my own throat I slip the toothed material around. And the person on their knees? The one I'm protecting? In my dreams, that's me too. And I never woke up crying either. I just woke up free.

—

I'LL HAVE HIM PUT SOMEWHERE HE'LL NEVER BOTHER YOU.

Who has a post in the wastelands that they cannot leave, but still has to live alone?

Who walks too heavy for their frame, not because they are a coward wearing body armor, but because the collapsible scythe weighs as much as the guillotine it was made from?

What post would be so morally repugnant that Cheeks could easily convince the emperor to use it to test a holy runner he didn't trust?

What post is so secret you get an emperor's mark just for taking it?

Jack Ketch.

I think back to the scar on Cross's thigh. It was years old, easily. Has he been assassin since he joined? I try to remember the day they brought him down to the row. I'd never been so shocked to see a recruit. For maybe seven whole seconds I was curious, but then I was just angry. Being a runner was my escape from assholes like him. How old had he been? I try to picture him, too tall for his weight, swinging a scythe as big around as he was. Good thing Ketch's kills come willingly. He probably couldn't fight them down otherwise.

I bet his arms shook with the weight of the scythe at first.

I bet he cried the whole time.

I bet he still does, maybe later, when he's home in the dark alone.

I ache for my bike when the bogs start and I have to cajole four wheels to move like two. When it becomes too dangerous, I skid-stop, mentally giving myself the lecture I'd give any new runner who dared to do the same twice in one day.

Once we stop I turn to Cara to tell her to stay behind, but she's already opening her door.

"We're not supposed to be here," she says, and I don't know if Ruralites all know where the field of blood is, or if she can just *feel* the wrongness of this place the way the rest of us do. When I walk down into the crevice she follows fearlessly, which doesn't surprise me. The more I am learning about her life with Adam, the more I'm sure following a runner onto haunted ground doesn't even register to her as danger.

I'm moving faster than I like. Cara will know I'm running because I care. So will Cross. Whatever. I take the narrow path down into the south of the south as if there isn't a sheer drop on one side. When we reach the bottom I shiver. Not because of the hopeless dead, but because we are now in the one cold, dark place in the desert, the one place that smells like mold and earth, the one place light can't quite reach.

I know I've reached Akeldama because my boots start to squish. Any Ash kid will tell you that moisture is all the blood spilled here lingering forever, but it's actually just that this place is in such a low crack in the earth it approaches the water sleeping beneath all deserts.

There is surveillance here somewhere. The Wileyites who come to die willingly usually record their final goodbyes and intentions before arriving, but it's good to have a backup in case someone wants to point fingers. But for the life of me I can't see the gleam of a camera lens or mesh of a microphone anywhere in the dense, rocky crags surrounding me.

It takes me too long to realize Cara and I are not alone. The walls here are all cracks, bright spires beside the blackest shadows. His tall, square mask and floor-length poncho are painted to match, the striped tan-and-black making him seem like part of the wall behind him. Only the scythe helps me see him—long and shining and heavy. They say it wasn't just any guillotine. They say when Nik Senior beheaded the last of the disloyal, he had the metal saved and made into the executioner's scythe. Most of the people Senior put down were his friends, his family, and when you kill someone that close the weapon carries the curse. The metal could only ever do this work, death with heart. Killing with tears, with a thousand pounds of obligation and not one ounce of real hate.

I don't know if it's the shadow or the limited visibility of the mask, but it takes him a few steps to recognize me. In that instant I see Jack Ketch as we want Wileyites to see him: Imposing. Mythical. Inhuman. Moving so slowly he might be part rock, but so surely he must be a soldier. If you were at all afraid of death it'd make you run. Which is the goal, to make sure the people who make it to death's door really want to be there.

Once he notices it's me, or maybe once he sees Cara, he drops the act. His steps become shaky as he moves forward. He still looks like a creature made of stone, but less like a dirt mage now and more like a bad golem, all its joints cracking together slowly. He's almost made it to me when he falls to his knees. I take off the mask, which takes some doing because it's actually a long hood tucked deep into the poncho that covers the rest. As the material slides over his head, revealing his face, the lightness of his skin still surprises me. His eyes are even bluer now with the wet shine over them. Mr. Cross has been crying.

We're trained, I swear I was trained, to look for depression in other runners. To watch one another for signs of cracking. I've spotted it in others, been proud of how good I was at providing aid and care to my fellow Misters. But I hated him so much for so long I didn't see it in him.

No, I did. Once upon a time.

But it's not too late. I thought it was. After what I saw in the cave, I thought I was here to report a corpse. I must have been hallucinating. Or . . . maybe seeing something that hadn't happened yet? I push that thought away. I hallucinated. It was all just a water dream—the opposite of a fever dream, a fantasy born from drowning, not burning.

"Wellness check," I say, like this was ordered, like this is at all official. "You good, Cross?"

He's shaking his head before I finish the question. "I can't do this anymore."

Of course not. By my count he's been executioner twice as long as anyone is supposed to be, and to be stationed here with no partner? All alone in a crack of the desert where the wind already sounds like the voices of the dead? If he was posted right when he came in, he wouldn't even have had time to make the kind of friends in Ash that would make this life bearable, and he'd be forbidden from talking to anyone from the past. Even playing wolf, spending too long staring at a screen to see everything Cheeks did, must have seemed like a blessing.

"It's okay now. I'm going to fix it."

He nods, like he understands, but he doesn't. I know he doesn't, because the next thing he does is hand me the scythe. I take it without really knowing why, but he's bending his head down, waiting for me to make it better for him the way he has for so many others.

I've thought about it, you know? Right now—hair messy from the hood, bright eyes shining, small and on his knees—he looks exactly like the boy that tried to make me hate myself. But it wasn't ever about him, not really. I didn't hate him because he called me a sinner. I didn't hate him because he told me I was filthy and in need of redemption. I hated him because everything he said was true. Not because I fucked and let fuck for money. But because I'd killed a man who was a father to someone I cared about, even if he'd never been one to me. And because it wasn't spontaneous. I'd spent most of my childhood and preteen years dreaming of murdering my father; it matters little that when the time came it was a different dad.

The sound of the scythe falling to the ground is a dull thud that makes his head shoot back up.

"Come on, you're done here," I say, knowing what it will take to make that true.

He nods. I don't think I've ever willingly touched him beyond duty, but he's so unsteady it makes sense to put an arm around him and lead him up the hill like a wounded solider. It'd be easy if it was Cheeks. Cheeks comes to maybe my nose, and I can lead him most anywhere by the shoulders. But Cross's Wiley blood wars with mine, and we're both too tall for me to touch anything but the slender curve of his waist. He's falling apart, but he's still focused enough to grab the scythe he's not allowed to be without.

The runners didn't do this. That much I'm sure of. We took him in with cracks and we never even noticed. Just like his old home never saw them. Hell, growing up on fresh veggies and toxic positivity, Nik Nik probably thought Cross was his most stable runner. He probably thought he was giving hell duty to his least damaged soldier, because we all assume not living poor means not living hurt. I, of all people, should have known better.

I put Cross in the backseat, and he doesn't ask where we're going, doesn't ask if I'm going to report him for desertion. Cara slides into the back with him. Eventually she pulls his head down into her lap and strokes his hair. He closes his eyes. Strange. Every ounce of Esther oozes sister. Even the way she *doesn't* look at Cross is heavy with love. Cara interacts with him like a stranger trying her best. But she was his sister too, wasn't she? If the rumors are right, she's been living in the Rurals since she could write her letters. I was older than that when I got Nik, and he's as much a brother to me as a twin.

Once we're on the road I check my cuff. I've got about forty minutes to get Cross squared away and ask Nik Nik for forgiveness since I sure as fuck didn't ask permission. I try not to think about what this little stunt is going to cost me. Luckily, the path gets boggy, and I get to focus on not drowning us all instead. I grip the wheel and lead us toward the only place I know that can fix cracks as old as these.

CHAPTER SIXTEEN

"ABSO-FUCKING-LUTELY NOT."

Vex didn't even look up from his desk. It's like he rejected Cross by smell.

"Come on, V. *Pleeeeease?*" I ask, hoping sounding like a kid again will earn me some favor from back when he loved me.

Exlee hasn't come back from the palace yet, meaning Vex is running the House until they return. Vex is usually part assistant, part manager, but softer than Exlee on their best day. But once Exlee's out of the building he goes full drill sergeant, guarding Exlee's policies with such sharp teeth you'd think he'd just take up the leather already. The people who whisper about things like that say Exlee's inheritance box has always had Vex's name in it. Me? I'm not so sure. I think it was Helene's.

He leans forward.

"He can never partake of our services. He's permabanned. Hell, *you* voted to permaban him."

Right.

"I know, but—"

"Weren't you actually the author of the motion to ban him?"

Cross tilts his head at me. I close my eyes.

"Yes, co-author, *technically*, but that's not the point," I say. Vex gives me a loud look. "I know! Listen, *I* know. No one knows like I know. But . . . he needs help. The kind he can only get here."

Vex crosses his arms.

"Why should we accept the judgmental righteous when they won't accept us?" Good point. "Besides, Helene X hasn't been sent home yet. I won't desecrate her peace by giving him refuge here."

An even better point.

"It's fine. I'll go," Cross says.

I hold my hand to silence him while still looking directly into V's eyes. "Helene X voted *against* banning him, because she believed change was possible for everyone, because she was a better person than you, or me, and isn't offering space for him a better way of honoring her than being the shittier versions of her we've always been?"

He bites his lip. "If Exlee—"

"Send Lee to me. I'll pay in skin if they want."

He nods, and I feel the knot in my stomach finally release.

"Speaking of payment, he'll need a room . . ." Vex looks Cross up and down. ". . . and some time."

"Bill it to the emperor. Work-related injury."

His eyebrows go up, but then he just shrugs.

"None of my business if you're looking to get demoted," he says, and begins writing the intake. He motions to a new worker, one whose name I haven't learned yet, to ready a long-stay room. They smile wide and approach.

"Is it all right if I touch your arm?" they ask.

Cross nods, and they take him at the elbow with hands that are probably the softest thing he's felt in years. It's early duty, for those who are here for training but not yet interested in full service. This newbee's smile is just customer service, but when I was on early duty I was so grateful to belong I just permanently grinned like a stupid dog or stupider child when I got to lead someone.

I'm gonna have to cut through half the desert to get back to the palace for check-in, but when Vex asks which of us wants to see Cross settled, I almost nod before forgetting who else is in the room. I look back at Cara, who's been staring around the House like it's an old friend.

"You want to go with him?"

Her eyebrows rise, surprised by the question.

"No," she says, and it's not even heavy. "You go. I'm not the one who can help him."

I can't tell if she means Esther is the sister who could help him, or I am the one out of the two of us that could help him, or—most impossible but feeling the most true—she's not the *Cara* that can help him.

Once we're alone in his room, I say the thing that's been pinging around my head since I confirmed he was Jack.

"Esther. She said your dad killed himself . . ."

. . . and there's only one way a Ruralite can do it in their religion, only one way that doesn't dirty their hands or make extra work for those around them.

Cross is staring at the floor, and he goes on staring.

"He never knew it was me. I heard his confession, but I never let it slip."

I realize he wasn't doing the man a kindness. He wants me to know that even when he was severing his father's head from his body, he kept the emperor's secret. He honored the mark on his thigh.

I'm getting a clearer picture of what could have pushed Cross over the edge. Did my brother know he'd had to kill his own father? Why didn't he do something? I understand he couldn't have pulled him immediately, it would have looked too much like calling him broken, but he could have helped in some way. He could have . . . All at once it hits me. No, he couldn't have pulled him without being obvious. But he could give him another assignment, one that might force him to talk to others in his off-time. Like, for instance, making Cross wolf even though there was no credible threat against him. He could also assign him as partner to me, one of the few House-trained runners at his disposal. I think back to how defensive my brother was of Cross when he messed up in the office. They way he'd called him *Brother*, and forced me to do the same. He was avoiding stepping on the cracks I'd been tap-dancing all over.

"You did good. You're a good soldier," I say, because it seems to matter to him an awful lot. "Things will get better here. This is a good place."

"I know," he says, finally looking up at me. "I've always known. I was just . . . you don't understand how jealous I was of everyone and everything when I was young. I wanted to be here, anywhere, so badly. All that yelling about morals and heaven, it was just . . ."

". . . ripping the wings off a bird because you can't fly?"

He takes a second before nodding. "Yeah, like that."

Destructive envy? One of teen Scales's greatest hits. Besides homicidal rage, of course.

"I know a little about that," I say. "Exlee says jealousy is a poison you make for others but drink yourself."

He nods.

"I know a little about that, too," he says, reminding me, because if I look at him too long I forget about his past substance use.

"About that. You should know they don't discourage drug use here. Let your provider know if you don't want it around you, and they'll do their best."

His surprise is genuine, and I try not to be insulted by it. "I thought this place was about wellness?"

"It is. For some people, wellness is a little oblivion. If someone wants to use it to destroy themselves, better to figure out why they want to disappear than just make sure they never hold a blade again."

It's a line straight out of Exlee's mouth, but it's one of my favorites.

The House raised me, so I'm indifferent to drug use. Like anything else that doesn't deliberately hurt others, it's morally neutral here. Lots of people use with no harm done to themselves or others. Those that do harm themselves, well, I understand how strong the urge to self-destruct can be, no matter what form it takes. But I've seen it in people who lift or run until they're nothing, people who love only those that hurt them, people who spend their pay so quick it's like they want to starve—not just those who tap their veins looking for a way out. They all have the same thing in common: You can't solve any craving for excess by stopping the act. You've got to solve what made them *need,* which is a separate thing entirely. *Need* can make any act harmful. Even love.

"I just mean if you are using, they won't stop you, they'll just watch you. There's a room for it."

He shakes his head. "I'm clean."

I flinch. This was such a fucking mistake.

"Don't . . . don't call it clean. Not here. Nothing dirty about the opposite."

His eyes widen at that, and I'm guessing his Ruralite upbringing meant freedom to judge anyone and everything as unclean.

I give it one, *maybe* two days before I get the call that his self-righteous ass has gotten kicked out. But at least I can say I tried.

Before I go, I tell him it's going to be okay.

He doesn't believe me, which is just as well, because I can't tell if I'm lying or not.

—

THE SILENCE CARA AND I SHARED ON THE WAY FROM THE PALACE IS TWICE AS HEAVY ON THE WAY back. Eventually, when we're near enough to the palace that it's our last chance, she speaks.

"You know . . . I'm not technically blood. You don't have to report him seeing family."

I turn toward her, and I don't know what she reads on my face but it's wrong, because she continues.

"Please. I don't know how he'll take it if he gets kicked out. This wasn't his fault."

It's less impassioned than the emotional plea I would expect from a sister seeing her brother on the edge of losing the only thing that's been standing him up.

"You think I'm going to go running my mouth about this? I must've broken ten rules today. Shit, I pulled the hood off the executioner. That alone's my hide."

She's staring at me with those eyes dark enough to look like empty space, twin voids threatening to suck me in and see every part of my existence, inside and out. I wonder if that's how she got her job, how she kept it: seeing every damn thing and never letting any of it go.

"You're lying," she says.

"Lying? The rules—"

"You're pretending to be afraid. Why? You gave the emperor an order at the crash site and he didn't even blink. Are you immune from censure? How? You're not the emperor's partner."

I have to take each sentence separately. Her voice is as rough as any dirt-born git, but the pacing and patterns are almost self-reflective. Like someone who's been away a long time. I realize, all at once, that she talks like Adam. Is that just standard for ex-Ash? Like, some kind of warped anti-accent? What you sound like after you've tried taking the Ash out of your voice? Or did they work together for so long she's not even aware of how he's rubbed off on her?

"How do you know I'm not his? Think I'm too ugly?" I say, smiling wide to enhance my too-square jaw, forcing even smaller eyes already too small to be considered feminine.

It's an old joke to tell. Fifteen years ago it wouldn't have been a joke. It would have been a barely masked insecurity. But insecurity is a young girl's game and somewhere along the way I got to building exactly the kind of life I want, and those old concerns slipped away. If I got three wishes now I wouldn't use a single one on my appearance. If I'd gotten those wishes as a teenager? Would've wasted every one.

I answered her question with a question. She returns the favor.

"Is your rank high enough you've earned favor? How long you been in?"

"Fifteen years. House before that."

"House? I don't remember you," she says.

I shrug. "You didn't preach out like your brother. Weren't likely to cross paths."

"Right," she says, too quickly.

Cara's still looking at me like she can see everything I'm made of. You'd think it's the stripes on her face that make her impossible to miss or ignore. But it's not. It's the intensity of her gaze. She's never just looking around. Her eyes are never just open. She's always *seeing*. Always *watching*.

Eventually, she turns away.

"I knew you weren't his because you've never had the bones in your face broken. I know how rough he plays with those he claims to love."

I almost swerve off the not-road with that little revelation.

"You take that back."

She's surprised by my rage. "Take back what? The truth? That your boss doesn't know how to love someone without bleeding them?"

Beat on someone in his home? In his care? That he loved? The city would call it *domestic violence,* same as what my dad did to me. He's the one who saved me from men like that. Gave me hope. Sure he's violent, but only in his rulings. Only at his post. He's violent like a soldier, not a coward.

"You're a goddamn liar. He wouldn't do that. He wouldn't—"

"He would. He has. And he always will."

I shake my head. "Liar."

"I've got my own scars from him. You probably do, too."

"That's business! It's one thing to lay hands on someone who knows the penalty for disrespect. We sign up for that. But someone who loves you? Who trusts you? He couldn't. Lovers don't ask for that."

Children don't either.

"Why don't you ask him? It'd be interesting to see if this version of him can lie any better than the others."

"You know that's creepy, right?"

"What?"

"Referencing people's *other* lives. The otherworldly ones. It's none of our business. It's like seeing your own death. It's . . . wrong."

She's staring at me again. "I guess I've never noticed," she says, and looks back out the window.

I want to ask, but will goddamn bite my own tongue off before I ask, if she's ever witnessed her own death. I keep my eyes ahead, trying not to think about my brother, trying not to imagine the hands that pulled a bloodhungry child out from under a desk wrapping around a throat or balling into a fist for the one he loves.

It can't be true. Maybe it's true somewhere, maybe Cara saw it on some earth, but not this one. Not my Nik. I don't care about universes or possibilities or infinity. This *isn't* possible. Not in my world. I believe in precious little, but I'd stake my life on that.

—

BEING IN THE CAR WITH CARA GIVES ME THE GODDAMN CREEPS, SO I'M STOKED TO PULL UP TO THE palace . . . right up until I actually do.

Runners are gathering for the afternoon's work, waiting on assignment. There's a hush over the crowd that tells me that, though we haven't been officially assigned, people are hearing stories of what waits for us.

We all ready. We all ready differently. We ready by sharpening our knives. We ready by testing our gloves. We ready by taping our boots. New Misters ready by talking to one another, faking excitement to prove how scared they're not. Oldheads, like Blaylock and Black Dragon, ready by sitting against a wall, crossing their arms, and going to sleep. Or trying to while Sai excitedly shows them some new dance from the vidscreens.

Sai's our youngest and technically a year-one recruit. But they've been following runners around since they were eight, rubbing charcoal on their teeth and practicing our walk. Blay's from just after Tatik's time, but he dropped down to reserves after his son died. He's been volunteering more and more once Sai showed up, no family to speak of and eyes full of trust. We all pretend Blay's not too old for this. Just like we all pretend not to notice how much Sai reminds everyone of Blay's kid.

I find Nik offsides speaking to the organizing lieutenants. Once they leave, I approach.

"A word?" I say, hoping for some privacy in case I have gone too far for even blood to save me.

"This'll have to do. They need to see me," he says, which explains why his braids look neater than they did when I left, and why every ring he owns is on his hand. It's calming for the runners to see him alive and well. It's good for civilians too. The only time it's good to have a dragon in your backyard is when it's aimed at the thing trying to kill you.

No one can hear us, but I still pitch my voice to a whisper when I tell him what I've done.

"I pulled Cross off executioner duty."

His eyes go full-wide before narrowing in rage. "That's above your rank. You're not thinking. Now I have to deliver you up to Tear for censure and put Cross right back where you found him."

"What will it take? To keep Cross off?"

He tilts his head. He heard the desperation in my voice. He liked it.

"Only emperor and emperor's blood have authority over Akeldama. Right now . . . that's just me, and I'm not reassigning anyone. Things are chaotic enough as it is."

His price is exactly what I thought it would be. I take a breath.

"Fine. You win. You keep him off the scythe, I'll take my spot. Braid my hair, wear so many goddamn rings my arm falls off. Whatever you want."

He smiles. Showing the onyx teeth of the emperor. My teeth, soon enough. "Good to hear it. This is no time for a power shift, but once the moment comes . . ."

"I'll stand beside you."

"Head high . . ."

". . . hands ready."

I cross my hand over my chest and he touches my shoulder, accepting my vow.

"We're just announcing posts now, but you'll be on collections under Tatik," he says.

"Collections? It's the wrong season for collections," I ask, then it hits me. "We're not collecting tribute, are we?"

"Not the kind I want," he says.

So it's body collection then. It must be.

"We have a watch on Rust?" I ask, because if we're going body collecting, he needs to be far away.

"We need every pair of boots," Nik Nik says.

"Protocol is two weeks—"

"Protocol ended when we were delivered a corpse harvest," he says, his tone severe without rising. A warning. I lower my head. He waits, making sure I'm well in my place before continuing. "He's not on collection. He's patrolling for fakes. And he begged for the detail."

"You think he's looking for Brand?"

"Almost definitely."

And what would it matter if he found him? If I lost someone I loved that much, would I be happy to see a face just like theirs even though it would never actually be them? If Exlee had been a target, would I have even wanted to see the version of them that came over?

Yes. Yes, yes, and fuck yes. Like I said, I'm a simple creature. You heard about that study? Where city scientists put two fake parent monkeys in with baby monkeys? One fake monkey was hard metal and produced milk, one was soft and warm and gave no food. I'd choose the latter. I like comfort in any form—cold, false, toxic—and I'd starve to death happily wrapped in a soft warmth I'm only pretending can love me.

"I hope he finds him," I say.

"I hope he survives the disappointment if he doesn't," Nik Nik says.

It's a better wish than mine, and I tap two fingers on my bottom lip, then earlobe, then point up, sending the request to a universe that I hope listens.

THEY COULD BE ROSES. THEY'RE ALMOST EXACTLY THE SAME. THE VELVETY, IRREGULAR RIDGES, THE dark red getting darker the deeper you go, the jagged bloom like a spray of petals. But those aren't petals, they're bone shards poking through skin. And those aren't roses. They're bodies. I'm escorting my eighth body since I shifted from collection to identification. Have you ever had to pin a name on something that used to have a whole life, and now you can't even tell their height? They don't look human, and it's easier to think of them as flowers than anything that used to walk.

"Your name was Terrick. You had your mother's smile, and everyone who saw it loved you," I say to the mass sitting on the black tarp beside me as I tag it for the family. What I say to this corpse is true. I know it's true because I know his mother. But I've been fudging for others, trying to give them some story to find themselves, because in this state their flesh won't guide them anywhere clearly.

I lean down one last time, closing my eyes and whispering all I can to lead Terrick home before I seal the tarp.

I hear the high-pitched beep just as I finish, and I'm in motion even before my brain has processed the sound. My feet know what to do, and so do my hands. The Wileyite already has his hands in the air. He's backing up. There are types of Wileyites, and I call this one *artsy parental disappointment.* His blond hair is long, his clothes are trying for rugged with their expertly placed tears and purely cosmetic patches, but they're too expensive—the synthetic materials shining rich and complex beneath the sun despite everything being black. Not to mention the tech he's using could feed a family out here for months.

"Hand it over," I say.

"I upload instantly," he says. "Taking it won't do anything."

Like I give a shit? Besides, he's wrong. Taking it will make me feel better, will give me something to hate that I can touch, that I can fight, and that's exactly what I need.

I reach out and grab the optical band from his forehead. When most of us need a camera, we just use the scanner on our cuffs. Not this guy. I examine the tech. If I put it on, my vision would be framed exactly like the picture, and I would be able to change the settings and view the effects in real time. It'd be like standing in a virtual reality depiction of the picture or video I'm about to take. It's impressive, even without the add-ons that give it greater zoom possibilities and options like infrared and night vision. My boots are not impressive, are neither new nor innovative, but in the war between boot and facecam, boot wins.

"You just crushed my specs!"

"You're lucky it wasn't an implant."

"I'm suing."

"Good. Go file a claim at the courthouse."

"You think I won't?"

I shrug. I don't care. I hope he tries, because I'd love to know how long he'll look before realizing we don't have a courthouse, and he wouldn't like the qualification process for a blood tribunal. This won't stop him, or the next photographer, I know. Bored Wileyites hoping to turn our tragedy into a section of their portfolio have been shadowing us all morning. We got instructions not to kill anyone, but we're still allowed to keep up our reputation.

I haven't had to deal with them much. I'm ugly, regular ugly, not ugly in a *striking* way that would make me artistically valuable. I guess if they knew whose daughter I was—biologically or on record—they might become a problem. But for now they only follow subjects they can sell to Wiley news projections. Cheeks has had two shadowing him all night, but he's used to it. Cheeks has been in the Wiley news cycle for *years*. The first time a newsvid projected a picture of him, thousands of Wileyites ping-reacted with sounds of moaning. They then turned around and voted to increase surveillance on the border and waive the rights for runners caught violating Wiley's citizenship policy . . . so either they were doing it for show, or Wiley doesn't know anything about care for outsiders despite all that it's learned about lust for us. The city thinks Cheeks is one of the good ones. They don't know he's an enforcer. Me? I'm the one they think strips skin for a living, and before all this went down I was just the fucking mechanic.

Damn, if Helene was still here, all Wiley blond but Ashtown rough, they'd never photograph anyone else.

If Helene was here. It still hits me like a truck that she's not just stuck at work, not late because a client ran overtime. She's gone, forever. Maybe once we have the funeral it'll be easier to keep straight. Though, at this rate, we're going to have too many funerals for any of them to register. It's easy to feel loss—to focus on it, to mourn it—if it's just one. Too much missing? All those absences, all stacked up? That's just night. How can you tell the shadows apart to feel them when there's so much darkness?

I don't know, but I have to pretend I do. Every civilian that's laid eyes on me has searched my face for fear and confusion and

I've only delivered up our regulation mix of confidence and threat. We're supposed to stand steady when there are holes ripped through the world . . . It's just a lot easier when we're the ones doing the ripping.

So we'll clean up once-people mush like it's nothing. We'll deliver them to their families without so much as a nod of sympathy, like it's nothing. We'll even joke about it where civilians can hear . . . and save our crying for where they can't.

Suddenly, I'm greeted by the sound of vomiting so violent I can hear the splatter on the sand. I turn, expecting Sai, expecting anyone too new to ever have had to face a scene like this. But I should have known Silk would never assign anyone who still had light in their eyes this detail.

At first, all I see is blond hair bent over, and I think it's another gawking photographer who just realized they're in too deep. But when the sufferer looks up and wipes his mouth, the eyes that meet mine are eyes I have loved. No, Silk would never force Sai to do such dirty work. But he would absolutely force cleanup on those that made the mess.

I know better, but my first thought is still Helene X. It's her ghost that makes me walk over. Now that I've seen him, I scan the area quickly for the other intruder. Anna. I spot her over a body bag a few yards away, making notes with nothing on her face but determination. I imagine no corpse will hit her as hard as the one she made.

"You good?" I ask the bent form.

Not-Helene looks up, but keeps his hands on his knees. "I didn't know. He didn't tell us."

I believe him, not because I think he or Anna is trustworthy, but because I knew Helene X, and there is no version of her that would be okay with this kind of devastation.

Suddenly, something clicks into place. "You couldn't afford to come either. You were supposed to be with the ones who tried to kill us. That's why your feet were so fucked. You ran from them."

Not-Helene looks away.

"Why'd you do it?" I ask. "You don't have the stomach for this. Why'd you come?"

He looks like he might answer, but then his eyes shift past me and his mouth goes hard. I turn to see Anna glaring at him, all threat. We'll need to find a place for this version of Helene X. But Anna is covered in bits of corpse and still taking the time to intimidate a loose end into silence. She's already found her place, she just doesn't know it yet.

I look back at him, but it's clear he's done talking.

"Are you going to force me to answer?" he asks.

I could. I'm not an enforcer as a rule, but breaking things has always come easy to me. But right now, I'm just tired.

I shake my head. "Ground's been watered enough today," I say, and walk away.

CHAPTER SEVENTEEN

WHEN I LEAVE FOR THE DAY MR. SILK TELLS ME TO REST UP. SAYS I'M REALLY GONNA HATE THE DUTY I've got tomorrow. I can't imagine I'll hate it more than this, that I could hate anything more than this. I say I'm going to sleep the full twelve hours until my next shift, but that's a goddamn lie and I know it as soon as I say it.

I sleep six, but once the sky starts to dim I shower and dress fresh. I cover myself in sundust, an oil from creo bushes that hydrates with a yellow shimmer. I wear my deepest black leather vest and nothing else, all the better to show off the promotion marks sitting pretty on my sternum. The pants I wear sit low enough on my hips to showcase the tattoos I didn't earn, just chose. I've got the horizon line of Ashtown wrapping around my waist, but it's the view of the mountains and valley if the city was at your back. It's a single, thick black line that goes jagged black and red for the ridges of the mountains, then soft gray and green for the low marshy lands of the sleeping river.

People ask why I didn't have the artist include Wiley City's skyline. Sometimes I tell them it was too ugly. Other times, too expensive. Truth is, I didn't grow up looking at the city, staring at the way light turned fake as it entered the UV-protective dome, the way color became dull in the artificial atmosphere, the skyscrapers black against sunset like pieces of the world cut out. I grew up inside, looking out at these mountains like they were salvation. I dreamt of running away from the moment I could dream, and I never thought of going anywhere but the desert. Maybe even then some part of me knew where I belonged, where someone else with my blood was, waiting for me.

I take one last look at myself in the mirror, wink at my reflection, and go.

—

WHEN I PULL UP TO THE NIGHTFIRE I HAVE TO PARK THREE ROWS BACK. I SWEAR EVERY RUNNER NOT ON shift right now is here. It's an eternal burn located just outside of the Rurals, where runners come for precisely one reason. The crime of hitting on someone just trying to do their job still stands on the clock, but here approach is fair game.

I take up a spot *just* outside of the fire's light to take stock of the crowd. Standing in the shadow means I haven't made up my mind, so anyone interested has to wait for me to come to them. I see Reisha across the way, standing in the shadow just like me. We make eye contact, and she steps closer to the fire, signaling her readiness. You only step into the fire's light if you're looking to burn. I was hoping she'd be here. I was hoping she'd choose the glow.

Keeping eye contact, I step into the light as well. Traditionally, as the second person to enter the circle of want, I should go over to her. But that's not what she likes. Instead, I tilt my head back, looking her up and down like I'm still deciding. Her cheeks go red, and only partially from the heat. Finally, I nod and crook my finger to summon her. Her head dips down and her blush deepens as she comes over. I grab the base of her neck and pull her along with me. I'm moving her with the momentum of my palm solely, not allowing my fingers to dig in, following exactly along the perimeters of her fantasy. She slows down deliberately, earning a teasing squeeze along the sides of her throat, a throat that vibrates like a cat purring at the rough touch.

Sometimes we don't make it out of the desert. Sometimes we make it to my cycle but no farther. Today she gets on the ride facing the handlebars, which means we're going back to her place. I tuck in behind her, and can't resist sliding a hand up her skirt to feel her. This is a game we play. If she wears underwear, I scold her for not being ready for me when we get home. If she doesn't, I point out how much she wants it, the attention making all her shame-kinks flare while she squirms. Reisha used to be a Ruralite with a more boring name, and even though she left the vows behind as a teenager, that upbringing of religious moderation left a mark in the shape of her strongest desires.

It occurs to me—unhelpfully—that Cross was also a Ruralite. Before I can stop myself I'm wondering if this is what he would want, if he still craves the shame he was raised on, if he still feels most comfortable on his knees, if he's anything but a top.

I give myself a mental shake, backing away from the edge of what can only be a killing cliff. I've got a beautiful creature pressed against me who is—I nip at her shoulder—*not* wearing underwear, and I'm not going to space out on how lucky I am.

When we get to her place, Reisha doesn't dismount when I do. She holds her hands up in the air, so I lift her up. She wraps her legs around me and I carry us inside.

We were never going to make it to the bedroom. I didn't just want this. I needed this. Even before the world repainted itself in the blood and sinew of my neighbors, I needed the sweet breath of her to ground me. Between Cross, my brush with the future in the cave, and the tragedy of the day, I've felt helpless and cruel. Having someone trust you implicitly, having big brown eyes waiting to obey your every word, and having a body not tense in fear or flinch away, even when I'm touching her most breakable places—it's enough to make me feel worthy. My mouth must be good for more than pushing a man to suicide, because I can turn her to liquid with a few sentences. And maybe my hands are good for more than death, because it is precisely my hands she wants.

After she's done, she moves to her knees between my legs, but I pull her up into a straddle, just holding her close and breathing her in. I don't want anything, not tonight. I just want to give, to make someone in this world feel anything but miserable.

I don't notice the sound of the shower until it shuts off, but I'm too lazy to react when her husband walks into the room. Mr. Slate is just going in for his shift. I can tell, because he doesn't have the shadows in his eyes. He doesn't know what he's in for. He points to himself, a question. I nod, giving permission. We've fucked a few times, and I've always enjoyed it, but that's not why I nod. Slate doesn't yet know how much he's going to want some sweet memory to get him through the next few hours, and we could give him that. It's Reisha who shakes her head, rejecting his addition. She kisses me, then rises up on her knees for the leverage to press my face into her neck. She's holding me, just that, and I understand. Reisha went to the fire for me. She's doing all this, for me. She's even turning Slate away, so she can focus on me. Slate is a competent sexual partner, but not a nurturing one, not one who can see all your needs before you open your mouth, like Reisha, and like anyone else who'd been trained at the House. Reisha and I didn't serve at the same time—she's older than I am and had left by the time I got there—but she wears the same tattoo on her ankle that I have on my hip: a simple black V upside down over a line: an abstract house.

Exlee is not like Nik Nik. They don't require tattoos or any permanent obligation. But those of us who leave with good memories get the tattoo when we drop the X from our names. Not because we need to be reminded that we were providers, but because we're proud and we don't want anyone else to forget.

Slate leaves the room to finish readying. He must go at some point to report for his shift, but I don't notice. I'm too busy crying into his wife's skin while she shields my face from the entire world.

I spend the night thanking the universe for Reisha, for Slate, for Helene X, and anybody who has ever let me pass a too-dark night in their warmth. I was a violent child who committed the worst crimes; I was a broken child who had no reason to believe she wouldn't be broken forever, but through the love, care, and modeling of everyone around me I learned how to love and care for others. All because I wasn't thrown away based on how I behaved on my worst day.

I'm thinking about how I can survive life, how I can survive anything, as long as there are warm people who know what it looks like when someone is cracking, and know how to be the thing that holds us together, when it hits me: This will be the last time I can ever be with Reisha. Slate is too devoted. He once confided in me how he subscribes to the deification of the emperor, how he served him as a god. Having a sexual relationship with him and his wife after I'm crowned would probably fuck his head sideways. I should have cut this off the second he told me, but I didn't ever really think I'd get brought up. I definitely couldn't have predicted I'd give all this up to save Cross's neck.

Before I go I give Reisha everything she likes for the last time, trying to repay her, in some way, for never caring about my stained hands and crooked mouth. Without words, I thank her for every time she should have turned me away, and didn't.

—

SCREAMING. BLOOD. WAVES OF ENFORCEMENT. PILES OF DEAD.

I sit up in bed covered in sweat, the nightmare breaking apart around me. Of course, I recognize it. It was the same scene I witnessed in the water. Wiley bringing war, Ashtown losing. Dozens of enforcement officers marching through my streets.

But it's not real. It can't happen and, anyway, enforcement wears light gray–and–blue uniforms. These guys were wearing black. I check my cuff, see my morning assignment, and then briefly consider chucking the device across the room, leaving the runners, and changing my name.

I'm still in a mood when I report for duty half an hour later.

"Can't I go back to scraping bodies off the fucking asphalt?" I say, the kind of joke I'm only making so civilians can hear me making it, can see how unaffected all us runners are by the wave of death.

Mr. Raider laughs, but says nothing, an oldhead of few words.

Before us is a sight almost as disturbing as a thrice-broken corpse: a line of visitors from Wiley seeking entrance into Ashtown. This is usually duty for our public faces—Cheeks with his easy charm or Tear with her intense and serious persona. But they must be desperately needed running logistics for the upcoming town meeting, because there's no way my unfriendly ass and Refuses-to-Say-Three-Words-Together Raider were Silk's first choice for intake duty.

I've done border work before, even ran trespassers for a little while. But working with Wileyites when they were trespassing or visiting was easy. It was always one or two, a bit more on a market day but not all at once. Nothing like the sea of Wileyites whose applications for entry I am overseeing.

I glare at the next batch trying to gain entry into our town. This group has twelve, and they're all holding what look like garbage bags. I can't hear what they say when they walk up to Mr. Sai, who begins tapping into a screen the moment they approach. The group doesn't look scared. They should—Sai's a baby, but they've done basic training so they could kill them all twice before the first one hits the ground—but they don't. They are glaring at Sai like they're being inconvenienced.

"Your turn," Raider says.

"Yeah, yeah," I say, then watch as Sai hits the button that vibrates my cuff and makes these people my problem.

I don't have to fake a runner's rage when I walk up. My rage is real, and just gets realer when I walk up to their leader. She has long and artificially spiraling hair, and she looks relieved to see me, which I take personally. Am I not ferocious? Maybe I need to get some facial tattoos. Maybe mix in some decorative scarring like Black Dragon—numbers on my forehead, riddles on my cheeks.

I bare my teeth, but she still looks at me like I either am her friend or want to be.

"Thank *God* . . ." she says, and then just goes off complaining, despite the fact that I haven't addressed her and am giving zero indication I am listening. I crouch down, touch the desert with my fingers, then palm a handful of dirt. While she talks—*still talking*—I tilt my head back and waterfall the sand from my closed fist into my open mouth.

Now she's quiet, mouth agape in horror. That's more like it.

She's got to know what's coming, but she's still standing right in my face. We're just staring at each other, until she eventually opens her mouth to restart her tirade about Sai's customer service.

". . . and then *this man* said we weren't allowed without a pass, but . . ."

I look at Sai. Sai nods. I spit the mud mixture in my mouth directly in her face and man, it's a beaut. It's less a ball of mud than a wonderful brown spray that pixelates her face, though mostly concentrates in the middle, at her mouth and nose.

She starts crying. I realize that her friend is recording, has probably been recording the whole time. Welp. If they'd wanted charm they should've sent Cheeks.

I wipe my mouth with the back of my hand and turn to Sai. "Fuck do they want?"

"Said they wanted to make a donation. Himself hasn't put out a call that we need anything though. Told them they could buy a day pass and see, but they don't want to buy a pass because they're *helping.*"

The lilt on the last word means Sai doesn't like the look of their offerings. I kick over one of the bags. Tiny shoes and dirty clothes.

"Wiley can't do its own trash duty?"

I dig through the bag. The shoes are small, for babies and toddlers. Probably hand-me-downs from children who will never wear them again, easy enough to part with. But our kids don't wear shoes until they're much older than that. Their feet get trained from the terrain, and it ensures they're the first inside when a bright day is coming. The clothes are worse. Old Wiley fabrics, too thin to protect from the sun or sand if there's even a breath of wind, not to mention they're all at least a little stained or torn. Those in the wastes could do something with the fabric, pulp it into something new, sew enough together to make a decent covering. I have to be offended on their behalf.

I take a long time to respond, staring into the ice-blue eyes of the woman, trying to understand her. I shift my gaze to look at the woman beside her, the one recording.

"You all must love your city very much to think that even its trash would be enough to spare your life after trespassing."

Now they're scared. The mud-covered woman is crying more

heavily than I intended. Do people not get spit on in Wiley? I have a vague memory of it, but my early memories sometimes get corrupted with the past I've invented. This woman is certainly acting like I'm the worst thing that's ever happened to her. Good. Ash is to be feared. Not pitied.

I look back at Sai.

"You cleared for wet work?"

Sai nods. "Yessir."

"Okay. Kill them. Hide their bodies with the rest . . ."

. . . And they say Wileyites can't run.

Sai will chase at half speed, getting close but never catching them, so they'll think they've barely made it out alive and, hopefully, tell the story to their friends.

I look at the next person in line for entry. She's one of the few alone, not using a group of pale bodies as a substitute for bravery. She'd been standing off to the side, and had the good sense to move farther away from the last group after witnessing our exchange.

"You got a bag of trash you want to dump on us to feel good about yourself?"

She shakes her head. "Not trash, not exactly. I did come to donate, but I'll buy a pass. I'd like to stay and help, but if you aren't accepting volunteers I'll donate and go."

"What do you have?"

"My dad . . . he used to own shares of the mines out here. The ones—"

"I know the mines."

I don't, though. Not like the people who worked them. I'm too young. But I know the ones who did. Before he signed up, Blay used to work at the factories. That's where he lost three fingers from his right hand and gained a taste for strong drink he may never kick. And he was one of the lucky ones. He can still breathe without coughing. One of the few good things Senior ever did was seize and shut down the factories who refused to protect his people from toxins, injury, and future birth defects.

"Yeah," she says, a single word summing up that dark bit of

history. "Those ones. I inherited the profit from his shares, and I'd like to give it back. I don't want to sit on apartheid money."

My shock must show on my face, because she reads it instantly.

"We're not all oblivious monsters."

"No, I just . . . I didn't know you guys were using that word for this."

"It fits," she says.

No righteousness, no defensiveness. Only guilt, and not even the loud performative kind. It's rare to meet a Wileyite who acknowledges Wiley's role in keeping Ashtown down. So many of them want to be seen as missionaries, as saviors; it'd kill them to acknowledge that the goodwill they're giving is far less than what they've taken from us, far less than what's owed. I'm not sure I've ever seen someone who follows their guilt to accountability and action. Her hair is purple. I like her.

"Can you read?"

She seems surprised, but answers. "English, French, some sign."

My eyebrows go up at that. The city doesn't teach sign easily. They'd prefer to change or ignore anyone who'd use it. If she learned sign, she must have worked for it.

I turn around and wave Raider over. "You got badges?"

He nods and hands me an armband. I program it with my call sign. It turns purple.

I hand it to her. "Upper arm. Keep it visible and never take it off. You have problems, there's a panic button that will alert me. If I'm sleeping or unavailable, it'll forward to a runner named Cheeks."

Her eyes go wide. "*The* Mr. Cheeks?" The irritation on my face dims the excitement on hers. "Right, sorry. It's just . . . he's kind of a celebrity. Rumor is they tried to change the rules for the city's sexiest man contest to include noncitizens just for him."

"I'll escort her to processing," Raider says, before I can respond. Which means he must know I was about to go off, which means the runners must have heard about Cheeks and my fight at the briefing the other day. Gossipy bunch, runners.

"What do you need me to do?" she asks.

"We've got hundreds of families all sure their loved ones are among the dead, and even more witnesses wanting to give statements about what they saw yesterday. You good taking statements and descriptions?"

She nods, but there's a hitch in it. "Isn't . . . I mean . . . with everything I'm hearing about the bodies, are the descriptions really going to do any good?"

"No, but it gives them something to do besides yelling at us to work faster."

That's not the reason. It's Raider who tells her the truth.

"It's good," Raider says. "To let them talk about their dead. To see someone recording what they say. They won't have recognizable bodies. This will be their only clean remembrance."

This time there's no reservation in her nod. Raider leads her away and I look at the long line of unprocessed Wileyites like it's the road to hell.

—

I'M ACTUALLY GRATEFUL FOR HAVING SUCH A SHIT MORNING DUTY, BECAUSE IT MAKES THE PROSPECT of standing next to my brother on a stage seem less terrible. I'd thought we were having a runners meeting first, but instead they've got the stage set out front and a crowd was already forming when I entered the palace almost an hour ago.

I'm standing at attention, ready to be in the back of the train, when the emperor walks up and waves me forward to walk at his side. I'm surprised to be summoned, but I try to hide it as I fall into step.

Once I'm beside him, I lower my voice. "Are you announcing . . . ?"

"No. A world on fire is no time for a power shift. We'll announce after this is done. But it won't hurt to up your visibility in the meantime."

"I don't want to take Tear's spot."

She's always been the one at my brother's right hand while Cheeks took left, and if it wasn't for her love of her job she probably would have been promoted out years ago. But the higher up you go the less wet work you do and, what can I say? She's got a taste for it.

"You won't. Cheeks stepped out. You're taking left."

"What? Why?"

My brother doesn't answer, either because he knows I'm mostly asking myself out loud, or because he's the emperor and he doesn't have to answer anything he doesn't want to. We've all been a little off-kilter since we got a crop of corpses, but Cheeks especially has been ash-faced since it happened. At least, from what I can see through the distance I've been keeping.

I shelve the mystery for the current crisis. I'm about to stand center stage as an emperor's escort. I've filled in before, but never on such an important day, never for a crowd the size of the one I hear out front. I put a little iron into my step and bring my chin up until my form is as polished as the day I graduated.

Tear is waiting by the doors, and when she sees me she raises an eyebrow.

"You taking left?"

I nod, and her smile gets wider. "All right, ambition, I see you."

I smile back, but we both go stone-faced before the doors open. Civilians think we are heartless and bloodthirsty, itching for the kill. Ashtown only works if they keep thinking that. When we walk out into the light, we both glare at the waiting crowd. A man in front—tall, *visible*—isn't quite bowing his head. I look at Tear, she nods once, and moving with a quickness I reserve for showing off, I lash out and grab his neck. The crowd murmurs. I stare into his eyes like I've never seen a pair before, and bare my shiny bottom teeth like a dog with an underbite. He lowers his head fully, this time having to push into my fingers to do it.

When his head is the lowest in the crowd, I let him go. I spit at his feet, and take my place at my brother's left side. Everyone in the crowd hates me. I'm a bully and a monster. They'll never know that a monster is what I would be without the leather. They'll never know I'd die for them, each and every one.

—

NIK NIK DOESN'T SPEAK. HE'S A LOOMING OBSERVER AT THE BACK OF THE STAGE. MR. SPLICE IS ON mouthpiece duty, which is unusual for him, but we only have a few who do good public work and none are around that I can see. Still, he's doing fine. He's miles from the uncertain, quiet man I first met when he still kept his head permanently down. That was when he thought his inability to focus was something to be ashamed of. Before his promotion to tech proved that his tendency to deep dive—to fixate on one thing until there was no subject he couldn't learn, no skill he couldn't master—meant his mind was absolutely perfect. He'd just needed to find the right place for it. The confidence of being valued shows, and Splice speaks to the crowd now like he was born for it. He explains how from the moment we learned of our first body, the emperor—in his infinite wisdom—began working on a solution. Yesterday was our first confirmation that it worked, when our emperor was spared. He says soon Ashtown will have the security of knowing the emperor's wrath protects them all.

I'm not sure that last part is true, but if Ashtowners can trust anything, it's Nik's wrath.

I'm watching the crowd when something catches my eye. It's the wrong kind of shine. Glass. A camera? I press the shortlink on my cuff for a security request, then use the lasersight to mark the place in the crowd.

Moments later snakes of black leather swim through the mass of people, slick enough to not interrupt the speeches. They move like tree roots until they're ready to choke. I know they've found something because the black converges, and a moment later four runners are pulling someone off to the side. The camera is comically large. I've never seen anything like it. Then I see the body attached to it and I growl low in my throat. Wiley. The city was recording us. I look at Tear, but she's already all tension and clenched hands so I know she knows. Without turning his head, without giving any indication that he's noticed us at all, Nik Nik motions just slightly, his right hand flexing into a fist.

Stand down.

What? Stand down for Wiley? I don't show my shock. I trust my brother has his reasons and send the command along.

I tune back in to the talk just as Mr. Splice signals a woman in a long dress and too-clean apron who walks onto the stage and replaces him. I don't know her, but others must, because they're whispering long before she speaks. Apparently the Ruralites have decided to deviate from their usual reclusiveness. She says they are setting up a short-term center for those who feel lost and would like spiritual guidance. It feels like some kind of guerrilla conversion—come for the lemonade, stay because it's brainwashing—but then she says they'll be setting up in the activities room at the House to support the aid efforts already in place there. She even encourages Ruralites to come to the House if they are feeling overwhelmed or anxious about the recent events.

I can't help it. My stone face cracks, but luckily the crowd is just as shocked as I am. This person is speaking with the authority of the church. I'd heard Esther was more progressive than her predecessors. Word was she'd quietly removed sex provision from the Rurals' long list of sins after her inauguration, but this proves it. I wonder if her father's suicide made Esther finally appreciate the only place in the desert that cares for the mind as well as the body. Or maybe she just wants to give her father a reason to turn over in his grave. Spite can look just like care, if you squint.

When she finishes up, it's the House's turn to speak. Lexxi saunters to the mic, all hips and lip shine like the world isn't ending. He's an OG Housecat. He smiles at me and pretends to brush something off my collarbone with a wink before heading to the mic. I didn't know the Ruralite speaker, and Splice just drew the short straw, but Lexxi has been the go-to for the House's communications with outsiders since he retired from skinwork. What he has to say is unsurprising. The House is suspending rates for emotional services the way they always do during a crisis. They're also discounting the cost for skinwork, which *is* a trap, as providers are quick to refer a client they think needs emotional services in addition to what they've paid for.

Nik Nik doesn't speak, and there's nothing said about next

steps or the logistics of protecting civilians, which means this is only the first meeting I'm being dragged to today and the good stuff is being saved for later. This is just pageantry. Letting people feel like things are under control, letting them believe there is nothing to worry about.

It's bullshit, of course. At any moment that other world could go for round three, on an even bigger scale. How many will it be next? A thousand? Their whole stupid ark? It doesn't matter. We could do fuck all to stop it. We'd just have to stand with our best intentions and watch the people trusting us now get broken apart by nothing but air. And I'm sure they know that. If Ashtowners are good at anything, it's knowing when they're in the mouth of the shark. But they're nodding along, holding one another in relief at the charade anyway. They're just like me. All wrapped up in our soft lie of protection, not caring that we don't have a drop of milk.

CHAPTER EIGHTEEN

WHEN WE RETURN TO THE PALACE, NIK NIK FINALLY TURNS IN THE DIRECTION I'D EXPECTED US TO GO from the start: the runner's hall. This time when we walk through the door Tear and I break formation immediately. We trade our stank faces for wide, vicious smiles and bump forearms and fists and foreheads with the runners crowded around to greet us. I fake choke Sai, and the youngen laughs fearlessly along, before I'm picked up from behind by Dragon, to whom I will always be a youngen, who spins me around until I hook a foot behind his knee and send us both laughing to the floor.

It's one moment, a perfect one, of letting off steam, of feeling safe, of feeling sure. It's one moment that becomes more precious because we are all thinking it might be the last. Slowly, I realize people are quieting. Slowly, I realize something is wrong.

There is a runner on his knees before the emperor. Someone is asking for censure. In the middle of all this pain, blood, and suffering, someone is asking for a little more. For a moment, I think it's Cross—because masochism and holiness go together like flies and shit—but then I get closer. I'm ashamed to admit I'd know his back anywhere. The jokes are fully at an end now, and we form a semicircle around runner and emperor, some of us worried and others just curious, to hear what Mr. Cheeks has to confess. I elbow through a sea of backs, trying to get a better view. Runners are a nosy bunch, but they let me through to the front because they don't know exactly what we mean to each other, but they know that we do mean something.

Cheeks's eyes are wet as he looks up at Nik Nik, and it catches me. Of course I've seen him like this. When he talks about the mother he wants to love but doesn't really know, or the father he'll never know and always wishes he didn't still love. This moment stops me cold because every time I've seen Cheeks like this before, every time he was close to cracking, I saw it coming. But I was so distracted with Cross's depression, our mound of bodies, and my own flared up wounds, that I didn't see him. I think it's the first time since I decided I loved him that he wasn't my first and only thought in the chaos.

Imagine thinking you've lost the person you cherish most in the world, the person who filled the absence of your greatest loss, and you saw his corpse as a pile of mush. Seeing Nik undone must have felt like losing a father a second time, and if I'd been thinking clearly I would have spent the night talking him through it instead of fucking with Reisha. But . . . that would just be healing someone else instead of myself, wouldn't it?

Maybe choosing myself over him is *growth*. Maybe this distance is *healthy*, but right now it just feels like being a shit friend. Thinking Nik Nik was dead on the heels of realizing Esther was untrustworthy must have felt like losing a test from the universe itself. He must have seen Nik Nik walking back into camp like a second chance to do right.

Cheeks takes out a dagger and holds it up to his own neck. My first thought is Brand, slitting his own throat to spare his brother pain, and I lunge forward before I can stop myself.

"Settle, settle," Dragon says from my left, a whisper to preserve my pride even as he wraps a hand around my arm to hold me in place. While I was moving forward, he must have been shadowing me, knowing I would need to be held back.

A hand slides into my right, and I look down. And it is down, for as formidable as she is in every way, Mr. Em barely reaches my shoulder.

She squeezes my hand, and I settle calmer still.

If Nik Nik knows I almost broke protocol, he doesn't show it. He nods, giving Cheeks permission to proceed, and Cheeks squeezes the hidden trigger in his dagger's hilt and activates the wire embedded in the spine of the blade. He presses the glowing red metal against his neck, a blistering line cutting right through his highest rank.

I can smell his skin, skin that once drove me to delusion with wanting to taste, burning like meat. I begin to shake. Dragon and Em cradle me harder.

"I accept your demotion. Now I want your confession," Nik says.

My brother must be confused, even if I'm not. I know what Cheeks has been hiding, and it never once crossed my mind to rat him out. Just like it never crossed my mind that he would rat himself out. Nik Nik isn't showing emotion, but he must be feeling something. Hurt, surprise, fear—I'm not sure. But if you'd asked my brother to name the one person whose love and loyalty he could count on, he would have said Cheeks's name twice before he said mine. And now his favored one is on his knees, signaling that he has a betrayal to confess.

"I have fraternized with outside organizations," he says. "I told no secrets. I hid none for them."

"But you let your heart rest outside of Ash," Nik Nik says on a snarl.

Cheeks looks up. "Not all of it. Never all of it."

"All heart or no heart!" comes a yell from the crowd, and everyone picks it up.

All heart or no heart!

All heart or no heart!

I doubt they actually care about Cheeks mooning over an outsider. They're just delighting in the fall of the immaculate runner with the angel face the way insects delight in a new carcass. They'll slather themselves in his failure and pretend it's their own success.

Someone spits and it lands fat on Cheeks's face. Someone else kicks up dust to turn the wet into paste.

"If you repeat this contact, you will be exiled," Nik Nik says.

Cheeks nods.

"You know the punishment for first betrayal?"

Cheeks nods again, eyes still on Nik's boots. We all know it. The unluckiest of us have even acted as the emperor's hand to dish it out.

"What is your argument for leniency?"

"None. I don't want leniency," Cheeks says.

Someone boos. Someone mutters, *Kiss ass*. Someone is me.

Nik nods. The most severe is a full-on beat down. I would have begged for level two. A broken finger feels more than sufficient to square the ledger for a first offense.

"But I do . . . I do have a request for hand."

The crowd goes tense. Acting as hand of the emperor is no picnic. Beating on someone who may save your life later, but doing it hard enough to satisfy a man who you've sworn your life to, is like trying to balance lava with a blade: You're not going to win, and the trying is going to burn.

"Who is your nominee?" Nik Nik asks.

"Mr. Scales."

The breath goes out of me, and if I didn't have strong hands on either side of me I might have stumbled back. It might be the most idiotic fucking thing he's ever said in his whole life. First off, we're not so far from his outburst against me with Esther that I've forgiven him. Second off, I'm the highest combat-rated runner in the room. Third off, we're friends. We are very *publicly* friends, so I'll have to go extra hard to prove I'm not holding back.

Fourth off, and I'm not just bragging, I'm one of the strongest people in here besides my brother. I'm stronger than Cheeks and it's not close. Everyone in this room had a childhood of starvation, nutrient-light food, and toxic water that is possible to somewhat offset as an adult, but never fully. My Wiley upbringing doesn't just make me taller, it means I have more of my own teeth than most of them and, yes, that my bones will hold when theirs will break.

Cheeks may not know that last point, but he's felt the difference in our swings when we sparred. It's like he wants a new face or something.

"Approved," Nik Nik says, way too quickly. "Proceed."

I know what he's thinking. Having his old left hand getting broken up by his new left hand will make me look good. When my ascension is announced, Cheeks is the one people are going to wish was inheriting Nik's throne. This will shut those people up before they can speak. It'll put the image of my triumphing over Cheeks in their heads, and civilians won't care that he didn't fight back.

Nik Nik looks over Cheeks's head at me. "Do you accept?"

Cheeks turns back toward me, but he's no more capable of meeting my eyes than he was Nik's.

"I accept," I say, and crack my knuckles.

—

THEY WILL SAY IT WAS BECAUSE CHEEKS INSULTED ME. THEY WILL SAY, *OH YEAH, THOSE TWO WERE friends and she was the better runner, but she let him get ahead of her because they were friends. Then he fucked up and spoke cross-ways so she came for his job, his throat, and his skin.*

They'll pat me on the back and congratulate me on being the most get-evenest bitch in the dirt, for making *run up, get done up* my doctrine. When they find out I'm emperor's blood, they'll laugh even harder. They'll say Cheeks messed with the wrong mother-fucker. Of course I put him down hard. They'll say I made him confess, and bullied him into picking me as an avenger.

They'll never again talk about us like we are the same person. They'll never wonder which of us is in love, and which of us is in the dark.

What happens next will make it so the past decade and a half never happened. I'm already in mourning.

Cheeks strips.

I take off my shirt, because I can throw away the straps I use as a bra while I work, but I could never wear this shirt again if it had my best friend's blood on it.

The other runners are hooting. They like seeing me work. More than that, Cheeks has always been the best runner out here, and they've waited his whole career to see him bleed.

Because it's viewed as an uncontrollable impulse, Cheeks is allowed to fight back. But when he stands before me, looking me dead in the eyes, he folds his arms behind his back to grab his own wrists. He'll hold himself steady, no matter what happens. He won't fight, but we both knew he wouldn't. In response to the gesture, I slide off my gloves. There's a murmur of disappointment from the young, who love seeing what new tricks I've put into my hands, but a nod of respect among the old.

My body still knows Cheeks's body. I want to believe his knows mine too, despite never having made even half so serious a study as I have. I'm hoping we can have a conversation anchored entirely in the skin.

With the first blow, the flat of my fist against the fleshiest part of his middle, I say, *Your hair was short, when we first met.*

With the second, placed just to the side of the first, hard enough to qualify as punishment but close enough he won't feel it as an entirely separate pain, I say, *I was so afraid of you then, you knew so much and I knew so little.*

When I go for the face, I won't use my hands. I'm too good with them. I make it look to the crowd like it is the hard edge of my knee risking a break to his perfect mouth but it's just the flat plane of my thigh, and it's only the widest part of his chin. The concession tells him, *You are the most beautiful creature I have ever seen. You are perfect. If I could have made you love me back, I would have been able to love myself forever.*

After that, every blow just tells him I love him. I say, *I love you,* with a boot to the thigh. I say, *I love you,* with a rib kick that was more side of the foot than toe. I say, *I love you,* with a backhand. He moves onto his back, wheezing, so I straddle him and tap love out on his ribs until I'm worried they've cracked; then I switch to his collarbones because right now love means not giving him a punctured lung. And when the cracked and red skin of my knuckles meets his red-coated teeth, my blood against his bones and his blood against mine, that is when I love him most.

"I'm satisfied," says the emperor after I don't know how long, and the tension runs out of me.

I've still got my knees on either side of Cheeks's hips. At the cease order I fall forward and catch myself with my palms. He flinches, even though the sanctioned beating is over, and I understand. I let my head fall, my mouth and nose against the place where the skin of his forehead meets the thick black of his hair, and I inhale deeply, deep enough to embed the smell of him into my lungs like a cancer that I hope kills me, or at least is still with me on the day that I die. Because it's my last chance. I know he will never let me near him again.

I get to my feet and step away quickly. I wipe the back of my hand across my mouth like I've been devouring messy prey. No, not prey. It doesn't feel like I've killed something I was meant to kill. It feels like I've committed cannibalism but closer. Hurting him feels like devouring pieces of myself. As Cheeks is helped to his feet I see him notice me. He is injured as bad as he's ever been, and, for once, I will not be the one tending to him. I am more devastated than I've been in years, and he will not be the one comforting me. He stares at my face, taking in the signs that I'm trying not to cry like he's trying to decide if he cares.

He doesn't.

Our friendship ends when, and because, he looks away.

It's been ages since I've thought of a future, any future, with Cheeks. But it might have been. Maybe in a year, maybe in a decade, maybe when we were both old and gray at the end, it might have been. Having all those possibilities close off all at once is like seeing a cluster of stars wink out: It may not materially change anything, but I'll always know my world is darker now than it could have been.

I move as fast as I can out of the meeting room and burst into the nearest gym like it's a sanctuary. I hear the door open behind me, and turn to see eyes every bit as haunted as my own. Of course, a mandatory meeting would include those on leave.

"What do you want?" I ask, all bark but too pathetic for him to flinch.

I see it. I see how much he wants to ask if I'm okay. I see, impossibly, how he wants to help. And I see how he's finally learned me well enough to say, "You got anything left? I think this tired out, I can take you."

I look down at the mats under our feet, finally registering the gym around us. I should walk away. My hands are already beat to shit, but there is something in the throes of both mourning and hunger under my skin like an itch begging for a scratch. Like I need to hurt someone who will hurt me back.

"You as strong as you look, Cross?"

"Come try me, Scales."

I pull my gloves back on and the pain is sharp and exactly what I need. The tight material squeezes my already-swelling knuckles like a vise, and it lets me exhale deep.

I don't warn him before I strike, but he doesn't punish me for it. It only takes a few minutes for me to understand he's going easy on me. It takes longer for him to understand I'm going easy on him. He's been smart enough to never be on sparring rotation with me, and now I've finally got the chance to lay hands on the man I hate the most and I . . . barely hurt him. When I could rib tap him and instead spin away, it surprises us both. He knows I dislike him. He knows I'd rather be breaking my skin against his edges than Cheeks's any day. He's offering me the chance to get exactly the most toxic kind of relief, but relief nonetheless.

"I don't want to fight you," I say when we've only just started, surprising myself with the news as well as him. I don't just not want to fight him, I don't want to hurt him. No, worse than even that. I don't want him to be hurt, and I wish I could make him less hurt than he already is.

He's got a big-ass forehead, but his eyebrows manage to crawl almost all the way to his hairline. I turn away because I can't help his confusion.

I don't know what this means either.

"THIS IS THE BEST PART," CHEEKS SAYS.

We're sitting on his couch, and he's catching the light the way he doesn't know he does. I used to think it was such a shame, the way he'll never know the real color of his eyes. It's courting fire to take a mirror outside during a bright day, but it's the only way he'd ever see what a fucking vision he is in the full light of the sun. Maybe if he knew how beautiful he was he would have known to see me coming, would have known instantly how I felt, because he would have known it was inevitable that anyone who saw him alone too many times was at risk of loving him.

"This is the best part," he says again, and it's not the second or even the third time.

We're high as shit and watching the aftermath of a bright day, when all the colors that had been bleached to white rush back and everything looks rich and wonderful.

This was years ago. Cheeks doesn't even have this couch anymore, and I haven't been to his new place enough times to even really know what it looks like.

But he's right. This is the best part. It was. When we were young and the days felt long and empty and we had no obligations but to each other. It was my very favorite part. And it's over now.

The hard thing to accept is that it wasn't hate or indifference that ended us. It was love. If I didn't love him, I'd be able to be his friend after breaking him. If he didn't love Nik Nik, he would never have made me do it. Cara said my brother broke the skin of those who loved him, and she said it like he should be put down for it. But he isn't the one who's earned that punishment. I am.

I don't want to face that. I want to believe Cheeks and I are still watching the color burst back into the world, still giddy with the explosion. All that light and possibility, the blues so blue it's like we've never seen blue before. We laughed loud as morning birds on that couch, and I want to imagine us still there, still smiling, still safe from all the horrors love can bring.

PART THREE

. . . What have you in these houses? And what is it you guard with fastened doors?

Have you peace, the quiet urge that reveals your power?

Have you remembrances, the glimmering arches that span the summits of the mind?

Have you beauty, that leads the heart from things fashioned of wood and stone to the holy mountain?

Tell me, have you these in your houses?

Or have you only comfort, and the lust for comfort, that stealthy thing that enters the house a guest, and then becomes a host, and then a master?

—Kahlil Gibran,
"On Houses,"
The Prophet

CHAPTER NINETEEN

I DON'T EXACTLY GET WHAT ADAM IS DOING, BUT I HOPE HE DOES IT FAST. I HATE HIM, BUT WE NEED him. I wonder if this is how the city felt about Adam back in his day.

"You're not paying attention," Adam says, and it's not a question.

"Yes, I am." I'm not. "I just don't know what I'm supposed to be looking for. This isn't my kind of work."

While Adam studies the raw material from the cave, trying to figure out how to use it to protect a wider area, runners are on a rotating schedule examining readouts from just before each event so we can predict the next one.

"Things that are marked abnormal before both events. It's not that hard."

"How am I supposed to know what a *normal* amount of pressure per square inch is for the fucking world?"

Adam leans down. "Figure. It. Out."

I squeeze my gloves to heat them. "I'll figure—"

"Wait." Splice steps between us. "I've got something that can help. If I can use your workstation?"

I sneer at Adam, then nod and move to give Splice access.

He types so quickly it makes my earlier pecking seem like a toddler's walk, and when he's done, colors appear over the numbers I've been studying.

"There. I figured out our baselines and made a code for highlighting abnormalities. Red for excess, green for low. Now we just have to record the anomalies surrounding each body, and see if any happen before all . . . before each event."

Meaning we analyze the data around each and every corpse, to see if something happened before their deaths that we can trace. Then we have to work backward to see how long before each event the anomaly began, and we have a countdown. Sounds simple, but it's hundreds of data points to look at for dozens of bodies. Splice's code will help narrow down the time, but we're still talking ages.

Splice knows I can't quit. There are barely enough literate runners in the first place, and that's with Splice taking so many shifts I'm worried for his sleep cycle. Being Adam's research assistant feels like doing exactly the kind of job we became runners to avoid for exactly the kind of asshole we swore we'd never work for. But the work is important, and this . . . this giant piece of shit who happens to share my blood is currently our only hope.

"Thank you, Splice . . ." I say, then turn toward Adam. ". . . for being *actually* useful."

It's a lie, obviously. Of course Adam's useful. All our atmospheric data comes from satellites his company put into the air and the rest comes from collection drones his company funded to predict bright days. If anyone is useless here, it's me, and that's why I'm swiping at everyone around me like a sand cat. Because when the next batch of bodies arrives, and everything in my gut tells me it will, it will be a failure all my own.

That's why, for all my whining, I put my head down and record anomalies like office work is what I was made for.

I'm used to working with my hands on metal, and my eyes are burning with the switch to bright screens and tiny letters, but a few hours in I've begun to sense something beyond the killer migraine forming behind my eyes.

"Splice, are you seeing the localized pressure fluctuations?"

He nods. "Yeah, I think it's consistent but they only precede the event by forty seconds."

I hadn't even checked that yet. This is when I realize even if we find consistent readings spiking or dropping before each event, if it only happens right before, it will be useless as far as prediction or preparation goes. I realize then what Adam must know but hasn't told us: This might be for nothing. There might not be a fluctuation that happens far enough in advance of each event to be relevant. We're hoping we'll get a lifeboat out of this. It might just be rubble.

Is this what science is? Putting your blood and sweat into something that might be nothing? Well, I fucking hate it.

I finally begin to get excited when I notice a massive fluctuation across each of my files.

"I think I've got something with the temperature fluctuations."

"What? Ground or sky?"

I look up. "I . . . didn't realize those were different categories."

I look back at my screen. Yep. There's a little *g* at the top of one and *a*—I'm guessing for atmosphere—near the others, but I'd been logging them as the same. I'd been logging them as the same this whole time.

I kick the table.

"It's okay. It takes awhile—"

"We don't have awhile!"

We don't even know how much time we have, because my dumb ass can't even complete simple data logging without messing up.

"It's not your fault," Cara says, somehow appearing in the doorway.

She has a way of entering rooms where it never feels like she's arrived, just like she's always been. It impresses me, but my own incompetence just makes me resent anyone who is good at anything, so I give her a snarl too.

"I'm going to put a tracker with a proximity alert on you, I swear to god."

She tilts her head. "Bell'd be cheaper."

"I'm trying to keep Splice in work," I say, 'cause it's easier to lash out at the whole damn world than admit I'm mad at myself.

She smiles, a white moon peaking out in the cloud-streaked night of her face. Her reputation is so big, the stories about her so varied, I don't want this little thing to be missed: Cara has a great fucking smile.

It pulls me in until I'm staring at her a bit too intensely for a bit too long. I clear my throat and look down at my screen.

"You need something?" I ask, though I'm not sure what in the whole wide desert I could possibly give to her.

"Your station," she says. "I'm taking your shift."

"I thought you had business in the city," I say, even as I stand up and move away so fast you'd swear my chair was suddenly hot.

"We shifted things around. Dell's going to stay with the kids. I'll be working on this until we have a way to keep Ash safe."

Kids. Of course. I hadn't given much thought to what she and Dell had been up to in the almost a decade since she dropped off the radar, but now that she says it, it makes sense.

She takes off her jacket and settles into my seat. She stares for a moment, then turns to Splice. "You've flagged fluctuations?"

At first, he just stares, the magnifiers over his eyes making him look even more wide-eyed than usual. But then he sputters out a *yes* and a nod. I realize Splice hasn't been around her much since this whole thing started, so the mystique of her hasn't quite worn off. Probably still thinks of her as *the traverser* and not *Cara.*

She ignores his uncertainty and turns back to her screen. "Nice, this will be even easier than what I'm used to."

I tap into my cuff to log the reassignment. If we weren't in crisis, someone taking my job would mean I got the day off. But as it is, I just wait in dread to see where Silk sends me. This *all-hands-on-deck* mode of working has meant I've been shoveling some shit, and I can't imagine whatever I get next will be better.

I'm still waiting for my reassignment when I hear the gasp.

I look up to see Adam standing in the doorway, staring at Cara. She's glaring at her screen, very pointedly ignoring him but I can see her eyes aren't moving as efficiently as they were a second ago, and there's a new tension in her shoulders. She might be going for nonchalance, but she's frozen more like prey not wanting to be spotted. I bet she's real good at that. Blending in, not being spotted.

The whirring of Adam taking a step toward her is all that breaks the silence. I think even Splice and I are holding our breath, though I don't know why this moment is so tense. Cara and Adam have been stuck in the same room a dozen times now.

"Didn't think I'd see you working for me again."

"I'm not working for you. I'm working for them," she says.

She doesn't look up to say it. If she did she'd see the confusion on Adam's face is genuine, and so is the loss.

"This is what you did for him? In the city?" I ask, because the strained silence is killing me.

"No. I would have, if I'd stayed long enough to get promoted." After a moment, she sighs. "Before I found out how immoral the company was, all I ever wanted to be was an analyst."

"And all I ever wanted was for you to be my successor," Adam says.

Now Cara looks up, and her gaze is dagger-sharp. "You're confusing me with the man you killed."

She holds him in that thick gaze just a second too long, before finally looking back at her work. Adam offers a shrug. This is the gulf between them, I suspect. He doesn't understand why she's holding against him that he killed someone else. I mean, I only barely get it. But Cara isn't here for herself, or the emperor. She's sitting here doing a job she no longer wants under a man she never wants to see again, to save the lives of people who don't even like her all that much. You'd think she was a god. You'd think we were all her children.

My cuff beeps. I've been reassigned. Splice gives me a desperate *Don't leave me here with them* look, and I blow a kiss as I go.

—

"WORSE AND FUCKING WORSE," I SAY, KICKING UP DIRT JUST TO DO IT AS I STAND IN FRONT OF THE palace. The sun and wind are making me squint, but I'd be mean-mugging anyway.

If processing Wileyite volunteers set my teeth wrong, escorting Wileyite *special guests* is going to make them fall out of my gums.

"Least we don't have to be polite," Tear says.

I nod. We've been instructed to dial up the quiet-scary runner charm for the visitors. No jokes, all scowl. I stretch out my shoulders and wiggle my arms, knowing I'll be walking extra-stiff to complete the image once they arrive.

The ride that pulls up is a too-shiny silver that reflects the sun at us like an assault. It's low, and I flinch when the front scrapes as it enters the palace's long driveway. I bet I could crack the oil pan with about twenty minutes of off-roading. If it even has an oil pan? These electric jobs from the city all look like puzzles inside to me. They aren't meant to be worked on easily with your own hands. They're meant to be turned in and picked up again.

Two more Wiley rides pull up behind the first, and beside them are the four cycle runners who were supposed to escort them in . . . though they may have played it like a hunt. I wave to Mr. Em, who waves back before peeling off and heading back to border patrol.

"Not it," Tear says as we're walking to greet the newcomers.

"Ass," I say, as I walk up to the driver's side door and, sigh, *open it* for the Wileyite.

We've got it wrong, I realize. Nik Nik always insists on driving himself, so I opened the driver's door. But the driver scrambles backward to open the door to the backseat instead, allowing the two women to step out.

"Mr. Mayor," I say, nodding at the first woman before turning to the second, "Mr. Vice Mayor."

I know good and damn well they don't use "Mr." like we do, but I like seeing the mayor's little shudder. She opens her mouth, but the vice mayor taps her wrist.

"Mr., it's a term of respect here, right? From your prior ruler?" the vice mayor says, and I remember what feels like an eternity ago in Adam's living room. I watched these women on TV, and he told me the mayor ran on a platform that threw us under the bus to get elected, while the vice mayor didn't.

"Yes," I say, a little thrown by her pride and excitement in knowing.

The vice mayor, still inexplicably excited, whispers to the mayor, "A former ruler heard that you use Mr. before someone's name to show respect, but the person who told him that didn't explain that it only applied to men, and the ruler had as many female generals as male, so they all became Misters."

They tell this story a lot. Some of us even tell it too. But mostly using *Mr.* was just a way of weaponizing the gender roles of Senior's enemies against them. A rival could intercept a message saying, Mr. Tatik is going to rob you tomorrow, and still never see her coming.

"Well, it means *man* where we come from," the mayor says, visibly upset. "And calling us that is an insult."

I've been gone long enough to have forgotten how hard up the city is about genders. They want gender like a border, something fixed, something to be defended from trespass. We like genders like landmasses here, like puddles that congregate, evaporate, and re-form. Even at the House, you choose *each day* which stage you want to dance on, and only then have you announced what space you're occupying. Someone might bounce between the masc and femme stages, or they might exclusively dance enby. Helene X was the rare bird who danced on the same stage most of the time, but I understood that. In the city, she'd had to fight to be called what she was. Couldn't blame her for never wanting to let it go. I wonder what this woman would call Helene? Would she acknowledge Helene as a woman? Or would it be just another gate she'd thrill to keep?

The mayor and vice mayor are both blond, but the mayor's hair and eyes are darker. The vice mayor is true Wileyite, all ice and white-gold. The mayor can't be more than a few generations in. I wonder if her own imperfect belonging would make her more open to protecting others. Or maybe it's the opposite. Maybe hating others is the easiest way to prove you belong, even if you're just doing to others what someone wants to do to you.

"*Another* word for man? Seems like overkill. Maybe that's why we took it away," I say, my voice lower and more robotic than strictly necessary. I gesture toward the palace, where two runners open the doors. "This way."

Once we move toward the building, four enforcement members get out of the car behind them and my heart stutters. I remember enforcement wearing pale gray and blue. These ones, these ones are wearing all black. I'm too struck to move, but Mr. Tear blocks their path. She doesn't saying anything, though. She doesn't have to. She said, *Not it,* so I have to pretend to be in charge.

"Two," I say. "No more. The others stay behind."

These are orders straight from Himself, not just us being assholes, but truth be told I'd do it anyway. God, I hate their faces. When I say only two can go, they look at one another like spoiled children.

"Or none?" I offer as an alternative.

"You two," the mayor says, indicating the nearest.

The ones left behind get even stankier stank faces, dwelling on their own lack rather than their teammates' win. They say runners are bad, but we're nothing like this. They may be a group, but they're not a team. Not the way we are. How can you swear you'd give your life for anyone if you'd slit your fellow soldier's throat just for getting a better detail than you?

Overall, the city's finest leaders and officers have not impressed me. Which is why it sets my jaw wrong to hear the mayor say, after a dramatic sigh, "Come on. Let's get this over with."

The vice mayor, to her credit, doesn't look like she wants to rush. She's looking at everything from the carving on the palace doors to Tear's silver tattoos like there's nowhere else she'd rather be, like the whole world is brand-new.

We walk to the right, avoiding any dungeon entrances, and take our guests down the very long hallway to the least used room in the whole compound. Though you'd never know it. When the double doors are opened, the throne room is shining from the dark-metal chandeliers and sconces—precisely the same deep obsidian as the emperor's teeth—to the accents winking from the velvet wall hangings. It is lush and cool, and in the center of the stage at the back of the room sits the emperor in the black-and-gold oversized throne that gives the room its name. He's wearing his showcoat, and it pools beneath him like some kind of massive pet warming his feet. His posture is disrespectfully lax, leaning back with one leg pulled up on the chair beside him, a hand casually dangling over his knee. It looks like effortless posture, but it's really just him highlighting his most dangerous rings. The emperor's rings are the subject of so many stories in the city, I imagine just having them out will set the tone for the meeting.

I go to my knee before my brother.

"Mayor O'Connell and Vice Mayor Hawthorne, Your Majesty."

He waves a painted nail, freeing me to stand and move beside the throne.

The mayor nods, but the vice mayor crosses an arm over her chest and lowers her head. Jesus, what has she been reading? I'm still not sure who annoys me more, but I can see the second has my brother's attention. He waves again.

"You may approach," I say, ushering them forward.

"I was surprised to receive your ping . . ." the emperor says.

He's trotted out his gruffest voice for them. It makes him sound removed, not just like English isn't his first language, but like human isn't his preferred tongue.

". . . What can I do for the city of glass?" He smiles so wide on *glass* his teeth shine like razors.

"We have a credible report that you survived the kind of attack we've been dealing with. We were hoping we could share knowledge, resources. Face this threat together."

Nik Nik . . . stares. No blinking. No breathing. Just eyes undoubtedly darker than any she's been in a room with in years emptying into the mayor. Then, precisely on cue, Nik, Tear, and I all begin laughing the runners' laugh, the braying echoing off the floor and ceiling both. The most important part of a runner's laugh is keeping your mouth wide enough to consume your enemies. The second is keeping your eyes dead and mirthless.

The sudden sound startles enforcement, and they jump and turn around mistaking the echoes of our voices for new soldiers. The mayor does the same. The vice mayor . . . she's recording on her cuff. I could probably gut punch her and she'd smile. *A real runner sucker punch! How novel.*

"Scales," Nik Nik says after even the echoes have died down, "tell the mayor why we're laughing."

I clear my throat and do my best Wileyite impression. "'We don't know anything concrete, but we would be naïve not to look at the savages outside our borders.'"

The impression is a good one, too good, and it's my mother who has come out of my mouth.

"We had no data," the mayor says, a panic in her voice I could lap up all day. "It would have been reckless not to entertain all possibilities."

"And then you used this tragedy to increase funding and approve force allowances against noncitizens," Nik Nik says. "Meaning my people. Meaning me."

"Action reassures panic. Plans calm people down. Making a funding motion eased their dread. Come on, you've seen these bodies, you can't let us all suffer that fate because I publicly considered the possibility of your involvement."

Nik is still staring at her. "Tear, how many of my people have been killed on bright days while Wiley refused to open their doors?"

"Two thousand four hundred and six," Tear says.

"Oh, now, Mr. Tear, that's not fair. Tell me just how many it's been during the mayor's reign."

"Seventy."

"Well, there you have it. I'll let sixty-five more of you die, and then save the seventy-first. And the scales will be even."

"Sixty-two," says the vice mayor, speaking to him for the first time. "You'd only need to let sixty-two more die. We haven't been . . . fully transparent about our casualties."

Nik Nik and I share a look. Splice's tech had only recently picked up chatter about the additional three bodies, and we'd wondered if the city would ever be open about them. The Wileyites who died were disgraced, the bodies managing to stay out of the news only because they were all incarcerated.

"Look, I'm sorry. Is that what you want to hear? My people were scared. They thought it was God or ghosts and that kind of uncertainty is—"

"Bad for your market?" Nik Nik cuts in.

The mayor takes a breath. "I'm sorry. They needed an explanation, and I gave them one. You'd do the same. I know you would."

That's the sound of me losing first pick at next shift. I'd bet Tear hard that the mayor would go dodgy and blame a publicist or speech writer or something. Still, I don't expect my brother to nod, as if the excuse is sufficient. This must be diplomacy. Or a lie? Or maybe they're the same. Nik Nik gestures toward one of the runners by the door, who nods in response and leaves.

The black-jumpsuit crowd gets nervous yet again when they hear one set of footsteps come back with two. These kids are looking for violence like they're afraid they'll miss the opportunity to use their fancy new stun sticks. Runners get to be calm, always assured that violence will come, and when it does, we'll be ready.

They relax, but only slightly, when the second figure isn't a new soldier, but a Wileyite.

Adam doesn't employ half the flash of Nik, but he's certainly cleaned up to put on a show. He's changed from the crumpled suit I'm used to. Now he's not wearing a suit at all. It's black pants with legs too wide to be practical, and a shirt whiter than anything I've ever seen in the palace walls. He's using the same walking aid as before, but the dust that's been settled on the dark silver has been brushed off.

"Macklyn," he says, nodding to the mayor, before turning to the vice. "Abigail."

"This is where you've been?" the mayor asks, equal parts confusion and irritation at seeing him, so we have at least that in common.

"We've met?" the vice mayor, Abigail, asks.

This sets Adam back on his heels. It hurts him, being unrecognized. I don't know if it hurts worse thinking it's because he's become visibly disabled, or just that he was never as important as he thought he was.

"Adam Bosch," I say, as if announcing him to the emperor.

Abigail's eyes go cartoon-wide. Adam smiles as he scales the stage to stand beside the emperor.

"This man is not to be trusted," the mayor says. "There's no telling how many crimes he's committed."

"Now, now. If that was true surely you would have had your people charge me," he says.

Her lips go tight. I know that look. I'm betting Adam spent his time in the city accruing threats and insurances to become untouchable. Untouchable, but not un-exileable. I remember his house, so many floors down the mayor could pretend he'd seen some kind of justice.

"This man is our negotiator. He'll name our price," Nik Nik says.

"I'm listening," says the mayor, but she's clearly not happy about it.

"The attacks are multiversal, coming from a world very much like our own."

The mayor rolls her eyes. "We have our own experts. We've been briefed on dop backlash."

"We've discovered a compound that, when encapsulating a person, deflects the attack back to its originator."

The mayor uncrosses her arms to step forward.

"That's how you did it," Abigail says, looking at Nik. They must have seen images of the body, must have thought for a moment their biggest enemy was no more.

"This material, is it part of the Eldridge research you never handed over?" the mayor asks.

I remember him saying it was the same compound his company used in the machine that let people traverse, but I keep myself from nodding when I see his blank face.

Instead, Adam shrugs. "Who's to say?"

I wonder what the consequences would be if he'd said yes. Jesus. This is why I hate bureaucracy. Every word a land mine.

"*Anyway,*" he says, "we need a more efficient delivery system. The substance seems to work regardless of dilution, and it'd be best if we could cover as much space as possible . . ."

". . . You want access to our atmosphere. To infuse this material into it?"

"Precisely."

"Can you provide data that says it's safe for a general population?"

"Of course. It's already passed human trials and has long-term experimentation showing no . . . unusual setbacks."

"Human trials like your former employees?"

Adam's smile is wide. "Wouldn't that be something?"

The mayor sighs. "The environmentalists will shit, but I can invoke emergency protocol to get it through." Her eyes narrow and she looks back at Nik Nik like she's just remembered something. "And? What's the price?"

"You have to share. You must allow Ashtowners into your walls to use the coverage until the threat has passed."

"Out of the question!"

Nik Nik's eyes slit in a flare of rage, but Adam's anger manifests in a smirk, a smirk that sits below eyes glaring with every bit of the emperor's anger. They don't just look like brothers now; they look like twins. Twin demons, earthbound and endlessly powerful.

"That part is nonnegotiable, I'm afraid," Adam says, the politeness doing nothing to take the edge from his voice.

"I would be unelectable," the mayor says, calmer now, like she's finally sensing the danger.

"Yes . . . but you would be in one piece. You must know it's the elite coming over. You may not be as important there as you are here, but your time will come. I've checked the file. You are alive there. I trust you've seen the bodies. Is that a fate you'd chance?"

"Just because I'm alive there doesn't mean I'm coming over."

"Well, you know yourself best. Do you think you are the kind of person who will do anything to survive? Do you think you would be so ambitious to claw at life at any cost? If not . . . then you have nothing to worry about."

Wileyites always sweat when they leave their atmosphere, but the line of wet on her brow looks like pure fear. To go from import to mayor in a few tiny generations? Yeah, I bet the mayor has ambition in spades.

She must have that same realization. She clenches her jaw one last time then nods.

"Fine. I'll do it."

CHAPTER TWENTY

"... HOW MANY ARE WE EXPECTED TO HOUSE?"

"Just the ones at risk, those who are alive over there, too."

"If you infuse our atmosphere, Ashtown can have the bottom ten levels."

Sounds good to me, but Adam scoffs.

"Be reasonable. The bottom ten floors are full of the equipment that keeps the city alive. You intend to put cots around your sewage processing? Sleeping bags on your water filtration plant?"

She sets her jaw hard, and now I understand the wisdom of having Adam negotiate. We could never have known that, and they would have done to us precisely what they did to those who built the city's wall all those generations ago. Another stack of false promises from the city built on them.

"Ten floors. Twenty-five to thirty-five. One family per housing unit."

"The student and retiree housing," she says, understanding.

"Yes. Your least desirable and least inhabited floors. You can give floor upgrades to the current residents using your eminent domain funding, or throw a hardship tax break their way."

"Higher floors would feel like we're devaluing their progress," she says.

"And you know as well as I that there are more at the bottom than the top. Do you want to secure your reelection, or your dinner party invitations?"

"Both, ideally," she says.

"You let the Ashtowners in, and I'll make sure everyone is still alive and in one piece to sip champagne together when this is all through."

"No, this can't just be a ploy to bypass immigration. The day you begin synthesizing the atmosphere, we'll let them in. Not a moment sooner."

Adam tilts his head. "If you go back on your word, I'll abort the process and save myself alone."

"I wouldn't expect any less," she says. "I'll discuss it with my cabinet. If they agree, I'll have a treaty drawn up. How soon can it be ready?"

"The synthetization should be completed by week's end. The technology to anticipate and predict the attacks will be ready much sooner, and I'll throw that in for free."

"I am simply stunned by your generosity," she says, voice so flat it makes me proud.

"Who could blame you?" he says.

She opens her mouth to say all kinds of colorful things, I'm sure, but then she thinks better of it. "Let's wrap this up. What else?"

At first his face doesn't change, but then he allows confusion to enter it.

"Else?"

"Well, aren't you going to ask for some kind of finder's fee? To regain control of your assets or something?" she asks. "You can't expect me to believe you did this out of the goodness of your heart and your only condition is we save a bunch of dirt eaters."

He masks his reaction before she can see it, but not before I can. The mayor is precisely right. Adam Bosch absolutely did this all for no reward.

He looks over at Nik Nik. "I assure you, my compensation is handled elsewhere."

Oh, that will keep the city on its toes.

"Should have figured," the mayor says, sounding less like the floor she lives on, and more like the floors her parents probably came from. She looks at Nik. "I shouldn't have to warn the likes of you to be careful . . . but a snake beats a dog every time."

She sounds so sure, but Nik Nik, Tear, and I share a confused look. A snake beating a dog? Unheard of. Even the smallest surviving breeds have adapted to bite the head off anything that hisses.

"Spoken like someone with little knowledge of Ashtown hounds," Nik Nik says.

"Fair enough," the mayor says, then turns to me. "We're ready."

I nod, and escort her back outside.

In the hall Cara is carrying her screen. Her face softens when she sees me, but then flashes to something guarded when she looks at my charges.

"Thompson?" she asks, and it takes me a second to register the enforcement officer she's addressing.

"Pigeon," he says, like it's a name.

She reaches up, touching my bicep without thinking. I've been doing this dance where I've decided to pretend Cara is interesting rather than attractive because I would never in a million years act on it, but the contact is a quick lightning strike that makes me meet her eyes. I must look at her like I want something, because she swallows and looks away first. Of course, she's got something to lose. Monogamy is about fifty-fifty in Ash, but the default standard in the city. Having seen Dell up close, I wouldn't risk it all for a roll with me either.

"A meeting," she says. "Can you call one?"

I nod. "The usuals?"

She nods, then melts back toward Adam's workroom that used to be an office. I watch her go, getting the feeling that I'm not the first, twentieth, or last to watch her dark form disappear into a space I can't see.

The mayor clears her throat.

I look at her for an extra second, just long enough for her to remember that I don't work for her, and the man I do work for thinks of murder as more of a tool than a sin. But eventually I continue on my way, anxious to get this particular group out of my palace.

I almost correct the thought to *Nik's palace,* but it's not and I'll need to get used to owning what's mine.

—

I'D CUFFED FOR A MEETING WHILE I WAS STILL WALKING THE WILEYITES OUT, BUT I'D PUT IT AT HIGH alert since Cara seemed pressed. I take a minute to commiserate with Tear about how much we hated every inch of that visit, before heading to the office-turned-lab for whatever briefing Cara needs to give. I'm not quick enough, though, because they've already started fighting.

"What if she finds out?" Cara says.

Adam practically pouts. "O'Connell? She was vice when I operated and she never found out so much as my grocery list."

"*I* found out your secrets. You're not that slick."

"*You* are nosy and bored. *She* has a job."

"You're risking the deal."

"I made the deal!"

Splice has been made small in the corner, so I walk over to him. "Care to share?"

"Adam Bosch secured safe passage for Ashtowners in the city."

"Yeah, I was there. That a problem?"

"He did it by scaring the mayor with her own death."

I smile at that. "It was a beaut."

Cara turns to me, her hate for Adam finally clearing enough that the rest of us exist.

"Except it's not true. Her people never made it to the city in the other world. She starved to death as a child out by Ruka City."

I whistle low. "The other world still has Ruka?"

That eastern monolith was destroyed before I was even born. If memory serves, it was taken apart piece by piece by its own starved people.

"Not the point," Cara says. "If she finds out . . ."

I shrug. "So we don't let her."

"You're just like the rest of them," she says. "You think people are stupid and easy to manipulate"—she turns toward Adam—"and look where underestimating others has gotten you."

"I was in the room," I say, anything to keep her attention off him and prevent a whole new cycle of shouting. "He suggested it *before* mentioning her death and she bucked like a dragon dying. She wasn't going to budge. Selfishness is all that works with some people."

Her eyebrows knit, and she turns back to him. "Why didn't you say that?"

"Didn't I?" he asks, innocent as a goddamn demon.

"Stop it," I say.

"Stop what?"

"Stop pissing her off just so she'll talk to you. She's not your employee anymore, and it doesn't sound like you were ever a very good friend. If you lost that, it's good and lost. Let it go."

Cara looks between us. Mad at him for playing her. Mad at herself for falling into it.

"Can't blame me," Adam says. "She used to look at me like I was the smartest man in the world, you know."

"I didn't look at you because I thought you were smart. I did it because I thought you were kind," she says. "And that's why I'll never respect you again."

We sit in silence that I'm praying lasts until Himself arrives. Cara is twitchy with whatever she wants to share, but she's still Ashtown enough not to risk telling us before she tells Nik.

Finally the door opens.

"We've had a breakthrough," she says so fast and excited she's practically a chirping night bird. "Splice and I, I mean. We can predict the next event."

Nik Nik's taken off his costume. He's ditched his long robe, and even his extra rings. But he's also ditched his carefree, indulgent ruler guise, so he's all seriousness and intensity when he says, "Tell me."

Splice steps up. "We thought it'd be atmospheric, or geologic. But after talking with Cara about the prior process for traversing, we had a breakthrough. It's *sonic*. The earliest anomalies to begin, they're auditory."

"Lead time?"

"Right now it's thirty hours . . ." Nik growls. ". . . but we can restart our anomaly search around the beginning of the sounds. If we find a symptom for the first symptom, and on and on, we may get even more lead time."

But no promises. Splice knows better than to risk death over a promise to the emperor unkept.

"Double shifts till it's done," Nik says. "Are there any literate runners who haven't joined the rotation?"

"I can hop back on, if it's all hands on deck," I say.

Nik looks at me, and I know what he's going to say so I object before the question in his eyes becomes an order.

"It's a health leave, Boss," I say.

"He's got closer ties to the city than any of us. It'll be his own neck he's saving."

I open my mouth, then close it and look down.

"Objection, soldier?"

I take a moment trying to talk myself out of risking my neck for someone I wouldn't have saved from a fire a week ago. No good. I've got to try.

"I thought we didn't work to death. Thought we stopped letting folks get used all the way up when we rode on the city's factories."

I wouldn't dare say it if I wasn't about to ascend, and if I didn't need to protect Cross to keep my own conscience clear.

Nik inhales, nostrils flaring while he decides if I'm getting a backhand or a nod. I've gotten the hand before, especially early on when I deserved every inch of it.

He spares me this time. At first I think it's just so I won't be bruised for my inauguration, but he must think I'm right because he doesn't just not punish me—he gives me my way.

"Go to him with an *ask,* not a command. Treating him broken without giving him a voice is no kinder than compelling him to pretend he's not."

I nod, because he's right. Looks like I'll be headed for the House tonight.

"Anything else?" Nik asks.

Cara shrugs. "Just the obvious about enforcement, but Adam's probably already told you."

"Told me what?" Nik says.

"Yes, told him what?" Adam says.

Cara looks between the two. "You didn't recognize them? Thompson was there, and I think Ellis too. Those weren't enforcement like we're used to. They were maintenance."

Adam groans.

"So they got a promotion?" I ask.

"It's a euphemism," Adam says.

"They were his," Cara explains. "Adam's old murder squad has been recruited to Wiley enforcement."

—

SPLICE HAS VOLUNTEERED TO INVESTIGATE WHY THE MAYOR'S PERSONAL GUARD IS FULL OF WET workers, which means there's nothing to stand between me and the work I don't want to do.

Vex tells me Cross is in care, and gives me authority to go through the beaded entry to the back rooms despite being neither guest nor worker. Still, I drag my feet like I'm sneaking as I make my way down the hall. I wasn't looking forward to interrupting Cross getting the kind of looking after he's needed for years, but when I approach the glass room he's not getting care, he's giving it. He's sitting in front of someone else, guiding the guest's meditation.

I watch him for too long, the seriousness with which he delivers instruction, the smile and emphatic nod he gives when the guest remembers their breathing. He'll be great at leadership, once he gets back. We weren't just hurting Cross by keeping him as executioner all these years, we were denying ourselves a valuable resource. Patient teaching is a rare skill among runners, and, outside of Mr. Em, there aren't many who have it. I myself have been told my mentorship style falls somewhere between a snarling beast and a volcano threatening to explode.

"He feels most at peace when he's giving to others," says Exlee. I'd heard them making their way down the hall—rather, I'd heard the swish of their train dragging like a croc's thick tail—but I kept my eyes trained ahead.

"Once a Ruralite," I say, not totally able to keep the sneer out of my voice.

"You'd be surprised. Most Ruralites serve when they have to, but it's not an instinct. Goodness, it's an instinct with him."

I turn toward them. "You're not mad I brought him here?"

"I'm mad you didn't bring him sooner. That boy was half eaten with self-loathing. You cut it close."

"But he's . . ." I wave my hand like it encompasses everything I hate, or hated, about Cross.

Exlee makes a disappointed clucking sound with their tongue. "Are we judging someone based on who they were at their worst? Is that what I taught you?"

"He's a Ruralite. They've had enough privilege. They don't need our grace."

"Ah, so we are only restorative when it comes to ourselves, and with everyone else we act like the city?"

"No! I just . . ." Anything I say next will sound like a defensive child, which, for the record, is precisely what I feel like.

"It feels good to criticize others into the ground when we are right and we know they are wrong. But it's not good, it's righteous, and the two seldom have anything to do with each other."

"I know, Boss."

I remember this lecture. It was in frequent rotation when I, or any other new provider, wanted to go out and spit in the face of every Ruralite who so much as looked at the House.

I want to show Exlee how much I've changed, but sometimes the girl I was is sitting right beneath my skin, as toxic and reactionary as ever.

". . . I'm glad he's doing well here. Honest. I'm not chipping my own shoulder anymore."

The smile that crosses their lips is sly and knowing. "I can see that."

Cross has finished. He dismisses the guest, and I see them open their arms, a request for a hug. Touch is common and casual in the House, but a rarity in the Rurals, and it's his upbringing that shows on his face as he processes the request. Eventually he does nod, awkwardly hugging the much shorter form.

I wait until they separate to walk in. Cross looks at me like an expected ghost, the horror he knew was coming. He nods before I even get the chance to speak.

He says, "My room? I'll need to change."

It's my turn to nod, and he leads me away.

Exlee watches us go, but I couldn't read their expression if it meant my life.

—

CROSS HAS BEEN MOVED FROM THE INTAKE ROOM TO A SUITE. HIS ROOM HAS A WIDE, LOW BED THAT looks like an invitation and a mat on the ground that I'll pretend I don't know is for prayer. I wonder who furnished the room, who wants to tempt Cross back to belief.

I whistle low. "Himself must've opened his purse wide."

I walk to the back wall and move a curtain to reveal double doors leading to the springs out back.

"I'd assumed it was you," he says.

That surprises me. Not that I wouldn't do it, but that he would know I was capable of this level of kindness after all the shit I've fed him.

"*Psh,* I don't have it like that. I get paid the same as you."

He shrugs and takes off his shirt. "Still . . . I owe you."

I'm no prude. Runners regularly bathe together, massage each other, hang out naked just because it's too damn hot to do much else. But I'll tell the full truth: When he takes off his shirt, I look away. The lights are on in this room, plus it's dark out, so staring out the back door is just looking into a reflection, but I pretend I'm studying a horizon I can't see while he changes.

"We're runners. Runners do for runners. There's no owing in it," I say into the glass.

"You could have left me. I know what you think of me."

I turn around, not realizing he's moved closer. He's standing right behind me now. I let out a surprised breath.

"No . . ." I say, rougher than I mean. ". . . you don't."

"Why are you here, Scales?"

I'd step back if I could, but it's just the door behind me. "We need readers to analyze data so we can predict the next events. But it's not an order. I cleared it with Himself. It's just an ask. You can say no."

He smiles with just the left half of his face. "You stuck your neck out to keep me from being ordered, and you still say I don't owe you?"

I lower my head. "Don't act like you don't know. It's less risky for me than others."

At this, his smile finishes crossing his mouth. "You forget I've been a younger sibling too. It still costs."

"Don't it just? He can be such an ass! Big brother loves the grovel."

"Esther would watch me doing something wrong, cooking or planting, just to come in with the *Here's how you messed up* after it didn't work."

"Gah! That's Nik all over. Don't waste my time with a lesson when you could have just told me!"

We share a laugh about that, and it feels so good to get to talk about Nik being a pain in my ass to someone. But then after a moment I remember that, for all that I am a secret, I still have an older sibling. In every way that matters, Cross has lost his.

Now we're just two sad people standing too close together, and nothing good can come of that.

"We should go, if we're going. But you don't have to."

He moves, finally, thankfully, away from me. He opens a chest in the corner of the room and pulls out a stack of leather.

"Where's the hood?" I ask.

"Exlee took it with the scythe back to the palace. They've already crowned my replacement."

Of course. In the decades since Akeldama was founded it has never been without an executioner for long.

"You sure?" I ask as he begins to strap up.

He nods. "I need to talk to the emperor anyway."

"I can relay a message."

He shakes his head. "I owe you enough, and you don't let anyone repay, so I need to stop accumulating debt."

"No one's keeping track but you," I say, and walk out.

I'm off shift, so when we get to the palace I don't get off the cycle. He hesitates before going inside, like there's something he wants to say. I am begging him not to say it. He doesn't. He turns away and disappears into the building like a man being swallowed by the beast he's already escaped once.

—

I WALK INTO BLAY'S FOR A DRINK AFTER SHIFT, DESPERATE TO SHAKE OFF THIS FEELING OF DESCENDing doom. I don't know what's got my skin tight. Might be Cross. Might be the knowledge that everyone I see could be ripped apart in front of me at any second. Might be my recurring dreams of war. I walk in and shake some hands and take the shoulders attached to those hands into my chest. Blay's is a runners' spot, primarily, and the sea of black tells me I'm not the only one on edge.

I sense him more than see him. It would take a room twice as big and three times as crowded as this to keep me from picking him out instantly. But for the first time, when I see Cheeks he doesn't lift a glass to me. Doesn't wave me over with a smile and put his arm over my neck.

Our eyes lock for a moment, and I think, *I love you. I miss you,* as loud as I can. He turns away first. I make my way to the bar.

"So when's the promotion?" Tear asks. She's slightly drunk and covered in sweat, so I know I've caught her in a moment between dancing.

"You know something I don't?" I ask.

"I know you beat a second's ass and have been taking the left ever since," Tear says, which is not, actually, the order those things happened in. "Thinking some ink might be on the way."

"What you get for thinking," I say, nudging her with my elbow, then I throw her a bone. I stroke my throat. "I mean . . . I might do a little something. Just for aesthetics, you know."

"Oh sure. Black's slimming. Get promoted to second just so you can properly accessorize that long-ass neck."

"You mad you short."

"Huh? Can't hear you up there, with your giraffe ass."

We love on each other a little more—because make no mistake, that is what this is—before she clears her throat. "How's office work?"

I shake my head. "It's murder. Actually, I'd take murder. I don't know if we're doing any good."

I stop when I clock the fear in her eyes. Honesty was a mistake. She wasn't coming as an equal, she was coming as a scared citizen.

"But damn, that Wileyite's a smart one. The traverser, too. She found a way to predict these events two days in advance, and she's looking into a way to predict it even longer ahead. We just have to hold out. Me? I'm just a number jockey. Boring stuff."

Cara's an easy grab to reassure her. People still look at Cara like she's half supernatural creature, half philanthropist. She's already legend and she isn't even dead yet. Knowing the traverser—the only creature who seems as unknown and otherworldly as the murders themselves—is on the case is like having an angel show up to fight your ghosts.

"Should be you in there. Your attention to detail is better than mine," I say, and it's not bullshit. Tear can stare out at the desert for five minutes and tell you the story of its last three months without trying.

She shakes her head. "I've been learning, but I'm still too shaky on my letters to bet lives on it."

I nod, respecting the acknowledgment of her limitations, never easy for a runner.

Blay comes around and slides me a drink I haven't ordered. I don't understand, but then I see the wide, white flower petal tucked into the side.

Tear clucks her tongue. "Looks like Ruthless would like a word."

I nod to Blay and push out of my seat. "She's just Ruth now," I say, which is technically true, but only technically. I don't have to say goodbye to Tear. She knows I have to go. She sends me off with a nod, and I make my way to the back of the dim room.

CHAPTER TWENTY-ONE

THE FORMER RUNNER, IF THERE IS SUCH A THING, IS SITTING AT HER USUAL TABLE. NORMALLY I'D have to wait for Ruth to wave to me, but the shard of flower in my hand is an invitation.

I sit down.

"General," I say.

"Not in a long time," she says, but the title makes her smile just the same.

She's been around so long she never served Nik, only Senior. While Tatik has turned to iron with age—eyes and hair shading into gray from the deep brown-black they used to be, Ruth is as clay as ever: rich, light brown clay of the hills in her skin, red earth of the valleys in her hair. She, Tatik, and a dozen others make up the old guard, those who were there for the earliest rides. She was Mr. Ruthless then, and they say the name picked her.

"Things good?" I ask.

"You tell me. Not a lot of information leaking out of the palace."

Of course not. Everyone wants to know what's going on with the bodies, but only literate runners are working hands-on. Ruth's informants are as oldhead as she is. Few back then had their letters.

I know my brother. I know his policies on spilling, but I also know his exceptions. Anyone who ever saved his father is granted a pass, and Ruth's got stars up to her eyes saying she has, so I spill. I've learned from my mistake with Tear, so when I tell her the plan I make the science sound optimistic. I make it sound like I believe everything is going to be okay.

Still, Ruth grunts at the end. "Bad plan."

"Which bit?"

"The bit where we expect the city to honor a treaty. Bet you when we infuse that atmosphere, those doors lock down twice as hard."

I turn the glass at my fingertips. "Scientist said he'd stop infusing if they did that."

"They're jackals. They'll find a way," she says. "Given how your parents went, I'm guessing you've already thought of that."

I nod, because, fake as they may be, the memory of my not-parents has crossed my mind more than once since I heard Adam make the deal.

"Bet the boy hopes they do it anyway."

This is how long Ruth has been around. She calls Nik *the boy* and lives because she called him that when it was still true.

"What do you mean?"

The smile Ruth gives is slick as oil and twice as dark. "Natural disaster's a great time for war. Let the city wrong us, then hit them hard while they're already scared."

Once was I'd cheer the idea of war with a bunch of Wileyites. But that was before I fell into water that whispered the future, before I dreamt of fire and death.

"The coalition would destroy us," I say, which is true.

While each city manages their own domestic troops—stunners, enforcement, petty drones—only the council of cities can approve mass destruction. They've done it before, protecting cities from those outside their walls by burning them to ash.

"Didn't bomb us over Wills," she says, referencing not Travin Wills, but the officer we skinned in response to his death.

"That was different. It was retaliation. The council didn't care because we had beef with one city, not *cities*. They only attack us when they're afraid we'll give other territories ideas, when we threaten the structure's existence. If we act because we're owed loyalty, that's exactly what we'll be doing. We attack now, they'd never let us survive it."

"So you wouldn't ride, if Himself asked?"

I swallow hard. "Of course I would," but it's just my mouth moving. Truth is I'm not sure.

Ruth can tell.

"Word of advice? Decide now if that's a risk you're willing to take. You dedicate yourself to killing long before you plunge the blade. In the moment, hesitation kills us all."

But there's no reason to decide if I would support a war, because we're not starting one. Right? But what do I know? Nothing. I'm not the emperor, not yet. I'm just a stupid soldier, and Ruth was a general with decades on me. Sure, the ruler she knew inside and out was our father, not my brother, but I'm less and less sure there's enough difference between the two to matter.

"Thank you. For the wisdom."

"You want another bit? I'll give it for free," she says, and there's only one answer.

"Always."

She takes a hit of the long pipe that's never far from her.

"Snakes don't cry over their skins," she says, exhaling an expertly round puff of smoke. Her eyes go sharp and sideways. I can see from my periphery that she's cut her gaze toward Cheeks. "Don't mourn what you outgrow."

I take the drink in a single swig and thank her again before leaving, but this time I don't mean it. 'Cause I bet snakes do mourn their skins. I bet they crawl back inside sometimes, wishing they could fit. I bet they rub their old skins all over, trying to cover themselves in the smell of home. That's all growth is, getting too big to stay somewhere that used to feel good. Just having one less place in the whole world that fits right.

All Ruth's talk of loss has dragged my night way down, and after I've shown a bare minimum of careless joy, I make excuses to head out. I would have left right off, but everyone knows I'm working inner circle on this case, and if I look too down word will get out how fucked we are. When I head home I think the day has reached its peak of confusing shittiness . . . but then I walk in the door.

"You are the absolute fucking worst," I say as the lights come on.

Cara is sitting—*sitting!*—on my—*my!*—kitchen counter. Her short-ass legs are dangling above the ground like we're just hanging in a clubhouse. I'm picturing the satisfaction of throwing the git over my shoulder and tossing her into the dirt outside, when she stops me cold:

"Adam Bosch is hiding something, and I need your help."

—

"GET YOUR BUTT OFF MY COUNTER."

Despite my growl, she relaxes and hops down, because it's not me throwing her out. I walk toward the fridge to grab a hydration pack to offset the drinks I had.

"What do you have?" I ask. "Or is this just history coloring your judgment?"

"It's not history. It's experience. Adam's a monster."

"So are we all," I say, already bored, and take a heavy pull from the pack.

Cara's moral compass points too north for my blood. Best I can tell, Adam's killed a bit and lied a bit. Neither costs me an ounce of sleep, especially if he did his deeds to the city.

"Is betraying the emperor something you're okay with?"

I wipe my mouth with the back of my hand. "I'm listening."

"Splice and I found a way to predict the anomaly, right?"

I nod.

"So after you left, I said we should look backward in the data even further, see if it happened before."

"Why?"

She levels me with a look. "Because when traversing started our Adam didn't start off sending five people. He started off sending one. Seems reasonable the other world's Adam did the same."

It makes sense. "You think there's an earlier body, something that got missed . . ."

". . . which means there might be an imposter that got missed too," she says. "But Adam said not to look. Then he told Splice he'd already checked it, but how could he when we'd just discovered how to track the anomaly?"

"So what happened when you tried to look behind his back?" I ask, because I know her at least enough to know she would have tried.

The stripes on her cheeks curve with her wide smile.

"He locked the data. All of the information we're using from his satellites, all of his atmospheric readings, all the scanning drones—anything from before the date of the five deaths isn't cleared for all users. I think he's hiding the first. Using it for leverage, or playing some longer game with the other world."

"Or he saw your interest and protected it just to put you on a scent. I saw how he messes with you. He's desperate for attention and you always deliver."

"I'm not stupid. I know I fell into that trap earlier and I have considered it. But worst-case scenario if I'm wrong is I waste some time. Worst-case scenario if I'm right . . . with him? There's no telling."

I cross my arms and lean back against the fridge. It tilts back a little against my weight and I shift my feet to pretend it was intentional.

"So? What do you want me to do about it?"

"It's a permission lock. Meaning he's put our stations at a lower trust level."

"But you think since his station's the master, it will have access."

"Exactly. I waited around all night for him to leave, but he wouldn't go until I did. I'm not staying at the palace, and he is."

"Which means you can't enter the palace after dark without a runner escort. You want me to get you inside?"

"It's all I need. Second shift leaves at midnight, first shift comes at six, as long as we're in that gap we're golden."

That's the part that hits me sideways. "If you just need a runner's pass through the front door, why didn't you ask Splice?"

My question has made her suddenly interested in her shoes, and the nervousness of the action makes her seem young. No, not young precisely, but human at least, when she so rarely seems that.

"Splice is a nice kid."

"And what the fuck am I?"

She looks up, and all at once I feel too close to her. Those eyes feel like liquid. They feel like drowning.

"Strong," she says. "I don't trust Adam not to retaliate."

"And I've got a better chance of standing it than Splice," I say.

"You don't even fear consequences from the emperor. If you're not safe, none of us are."

Flattery will get you . . . pretty far with me, actually.

"All right, let's go."

"Tonight?"

"Yeah, tonight. You think I want to sleep on this?" I check the time on my cuff. "Get your shit."

—

DO I THINK ADAM BOSCH IS SHADY? AS FUCK. DO I THINK HE'S PLAYING SOME KIND OF DEMENTED chess that ends with us getting ambushed somehow? Probably not. Truth be told, Cara likely wants evidence of his continued villainy to help her sit right with whatever she's done to him. I'm probably wasting my time. But ever since I saw the bloody end of everything in my water vision, I've been tense. Now I'm hoping being proactive will chill my nightmares.

When I pull up it's Sai on night watch, which is lucky because I trained Sai up and they'd trust me to the teeth.

"World walker left something. I'm escorting in."

I needn't have bothered with an excuse. Sai barely looks away from the horizon. They're not concerned with familiar threats, just whatever great unknown sits beyond our vision. We enter the palace and it's so easy I just know I'm wasting my time, but when I too-confidently try to fling open the office door, I find it locked. At first I scan my cuff, thinking it's clearance locked. But even after the panel glows the door stays. It's physically locked, with the bolt thrown.

"Do we need to call someone to open the lock?" Cara has the raw, unfiltered audacity to ask.

Giving her a silencing glare, I pull my magnet set out of my side pouch and unroll the pack. I slide two out, and slip one beneath the lip of the metal door to the other side. I slide its partner on our side of the door, guiding it up to the bolt on the other side. *Call someone.* The nerve. I stare at Cara as the latch gives and the door opens. It's been years since I was a regular at breaking in, and it still took less than a minute.

Cara doesn't even have the grace to fake being impressed. She just pushes past me and heads for Adam's desk.

"Shit," she says.

"What? Did Adam lock it?"

"No, it's just . . . it's a palace log-in screen. Do you have access? Splice keeps our stations logged in with his so I don't need one. I didn't think Adam had one either."

"He shouldn't," I say, but he must have one if we're locking his station. Did Nik give Adam that kind of access? Did he trust him that much?

"Can you use yours?" she asks.

"I'm a row mechanic. I don't have a palace log-in."

"Any chance we could guess it?" she asks.

I shake my head. "Splice gives the passwords. They're all random characters and numbers."

Cara begins looking around the desk. "Maybe he left some other device around, something logged in."

"He doesn't have another device," I say, remembering how he just uses his arm or eye projector when he needs something portable. "He *is* the device."

Still, I help her look through the odd collection of samples and data around the office. Once it becomes clear we're wasting our time, I turn away from the desk.

"We'll call Splice."

"No, I just need to figure something else out. I just need time."

"Time is what we're wasting. I'm bringing him in."

"No!"

The yell surprises us both, but Cara worse despite her being the one who did it. She's breathing hard. She sits on the floor, drawing her knees up to her chest, her breath still rapid but slowing. I go down in front of her in a runner's squat.

"Splice is . . . curious," she says, looking down at her hands. "So was Jean. He was my mentor and friend. He was curious, and hard, but kind and resilient . . . and optimistic, even at the end." When she looks from her hands to me, her dark eyes are wet enough to shine like stars. "And I got him involved in my vendetta against Adam, and Adam killed him for it. I won't do it again. I won't . . ." She bites her lip, because it's better than letting the sob out. "No one vulnerable. No one . . ."

". . . kind?" I ask.

She nods. It's all she can do.

So this is why she took Adam's eye. It wasn't because he was operating a corrupt company, it was nothing as large as that. It wasn't righteousness, it was vengeance. Payback for her friend. I can respect that, even if it ties my hands. If I bring Splice in behind her back, and something happens to him, she'll consider it her own sin, even if I'm the one who makes the call.

"Splice isn't the only one with palace access," says a voice at the door, and I pop up so fast I almost topple over.

I catch my breath as Cheeks looks at me, too much passing between us to ever say out loud.

"Why are you here?" I ask, and it feels like I'm dreaming.

"Motion sensor on the door. It pings me if someone comes in after hours."

"Why would you have an alert on the office . . . You don't trust Adam either?" I say.

Cheeks finishes moving into the room, closing the door. "Gah no. Man's a fucking snake."

I've only seen him from a distance since I put him down, and seeing him now hits me right in the gut. His face is a garden of bruises with his bandaged nose sitting center. He's got a cast on his wrist, and, judging by his stiff posture, his ribs are bandaged up too.

"How much of that did you hear?" Cara asks, though her face is so shuttered now you'd swear we were just discussing the weather.

"Enough," he says. "But I've sparred with Adam before, and I came through just fine. You'll need no tears for me."

"Like I'd cry for you, Cheeks. Adam's a snake, but you're a dog," she says.

"Fleas and all," he says, giving her his trademark charming smile.

Their easy camaraderie while I'm sitting here awkward as a Ruralite in the House even though he is—*was*—my best friend puts me in a mood.

"We here to banter all night? Or do you want to log in to the station?"

The mirth goes out of his eyes when he looks at me. "Sure, once you two spill what you're sniffing after."

Cara's still explaining her theory when Cheeks begins entering his credentials. He took little convincing, and I don't know if it's because he distrusts Adam or because he's still in love with Cara's sister and doing her a solid is the closest he can get to touching Esther.

He whistles low. "Nothing looks password protected but . . . he's got a real needle-haystack approach to his file organization."

The transparent screen of Adam's station is filled with the blue light of file names. All with no descriptions, only numbers ascending from one to . . .

". . . Christ how many are there?" I ask.

"Five hundred?" he says. "Give or take."

Cara leans forward, typing. "They're obviously dummies. We just need to organize by file size to weed out the fakes."

I see her touch the screen, trying to access settings or properties or some techy thing better left to someone other than me. And I see how nothing happens in response.

"It's like we're not even in the system. It's like this is just a picture."

I can see the frustration rising in Cara. Her foot starts tapping. The familiarity of being up against Adam is probably compounding the annoyance.

"Maybe it is? Maybe it's a dummy version of the palace's system to protect his files, and you've got to click on the right one to get in?" I say, anything to keep her focused.

"Don't suppose you know his favorite number?" Cheeks says.

Cara closes her eyes and drops her face into her hands, taking a few deep breaths. Cheeks looks at me, I shrug, but we both keep quiet while she processes.

When she snaps her head up, we both flinch.

"Seventy-eight."

"You sure?" Cheeks asks. "He's probably got something nasty planned if we pick wrong."

"It is. I know him."

She reaches to touch the screen and select the file. I grab her wrist.

"You sure you know him? Or do you just think you do?" I ask, forcing her to look me in the eyes. "You might not get another chance."

She takes a breath. "It's just like earlier. The way he deliberately let me hear that he lied to the mayor to rile me up. He wants to be found out and he wants *me* to do it. Seventy-eight was the floor he pretended to hide his secrets on when I worked for him. It was the floor I broke into to find the truth. If it's a game he's playing, he wants to play with me."

"Fair enough," I say, releasing her.

Cheeks and I hold our breath. All we can do is look on, trusting Cara as she raises her hand to tap the file.

MY BROTHER IS IN THE SPACE HE'S USING AS AN OFFICE NOW THAT ADAM'S MADE HIS INTO A DISASTER-response lab. He's looking at a map, and then sliding through close-up pictures of faces. The dead, I realize. He's looking into the face of every citizen he failed to save.

I clear my throat, and the way his face is guarded when he looks up at me but then drops to let me see his sorrow is as intimate as a hug. *Oh it's you,* his expression says, *you can see me.*

Whatever he sees in my face prompts him to do away with niceties.

"Problem?"

"Adam Bosch has been hiding something from you. From all of us."

He takes a moment, then sits in his chair and tents his fingers on the desk in front of him.

"I see."

I take that as encouragement and step forward. "He isolated an earlier incident, a crossing-over that predates our first kills."

"Do you know who crossed over? Who was killed?"

The question I can't answer stops me. "No, but the signal was detected at Wiley's city hall. It could have been the mayor's living quarters," I say, then add, because he seems to be missing the shadiness of it all, "Adam had the anomaly flagged, but he didn't tell the rest of his team."

He takes a moment, looking down at his rings. "Maybe he looked into it separately. It might have been a failed attempt, not a crossover."

"Then why did he lock out Cara's and Splice's stations to keep them from looking backward and finding it themselves?"

His eyes flash up to mine. "Did Cara bring this to you?"

The question derails me. This is not how I thought this was going to go.

"Does it matter?"

"This is a wild hunt. We need people looking forward, not wasting their time looking back before our first incident. Maybe that's why they were password locked. I'm sure he has his reasons."

My brother, famously suspicious at the slightest hint of sabotage, is making excuses for a Wileyite stranger.

"Like he had his reasons for shoving me into toxic fucking sludge?"

"Are you wasting my time with a vendetta?"

"No! There is something going on. I've already started looking into it. I couldn't get into the interior surveillance videos remotely, but I was able to check the security logs. The mayor called security just a few minutes after the anomaly in the middle of the night, but then canceled the call and said nothing was wrong when they showed up."

I'm saying *I* instead of *we* and hoping he doesn't think to ask how my ass got any of this data when I can barely type.

He leans back in his chair. "You think the mayor of Wiley City is a dop."

"It fits. I just want permission to tap into her interior surveillance to see the footage from inside her quarters that night. A spider team, not a pack. Three people, in and out, quick."

"This is a distraction we don't need," he says. "And the mayor isn't even alive on the earth that's coming over. I thought Adam said—"

"Adam is a fucking liar!" I'd felt the yell boiling up inside me, but I didn't expect it to come out right then. "The blood between you doesn't speak to him. He's not one of us, Nik."

He doesn't love you like I love you. Doesn't love Ash like I do.

His expression is dangerously shuttered. I think back to what Cara said, about Nik breaking those he loved. I'd told her it was impossible, but the way he looks right now, I'm not so sure. I've never been so scared of him.

"Neither were you, once."

The silence after his sentence, where he is intensely staring at me with his chin tilted up, is a dare.

"Guess I'm wasting both our time," I say, and, for the first time in my entire life, I leave the emperor's office without being dismissed. I don't slam the door when I enter the hallway—letting my rage be visible would force my brother's hand—but I wish I could.

CHAPTER TWENTY-TWO

CHEEKS AND CARA ARE WAITING BY THE DOOR. AFTER WE'D SEEN WHAT ADAM WAS HIDING WE'D parted ways and met back up this morning. By virtue of being the one Nik was least irritated with at the moment, I was elected to go tell him. For all the good it did.

"He wants no part. Doesn't think it's important."

"What?" Cara says.

"He thinks it's a distraction. He wants the focus to be on increasing the lead time on predicting the next event," I say.

Cheeks nods, the light catching on the metal splint on either side of his nose. I don't know if I'll ever stop feeling guilty about all the pieces he's in.

"He's probably right."

"Kiss ass," I say, because feeling guilty about his lumpy face isn't going to keep me from telling the truth.

"I said he's probably right. I didn't say we shouldn't do anything about it."

That's the Cheeks I want. "You thinking what I'm thinking? Same plan as before?"

He nods. "Three people, in and out. Get the footage, hand deliver to Splice so there's no tech trail leading back to him."

"I'm in," Cara says.

I shake my head. "No, you're not. Emperor's right about this being a distraction. I'm not going to pull our best bet at prediction off the job."

Cara stares at me. Her face is still but I know she wants to disagree, and is just waiting for some good argument to rise up. Eventually, she sighs, and looks away.

"Fine, who's going then?"

"Me," I say.

"And me," Cheeks says.

"No," I say. "I can pass a civilian scan. I won't risk anyone that can't on an unsanctioned run."

"Tough shit. This job needs three. One runner with rabid enforcement is just asking for a disappearance."

"Yeah, but you know how they like to rough us up when we're caught before letting us go. You're already half broken," I say.

He opens his mouth to bray about that, though it's true and we both know it, when Cara raises a hand between us.

"Okay, so I get a day pass for Cheeks. Who else?"

Cheeks and I both blink at each other, the void where our fight was leaving nothing between us but awkwardness.

"It's gotta be Cross," Cheeks says.

"Jesus," I say, because I know he's right. "Maybe if I stack you two on each other's shoulders I'll have one whole runner."

"Even bruised I'm twice the runner of anyone else."

"Might take that serious if you weren't wheezing through broken ribs."

He looks past me to Cara. "Cross'll be off at six tonight. We can wait for him to do his shift and then use the setting sun to hide our entry."

It's the only way we can approach the city hidden without involving Em, or Silk, or any of the edge runners we use for drone distraction.

"I hate this," I say, which is as good as signing the order. "I'll get a ride, you get Cross."

THINGS I REMEMBERED TO BE AFRAID OF PLANNING THIS OP: ENFORCEMENT, TO WHICH THE NEW mayor has given free reign to do whatever they want to runners caught trespassing; drones, which are not supposed to fire autonomously but do often enough that the animal rights people get mad at the number of stunned or dead creatures found in the border between Ashtown and Wiley; Cheeks being out too soon and setting back his rib recovery doing something as basic as marching up stairs too hard; the desert in general, whose dangers and mysteries are too vast to be contemplated.

Things I forgot to be afraid of: Sheer. Fucking. Awkwardness.

It settles between us while I drive the mirrored cutter through sunset. The vehicle is low, shaped like a wedge, and covered in neo-chrome so if they see us at all we'll just look like a heat mirage. Despite its sleek silhouette the ride can seat five easy, which is why it doesn't make sense that it feels too crowded with just me, Cheeks, and Cross in it.

At first, I thought it was just the absence of Cara. She's like a black hole, or a human being quickly turning into one, and when she was between us Cheeks and I could be pulled into her and ignore each other. But it's more than that. Cross is making it worse, the way he isn't looking at Cheeks . . . and the way I'm not looking at him.

"No chatter," Cheeks says, putting away his scanner as we approach the wall.

I nod and shove free the fake section of wall, then hit the switch on the side to deploy the hologram that will enable our quick exit while concealing our means of entry. It looks just like the metal exterior—uninterrupted, solid—and the illusion is so good in the low light that when Cheeks passes through it it's more like I've watched him become a ghost than walk through an artificial wall.

"Huh," I say, signing us in to the tunnels so if, god forbid, something happens there will be a record of where we last were.

"What is it?" Cross asks.

"Nothing, just . . . there's been a lot of traffic in the tunnels since the incident," I say.

I wonder if it's runner superstition, spending their off-hours in the walls' tunnels hoping it will protect them from whatever is tearing people apart outside. I guess the walls, built with the blood and sweat of people who still hoped for better, are as good a sanctuary as any church. A week ago I would have known for sure, I would have been invited along, but being sequestered on data duty with the other readers has isolated me from the rest of the runners.

The largest chunk of Ashtown are the descendants of people brought in to build this wall, only to be denied entry when the city began operating. We left these holes, little places where we could hide and enter, as unerasable proof that this entire city was built on our uncompensated labor. Many of the original smuggling tunnels into the city have the names of ancestors carved into the archways. In the city, the streets above are named for their heroes, but down here everything is named for our dead. Maybe runners have been coming here like a homegoing, feeling closer to those who made such feats possible. Maybe it isn't about being safe from the force outside at all, but about choosing to die where your roots are. I don't know. For me, being in the wall while being denied access to the other side doesn't feel like a privilege. It's just a reminder of everything that should have been ours, but was kept from us by those who never even worked for it.

After a few floors, Cheeks calls out, "Break," while cradling his ribs.

I stop, but Cross keeps climbing. I reach forward and yank his shirt.

"Cross. Break."

His eyes narrow as he looks at Cheeks, but he nods.

"We need to sit and wait out the daylight timers anyway," I say, to ease the tension between them. It doesn't.

We've got fuck all to do until the timer ticks over, but you'd never guess it by the way Cheeks has an earpiece in and his eyes glued to the scanner, like we wouldn't get an alert for new activity if we'd been spotted.

I've got no problem working clear-headed with even my worst enemy, but I can't risk their tension affecting us topside.

I sit on the floor between them, legs crossed, preparing. I'm not *stellar* at mediation, but I've taken my conflict resolution classes along with the rest of them. How hard can it be?

"You guys okay?" I ask.

"Fine."

"Great."

The words might as well be barks, they're so short and sharp.

I sigh. Cross is reasonable and levelheaded eighty percent of the time, so I turn to him first.

"Listen, I know you're all huffy 'cause he's dating your sister. But—"

Cross turns, eyes like hellfire. "You're seeing Esther?"

Cheeks glares at me and crosses his arms. "Not anymore. What of it?"

I push up to my feet. Okay, so conflict resolution was a bust, but I'm great at keeping two people from hitting each other, and it feels like that's a skill set that's about to get some use.

I put my back to Cheeks and hold my hands up to Cross.

"You're not good enough," Cross says.

"Whoa, let's not say anything we'll re—"

"You're a fucking coward!"

Have I ever heard Cross yell like this? Have I ever heard Cross say *fuck*?

"Say that again," Cheeks says, pressing against my back, knowing I will keep him from getting hit, but also needing to puff up from the insult.

"Settle," I say at Cross, then look over my shoulder. "Settle!"

Cheeks throws his hands up, but moves away. He could kill Cross, even injured, but it would cost them both something. Whatever Cross may think, Cheeks is at least worthy enough to not want to body the only brother of the girl he's in love with.

"What is going on with you?" I ask Cross, because Cheeks acting out is as familiar as a sunrise, but Cross is usually calm logic with a hint of faith. "Why are you so tense with Cheeks if you didn't know about Esther?"

Cross glares past me, then softens his gaze when he looks down at my face. I'd swear his eyes are full of pity.

"Because I was his wolf. I was copied on all of his official messages. I heard every conversation through the official channel."

I wait for Cheeks to lash out at this revelation, but he just tilts his head toward Cross.

"It was you?"

Cross nods, but then looks at me with a question he won't say out loud. He's surprised I kept it from Cheeks. That I would protect him instead of telling Cheeks. I can only shrug. I'm surprised myself.

"Was it you the whole time?" Cheeks asks, thankfully pulling Cross's too-intense attention away from me.

"The whole time. No one else," Cross says.

"I don't get it," I say. "Why does that make you angry?"

"Where were you four weeks ago, the night of the solstice, after the weekly meeting?" Cross asks.

My neck could snap from the speed of the subject change, but I know the answer easily enough. "Cheeks and I went riding. The moon was huge."

"You were together."

"'Course. Not going to risk a broken spine in the middle of nowhere with no spotter." I laugh a little, but it doesn't lessen the tension in Cross's shoulders.

"He marked himself as alone," Cross says.

"What?"

"Whenever he had to give accounting for his time, through the whole investigation, anytime he was alone with you he told everyone he was by himself. That's what made me suspicious in the first place. All of his unaccounted-for time."

I look at Cheeks, but he doesn't raise his eyes. It's not like he's ashamed, but more like he thinks this whole conversation is beneath him.

"When others would ask about you, he'd act . . ." Cross shakes his head. "He's not good to you."

"What does that mean?" I ask, but the words are hollow.

"It means he's a shit friend. And now he's pouting to punish you for his injuries, running around talking shit about how rough you were, when he's the one who requested you as hand. It's just another situation he put you in. He made you hurt him and now he's making you feel guilty for hurting him."

"You don't know anything about our friendship," Cheeks says, stepping forward.

I should step between them. Calm this down. Save Cheeks from picking a fight with fractured bones, because he will. But I'm just frozen. Staring.

". . . Why did you lie about hanging out with me?" He doesn't answer, but he does look down. "Is it because of the rumors about the emperor? Because people thought I was his and you didn't want to get in trouble?"

There. I've given him an out, but also given myself one. If he says yes to this version of reality, if he even nods, it will be true, and I will understand, and we can both keep on going in a world where my best friend has never been ashamed of me.

He doesn't.

"I just didn't want people to get the wrong idea . . . about us."

At first I think, *That's reasonable.* Which is also the part of me who doesn't want to know any more saying, *Stop looking at this.*

"Why not?"

The question catches him sideways, and in the moment before he fixes his face there's real horror there.

"Because we're not together."

"You aren't with Tear either, but everyone thinks your reading practices are cover for sex and you've never lied about them. Same with your and Em's charity projects. You don't lie about those. Why only with me?"

I know the answer, obviously. I knew before I asked the question.

Tear is beautiful. Em is beautiful. I am not. It's never prevented me from finding companionship, so I didn't think it mattered this side of adolescence, but apparently it does. To the man named after his own face, it still does. No, that's not fair. This isn't vanity, or shallowness. This is the shape of his trauma. Mr. Cheeks wants to be loved and accepted and judged worthy by the entire world, to make up for the one retreating silhouette in his childhood. If I wanted to hurt him right now, it would be easy. I'd say something like, *Fucking only beautiful people won't bring your father back.* But I just stand there, more astounded than hurt, as Cheeks fails to come up with an answer.

"It's fine," I say, because it is, in the worst way. I feel the part of myself that cared about Cheeks, that cared that Cheeks respected me, wither and fall off.

"I wasn't punishing you for beating me. I know I asked for that," he says, eager to defend himself from the piece of Cross's accusation that was untrue.

"Oh?" I say, sarcastic enough to convey *I don't give a shit.*

"I was just sad. I missed you. I thought at some point you'd show up to check on me, comfort me. But you never did. Not once."

"You never called! I had a shitstorm on my hands with all of this, but if you'd missed me and called I would have shown up."

"Called?! I saw Nik Nik's corpse. I found it. You knew how much that would fuck me up, but you never even cuffed me."

A lot of responses come into my mouth. *I'm sorry. I was busy. I was doing my job. He's* my *fucking brother, you git.* But the strongest, the most unexpected, is this: *I hate you.*

"My father died a week ago," I say.

Cheeks shakes his head in confusion. "Your parents . . ."

"Not my biological father. The man who raised me, who abused me, who treated me like shit for not being his. He died and I didn't tell you because it would take too much time. You didn't even know who he was. But I know your father left when you were four, and I know the story of every time he's ever let you down. I know the name of the man who hurt your mother, how your grandparents met, your worst fears, and you don't even know my name, D'Angelo. So I'm sure not having me come around to wipe your tears was a real fucking shock and a letdown, but I've been keeping my own head on straight. I've been being exactly as self-protective as you have always been in our friendship, but you can't stand it."

I wipe at my mouth, like it will stop my lips from moving. Keep whatever else I have to say inside. But it's no use. I'm not done. And I won't stop until I am.

"I'm not even mad about you saying I was jealous of Esther anymore. I'm mad that you expected me to get over it. Because I always do. Every time you've misstepped, or lashed out, or fallen down, I have been there to comfort *you* through what you've done to me. I have watched you cry, and talked you off ledges, and made peace with people you've wronged, and I have never asked for anything in return. Cross is right. You're a shit friend."

At first, it's like I've taken every drop of air out of the room. It's like the oxygen is gone and we're all just husks who would shatter if we dared speak again.

It's Cheeks who finally breaks.

"I know you do a lot for me. But don't pretend you'd let me do anything for you. You never open up. You never ask for help. You don't trust me. You think I don't realize it's one-sided? When I am hurt I go to you, and when you are hurt you go . . . to the House? To the nightfire? I don't even know because you don't tell me. After Helene X died I asked you how you were and you told a joke, like I didn't know you were close. You think that doesn't hurt me? You think that doesn't insult me after all this time?"

This time, I look away. I don't mean anything by it, but he seizes on the movement like it's hope itself. He reaches out, touches my arms.

"I'm sorry. I was a shit friend and I'm sorry. I don't want to lose you," he says, and at least that last part, I know, is true. "You want to break my nose again?"

I shrug out of his grasp.

"Maybe later," I say.

The truth is I don't know what later means. I need time. Time to understand if the story he is telling is one I want to believe, one I can make true by believing.

He gives me space, and none of us dares say anything else. Cheeks sits at the floor of one wall, so I sit against the wall across from him. Cross sits beside me. We do nothing more than listen to the sound of one another's breathing in the small space, which is really listening to the sound of our breath becoming one in the air above our heads. I close my eyes and imagine floating there, all three of us, without all the shit that makes us separate: Cheeks without his abandonment issues making him over-prioritize romantic relationships, me without my abusive history keeping everyone at firing distance, Cross without the self-loathing he was taught to call holy. I wish fiercely that we were kids together and this was a clubhouse, before the world taught us its many disappointments.

Eventually an alarm goes off on Cross's cuff and it doesn't just startle us but resurrects us, puts us all back into our flesh.

"The lights shifted," Cross says, even though we all know what the alert was for. "It's dark now."

I don't know if I hug Cheeks or he hugs me, I just know we're hugging and I care enough about his ribs that I resist the urge to squeeze him. We step away, and then—*ah, fuck it*—I hug Cross too. He smiles. It surprises me, because I don't know if I've ever seen Cross smile like this, or if I've just never been this close to him when he did. It makes me wish we were on the other side of this going home, that our next move was to drive into the desert together, and maybe we'd share a drink as the sky goes purple. But that's not the case. This? This was the easy part. Now the mission begins.

—

CROSS AND I ARE IN AN ALLEY TWO BLOCKS FROM THE MAYORAL COMPOUND. THE MAYOR'S AND VICE mayor's mansions border City Hall, and they are all lit up like daybreak, bright enough that we can see the glow even from here, so it's safer to tap in from just outside visibility. The brightness helps us, actually. The holographic wall I've deployed to hide us in the alley is the portable kind, which just automatically scans surroundings to replicate the image. It's not like the stationary ones we've painstakingly programmed to hide our entrances in the wall, and its image would never pass inspection if everyone passing it wasn't having to squint against the hallelujah of white at our backs.

Cheeks is up high, scanning digitally and visibly for anything in a uniform that might be coming our way. I've just finished anchoring the projector for the wall display, while Cross puts Splice's hack into the system to seek out the security feed we want like a squid with a scent . . . At least, that's how I've always pictured the dynamic code working. But now that I'm saying it to you, I'm not sure if that's how squids work. Do squids have noses? No matter. I don't know from sea life, or technology, but I know that it moves through data grabbing at things like something weightless with more than two arms and, to me, that says squid.

I crouch beside Cross, back against the wall, as we wait for the hack to do its work.

"How are you?" he says. "That conversation was really intense for you."

Like he wasn't the one bright red with a vein in his forehead over Cheeks.

"I'm . . . I'm okay, I think?" I say. "Thanks for asking. Exlee really is rubbing off on you."

He smiles, again, which must be some kind of record. "I'm afraid checking in with others was something I learned from my father. More Ruralite residue, you would say."

He's wrong. I would have said *scum* not *residue,* but I'm not saying it now.

"Your dad, was he good?"

Cross nods. "Tried to be, for those that fit. He never knew what to do with me. Wasn't his fault. I'm not great at fitting, and watching him try to pretend I belonged hurt worse than not belonging."

"When they . . . come to you. Back at Akeldama. Do they ever tell you why?"

He takes a breath, sensing the trap. I pushed too hard, too fast, and when he looks at me his eyes are narrowed with suspicion.

"Are you asking out of curiosity about my father . . . or are you asking out of curiosity about yours?"

I don't answer. He already knows.

He shakes his head. His smile, always elusive, is long gone now. "Should have guessed you'd figure out what happened to him."

"He showed up on the border patrol intake, his death was announced the next day. I was at Viet's when you came up from Akeldama, the way you looked . . . I didn't get it then, but you'd just had to kill someone, hadn't you? That wasn't long after he died, was it?"

"I can't say," he says, which is just a yes that doesn't threaten his emperor's mark.

"Did he say anything? Was he . . . was he . . ."

"Sorry?" Cross asks, and I can tell from the pity in his eyes that Jeffery Ackerman did not come sorry. "I wish I could tell you that he was weeping, sorry for whatever he did to you to make you . . ."

". . . a stunning conversationalist?" I say with my fakest smile.

". . . affection avoidant," he says, which is real polite. "But Jeffery Ackerman died in the same way I imagine he lived: thinking of, and talking about, nothing but himself. There was some kind of investigation that intended to make an example of him. He talked about his own death like beating them, like winning. When I realized your mother was still alive, I was shocked. He hadn't even mentioned her."

"Fucking bastard," I say.

This shouldn't matter. I've been away from that man for twice as long as I was with him. But it feels . . . unjust. It's an ending, but not closure. More like a closing off of possibilities. I need Cross to stop looking at me, to stop staring at me with eyes shining in half pity and half pride. He places his hand, carefully, beside mine. Not on top, not touching, he lets it sit in case I want it the way wastelanders will leave out food to tame a sand cat.

I lift my hand, then lose my nerve, and set it back down. I'm just thinking about trying again, when Cheeks comes down the building and saves me from doing anything that would go nowhere but down.

"How long?" he asks.

I pop up, eager to get away from Cross, and check the screen. "Three minutes."

"That's a problem, because enforcement is one minute away."

CROSS HOPS ONTO HIS FEET. FOR WHAT? I'M NOT SURE, BUT THE ADRENALINE OF THE COMING THREAT is making me bounce up and down, so I can't blame him.

"How many?" I say, squeezing my fists.

"Too many for what you're planning," Cheeks says. I open my hands.

"Then we have to pull it. We have to abort," I say.

"Too late for that. They're on the street. They'll see us once we leave the wall anyway," he says. "It's the mayor's squad again. The black jumpsuits. I've been on every inch of the scanner. They aren't getting their information from an official channel, but they definitely know something is up."

"Can we count on the wall to hide us?" Cross asks.

"Not if they know something's here. If they walk too far into the alley to investigate we're fucked," he says.

"Not just us. They'll know how every runner gets in and out of the city without them catching on," I say. "It can't come to that. We've got to give ourselves up before they confiscate the hologram."

"Not all of us," Cross says. "I'll run out. They'll rough me up, and you'll pick me up tomorrow."

"These guys were a kill squad under Adam, and they aren't using official channels. We don't know how far they'll go," I say.

Cross shrugs the information off, like it changes nothing.

"You're the least ranked soldier here. It can't be you or it's both our hides," Cheeks says.

We both realize, at the same moment, that it has to be me.

"When you get the data don't forget to check the footage from the days after our first incident too. I'd bet teeth Adam's made contact with the dop," I say.

I walk past the holograph, appearing in the alley from nowhere to anyone watching. I begin to stretch. If I'm gonna get nabbed by enforcement on purpose, I'm gonna make them work for it.

"Yeah, one thing," Cheeks says, stepping into the alley.

"What?"

He grabs my shoulders.

"Can't let you do it."

I don't have time to process. He uses my surprise to shove me back behind the holographic image of the alley.

"Hold her!" Cheeks yells, and it's an order.

I collide with Cross, who wraps one arm around my waist

while the other is a bar across my chest, as Cheeks runs out into the street. A pack of black follows after him like a rabid hunt. I try to lunge forward, just like he knew I would, but Cross holds me firm. I don't know I'm screaming until he claps a hand over my mouth.

Cross's whispered "It's okay. It's going to be okay. I'm sorry. I've got you. I'm sorry," is a rush of air against my neck, but all I can hear is Cheeks, sitting on his couch, looking over at me.

This is the best part.

I have never, not once, believed someone like Cheeks could really care about someone like me. In the smallest part of my mind, the part where I am an unwanted child wrist-deep in other people's blood, I've never believed I was worthy of our friendship. Only now, now in this moment that is far too late, do I believe.

Maybe it's my imagination, but I swear I hear every step Cheeks takes away from me.

I swear I can hear him laughing as he hits the ground.

CHAPTER TWENTY-THREE

I DON'T OFTEN GET TO SCARE MY BROTHER. NOT BECAUSE I CAN'T, BUT BECAUSE I DON'T TRY. MOST OF the time, I try to keep him from remembering there are reasons to be afraid of me.

But not tonight.

It's been hours since Cheeks was taken and no word has come. They're keeping him until he talks. He's never gonna talk. No matter how many of the wounds I put there that they reopen.

That's why I'm sitting in the dark, waiting in the room Nik thinks can't be broken into.

He must have had meetings because I can hear his coat dragging behind him. He turns on the light and jumps when he sees me, perched on the back of his chair, my feet dirtying up his cushion and something in my hands that might look like a blade at first glance.

He doesn't yell, not even a *yelp* in shock, I'll give him that. His face goes stone and he reaches for something in his coat, before he processes that it's me and relaxes. He can tell something is wrong, but he believes I won't harm him. I used to believe that too. Now I'm not so sure.

I press to project from the fob in my hand, and the video Cross and I found rolls on the wall behind him.

It's the date of the first anomaly, before all the others, the anomaly Cara found that Adam tried to hide. The image shows the living room of the mayor. She enters the frame with a stunner in her hand, a weapon non-officers aren't supposed to have.

"Oh, Jesus. It's you," she says, as a flash of blond enters the frame.

It's the vice mayor. The too-sweet woman who looked around at the whole wide world like it was new.

The mayor lowers her weapon. "What are you doing in here? I called enforcement. I thought you were an intruder."

"Sorry, I'm . . . I guess I'm lost. I was . . . sleepwalking," the vice mayor says, an unconvincing lie given that she's fully dressed.

"Sure you were. I don't know what you're on, but the vice mayor's residence is across the compound."

"Sorry," she says again, moving from frame.

I cut the feed.

"So it's the vice mayor, not the mayor," Nik Nik says, looking back at me.

I don't respond. I raise the fob again and press play on the next clip. Because I wasn't arrested, I got to do myself what I'd asked Cheeks to do. I went through all footage of the vice mayor's complex since we began working with Adam.

I play the feed. The vice mayor is in her living room when Adam enters without knocking. Judging by how clean he is, this is the same day she and the mayor visited our compound, just later. I should have figured he'd insert himself into her life after she dared not recognize him at the meeting.

On the feed the vice mayor screams when she sees him, standing and running toward her security panel.

"What are you doing here?" she says, voice pitched toward hysteria.

"I used to come here a lot. I understand I must look very different from the Adam you're used to, but I assure you, I knew the woman you are pretending to be quite well."

It takes her a second, but not long. The hand that was reaching for her security panel drops slowly.

"What do you want?" she asks, and Adam smiles. He smiles like that is his favorite sentence, like it's the sentence he's heard most often in his life, the sound of another person's desperation the lullaby that sends him to sleep.

"The emperor would like to see you again. Just you this time. The winds are high tonight, so get your coat."

I pause the feed on that smile. I stare at my brother. I wait.

". . . I heard about Cheeks," he says, carefully.

"Cheeks is down because you lied to me. Because you could have told me the truth but you decided you trusted me less than that fucking—"

I throw the fob at Adam's stupid projected face just to hear it shatter on the wall behind it.

"Cheeks is a soldier. Whatever happens, it's not your fault."

It is. It is. It is.

"This isn't about—"

"Yes, it is. This, all of this, is about the guilt you are feeling right now."

He sits in a chair across from me, his coat pooling at his feet. I'm desecrating his chair, which means the one he's sitting in is usually for guests. His chair sits higher, better for attacking. He must know that. I hope he feels it now. I've been the only one walking out of a room that an emperor and I walked into before, and I'm so full of rage now it could easily happen again. I wonder if he regrets putting my name in his inheritance box yet.

"You had a successful mission. You got the data you were looking for, but you won't let yourself feel that victory because you lost someone in the process. It isn't about winning by any means necessary with you. It's about being . . . good. I didn't hide my plans from you because I didn't trust you. I hid them because I didn't want to burden you."

I swallow. "You're lying."

"I'm not. You and I are different. We have always been different. I was raised by the man you wouldn't tolerate existing for more than an hour. I watched Adra take what my father was doing to me that day a hundred times. He watched me take it the same. You couldn't watch, not even to protect your own life. You are the best of us. You will always be the best of us. Adam is as ruined as our father on his worst day. I can't corrupt him. He's already rot. But you . . . there are things I would keep off your hands."

I have never seen him like this. It makes me think I don't know him as well as I thought I did.

"Cara, she told me you break your lovers. Says you hurt them bad."

"No, I . . ." But then something happens, someone's face passes behind his eyes, and his confusion turns hard. ". . . Not in a long time. Not since I was young."

I look up, forcing him to meet my eyes. "Not since I came?"

"No one had ever protected me from harm before. Not my mother, not my older brother. No one. But when you came, you stopped it like it was obvious that it should stop. I realized I was wrong about everything. I still don't *understand* like you do. Not in my heart. But I have learned from watching you. I have learned what is too much. I've since gotten . . . help, with my heart."

Help? Did he see someone at the House? Is that when he got so close with Exlee? I think back to our disagreement about forcing Cross out of treatment. The way he looked at me before caving in. He was listening to me. His instinct might tell him to use everyone around him to death for victory, but when I disagreed he listened.

"You've cleaned me up after killing two men with my bare hands and decided to make me your moral compass?"

"You killed Senior for what he did to me. You killed Ripper for what he'd done to other workers. We don't live in a place where nonviolence is an option, but you are precisely the person who needs to be holding the sword." He looks away. "What Adam and I have planned is bloody, bloody enough to ensure your reign will be peaceful."

My reign is a concept I reject instantly. I don't want to imagine outliving my brother. I don't want to imagine standing alone in the place where I used to stand beside him.

It is tempting, though. To sit back, let something bad happen, then call myself innocent.

"No," I say. "I don't want peace bought with the blood on my brother's hands. If it's *for* me, let it be *on* me."

He can't be surprised, but he does look impressed. "Are you sure? You can't know the burden I am about to take."

"I've killed lots," I say, irritated at all this concern for my morality.

"You've killed lots, but you've only murdered twice, and this will be much, much worse than that."

I shake my head. "What could be worse than murder?"

He leans back in his chair, and suddenly he looks older and more tired than he ever has. He looks, just a little, like the first man I killed.

"Letting some of your own people die to save the rest," he says.

I sit back down to listen and, slowly, begin to understand.

My brother doesn't want to start a war. He wants to change the world.

—

"THIS IS RECKLESS," I SAY. "THE RISKS ARE TOO HIGH."

"They're as high as the reward," Nik Nik says. "And we'll never get a chance like this again."

Ruth was right. I should have known. The oldheads are always right.

"There are so many ways this goes wrong."

"But it might go right."

"Say it does," I say. "Say it goes smooth as glass . . . and then the council of cities bombs us to shit anyway."

The question hardens his face, takes the hope out of his eyes. It's a question we can't answer. No one can.

"We have to move forward as if they won't."

This is crazy, and I'm so past protocol I don't even try to keep the judgment out of my voice. "But you don't know. You can't."

"Fifty percent chance."

"Fifty percent chance that *we all die*. You, me, our soldiers, our citizens, everyone. There are no survivors when the council makes an example."

"And fifty percent chance that we thrive in ways our father could only have dreamed of."

He's right about one thing: The possible reward is too great. I'll never be able to talk him out of this unless I know for sure it's a disaster.

I stand, too quickly. Nik stands, too.

"I have to go," I say, marching toward the door.

"Where?"

"To find out if you and your brother are about to get us all killed," I say, and move as fast as I can to the darkest place I've ever been.

—

WHEN I LEFT MY BROTHER I DIDN'T THINK ANYTHING COULD LIFT MY MOOD, BUT SNEAKING UP TO THIS small house in the desert comes close. I want to creep up and yell *Boo!* to pay Cara back for always slinking around, but when I walk toward the house she's already staring out the window. At first I think she's seen me and ruined the surprise, but she can't possibly because all the lights inside her house are on and outside is as dark as my future.

I hear the ground shift beside me, not too late but close, and make out the shape in my periphery.

"So you're the one who taught her to walk like a ghost," I say, not turning my head to face Dell, though I watch her from the corner of my eye. In one hand she has a weapon, in the other she has a portable perimeter scan. It must have alerted her the second I stepped onto the property. I know for damn sure I didn't trip any lasers, so she must have the fancy satellite version, because of course she would.

Dell lowers her stunner, and I see her smile for the first time.

"You greatly misunderstand her nature if you think I could teach her anything." There's so much love in her voice, it's not even a criticism. It's awe. "Have you come here to prematurely disturb her peace?"

"Prematurely?"

Dell nods, shifting beside me to stare at Cara through the window. "She knows something is coming. She often does."

Now we're both watching the woman she loves, and I see what she means. Cara's arms are crossed, and her face is tight, like she's trying to work out a problem no one else can see.

"I'm not buzzed to be bringing you trouble. I wouldn't if I had a choice," I say.

"I'm giving you a choice."

"I need to speak to her. It's about . . . traversing."

Dell regards me with new interest, and I wonder what she thought I'd come for. It clearly wasn't this.

"What do you want to know?" she asks.

"I need to ask her how she controlled it. If the worlds are so many, and movement so open, how did she find the way to where she wanted to go?"

"She didn't control where she was going," Dell says. "I did."

Seeing Cara so obviously upset has killed my desire to disrupt her night, and now I genuinely don't have to.

"How is it done? Tell me and I'll go."

"Would you like to know what the scientists believed, or the spiritual?" she asks.

It's a nonsense question, which is why I'm surprised I don't have an answer. "Which are you?"

"Both," she says. "I've been both from the moment she walked into my life."

"Then you'd better give me both."

"The science involved sound. Each world has its own unique frequency, and I would tune the material in the hatch to match where we needed to go."

She says *we* needed to go, but I'm sure she never traversed herself. It must have felt like it. I bet it felt just like her own heart was leaving every time.

"And what would the spiritual say?"

Dell looks away from me, back at Cara who is now looking down at a screen, reading something at their table.

"Cara was the only one who came back every time," Dell says. "And she was the only one whose handler was in love with her."

"You think it mattered?"

"The science of sound and a mineral compound is what you need to send you. But sometimes it felt like my own will was bringing her back."

I swallow hard. It's not good news. My strongest connection is my brother, and even that link has frayed to a near-break now that his secrets might have cost Cheeks everything.

"And what if . . . what if no one loves you?"

I'm grateful Dell's face is so unexpressive, because I'm sure it would be covered in pity otherwise.

"If you had no love in your life, you wouldn't be taking the risk traversing in the first place."

She starts to walk away, signaling that she's said all she's going to. She's said enough. I owe her.

"Adam's been saying some things. He says . . . he says he did something to Cara that'll make her outlive you. I wasn't sure if she told you."

The surprise on Dell's face is real, and she looks at Cara inside quickly before turning back to me.

"That explains the mood she's been in," she says, and there's almost a smile on her face.

"You're not upset?"

At first it's like she doesn't understand my question. "I've had years of Cara leaving me behind on this earth. I don't think I could survive it again."

She walks inside the house, but I stay standing long enough to watch a bright change come over Cara's face when Dell walks in. I've never seen her look like that. I've certainly never seen anyone look at me that way. In that look, I have my answer.

I leave the lovers alone and ride recklessly home. I tear apart my already messy room looking for a gift from so long ago I don't even have the same name anymore. I find it shoved in a drawer: a bit of amethyst on a long metal chain.

What is it for?

It helps you find your way.

It's a reminder of the truth Helene X and I share. Because maybe no person loves me with the strength that Dell loves Cara. But I have been loved. I have been cradled, and healed. I have been called back from another world and welcomed home when I arrived.

It's Ashtown. I'll traverse for Ashtown, and my love for Ashtown will bring me back, just like it always has.

—

IT'S TWO DAYS LATER AND EVERYONE IS DEAD. I WATCHED THEM DIE. WE FOUGHT WELL; WE FOUGHT better than they did. But the blood and the smoke and the screaming still come. Cross dies last and he dies in my arms. He tells me he loves me, but he's gut sliced and bleeding heavy, so I don't know who he thinks I am. The shadow that falls over me belongs to a man who has killed me before and who will kill me again. The black of his jumpsuit crinkles as he crouches down to put his blade against my throat. I don't close my eyes. I stare into his face, not because I care who he is, but because I want to haunt him.

I open my eyes, gripping the pendulum I've wrapped around my palm. Gasping, I roll onto my side and vomit black water onto the floor of the cave. We all died. Again.

Two things have become clear: First, no matter what the treaty says, when the next wave begins, Wiley City is not going to open its walls to us. Second, if we fight them for breaking their word, the council steps in and we will all die anyway.

My plan was to get concrete visuals, convince my brother that the council will kill us if we repay the city for betraying their contract. And in some worlds, I do just that. But it doesn't matter. It was too late to turn back before I ever entered this water. The moment those first bodies broke apart badly enough to give the city something to fear, we were already as good as dead.

At first, I was just reliving the same failed battle over and over again with no control. Then I remembered Dell saying how important sound is to this process, and after I'd go into the water I'd begin seeking places that sounded different so that I could see places that *were* different. I have seen futures where we strike earlier, where we strike later, where we wait for them to strike, where we have different captains lead, where we are less or more aggressive. They are all there, the endless possibilities of different future universes. And in all of them—Every. Single. One.—we die. The cities don't care that Wiley broke their word. They side with them against the faceless dead Ashtowners. We don't matter to them. They will incinerate us for daring to think we deserved the respect of a promise kept.

And if we don't fight? If we let them close us out? Then I watch my friends and neighbors transform from human beings into exploded abstractions of blood and bone. And then, and here's the kicker, the black jumpsuits come for the rest of us anyway. Nik Nik understands that this unprecedented event is an opportunity to upend the status quo, but Wiley's mayor does too. So, after we're rendered weak by the other world, the city will come. They will seize land regardless of sovereignty, regardless of rights, and reopen the earth-and-people-killing factories and mines that only we stood in the way of. The nomads in the deepwastes will be rounded up, forced to take names and social security numbers, just to be left out in the desert again, because someone will need to work for nothing in the desert, and the rest of us will be gone.

I try to stand and come crashing down, my eyes swimming with bad light. The first few dives I got a headache. The next few, muscle cramps. The voices, indistinct whispers that come from all sides, happened a few dives after that. I don't know how long ago the vertigo started, but I know I can't stop, because I don't have an answer. I try to stand again, but it's no good. I crawl to the edge of the pool, and wait. I'm too hurt to walk in, which means I won't be able to get myself out. I might find out what we need and drown before I get the chance to tell anyone. Is it worth it?

I look up, and see her face. I don't know when Cara entered the cave, but she's standing in the dark, her obsidian eyes catching torch shine like a creature peering out from behind reeds. She looks from the liquid pool, to me, and then nods. This is not a promise. I understand instantly that this is not her telling me she will pull me out if I go in. It is an answer: The risk is worth it. That even drowning in this sludge is a kinder fate than seeing what will come if I don't figure this out.

With no assurance of survival, I plunge into the dark.

—

YOU'D THINK I'D BE GETTING BETTER AT WATCHING IT, BUT EVERY TIME IT'S WORSE. IT'S WORSE BEcause I know these aren't dreams. These are worlds. This isn't fantasy; it's reality. Even worse, soon it will be history. We'll all just be so much history. It's already happened on other earths, and in other places on this earth. Civilizations once strong wiped out by those greedier, more religious, more self-entitled. Inventions uninvented. Poetry, not just unwritten, but the very words that would have made it up lost forever, the very tongue it was written in cut out and excised from reality. Nik Nik used to tell me these stories, the fallen empires. Places that had plumbing and sewers and writing before anyone else, but they were nonviolent, so they were killed by hordes who called them heretics and shit in their water basins and used the sewer for food storage because they didn't know what it was. I know that it happened; I just didn't think I would ever see Ashtown turned into deadland, turned into museum fodder. And I have no doubt that if I look far enough into the future, Wiley will have whole exhibits about the people we used to be. Their kids will dress up as us for school projects. Their eccentric artists will take names that sound like ours and say stupid shit like *Spiritually I am an Ashtowner*.

I go through it all, again and again and again. There are bodies I have seen so many times now they have become geography, people who die so consistently I can visit them like the friends they used to be. Ruth, always with the other oldheads, killed in her private compound. Exlee killed in the palace's safe house. Every worker, runner, garbage git, and Ruralite together in their deaths in ways they would never be together otherwise, because the people killing us can't tell us apart anyway. There is no distinction to them. We don't have different religions or cultures. We're all just Those Outside the Wall.

I cycle through possibilities again, but then I hear something. It feels significant. It feels like a clue. I draw closer to the sound, soft, irregular. It's the sound of me, crying. A name floats up from the void: *Travin Wills*. It's not an answer, but it's close. What does a man who became a martyr before I even took the leather have to do with this? I almost have it, I am *so close* to making all the poison I've consumed worth it, when it's pulled from me in an instant.

—

"NO!" I SAY, OR START TO SAY, BEFORE I BEGIN RETCHING. I THOUGHT I'D BEEN CAREFUL TO KEEP MY head above water, but I must have taken some of the liquid in because I'm vomiting and dry heaving like my body has no more use for a stomach.

"You shouldn't be here," Esther says, sidestepping the fluid that's gathered around me.

I want to argue, or explain, but then the seizure comes, and my whole body goes rock-rigid, all my limbs extending wrong.

"You need a doctor," Esther says, crouching down. She wipes my brow with the hem of her skirt. The concern on her face is real.

"I need . . . to go back . . . in."

"Absolutely not," Esther says.

"I have to." I want it to be a yell, but it's a whimper. People are supposed to fear runners, but I'm so weak even this Ruralite doesn't flinch at my rage.

I settle for pleading. "If I don't, everyone dies."

She kneels down, her face still hard but her voice sad. "No, they won't. That water . . . it plays tricks. It poisons your mind. It makes you destroy yourself."

I think about how horrified she looked after I fell in the first time, how careful she is not to touch the liquid now.

"You went in?" I ask.

She recoils like the words have dripping fangs. "Never."

I close my eyes, and man it feels good to rest, to just lie here like this, if only for a second. When I open them again, she's still looking down.

It makes you destroy yourself.

"Your dad?" I say, my tongue not quite cooperating.

She cocks her head in that particular way I've seen Cara do so many times now. I don't know where Cara goes when war breaks out. I've never seen her body, but I'd bet it's somewhere only her sister knows.

"... Yes," she says, finally. "My father fell in shortly before he left us."

He knew. He saw everything he'd ever known end in ashes, and probably couldn't live with it. I wonder if he had the nightmares like me, or if it was worse. If he had to watch what happened to his children over and over again, and cracked. I wonder if he saw me, always somehow holding his son when he died, and wondered who I was.

I can't let it happen. Standing up is too impossible to even be a dream, but I try to turn over so I can crawl. No dice. I begin to rock myself back and forth over and over again hoping to gain enough momentum to turn onto my stomach. It works, but I've pinned my arms under my chest now, so I can't even crawl.

I turn my head, seeing Esther staring down at me in equal parts revulsion and pity.

I take a breath, and say the word I hate the most.

"Help?" only the *L* doesn't come, so it's more like *hep*.

"Is there someone who can take you home?"

Yes, but no. Not yet.

I look at the liquid, too still now that I'm out of it. It looks like solid black glass, like if I try to go in I'll just slide across the surface.

"Put . . . me . . . back."

"Absolutely not. You're half dead as it is, and I barely got you out the first time. Let me call someone for help."

"Put me in . . . then call."

She rolls her eyes.

"It's important," I say, before adding my second-least favorite word. "Please?"

She sighs, but I know a forfeit when I hear one.

"You'll have to help me."

She puts a hand on my side and begins to push. I rock with her, and we roll me over and over with my waterlogged-leathers squelching with every turn, toward the pond. By the time we make it she's out of breath and I'm feeling remarkably like a moist meat lump over a bonfire. It certainly doesn't look—or sound—like the bravest thing I've ever done, but it is.

Just before I go back in, she stops me.

"Who should I call? To get you?"

"Cross," I say.

When her eyebrows knit I know it's more disbelief than confusion. She must know her brother's new name, after all these years.

Still, I humor her. "Michael," I say.

She nods, though it's tense. She grabs some dirt from the floor of the cave, and looks up to a sky we can't see.

"I call as your servant, sanctify the actions of the day. Guide this child through light, but bring her home to ash, and dirt, and oil."

She takes the dirt and smears it on my forehead. I don't know if it will bring me home, but the cool of the earth and the warmth of her hand feel as divine as any deity. Maybe that's all holiness is: the dirt that raised you in the hands of someone who cares.

"So let it be done," she says, pushing me into the darkness for the last time.

CHAPTER TWENTY-FOUR

EVEN WITHOUT THE WATER, I WOULD BE VOMITING AFTER WHAT I'VE SEEN. CROSS PULLED ME OUT, BUT I was ready to leave the water long before he did.

"You're all right. You're okay."

I've seen too much now. I've seen his whole life. So I know that while his sister trained in leadership, he trained in aid. She prayed over the dead; he tended to the sick. It's how he got access to the substances that almost unmade him. But it's also how he's able to kneel beside me in the dirt outside the cave, unbothered by my retching, placing a cool hand on the back of my neck precisely where I need it most.

"I need to get you to the hospital. I'll have to pick you up. Nod if that's all right."

I don't know how he knows I can't speak, but I'm grateful. I nod, and I'm even more grateful to feel suddenly weightless. I don't ever want to walk again. I don't want my legs to be my legs or my body to be my body. I would forfeit my eyes to ensure I would never again see what comes next. Cut off my hands to stop them from doing what I know they have to.

His sister must not have told him why she was calling him, or he would have brought something other than the cycle. He places me on the bike ahead of him, then gets on behind me, arms wrapping around to get the handles. It's dangerous. But I don't want him to think better of it. Pressing against him I slowly put myself back in my body. Listening to his heart reminds me I have a heart.

Feeling him breathe helps me remember how. There's nothing physical in the dark water. And it felt like I was there for a very, very long time. I watch his hands tighten on the handlebars and flex my own fingers in response. If he talks to me enough, I know I will remember how.

—

THIS TIME WHEN I WAKE UP, I'M IN A STERILE INFIRMARY RATHER THAN THE MUDDY GROUND OUTSIDE OF a cave. The light is almost too bright here, and I wonder how long I was in the dark. It felt like years, traveling through the same set of days over and over again, but who can tell? I'm not sure how to measure time anymore. How to treat it like it's not a living thing, ornery and unpredictable.

I sit up, but the room shifts out from under me. It shifts. It is the room, then it is the smoldering remains of the room, then it is the hundred-year-old ruins of the room in the future, where kids will light fires and tell scary stories, and then it goes backward, to before the room, just ground and brush and life. I move my legs over the edge of the bed, and suddenly my feet are dangling over the ocean floor that this part of the desert used to be. I close my eyes, and wait for the world to right.

"The side effects of the exposure should pass once the deferoxamine works through your system."

I open my eyes and see Adam, then I look sideways at the glass bottle dripping liquid into my veins.

"I'll need it in a syringe," I say. "The next wave is coming in around thirty hours, and I need to see my brother."

Adam tilts his head. "My sensors haven't detected the next—" He stops, looks away, then back at me. "Well done."

My cuff flashes red with the notification going out to all runners. A thirty-hour countdown flashes between instructions to report in.

He looks away from the new intel to me. There's no panic about the countdown, about the war we both know is coming; he just looks at me with a curiosity that verges on desperation.

"Fascinating," he says. "I trust you know what it will take, for us to survive this."

I nod, tense. I want him to know that I hate him. Even if this isn't the moment to do anything about it.

"Then the question is, are you going to do it? Or am I?"

I glare hard for as long as I can take, wishing I had another answer to give. But there's only one. There's always been only one. Adam Bosch is one of the coldest people I have ever met . . . and we are on the exact same side.

"I'll handle it," I say.

He comes over to remove the tube from my vein.

"When I tipped your whereabouts off to the mayor's kill squad, I wasn't sure who would be taken. But I am glad, now, that it wasn't you."

I want to square up on him then, to spit in his flesh eye and take all my rage out on him. But then Cross comes in, as I'm sure Adam knew he would, and I can't react, because I can't explain.

I turn to Cross, and can't breathe. He is Cross as I know him, but he is also older, wearing the marking of a general and a scar across his eyebrows, and he is younger, a boy in a tunic whose eyes never carry a hint of light despite being the color of a bright sky, and he is the age I know him now, but dead, eyes empty and a blood curtain across his chest.

"What's wrong?" he asks.

I turn away, shutting my eyes tight.

He touches my arm, and I look at him, the contact grounding me. It also locks him as the version I know, so I put my hand over his to keep it there.

He looks over at Adam, then back at me. "Is there something wrong with the medication he gave you? I looked it up. It is supposed to be for metal poisoning."

"It's fine. I'm fine. Just . . . just shaky," I say.

Adam comes up from behind me and claps a mechanical hand on Cross's shoulder, touching only and always the people who don't want him near.

"I'll give this one the syringes for your next dose in a few hours." Then he holds my gaze. "I believe you have places you need to be."

Cross doesn't like the sound of that, but I pretend I don't notice and nod.

"Do you know where Himself is?" I ask.

"He was in his office, but he probably won't be for long," Cross says. "Cheeks is back. He's in recovery waiting for Viet."

I look away when I nod, because I already knew where Cheeks was, and I don't want to explain why hearing good news puts tears in my eyes.

"I'll see him next," I say, and leave the room.

—

OUR WAY OUT WAS OBVIOUS, ONCE I FIGURED IT OUT. STORIES. OUR SALVATION, OUR CONTINUATION, our whole existence, has always been sustained by the power of a story to determine reality. And if I do everything right, we might be able to harness that power like we did all those years ago.

My brother is not the first person I see. First, I go to Splice, then I message Esther, and then, finally, I find my brother. He's not in his office anymore. He's precisely where I expected him to be: waiting at Cheeks's side, holding his most loyal runner's hand and hoping he'll wake up.

"We need to talk," I say.

I hear injury in my voice. I hear how unsteady I am. He must too, because the concern in his eyes when he looks at me is almost as strong as when he was looking at Cheeks.

"Tatik messaged me. You've been giving orders. I take it you saw something?"

I start with the easy part.

"They target the children. They kill them or kidnap them to make them Wiley. Instead of the shelter, I've arranged with Esther to have the young and infirm go to the cave. It's not on any maps, it won't be found, and that way if we lose . . ."

". . . there will be something of us left," he says.

With all his arrogance and Ashtown pride, I'm not surprised he couldn't plan for our death. He assumed the children would be held until we returned victorious, because of course we would. But we need to plan for our own annihilation.

"And you can't lead the charge," I say, and he immediately bristles, but I cut off his objections. "You can't. This only works if you're in the city with Adam infusing the atmosphere. The sight of you on the battlefield wins us zero popularity prizes, and sometimes . . . the dops start coming before we infuse the atmosphere."

"My dop already came. I won't be in danger."

"No, but seeing it happen ruins you. You become tactically useless and an easy target."

I don't add that Exlee dies in his arms the same way Helene died in mine. I don't add that I finally know, for certain, who he is in love with, because I watched that love turn like a hatchet. When my brother goes screaming into the city, a machete in each hand, he is glorious as he cuts down a dozen Wileyites for the crime of barring the doors, but it is just the spectacle they need for the coalition of cities to approve air raids and mass destruction.

"The runners need a leader. They need a symbol."

"I know," I say. "It's going to have to be me."

Even through all this shit, he manages to smile a little.

"You want to ascend before the charge?"

I nod. "Send for the braiders."

He rubs his chin. "If I had more time . . ."

"You'd what? Make a custom cape in the style of your mother's but reflecting my history instead?"

He smiles widely. "I like being prepared."

"Just go get it."

"Report to the west wing when you're ready. My mother's suite will be yours now. I'll send the dipper there too." He grabs my chin and tilts it up. "Your teeth are so sharp, they'll hardly need filing. We'll have to reinforce your nails though. You keep them too short. That will have to change."

I nod. That, and so much else. I will not be the same person when this ends as I was when it began. But maybe that was always true. I've had to be so many versions of myself in the last few hours, maybe I can never really lock down into the old one again. Maybe I'll spend the rest of my life feeling like I'm floating, like I can't get my feet to stay on the ground. I wonder if this is why Cara is always so hard to find, rootless as she drifts between the city and Ash.

"Can I ask you a question?"

My brother nods.

"How did you know Adam wouldn't betray us? How were you so sure you could trust him?"

This is the part that baffles me. I looked into futures beyond counting, and in every one Adam is loyal. Not just loyal, he does what he can to save us. Even in worlds where it costs him what little he has left in the city. Even in worlds where it costs him his life.

"The substance in the cave."

"Barsamin?"

Nik Nik nods. "It's the name of the god in the sky in the stories our mother used to tell us. He said he named it. After all this time, he carried it with him."

There are those who choose the city because they've genuinely absorbed Wiley's values so they've learned to hate the way their parents talk, the town they were raised in, their own names, their own skin. But then there are those that shed those things, not because they hate themselves, but because it is the only way to really feel safe. The only way to reach a place in life where you no longer feel like you're always just barely not-drowning. I'd always assumed Adam was the former. But maybe, maybe he's the latter, viewing Wiley as a tool not a salvation.

I was dead set on Adam being evil, because I've been looking for a villain this whole time. Every story needs a villain, especially one with as many dead as this tale has.

I just didn't know it was going to be me.

I take my brother's hand in both of mine and kiss his knuckles, swearing fealty to him for what will be the last time.

"I need a minute," I say.

At first he looks confused, then his eyes dart over to Cheeks, and he nods.

Once he leaves I approach the bed, and take Cheeks's hand.

They've beaten him, again, covering over every bruise I gave him with their own. Not one of these blows told him they loved him. They told him the opposite. They told him the world didn't want him. They told him no one and nothing would ever love him.

I don't know I'm crying until the tear drops. I don't know I'm hovering over his face until it lands on his bottom lip. I want to wipe it away, but it's too intimate, it's never been my place to touch his mouth. As I watch, the tear slides into the gap between his teeth. He will wake with my tear on his tongue. He will wake tasting salt, and he won't know why. He will wake, though, that much I know.

I tell him every good thing I know about him. I recall for him every moment I know he was happy, the names of everyone who loved him, and it is such a long list.

But that's why this is happening, isn't it?

I'll admit that I looked. I scoured the universe to see a time he would end up happy. Mostly, he survives the battle because he's here. When we lose, Wiley takes him. They call him a war criminal and force him to live his life in a cage, with the city giving access to every curious journalist and historian and sociologist. They say there was a time they would have hung him in public, would have turned his skin into purses and displayed his head and knuckles in a case for daring to rise against them. They never realize the glass-walled cage is no different: the preservation and display of a trophy.

I did, eventually, find one Cheeks that gets to be happy. One single version that gets peace.

But it's not this one.

Twelve minutes later Viet is telling me he's gone, and the room fills with oil as the preparations begin. I leave, tears streaming down my face, and go to select my crown.

WE LET THE STORY LEAK. SPLICE POSTS ABOUT CHEEKS'S MURDER ON CHAT ROOMS, LETS THE WILEY City newsvids pick it up. Just enough to know he's been killed in the city, just enough information to make them hungry. No one likes an unfinished story, so they fill the gap with speculation. People who hate us, people like the mayor, suggest he was killed committing a crime, or he'd overdosed on the wrong side of the wall. People who know us go straight to blaming enforcement. Enforcement denounces the possibility loudly, just as we knew they would. They open their records. They tell their trusting citizens they have no evidence of an interaction with the runner, though he did have a day pass for the day of the alleged interaction. They might even be telling the truth. The mayor's squad wasn't on any official channels. But the black jumpsuits are just the bluntest version of every value the rest of the city doesn't even know they hold. Even the mayor who hates us is just the one willing to say the quiet part out loud. It doesn't matter who knew what, or which officers were actually there. The whole system is guilty.

We wait until enforcement denies ever seeing Cheeks, and then we release the file. A story gets extra legs when it counters the narrative, and this one does. The info packet we release is picked up by Ashtown cuffs and Wiley TVs alike, and it opens up with pictures of Cheeks. Pictures of him grinning with a charm you can feel through the lens, pictures of him serious, covered in dirt as he worked to help others after the last anomaly. Splice decided to circulate images Wiley photographers took too, images of how the city would remember him. Once those have been out a few hours—long enough for the newsvids to get bored and become hungry for more, newer content—we release the recording of his attack. The footage of the mayor's private enforcement team surrounding him. His hands are in the air in a show of peace. He points to his cuff. The audio clearly picks up his voice: "Calm down, I've got a day pass."

As far as the world is concerned, those are the last words he ever said. He goes down in a sea of black jumpsuits, and we force the world to watch.

Enforcement scrambles. The mayor scrambles. The tone begins to shift as the city decides on its story, which of the whispers it will legitimize.

They say he was the mayor's lover, and she was covering it up.

They say the mayor's secretly addicted, and she killed her supplier so he couldn't tell.

Then, finally:

They say he'd found out the mayor was going to violate the Ashtown treaty, and she ordered his death to silence him.

This last one is the version that spreads: Cheeks as the hero of Ashtown taken out by a Wiley City villain.

The vice mayor's office legitimizes it by responding. She issues a statement saying she has no knowledge of any plan to violate the treaty, and that she denounces vehemently the xenophobic violence displayed. She calls for a full investigation.

The mayor's office is unavailable for comment.

In less than a news cycle, the city has decided on reality, and now, we just have to hope it's enough to keep retaliation at bay. Then the new discourse begins. New among Wileyites, because they are just now asking one another the question we have been asking the whole time:

Do you think the mayor's going to back out of the treaty?

I HEAR THEM. THROUGH THE DOOR, I HEAR THEM. IT'S SUNRISE. EVERY ASHTOWNER, RUNNER AND CITIZEN, is outside waiting for their instructions so we can efficiently lead our people to Wiley's walls. Walls we already know will not open for us, and soon, the entire world will know, too.

I look down at my hands, but they don't look like mine. No part of me looks like it's mine, not anymore. My nails have always been short, so to approximate the weaponizable nails every emperor has, the royal blacksmith has made me special prosthetics, black metal rings around the top of each finger with a retractable razor on each end. They were the last part of my outfit, and I've been nervously deploying then retracting the eight blades ever since. I like my hair short, so braids like my brother's won't work, but the top has been put into three neat rows, one on each side and a large one down the middle. Like my brother, I don't think I'll keep the chrome-dipped hair after today, but it's important my first impression be a total one, so the three rows on top of my head shine. We thought it best I wear my leathers—vest, pants, boots—though I've chosen my best ones, the ones that are still more black than deep brown, that aren't stained or roughed up. Not that anyone will notice, since over it all I am wearing the dramatic cape my brother has waited years to put me in. It's reptile hide on the outside, spider silk on the inside. The exterior is three different reptiles, actually. Two are crocs I took down myself that my brother saved, the other one he went out and hunted as a gift. Now I have a cape that is stunproof and, on the side that isn't the silk touching my skin, just toxic enough to be an advantage in a fight . . . or, as a last resort, a way out.

Outside, my brother is onstage speaking. He rarely addresses crowds, so I'm not surprised at the semi-constant cheering. Part of it is the result of his attempt to encourage his people . . . the other part is fear of what will happen if they don't cheer loudly enough. I've worked the streets for years, and before that I knew most citizens from the House. Will the people who've always trusted me start to fear me that way? Start lying to my face to spare their own necks? Maybe. But it's too late to mourn my place in the community now. My path is set, and it's the only one that leads somewhere other than total annihilation.

The people outside are cheering again, which is not my cue. I hear my brother quiet the crowd and I know from the severity of his tone that my moment is coming soon. The end of my life. The end of Mr. Scales. The death of who I used to be. But I'm already dead, aren't I? I cut a piece of my hair to lose Ackerman and change Devon to Dex. I killed the Ripper, ending Dex and making Mr. Scales. Now I'm Devon again, but Devon Nazarian, and getting to share a last name with my brother only mildly takes the ick out of sharing a last name with our father.

These aren't my hands, my cloak, not even my teeth, newly shaved and dipped in the emperor's onyx. I think I died, and I don't know if it was in that black pool or hearing Cheeks breathe his last, but somewhere along the line I became a ghost.

Well, that's fine. All good stories have ghosts. Let me be a vengeful one. Let me be the bloody kind men hear shrieking in the night before they never wake up again. Let me be the ghost of all our dead come back armed and rabid.

It's this that I hold on to, this wish for rage that I keep on my face when I hear my brother say the words *sister, and emperor,* sending a confused murmur over the crowd. That is my cue.

I knew the double doors would be pulled open by two high-ranking runners; I didn't know it would be Tear and Dragon. Dragon smiles wide, forgetting himself and crossing a fist over his chest like he's always been ready to accept me as ruler. Tear looks down at my ring finger, then back up. I smile wide with onyx-dipped teeth, and that makes it real for her.

Her back goes straight, and she half bows and crosses an arm over her chest before turning and marching runner-perfect beside me to the stage. There are no stolen glances or secret smiles, none of the jokes we used to play walking beside each other. All at once, she's acting like she works for me, and, I realize, she does.

Nik Nik takes my hand when I step onstage.

"My blood, my heart, my sister," he says. I am numb as he raises my hand above my head. "She has long been your protector, and now she dedicates her life, stepping in line for the throne."

I open my mouth wide to show my crown of sharpened teeth, and they cheer twice as loud.

Just as my official robes will always be monster skin, I've opted to have all my top teeth sharpened and dipped. My brother went for wide, long incisors, but he's always been a lion. I'm a thing with poison skin that licks the air, a thing that kills you long after she's bitten you. I let the bundle in my other hand drop, revealing my father's bladed whip. It was my first weapon, and the only thing I would dare take into my first war. The blades have been coated with my brother's poison. Our compromise, since I am still a mechanic at heart and bulky rings will only ever feel like a way to get your finger ripped off.

I may never get to be a runner again, but let them always remember that my name was Scales.

THE SMELL OF EXHAUST IS AS OVERWHELMING AS THE SOUND, THE SOUND OF RUNNERS. THE SOUND OF anxious soldiers laughing too loud, the sound of weapons being sharpened. I'm going through, speaking to unit heads that outranked me yesterday, their eyes filled with questions they dare not ask me now. I know that coming out like this will cast a cloud over my reign. I'll need to do work to earn their trust if I don't want to rule through fear like the emperors before me.

I'm halfway through preparations when I see it, a dark shape, already small but making itself smaller. Someone who wants to be here to help, but doesn't want to see me. I use the fact that my legs are twice as long as hers to cut the distance quickly, and am lucky to catch her at the edge of the building, which gives us a little privacy.

"I don't have anything to say to you," Cara says. Her eyes are red for Cheeks, and I wonder if she's spent her morning comforting Esther.

"That's why I'm the one doing the talking. You're riding in the VIP caravan to the city. You'll be with Adam and the emperor when they infuse the atmosphere."

She wants to tell me no. She wants to reject the order. She can't. Her eyes narrow, taking in my cape, teeth, hair, and nails like a confession. "The *other* emperor, you mean."

"This was the only way."

"Death is never the only way. It's just the easiest."

"You didn't see the things I saw. I am trying—"

"You think I've never had the visions? You think I have never seen how removing one person from an equation could simplify the world? But you can't give in to it. Soon you'll be slitting the throats of babies because of who their grandchildren will be."

I swallow, because she's not wrong. "Isn't that what you did when you tried to kill Adam?"

"No, I hit Adam for crimes he *committed*. I didn't kill someone innocent, someone *unconnected* just so the aftermath will shape the world in the way I wanted."

"Be honest with yourself. You just don't like that this path runs through a war on the city."

This hits her, and her shoulders relax, the closest thing to backing down I've seen from her yet. "I don't like unnecessary death."

"Maybe, but you also *love* the city. You can pretend you hate them, but deep down you're just jealous. You hate them for rejecting you, but you love what they stand for."

"That's not true."

"All I want is for the city to stop existing. To snap my fingers and wake up in a world where they are a million miles away and have never heard of us. All you want is for them to open their arms and take us all in and for the differences between us to disappear."

Her eyebrows knit. "I want us to exist peacefully. That's not a crime."

"The city only exists in peace with itself. Peace will only come when we stop being us, and they can pretend we're just like them. Your peace is genocide."

"You aren't being practical," she says, which is probably true. "Yeah, it'd be great if we could snap our fingers and pretend they never came to our desert, but they did and we can't. We have to figure out how to coexist."

"That's what we're doing. Teaching them the lessons they need to learn to coexist with us."

She must read everything I'm not saying, or maybe it's our fight from earlier playing across her face, but no one has ever looked at me with as much disgust and disappointment as Cara's giving me now. This is Ashtown's irreconcilable difference: to assimilate and reduce suffering, or to remain ourselves and stay a target. We are standing on two sides of an issue that can never be resolved, and it's a shame because it's a fight we didn't start. They did, but it will tear us apart anyway.

"I'll ride in the convoy, but once this is over, don't call on me again," Cara says. "After what you did, I want nothing to do with you."

It doesn't hurt, because I don't much want anything to do with myself either. But I keep my face runner hard, no, *emperor* hard when I say, "As long as you keep what happened to yourself, you won't see my shadow. If Nik needs you, he will get you."

"I won't tell," she says. "But only because I know why you did it, and I don't want it to be for nothing."

I nod. "I'll see you in the city."

"And then never again," she says over her shoulder.

—

CARA IS ALLOWED TO HATE ME, BECAUSE RIGHT NOW SHE IS THE ONLY ONE WHO SEES ME CLEARLY.

Because she came to visit Cheeks after promising her sister she would. Because she was there—a shadow I've never quite been able to track or hear or anticipate—watching me kiss my brother's knuckles in fealty, and watching me slide off one of his rings and pour the contents into Cheeks's mouth.

"What is that? Is it medicine? What are you doing?"

When I turned there must have been some guilt, some admission, in my eyes because she understood instantly that I was not there to save him. I tried to explain. Tell her that when she told me to go back into the barsamin I did, and I saw us all die over and over and over again. Except Cheeks. In every version he survived by being in the infirmary, he survived to become a slave. Only when he dies do we survive this. Only when there is a singular face to make the tragedy legible does the council spare us and allows us to fight with Wiley in peace. It was the lesson Travin Wills taught us, and if this goes right, it's not a lesson anyone will ever have to learn again.

She disagreed with everything I said, but most important, she disagreed with my first sentence.

"I never saw you in the cave, Scales. I would never hint for you to look for other worlds. It will ruin your life."

I wanted to tell her it already had, but it would save so many others.

Instead, I told her to leave, and I walked toward Cheeks.

"I won't let you poison him anymore," she said, moving between us. So small, so determined. I wondered if she knew she is so hard to find. When I tried to look into other worlds, those in our time and those in the future, she's like a ghost. There but not. Present, but slippery. I don't know what that means, but it scares me for her.

It doesn't matter. We won't be friends after this. She'll keep her word to never speak to me again, so I'll never get to tell her that I do respect her. That I respect her and I know she's right and I wish being right was enough, but it's not.

I was still grateful that I wouldn't have to move her, wouldn't have to hurt her to do what I needed to.

Cheeks was waking up. That was all I needed.

"Cheeks," I said, looking at him over Cara's head. She was still standing, feet planted and two feet tall, as if I couldn't end her to accomplish my goal. So much runner in her for someone who resents us so much.

She knew I could hurt her, of course. She knew I could and she knew that I wouldn't. For as disgusted with me as she was, she still thought I was at least that good.

"Scales?" Cheeks asked back, his voice weak.

Hearing him say my name for what I knew would be the last time filled my eyes with tears. I tried to keep my face even—Cara had already seen enough of me—but it was no use. I cleared my throat, swallowed hard, and said what I had to say.

"Tell me you love me, Cheeks."

He'd chuckled at that. "I love you."

"Tell me you're in love with me and I'm the best runner ever."

He was still laughing when he spoke. "I'm in love with you and . . . and . . ."

I closed my eyes and looked down as over Cara's shoulder Cheeks began to writhe in agony, the lie he'd just told mixing with the serum I'd put into his system, exacerbating the injuries he'd barely survived, and turning them fatal.

When I opened my eyes Cara was gone and Cheeks was dead on the table, mouth full of blood from internal injuries that Viet is sure came from enforcement.

This was not me killing a man I used to love who never loved me back.

This was not me killing my best friend so he wouldn't suffer what was to come. I would have done it even if there had been happiness on the other side for him.

No. This? This could only ever be one thing: the moment I became an emperor.

PART FOUR

And when the cherry's white with blossoms
be ready and be brave;
and remember what we had here
when there was something left to save.

—John Darnielle,
"Magpie"

CHAPTER TWENTY-FIVE

THEY CALL ME MR. SCALES BECAUSE . . . DO YOU STILL WANT TO KNOW? I WON'T TELL YOU WHICH ONE is the truth. It doesn't matter anymore what they called me, or why they called me it. I am not that person, and I can't ever be again. The multiverse is full of people you could be, sure. That's all anyone thinks about when they look at Cara. But I am here to tell you the multiverse is also full of people you can never be. Of paths you can never take. Of rooms with only one way out.

Possibilities, when you get down to it, are rainbows: beautiful and meaningless.

Now they will only ever call me Sir. And I will only ever call myself a murderer.

—

I AM STANDING ON A RIDE WITH TIRES AS TALL AS TWO HUMANS AND TWICE AS WIDE. I'M A MONSTER riding atop Beast. I never thought I'd see the world from the top of my father's most destructive ride, but here I am. I feel so high up, even higher since I have to stand to operate it, and I hate how small it makes even my runners look. From this high up, no wonder the stories say my father never flinched no matter how many kids he crushed. You could just pretend they were animals, some kind of rodent. The top's been taken off and the body lifted, so that I am visible to all who wait revving their engines and chewing their lips. We are runners, and we are about to parade.

I can't explain to you the feeling. I'm tempted to say it's electricity in the air, raising hairs on your neck, goosebumps on your arms. But it's nothing so technical as that. It's earthy. Tangible. It's the way a vibrating engine challenges your heart to match it and leaves you gasping. The way when some fluids get hot enough to scorch they smell exactly like spilled blood, and force you to remember that you are also made from parts mined in the deep. That you are just as much an engine, your blood just as much iron, as anything beneath you.

Runners don't love their rides out of pride, or out of some greedy fixation on objects. Runners love their rides because we know what everyone else wants to forget: The line between hot stuttering machine and the human body is thin enough to barely see light through. Especially when the latter is flattened on the ground, twitching without thought because all machines take awhile to wind down once your foot's off the gas.

That is what we've been prepping them for. We are murderers. We are meant for murder. The last few weeks have been a scramble to protect our people, but at the core of that protection is a promise to rise to violence. This is the step some civilians don't understand, the step Cara rejects: We can *only* make good on our promise of protection if there's blood on our hands. We can't bluff. The city only speaks the language of power, and we have to speak it right back for them to listen.

I am about to start my engine, a sign to the procession that we're going to take off, when a roar comes toward us. At first, I reach forward, my hand hovering over buttons that can bring whatever manner of pain I choose. But then I recognize the ride in front—fire-red with gilt edges. It's a vehicle that used to strike fear on sight alone, but it hasn't run in decades.

I look down at Ruth, who is either wearing her old leathers or has had new ones made that look shockingly similar.

"Out for a drive, general?" I ask.

"Slow day. My friends and I thought you could use an escort."

Her *friends* are a collection I know well. The old guard. The runners who taught the rest of us what running means, retired but ever-ready.

I want to smile, but first I have to say, "You know how dicey it'll get. You're not required to do this. Conscription doesn't apply to you."

Ruth chuckles, pulling her goggles back down. "Don't tell me the conscription parameters, I wrote them. We're here for Cheeks, and you'll have to chase us off to keep us home."

His name puts a lump in my throat, and I struggle to swallow around it.

"You still favor the left?" I say, signaling Silk to accommodate them.

"If it's not too much trouble," Ruth says. No, not Ruth. She's Ruthless again now, and seeing the ease with which she slips back into the fight lets me know she was never anything else. Ruth was a mask, with Ruthless always waiting underneath.

I have seen this battlefield a hundred times, but today will be the last. No more do-overs. No more test runs. When I see these runners die, I will never see them upright again. But Ruthless and her friends weren't around for most of the failures, and that gives me hope.

I start my engine, a signal for everyone else to start theirs, and when the roar comes from so far in the distance it feels like I'm in the center of one large wave of machinery, when the sound is so loud it syncs like it all comes from the same beast, I raise a fist. The unit heads each raise theirs, signaling to their groups. At the same moment I punch forward and hit the gas, I open my mouth wider than I ever have. I risk exhaust and dirt clogging my lungs to let out the loudest, pitchiest runner cackle the desert has ever heard.

The parade has begun.

WE ARE NOT AN ARMY; WE ARE A CREATURE. AT LEAST, I AM SURE THAT IS WHAT THEY SEE AT THE wall. Driving wheel-to-wheel, we move like a sideways centipede, skittering toward the city on a thousand legs of unified purpose. I am the tallest figure in the center, the head of the beast, but above and behind us rises our carapace: the wide, round cloud of dust that is reaching to heaven. It's larger than I've seen it, even in my visions of this day, but that's because Ruthless's people are here and the old rides have teeth for treads that tear up the earth like they want to see the other side.

The important thing, the *main* thing, is not how we look: It's how we sound. You'd think the engines and wind would be too loud for the stories of the runners' cackle being the loudest part of the parade to be true. But it is the loudest part. We are a roar as we come up to the city. I wonder if the mayor can hear us. I wonder if she is watching and sweating. Or if she is so sure she's sleeping easy.

When we get to the front entrance of the city, I check my cuff, the red countdown reminding me of the consequences of failure. I need to get this over with, so that my people can be spared the broken agony of the other world coming over. A sea of black stands in front of the wall. Enforcement looking more like us than they ever have in their dark jumpsuits, though those clothes are for easy cleaning, not protection like ours. The biggest difference, though, is that they had a choice. Enforcement in the city isn't keeping anything alive, isn't vital to anything. They just protect rich people from minor inconveniences. They could stop working and their world wouldn't fall apart.

That is what I will tell myself when we kill them.

The figures are still pouring out. We are less equipped. They are outnumbered. We are less eager. They are outmatched. I look up. There are two drones in the sky. One is theirs. One was theirs this morning, when I sent Mr. Em to harvest it. She made them crash like always, but this time she kept the corpse and brought it to Splice to refit. Now it's ours, and it's broadcasting video and audio. No matter how this goes, we will hold Wiley up to a light. The oldest way to beat the dark: Shine the light of truth upon it.

I grab the small box on the front of my steering wheel and hold it up to my mouth. I have another mic that transmits just to unit leaders for instruction, but this will amplify my voice for those not on our network. I'm careful to switch the internal mic off first, so I don't blow out the eardrums of anyone listening on our channel.

"I am the emperor of Ashtown. The infusion of your atmosphere began an hour ago. We seek entry into the quarters prepared for us for refuge, per the agreement signed by your leader."

Enforcement laughs, and sneers break out around me. The leader pushes through to the front, activating his own mic. His isn't a wired box like mine. It's a wireless, digital screen. It's hands-free, emitting from a device near his ear.

"Do you have a day pass?"

The black jumpsuits laugh even harder at that. I don't know if they're laughing because they somehow learned the backstory of the runner who would be leading the charge, or just because schoolyard cruelty when you are actively condemning others to death strikes them as the height of cleverness.

Those around me stay silent. We'd discussed this.

I say the next bit loud, loud enough to ensure the drones can pick it up.

"Are you saying that you will deny us entry despite the treaty?"

"No day pass, no entry."

"We are entering the city to inhabit the quarters prepared for us as part of the treaty signed by your leader. If you attempt to stop us, you will be violating international law. If you have orders to stop us, you will be following corrupt orders. We are coming in."

The words were written for me, so I'm careful to use them exactly as they were given. I'm doing everything I can to telegraph to Wiley's people, and the council undoubtedly watching, that I am acting on the side of legality, of law and order, and shouldn't be considered a target for incineration. This is another reason Nik couldn't come. Keeping his temper with those below him has never been his strong suit.

"You are trespassing," he says.

We are not. This is public land. But I'm sure he knows that and is just choosing to ignore it because he doesn't serve any law beyond following orders.

"Return to your homes peacefully," he says.

Yeah, and peacefully wait to die? He must know we can't do that either.

I put the speaker down and turn my comms back on. "Tech one, quiet the speaker."

The shot comes from above, and hits the man perfectly, though he doesn't know it. It pulses once, ensuring that the remote mic won't work anymore. A lot to be said for old-fashioned speaker boxes.

A voice comes over my comms.

"Say, 'This is public land and cannot be taken from the people without legislation. You cannot trespass on public land,' " Dell says, and I wonder who all is watching and listening on the drone above.

"Unless you have passed a law taking yet more land from the people, this land is public," I say, which is true of everything up to the wall itself. "We have authorization via treaty to enter these walls, and so we will. If you use force against us, you will be doing so on orders you are aware are illegitimate."

The speaker says something, looks confused, taps his ear, tries again.

Eventually, he just glares at me. Adam warned us there would be phrases—rights read, intentions stated—that would make whatever brutality they planned sanctioned under their law. Now they'll have to act without their safety net.

"Let's go," I say, and the beast begins to lumber forward again.

—

THEIR FIRST MOVE IS TO FIRE PROJECTILES. STUN BLASTS, ELECTRIFIED NETS, BEANBAGS THAT ARE classed nonlethal but have blown out eyes, shattered organs, and, yes, stopped hearts.

So our first move is to send in the rockets: three small, low bikes equipped with the kind of tires that would do Ruthless proud, biting up the earth and putting a cloud between us. The sand is so thick, only luck would let them hit us, and it doesn't.

We raise our goggles and ride.

Enforcement shoots a front liner off her bike and she rolls to the ground. Her limp form is picked up by the runner behind her. I don't know how seriously she's injured and I can't afford to look back, can't afford to look anything but joyous as we ride for blood. Enforcement does their best to keep the game long-range, firing stunners and electrified nets wildly in the dirtfog. One hits my front tire, but these tires could swallow barbed wire without pausing to chew, and it passes harmlessly under. They are long-range fighters and we are short, but we are eating up the space where they have an advantage and closing in on the space where we do. I know this won't last, but I push ahead full speed, trying to make the most of this fog, this last moment of protection for my runners.

It doesn't last long enough. There's whirring overhead of a third drone in the sky. This one drops liquid in the space between enforcement and us, getting rid of our cover. Quickly, their weapons begin finding their targets. A line of ours goes down in a wave. Some are scooped up by their fellow runners, some are not. I try to count my losses, but can't.

I see Sai go down and it's all I can do to keep from screaming. It's a curse, this well-armored ride. It will never be me getting got. I will sit in my rolling fortress and watch everyone I love turn to dust. This is the nightmare of ruling. Dragon picks Sai up but there's no telling if they're alive or dead, and from here I can't see Dragon's face to tell if he's mourning.

I turn my attention back to the front line. They may have cleared our cover, but it was too late. Soon the time for projectiles will be over, and they haven't killed enough of us to offset the advantage we'll have in hand-to-hand. Now I don't have to fake my runner's grin or my laugh. They may have just taken down one of our youngest, but we're finally within range.

I lock eyes with the officer who had the speaker. *Do you have a day pass?* I wonder if he thought that was funny, as I lash out with my whip down below. He raises a hand, blocking the whip from wrapping around his neck by catching it around his wrist. He yanks, pulling it from my hand. He studies it, wrapped around his hand like a captured snake. He's probably already envisioning taking it home as a trophy of the battle. He never once wonders why I am smiling.

—

WAITING IMPATIENTLY TO GET MY INAUGURATION OVER WITH, I HEAR THE UNEVENLY WEIGHTED GAIT coming up behind me and hate that he's been around long enough for me to know his walk without looking.

"You moving up, too?" I ask Adam. "Letting Nik collect the whole set?"

I can see from his expression that the thought hadn't even crossed his mind. It's true, I never saw a world where he betrayed us, but I also never saw one where he claimed us in the light.

"No, that's your path. Mine was chosen long ago," he says, and then I notice the box in his hands.

"So was mine," I say.

He smirks. "I know."

And I think he's just saying it, but then he opens the box and proves he does.

There, curled up into velvet like a snake in its hole, is the sharded whip I used to kill our father.

I look up from it like it might actually strike. "Nik told you?"

"Of course not. But I know the only reason to lie to me about your age would be to keep me from knowing you were the right age to match the witness reports. And I know there is only one weapon in that room that can do the kind of damage that was done to him, even in the hands of one so young."

"Why are you bringing this to me?" I ask, because I don't see an ounce of the threat I expect in his eyes. This doesn't feel like leverage, and I didn't think he ever operated under a motivation that didn't give him power.

He looks down at the weapon. "You know he used it on me once? The day before I left the desert. He had it made specifically because he thought it would be the thing to finally break me. To make me weep for him. To make me compliant. When it didn't work, he knew he had to get rid of me. In some worlds, most by my math, he killed me. In others, exile. I was twelve."

"I'm sorry," I say, the words coming out without my permission, before I can catch them, before I can remember what kind of

person I am saying it to. But fuck it. I am sorry. It's not an excuse for what he's done. But I wouldn't be me if I couldn't feel sad to watch a child treated that way. If I could just turn off that part of my heart as long as it was an enemy suffering, I'd be no better than the one who did it in the first place.

The look he gives me when I offer my apology is profoundly confused. When he looks back down to the box in his hand again I can't shake the feeling that he's just hiding his eyes from me.

"Nik is right about you. You will be good at this, but not because you are kind. Because you earned it," he says.

He's the only one who knows how true that is. The only one who knows I killed both my father and best friend to get here. It seems impossible to live in a world where the man who understands me best is among those I hate most.

"Give me your hand," he says, and before this conversation I would have told him to fuck off, but I offer up my palm without hesitation. He slips a small disk against the leather of the glove that imbeds itself into my palm.

"Splice is brilliant, but he can't give you what you want. My recall isn't done with magnets alone," he says.

That's when the too blackness of the disk makes sense. "Barsamin."

He nods. "It's a sympathetic material. I have a delivery system that leaves a fine coat on small objects I want to recall. When I activate it, the material, plus the magnet, work together to bring them to me. Look at the handle."

I look down at the handle of the whip and understand. I smile.

"For killing my father with the very weapon he crafted to break me, this is my gift to you."

I FLEX MY HAND, ACTIVATING THE RECOVERY MAGNET IN MY PALM. THE WHIP LEAPS TO RETURN TO ME handle first, the bladed length of it gleaming as it rips through the leader's joint to get free. He goes to his knees, holding his brand-new bloody stump to his chest.

I lash out again, and this time he doesn't try to block it. I push the tank forward with one hand, my other hand using the whip to yank his body toward my tires. My ride, the heaviest on the field, liquefies him to the neck, and when I yank the whip back this time it sends his head flying toward his comrades. My runners cackle and hoot at that. They told us their jokes. Now we've just told them ours.

"Spike strips!" Splice's voice cackles in my ear, intel from the drone above.

I tell Ruthless's contingent to go wide. I give the order for everyone else to abandon rides and go to foot. Tear obeys first and eagerly. She revs hard and shoots past me, then abandons her bike by sliding it at top speed into a cluster of officers, yanking the dual machetes strapped to her back free as she runs in behind it.

The other runners of the front line follow the same protocol, abandoning rides that continue forward at top speed, then running in with weapons drawn. Now the battle is beginning in earnest as roughened leather clashes with its plastic equivalent. Even our clothes are two different kinds of violence meeting head-on: Their plastic jumpsuits don't require a carcass to make, but they take so long to decay we'll be finding them in the stomachs of choked birds for centuries.

For the rest of my and Nik's plan to work, I need to get to the runners' tunnels inside the wall after the second wave. I can see the nearest entrance, a perfect hologram prepped to invite me in. There are easily thirty enforcement officers between it and me, but if I don't get there soon there won't be enough time to save us from the new world's attack. We'll win the battle, just to be turned to pulp on the sand.

I ride for as long as I can, before my tires have picked up so many spike stripes their mass of twisted metal blocks my wheels from turning, and I enter the field. I'm a target the moment I step down, but I'm armed for the challenge.

I snap my left hand out, charging my gloves while my right hand grips the whip still dripping in blood, just like the day I killed my father. That moment is inexplicably connected with this one, like I had to kill him to be standing here today. Like from the moment I killed him it was inevitable that I would become him, hungry for blood and screeching in the desert. I meant what I'd said to Adam, my path was chosen long ago. But he was right too: I did earn this.

The first officer that sees me fires a blast from his stunner automatically, but I turn and catch it on the hide of my back, before turning again and using the whip to make his stunner mine. I use his weapon to clear the way until it's out of charge, turning my body to let my cape absorb shots as I go. The creatures my brother and I hunted to make this cape cannot be killed from a distance. Their skin resists electrocution and poisoning, and even sharp projectile weapons bounce against its thick armor. No, you have to get close. You have to embrace it enough to slide your blade between and beneath the plates of its chest and hope it dies of its injuries before you die from its toxic skin. No stunners for me. If enforcement wants me dead, they'll have to get as close as I got to Cheeks. They'll have to get as close as a lover.

I manage to trip up an officer in my way with the whip, but when I go to put him down there's an arm against my throat, putting pressure from behind. I can't breathe, but I won't say it. I never want them to hear another of us say those words again. I dip my chin, forcing it into the crook of his elbow, open my mouth wide . . . and bite. To his credit, he doesn't release me when my razored teeth have dug deep into his forearm, but when I begin jerking my head side to side, sawing more of his flesh away with each movement, he screams and lets go. He falls to his knees, and I boot him hard enough in the face to stop his crying.

Now that I've discovered how handy sharpened teeth can be, I make my way through the field quickly. Biting an artery is faster than choking, and I can move on toward my goal while I leave them too afraid to take their hands away from their necks. I'm still not great at the whip, but whatever. I'll be good at it eventually, and for now the officers who see it get real skittish and make obvious mistakes.

I hear a yell and turn, but I'm too late. Slate is on the ground, eyes and mouth open to the dirt, an officer slowly rising over him. I'm there in a second, reaching with my blade-tipped fingers outstretched to slice open the throat of his killer.

"Slate?" I say, but there's nothing there. I think of the last time I saw him, watching me and his wife with all the love in the world in his eyes. Looking like he thought he was lucky. But he wasn't.

I take one moment to bend down, to close his eyes, to lick my thumb and make a mark on his forehead that the dust will stick to, bringing him home. Then I am on my way.

There is so much happening that I cannot control. My own people needing help, needing to be saved, and there's nothing I can do. I need to get to the wall. If I stay here, fighting with them and never accomplish my task, it will be for nothing.

There's a grunt as Blay—too old to be out here, but too stubborn to be anywhere else—goes down in a circle of them. They swarm him like ants, until I can't see him; I can only see them kicking and kicking and kicking.

I move toward him without thinking. And when a hand grabs me, I turn on a hiss.

"Your Highness," Cross says, nodding toward the wall.

He's one of the few I've told the full plan, because somewhere along the way my worst enemy became someone I trust.

I look over to where Blay fell. Cross is right. It's the wrong direction, and I'm cutting it close as it is. But I still can't bring myself to move away.

"You have somewhere to be."

He's right. I know he's right.

"I'll meet you there," I say.

He leaves without argument. Because I'm the empress or because he knows firsthand what a stubborn shit I am.

Before I can close the distance to where they've downed Blay, another shape jumps ahead of me into the fray. It's Tear who makes them pay, and she doesn't need my help. I'll need to thank her later.

I turn to follow Cross to the wall, but then Splice comes in on my earpiece.

"Second wave, incoming."

Right. Because we hit them with everything we had, but they held a fourth of theirs back. I knew this was what they would do, but it still hurts. We were winning, but not by enough of a margin to handle that kind of influx.

They needed the fresh blood, and not just for numbers. The enforcement officers in the field have lost their smiles and their will at the reality of being violent against those fully ready to return it. But these new officers are still young with the thrill. I'm sure they *think* they've been in fights before, but kicking or choking an unarmed civilian while your friends hype you up is not a fight. They're about to find out the difference.

With a portion of enforcement going to assist the officers emerging from the city, the path to the part of the wall I need to get to has never been clearer. All it would take is me turning my back.

What a good leader knows is how to trust. Learn to use your resources, Beloved.

And so I trust. I trust that my brother was right. I trust that my runners can fight as long and hard as we need them to. And because I trust Tear to lead them, I use my cuff to activate her armband, a blue light shining up in a quick burst. It's a promotion and a burden. I am telling the runners that Tear is in command now. I am telling Tear that she's been made general. Even among the bloodshed there are whoops from the runners.

I head away from the conflict. Two officers see me and break off to get in my way, but they've been out here too long. Their heart's not in it. The sound of enforcement coughing has become as common as battle cries, and their eyes are already red with the dual exposure of real sun and kicked up dust. Not us, though. Every hard thing the desert has thrown at us is worthwhile now, watching enforcement red-faced and struggling with their first taste of the things that raised us.

I use my nails across the face of one, then retract them to beat the other the old-fashioned way.

"Something's happening," Splice says, and I have to fight not to turn and run back.

Of course something is happening, but I've already made my

decision. I move toward the wall, because I don't want to see whatever destruction my absence allows. I left them alone, all of them, in the face of the second wave and I . . .

"Would you look at that," Splice says, and only the laughter in his voice lets me turn around.

I can see, technically, but my brain has trouble processing the sight before me. Jesus fuck. It's Wileyites. Dozens of them have pushed through and are blocking enforcement's path with their bodies and large plastic sheets to obscure their vision. I see a flash of familiar purple hair and I've just managed to grasp that these Wileyites are putting themselves in front of weapons to protect us when I see the second group. These are dressed like the first, but they aren't pale. They're Ashtown. The children we sent away, the adults who managed to immigrate, the ones I always thought never looked back. And there, at the edges with their sleeves rolled up, is Jax.

I knew I would cry today. But I did not think that the first thing that would bring tears to my eyes would be this unexpected sacrifice. I'd prepared to feel so many things on this battlefield, but now I am overwhelmed by hope.

Young Wileyites are keeping the officers from attacking us. The officers are pinned. They'll need to either shoot or trample their own kids to join the fray, and each of the Wileyite civilians are wearing recording face cameras. They'll need to arrest them, one by one. And they'll need to do it gently, wasting more time, or let the whole city know exactly how vicious they are.

We'd broadcasted into the city, but it wasn't a call to action. We didn't have enough hope for that. But it became one. Now dozens of young Wileyites are standing in front of enforcement shouting that the whole world is watching.

I leave the battlefield overwhelmed by the unexpected. I wonder if the Wileyites came to help because they've only met Ashtowners like Cara so they think we all want peaceful coexistence, even if we're the ones getting choked. Would they have come out if they knew I planned to destroy their entire way of life?

There's no telling. And anyhow, it's too late.

I disappear into the hologram of the wall.

—

"YOU FINALLY MADE IT," CROSS SAYS WHEN I ENTER THE TUNNELS.

He's bandaging up his own arm, and seeing it sends me back to my time in the pond, watching him train to care for others. I see the deep cut on his forehead and know, because I still remember the visions I had of him as a general, that it will scar. I'm cataloguing the abundance of other injuries on him, but when he looks up at me he's horrified.

"What happened to you?" he says.

I reach toward my throat—almost forgetting my claws and giving myself a new bloody smile—but then I realize he means my face. I've bitten through a few more arteries on the field, and that means blood has poured from my lower lip down my chin and neck. No wonder I made them afraid.

"It's not mine," I say, which doesn't put him at ease.

"Some of it is," he says.

"So what? Your lip is three times its normal size."

He smiles, threatening to resplit the aforementioned lip. "Yeah, but I'm not *royalty*."

A past me would have said, *Of course you are,* would have called him a holy prince, and spit when I said it. But I don't want to hurt him anymore.

"*Psh,* fuck off," I say instead.

We manage to work side by side in the tunnels for a whole thirty minutes before he pulls a Cross and opens his mouth.

"Are we going to talk about it?" he says, grabbing the puddy I'm holding and applying it to the wall.

"Pretty sure I can order you not to," I say.

"Pretty sure you won't," he says back, and he's right. He's known longer than the others that I was emperor's blood, so right now being alone with him is the most normal I've felt since my ascension.

That's probably eighty percent of why I did it . . .

He pulls himself up on an overhead rafter with one arm to check the puddy's placement.

. . . maybe seventy percent.

Okay, *yes,* after Cheeks and before my coronation, up to my neck in grief and guilt I went to get my injections from Cross and found myself wrapped around the person I would once have licked a running fan belt before I let touch me. And boy oh boy did I throw myself at that mistake, only for him to step back, push me away, and send me home.

"Nothing to talk about. I misread some signs. Happens. I said I was sorry," I say, checking my cuff even though we're in a holding pattern until I get the green light from Nik.

He stops and turns around, making me wish for the millionth time that he were shorter.

"You didn't want me," he says. "You hate me and you wanted to punish yourself for Cheeks by letting someone you hate touch you."

My mouth goes dry. He can't know. How could he know?

"What are you talking about?"

"It was your mission, he was previously injured because of you, he gave himself up for you. I know you blame yourself for his death."

I look down again at my cuff, but the screen's still dark so I might as well be staring at my own boots for how subtle I am.

"This the part where you tell me it's not my fault and I have nothing to feel bad about?"

"No," Cross says, and thank god for that. "This is the part where I remind you that Cheeks was a runner. We sign up to die, and die well. If you'd pushed him off a ledge for something to laugh at you could feel guilty. But I saw the vids Splice sent out. Cheeks died for something. That's what we're meant to do. We consent to it when we take the vow. Don't turn him into a civilian with your guilt."

It's the closest I've felt to comfort since I asked my best friend a question he could never have answered honestly, and it makes me mad at Cross, because it's a balm I don't deserve.

"Let's just finish checking these floors," I say, and we both pretend my voice doesn't crack a little.

I go quiet and he lets me, the way he always lets me, and it gives me just one more thing to feel guilty about.

"Listen, I'm a mess. I can't promise I'll ever not be a mess, but I'm definitely a mess now and that's why I shouldn't have gone over last night," I say. "But it's not because I didn't mean it. It's not because it wasn't real."

He looks . . . surprised. Like he just heard something impossible but, also, something he definitely wanted to hear.

"Whenever you're ready, you just say my name."

And we both know he doesn't mean Cross.

And we both know I'm going to.

WE'RE JUST FINISHING UP THE JOB WHEN I GET A CALL FROM SPLICE.

"I've lost audio, so I don't know what's happening. I just thought you should see in case something's going wrong."

As he speaks he sends over a feed. It's a room I've never seen, and it takes a second for my context clues to tell me I'm looking at the infusion room, the beating heart of Wiley City's artificial atmosphere. Adam is supposed to stall, pretend he's refusing to infuse the atmosphere because they won't open the doors, but he's typing furiously . . . and against his will. The back of his shirt is ripped open, and the mayor has a stunner aimed dead center at a collection of tech along his spine. Nik Nik and Cara are there too, surrounded by enforcement with weapons trained on them.

Is this part of the plan? I can't tell. Adam's body language is certainly projecting duress, but he's the king of bullshit. I can't imagine him actually being coerced into doing anything against his will, and it's just a stunner after all. Unless . . . is a stunner as good as a blade if your body is mostly tech? Is she threatening to stun him, or threatening to ruin his leg and arm and eye?

I can't tell. I stare at my brother's face on the feed, but he gives nothing away. I think I see his hand twitch, but is he playing with his rings in genuine nervousness, or counting down the seconds until he makes his move? Cara's too short for me to see her body language around the enforcement officers, and her face is the vast emptiness it's always been. I could see a thousand expressions there, or I could see the endless void of space.

I can't risk it. Instead of returning to the front lines as I had planned, I transmit orders directly to Tear's earpiece and send Cross to back her up on the field. Then I begin the climb that will lead me higher up in this city than I have ever been.

CHAPTER TWENTY-SIX

BECAUSE I'M NOT SURE OF THE SITUATION, THE BEST OPTION IS TO OBSERVE FROM ABOVE BEFORE DEciding what to do. The infusion tank was once on the highest floor, but like any ravenous beast the city keeps growing and growing, trying to eat the sun. Their ambition means there's ample construction scaffolding for me to climb for a better look. Normally, there'd be an annoying amount of enforcement here, protecting construction projects like real estate investors are the ones paying their salary instead of civilians. But we'd planned for that. With the battle below pulling resources from the city, there aren't enough people to spare for something as routine as patrolling.

Still, the mayor has retained four officers. She must know her battles—the one outside and the one to save her image—are going badly. If the other world comes over and takes even a single Wileyite's life, it will be the handful of dirt over the grave of her position. Will she even make it to reelection? Or will the Wileyites drag her out of her mansion and set her on fire? Okay, probably not that, but surely they have some method of angrily outing people in power. Something with paperwork, probably.

She's clearly working out of panic now. Holding her own—admittedly, least desirable—citizen hostage? Having her men detain the ruler of a nearby territory, making them AWOL for the battle below? She either thinks no one will find out, or she thinks no one will care.

Or, most likely, she just thinks that whatever happens to her, this will all be worth it. I don't have much in common with the mayor, but I do know the kind of desperation that alters morality. I understand her. Watching her so nervous—eyes darting around, the hand holding her weapon shaking like her whole world is falling apart and this one thing is all she has left—I know that whatever mistakes she's making, she believes in them. She didn't betray us for money, didn't campaign on hating us solely for power. She believes in everything she does. She's scared, she's always been scared, and she made her TV appearances and ran her campaign and passed her border laws to make everyone else as scared as she was.

And most of what she feared wasn't even real. No army of Ashtowners waiting to beat Wileyites to death, get their children pregnant, outlaw their gods. Just shadows being jumped at by someone whose only response to change is dread. Now it's time to make her dreams come true. Everything I know about cruelty I learned inside the wall, but I'll happily use Wiley tricks to give her an Ashtowner worth fearing.

I leap from the scaffolding, landing in the circle surrounding Nik and Cara so I can block stun blasts that come our way. I try to use my metal whip to wrench the stunner from the mayor's grasp, but this isn't a vidscene and I'm still new at the weapon, so all I manage to do is cut her wrist enough that she lets it drop . . . which is close enough for me to call it a victory. I turn my attention back to the soldiers around me, but there's no point. A flash of blue light surrounds us as my brother activates the trap he'd already set. My brother's hand wasn't twitching in the feed, he was tossing out the small, round conductors Splice uses to make electrified perimeters. The men never even realized they were standing on the mines until Nik tossed the active one, completing the circuit. He'd planned for this.

Establishing I'm useless here, I turn to see the mayor picking up the stunner in her other hand. She sees me coming and fires instinctively at Adam's back. I lunge forward, knowing I'm too late but needing to try, still expecting to get there just to hold my least favorite brother as he lies twitching on the ground. But that's not what happens. There are two flashes, one from the mayor's stunner, and one from the electrical pulse of it hitting an invisible force field that seems to be emanating from Adam's spine.

So his nervousness was bullshit. Of course it was. The first thing he probably did was ensure protections against stunners being used on him.

He glares at the mayor, who lets the stunner fall to her side, then he glares even harder at me.

"What are you doing here?"

I look from him to Nik, but they're both giving me the same eyebrow raise of judgment.

I smile crooked. "Saving you? Splice said he lost audio and the image on the feed looked . . . dire."

"He lost audio?" Cara asks.

"I knocked it out," Adam says.

"Why would you do that?" she asks.

"For the same reason I am about to knock out the video." He grins at the mayor. "No one needs to know about this."

He touches his eye, and I don't feel the change but I'm sure video's just cut out. Immediately, Splice cuffs me, confirming. I've just texted Splice not to worry when Adam holds up his palm, and the mayor seizes and goes down.

"You put a stunner in your palm? I just caught up with the magnets!" I say.

Adam winks at me, then says, "Visuals are out."

I don't realize he's not talking to me, or anyone else in the room, until the construction elevator rises in response to his words.

I'm surprised-not-surprised to see the vice mayor step off it. She looks at the mayor with no expression, no horror at seeing the twitching henchman on the ground, no surprise at seeing Nik Nik in her city.

"Are you ready to become mayor again?" Adam asks.

She nods, but not with excitement. I'd figured she was mayor on the other world. That's why she was first to come over, why she instinctively went to the mayor's suite. This mayor didn't exist there, so there was no one for her to lose the election to.

She crouches over the twitching form of the dark-haired woman who was once her colleague.

"I want you to understand, I'm not like you. This isn't about power. I could have come in, kept my head down, and let you stay. But do you know it only starts with Ashtown? The palace we went to, I'm sure you've thought about destroying it. My predecessor had already done that on my world. But that kind of destruction and hate doesn't have a border. It always comes back. It eats and eats and eats, finding new targets until there's no one left to swallow but the ones who sent it. It starts with those outside the wall, and it ends with the whole world."

Adam sighs, bored as ever. "You're new at this villain thing, but if you intend to kill them, there's really no point in explaining why."

The vice mayor turns. "I'm not a villain."

"Of course you are. No matter your reasons, there are people who will see nothing more than someone doing something terrible. Someone will come along that looks at you just like you're looking at her."

Her face had been so righteous, so certain, but now it was dimming. "You think we shouldn't kill her?"

Adam barks a laugh. "Please. I'd kill her for her haircut alone. People seeing you negatively is a terrible reason not to do anything. Sometimes, villains are precisely what the future wants."

"Stop infecting her with the lies you tell yourself," Cara says, but it wasn't just the vice mayor being infected. I'm not just listening to what Adam's saying; I'm praying it's true.

Adam looks at Cara, then rolls his eyes back to the vice mayor. "See?"

"Sorry, am I here to listen to your half-assed philosophy lecture, or do we have a job to do?" Cara says.

He huffs, but does make his way over to the infusion station. Cara must have been prepped, because she moves over to the console and begins working without needing additional direction, though she's careful to stand no closer to Adam than strictly necessary.

Adam takes a moment to look over his shoulder at Nik.

"I trust you'll take care of her?"

Nik Nik's been staring down at the mayor the whole time. "Can you stand?"

She sits up, moving shakily but eventually getting to her feet.

He doesn't move for a bit, his dead calm ratcheting up her anxious twitching. Even now, when he walks toward her, he moves slow. She's unsteady, but still holding her chin high, and I do admire that.

When she talks, it's the slow, telling fat-tongue of a stun. Adam's weapon must not be as powerful as the ones installed in Wiley's drones, or she wouldn't even be awake yet.

"I was just trying to—"

Nik Nik doesn't backhand her. He open-hand slaps her, curling his fingers at the last second to scrape across her skin. Four perfect slash marks. A death sentence.

"You have been found guilty of betraying Ashtown."

She swallows, the side of her face going red and puffy against the deep red gashes, but her eyes are still hard. She's still calculating.

"So what? I open the doors or you'll kill me?"

Nik Nik tilts his head. "We don't need you to open the doors."

"Then what do you want me to do?"

His look of elegant confusion doubles. "You've been found guilty. All you can do for Ashtown now is die."

And then my brother begins the slow process of beating a woman to death.

Cara is looking over her shoulder, but not interfering. I wonder how many warnings she got before they embarked on this plan. I wonder if she knew she was coming here to watch a murder. Another murder, I should say.

She looks at me and the hatred in her eyes makes the implication clear.

This is you. You're no different.

She's right. Trouble is, I take that as a compliment.

"Focus," Adam says, snapping her attention back to their work.

I don't look away. I make myself watch as the man who shares my blood reshapes the mayor in ways that make it look like the work of the universe. That's why we aren't using poisons, aren't throwing her over the wall so her body lands on the battlefield destabilizing her army even more. We need it to look like the same backlash from the incoming world that killed the others.

Earlier, Adam, Nik Nik, and I met up in his room to discuss who would do what. Nik volunteered for this job—to make a death so bloody no one would think it was human—but the startling thing, standing there with my brothers, was that any of us could have done it. For all our trying and drifting and name changing, we all grew up to be our father's children.

When he finishes, blood is splattered across his face as he reaches down and forces limbs to twist wrong, forces bones through skin. His work is thorough, and the mayor's body looks so much like Helene X's that warm liquid fills my mouth and I almost gag. But I don't. I keep steady, and when my brother—out of breath with swollen knuckles—turns to me and says, "Your turn," I'm ready.

I cuff Tear, giving the withdrawal order at the same time I contact the runners stationed at the tunnel entrances who've been warding people away. We might get most of them, but we won't get all. I cuff Cross with a countdown. My brother just killed one person, and it cost him pain and time and effort. But I am about to do far more damage, and I won't even break a sweat.

I get confirmation from Tear and the others that protocol is complete and they've withdrawn, so I use my cuff to pull up the screen my brothers decided I alone would be able to access. Nik didn't trust Adam with it, and Adam worried Nik would be too obvious a target and get captured before he could use it. This is my part, the last hard choice I will have to make. I take a breath. And hit the button.

It will be too late for the city to realize the fight outside was only ever a distraction. I told you my brother didn't want to start a war; he wanted to change the world. And now as the ground beneath us shifts and the loud roar of destruction rolls in, he has.

The mayor asked if we wanted her to open the doors.

No, that's what Cara would have wanted.

We want them to no longer have doors to open.

—

THAT NIGHT IN HIS ROOM WHEN MY BROTHER TOLD ME THE PLAN, HE SAID IT LIKE IT WAS HIS OWN, but I recognized Adam's fingerprints around the edges. The city thought we were making a treaty for Ashtown protection in exchange for Adam infusing the barsamin into the atmosphere. But we weren't. We were getting access to the atmosphere so we would never have to ask for anything again.

We knew the city would reject us, knew there would need to be a battle outside, but there's a reason there were no civilians with our caravan. We didn't come to win the fight. We didn't even come to get into the city walls. We came to distract them while we took those walls down. The influx of names on the tunnel logs weren't there because runners thought the walls would keep them safe. Runners were on the log because they were saying goodbye to the walls their ancestors carved while they laid out the stockpiled explosives to bring them down.

They won't be able to keep us out anymore, but they won't be able to keep their artificial atmosphere in either. Without the ring keeping the field concentrated, and with Adam increasing its potency to extend its distance, the artificial atmospheric field will radiate out, providing a shade umbrella for miles and miles. Yes, we'll get to benefit from the barsamin shielding us from other worlds, but we'll also get Wiley's artificial atmosphere. The carpet of dead plants outside of the city will turn into a garden again. No more bodies scorched by bright days. No more being limited to growing what can be kept indoors or what is charproof. No more skin sickness in our children or elderly. This will change everything, forever.

If I die today it will be happy. Those who built the city were never paid for their labor. They are never acknowledged in the city's history. That makes those walls and everything in them stolen, and everyone knows you're allowed to take back what doesn't get paid for. Really, they're lucky. We're only taking the wall. We're letting them keep their homes, and we built some of those, too.

I meant what I said to Cara. This is how we can peacefully coexist, the only way, when one entity doesn't hold the existence of the other in its firm grasp. We'll grow all our own food now. And if our people in the wastes get caught out in a bright day, they'll run toward Ashtown, not the city.

It's worth everything I've done. When I die, and Cheeks greets me with fire and rage, I'll tell him the same. I'll take nothing back.

—

I RUN TO THE EDGE AND WATCH AS THE SHOCK WAVE OF CRASHING METAL ECHOES ACROSS THE DESERT on one entire side of the city. We made sure that the pieces of the wall fell straight down, instead of laying the debris long across the desert. It's a fantastic crash, but once everything settles, Wiley will see how lucky they are. City ordinances stating that no construction can be closer than ten feet to the edge means we get to peel the wall away like fruit skin, taking only the exteriors of some older construction with it. There are a few floors too close to the impact zone to avoid the devastation, but those would be the very ones, in fact, that Adam had the city evacuate for our use. If they never evacuated because they never intended to give us refuge, then it's by their own ruler's hand that they die.

Decades ago, I watched from a view just like this as a family died under a light that was so bright I was only kept safe by feet of specially tinted glass. The window that separated us that day is broken now, and I watch as a blue glow stretches across the sky out into the vast desert. It will protect my people from one threat that is multiversal and new to us, and one threat so known to us it is kin, a threat as old as fire.

I close my eyes and breathe in a scent that is common to me now, but has never been detected in Wiley before: hot, dirt-scented wind. Wileyites are about to get their first taste of the desert they've lived in their whole lives.

The vice mayor—mayor now, though her people don't know that—is already gone. Down below, she will rally first responders, organize a head count, and stand on rubble while pretending she's not posing for pictures as she takes the mantle of city's hero. It will look like she rose to the challenge. It will look like she was meant to be mayor all along. It will not look like she was in on it, and had a week to make the best possible plan before the event happened.

I turn back to the infusion room, still giddy with disbelief, when all the joy drains from me.

"Um . . . guys . . . ?" I swallow hard, staring.

Adam doesn't turn, but Cara does, and she goes still when she sees what I see.

Outlined in blue-white light are Cara and Adam. Different versions of them, but still them. This Adam is still, visibly, only organic. This Cara's face has no lines save those made by her cheekbones. But they hover and stare with the same intense curiosity of their counterparts.

Adam finally turns and freezes. He stares at his own face, the face that used to be his, as if he's seeing it for the first time. I swear he doesn't even recognize the man in the suit with the meticulous hair, but then he blinks, looks down, and returns to the console.

"This doesn't matter. We still have ten minutes," he says.

"Are you sure?" I ask.

"You're questioning my math? Of all people?"

"I'm not questioning your math, I'm questioning his," I say, pointing to the other Adam. He looks at me when I do. "He can see us. Wouldn't he assume you're interfering and try to stop it? Speed up the timeline? What would you do?"

Adam pushes one final series of buttons on the console, then turns around. His other self is directly behind him, frowning as he takes in the modifications.

"He . . . he wouldn't trust anyone else to ensure his vision's safety," Adam says. He crosses his arms. "I would come over myself, and bring my most trusted assistant, and maybe some muscle, with me."

He looks at the blue-white-light version of Cara, and then at the Cara beside him. The Adam and Cara on the other earth are standing close together, too close to just be associates.

"The atmosphere is infused, it will be up to full potency soon . . . but I think it will be too late for you and me."

He keeps staring at her until I think, even now, she will ignore his existence, but eventually she turns.

"You knew," Cara says. "You knew there was a chance we wouldn't make it."

He looks up. Their blue-white-light counterparts are standing eye-to-eye with them now. The unmarked Adam and Cara staring themselves down. Are they marveling at how much their other selves have been through? Thinking about how it didn't matter, because it's the Cara who's seen less death that will win, and the Adam who has clearly never fallen that will be victorious?

The ghosts mouth something to each other that we can't hear. No, I guess the blue Adam and Cara aren't the ghosts. Ours are the condemned, the walking dead.

"No," Nik says, as if this is something over which he has domain. "No, there must be a way. You should have told me. We could have gotten you to the cave."

"That wasn't an option. I can't be in two places at once. I'm the only one who could do the infusion." His eyes flick back to the other Adam. "He's not the only one who wouldn't trust someone else with his vision."

Nik Nik grabs his brother's arms, to shake him, to squeeze him, to hit him, to dig his nails in and keep him here forever.

"Don't be dramatic," Adam says, though he looks like he might cry.

I think back to when we first met, all that chaos ago, in his low-level apartment. I'd wondered then if he had anything to live for, but that wasn't what he lacked. He was looking for something to die for.

"Should have known no one could kill you but you, Bosch," Cara says, wiping her nose on the back of her hand. "You're such a piece of shit."

Adam turns to her. "Are you mad I brought you? Who would you have stand here in your stead? One of his mildly techy runners? What's his name . . . Splice?"

She shakes her head quick, and I know she's thinking of the man we talked about, a man she still believes died because of her.

"This is the only thing you've ever been right about. It had to be me," she says.

"Is there anyone you want to call?" I ask Cara. "Do you want me to give Dell a message?"

I don't care that she thinks I'm shit. I'd let her berate me raw as long as it meant I got to know she was out there, somewhere, still alive with her bleeding heart and her lofty principles.

She shakes her head. "Dell should be back in the cave with the kids by now, outside of signal range. I recorded a vid before I left . . . just in case. Esther has it. She'll give Dell hers now and my kids"—her voice breaks here, but she works hard to get ahead of it—"she'll give them theirs when they're old enough to understand."

It's disrespectful to cry for her right in front of her face, but I can barely hold back.

"Right. Smart move," I say, wiping furiously at my face.

"Oh . . . oh! . . . that *is* unpleasant," Adam says.

He cradles his ribs and only then do I look, really look, at the clothes he's wearing. He's chosen this outfit—the wide-legged black pants, the white collared shirt—deliberately. He wants to die in it. Wants to be remembered in it. I don't have the heart to tell him how little of it will be left.

He goes to his knees as I hear the joints of his legs bend sharply, and in the wrong direction. The sound that escapes through his clenched teeth is half growl and half whimper. His organic arm snaps at the elbow, and he falls forward, catching himself on his mechanical one.

"I promised . . . myself . . . I wouldn't . . ." The popping out of his shoulder interrupts him, but he presses on. ". . . scream."

His spine begins to curve and he won't want to but I know he will scream, he will scream and scream and the damage will be so bad it will be all he can do. I don't want to watch, but he deserves my witness, so I keep my eyes open. His spine begins to stretch, and I prepare to see the most arrogant, intelligent, unbeatable man I've ever known broken in half.

The sound that rings out is so loud, I'm the one who screams.

When Adam falls over, a hole in his forehead and his rigid limbs suddenly at peace, I'm still not sure what has happened. Nik Nik is holding a right angle made of metal, its barrel still breathing smoke into the air, and it clicks for me. Nik Nik has finally used his secret gun.

There will be those that say in the end, Nik Nik never loved his brother, just used him up then paid him back for abandoning him all those years ago. They'll be wrong. Because there was nothing but love on Nik's face as he pulled the trigger, nothing but hurt on it after. Loving someone enough to put them down, even when you're the one who will miss them most, is a gift. I hope one day I am loved like that. I hope Cheeks knows he was.

No one speaks for a while, then Cara does at last.

"Didn't think you'd ever use it, Second Son."

Nik growls when he turns to her. "No one calls me that and lives."

"Don't worry," she says, cradling her own ribs while looking at the still body of Adam Bosch. "No one ever will again."

And just like that he understands. He'll never be the second son again, never be a little brother again. It isn't just Adam who has died, but a version of Nik Nik that only Adam could claim to know. One day, I know, this will be me. Nik Nik will turn to ash and with him will burn the one who made me a sister, who made me belong.

The light crackles over his body, and for a moment I see Adam the way I never knew him. He's standing over the body, looking as he must have before he crossed the wrong garbage git. His hair is still black, his face symmetrical, and he's staring with an intensity that scares me. He looks up from the mangled corpse of himself, and his eyes widen.

"Don't. I'm your—"

And Nik Nik uses his gun for the second time. The second Adam drops beside the first, head tilted to look at our Adam, just as our Adam's head is tilted to look at him. It's as if even in death the bodies of the other selves are seeking each other.

"Here it comes," Cara says, and suddenly my attention is pulled from the still bodies to the new one in the making.

My brother will mourn for Adam, but I'd have shot him myself to keep Cara here. It's not just knowing her. It's her special rareness. It's all of the impossible things she's seen. Watching her go won't even feel like witnessing a human dying. It will be like saying goodbye to another creature entirely, something that was the last of its kind.

She goes to her knees and sits back on her feet, face turned up like the sky is her friend and it's time to greet it. I move beside her. She looks up at Nik.

"Don't kill me, when I get here. I'm usually . . ." She clenches her teeth. ". . . pretty cool."

"Are you scared?" I don't intend to ask it, but it slips out. "Do you want to take my hand?"

She takes a breath. "I've been on stolen time for years, Scales. I'm not scared. Just grateful."

She turns back to the empty space where the blue version of her had been before it faded out, like she is greeting an enemy of old. And she must be. How many times has death courted her and missed? She's still sporting that amused smile, and I stare at her even though she's not seeing me. I want to be able to tell others—Dell, her children, anyone who will listen—how brave and defiant she is in this moment. I want them to know I was more scared than she was.

She flinches as the pressure increases, but her smile doesn't fade.

"Let's see what all the fuss is about," she says, and she sounds almost excited to see death up close for the last time.

But it's not meant to be.

The light gathers, but instead of breaking our Cara, a different, unstriped version of her falls mangled to the ground where she's on her knees. Even from here it's clear she's dead. In the battle of the universes, our Cara won.

Cara shakes her head. "No . . . no, this was it. Wasn't this it?"

"It's okay," I say, touching her shoulder. "You survived. Everything's okay."

She doesn't take it like the good news I mean for it to be.

I look over at the console. "The atmosphere has finished infusing. She must have tried to come over second and gotten caught, just like the other Nik."

She's not listening. She moves forward, shaking her double. Moving her like she's going to wake up, even though no body has ever looked as conclusively dead as this one does. Eventually she moves backward.

"This is a good thing," I say, and mean it. I didn't want to let her go. Didn't want to have to be the one to tell Dell that the star she stood watch over all those years winked out the moment she was in my hands.

"I can't die," she says, first as a whisper into her hands, but then she lifts her eyes to mine. "I don't think I can die."

Whatever is distressing her isn't going to be fixed tonight, and we need to move.

"We stay around here much longer, we're gonna find out," I say. "Tensions are high. Best not to be here when they find the mayor's body."

Nik Nik hasn't said a word since Adam's death, but he has been busy. He's taken the mayor's stunner and wrapped it with cloth to leave only her prints, then bashed the otherworld's Adam in the forehead with it until the skull caved, obscuring the bullet wound. He puts the stunner back in the mayor's hand, creating a story of her murdering the intruding Adam that will give her followers something to lick their wounds with. He uses a long nail to pop the bullet out of the wall.

"Ready," he says, picking up the body of our Adam. His Adam, really. *His* because only Nik will mourn him, and *his* because he is the one who killed him.

We've walked down ten floors when the dirt in my nose gets corrupted by something too sweet. Almost against my will, I slow to a stop surrounded by the smell of a familiar garden. We're taking the runner's path all the way down, so I can see through the false wall but my mother can't see in. She's standing outside, just like everyone else who heard the crash. Confused and curious, but not as relieved as you'd think. The people this high up aren't grateful to have dodged this tragedy, because they don't actually believe any bad could have happened to them. It's a spectacle; not a near miss.

And I have never been more sure that she is just like the rest of them. And I have never been more sure that I am not.

"What is it?" my brother asks, my stop allowing him to catch up despite his heavy load.

"Nothing," I say, and turn away for what I know will be the last time. I hadn't thought about it until now, but this is goodbye.

When we make it to the meetup point, a shape I mistake for a rock unfolds itself into a form that, I swear to god, is not taller than me. Being Jack Ketch has taught Cross how to blend in with his surroundings. He's more injured than I left him, but he's alive. Without a word he follows me to transport.

Before we head back to the palace, I turn back and look at the city. I'm emperor's blood now, and I'll never come back to Wiley City again. I wait for a moment, poking at my heart just to see if I'm going to mourn it. I don't feel a thing. Ruth was right. I told you: Oldheads always are eventually. Snakes don't crawl back into their old skins. They eat them for extra nutrients. Cheeks isn't the only old skin I've outgrown. Wiley was first. Now I've destroyed it to fuel my own growth. Just like snakes do.

With the wall gone, I can see into her streets, and, on the lower levels, into her buildings, little squares of things and people, like an open dollhouse. It's like seeing someone vain, someone who used to wear makeup and do their hair, with their face ripped off. It's all orbital sockets and teeth. I don't feel guilty. How can I, when if I lower my eyes to the dirt, Em is counting our dead. These bodies, these ones are mine. I went with this plan. I led them to death knowing it would be death. I added them to the pile I started with my father, more friends I've killed to keep Cheeks company.

Tomorrow there will be more collection, more identification, more families crying as they are informed. We will come together to mourn a crop of bodies twisted in violence. But it will be the last time.

As we make our way back to Ashtown, the story is set, though there will still be whispers. The city will never really believe Adam Bosch is dead. Ashtown will never really believe Cara is still alive. We are making our way into the night with two legends. Three, if my brother counts. Not me though. I'm just the witness. Just the storyteller.

CHAPTER TWENTY-SEVEN

OFFICIALLY, WILEYITES ARE ONLY ALLOWED TO BE BURIED IN THE SUICIDE BOGS, NOT THE ONES IN sunlight. But there's not much official about this funeral. There have been massive ceremonies throughout the desert, even a few in the city now that the threat from the other world has passed, filled with Ashtowners and Wileyites crying side by side. The mayor herself attended Cheeks's funeral. While we were infusing the atmosphere, a few of the other world's dops managed to come over, bringing a wave and panic and horror perfect for the new mayor to ride. And she did. She emerged as their protector. Afterward, she gave speeches about how hate and separation led to this destruction, and how only love and togetherness can mend it. It is the first time the same thing had come to kill Ashtown and Wiley both, and overcoming it has bonded us somehow, temporary though it may be. She even cried good fake tears at the other mayor's funeral, though I didn't attend that one. I heard Cheeks's was bigger, and less protested. So there's that.

We still call the local drinking hole Blay's, but Ruth has been running it since the battle. Blay didn't die on the field, but seeing Sai go down mixed with his own injuries reawakened every ghost of battles past, and the only way he knows to quiet them is drink. Most days he's in the alley by the House—sitting under the shade of its wide awning that is now a luxury, not a necessity—or walking through the newly resurrected garden grabbing something to eat. We pass him rations when we see him, even buy him a bottle or two when we're flush, because it's the least we can do. He's our reminder that doing the right thing doesn't protect you from consequences. All the medals in the world won't take away the scars. Once, I nearly gave myself a heart attack dropping off some spare meals for him, when I saw Helene X bent down to give him water in the alley. I thought it was Blay's homegoing and I was seeing spirits, but then Helene looked at me and I realized I was wrong. I nodded and left the food in the alley, without making a comment about how long Helene's dop was letting his hair grow, or how interesting it was that he'd ended up at the House too.

In the wake of the battle, Splice dealt with his survivor's guilt by going online under a hundred usernames and blaming just about everything he could on the dead mayor. Even down to the wall compromise being her fault, for caring more about funding enforcement than infrastructure. Most everyone knows we're the ones who took out the wall, but they generally buy that it was an act of desperation that she forced.

I bet Cara'd love this, Ashtown and Wiley together in giddiness over their own unexpected survival. But I'm not sure she's paying much attention to the world anymore. The last time I saw her I dropped her at the cave with her family, but her eyes were somewhere else. I gave her a message to give to Esther, and she agreed to do it, but her voice was like an afterthought. Like she wasn't speaking, just had spoken, and my brain was remembering it like an echo.

"No one else can come here," she said. "Like you did."

I nodded. "We'll make sure of it."

And she knew I didn't mean the *we* of Ashtown or the *we* of Nik Nik and me. It is the *we* of me and Cara, the only two people in the desert who know what it's like to let too much of that darkness in.

Dell walked out of the cave, and Cara let her hold her for a moment before retreating into the shadows. I couldn't shake the feeling that she was disappearing into a different darkness altogether, that the second she faded from my view the inky black that lives between worlds would swallow her up forever.

"How do you do it?" I asked Dell. "How do you love someone who feels so out of reach?"

"Loving someone who feels larger than life, who feels too close to power you can't comprehend? It's easy, once you learn to be grateful for every second, and not assume you'll be granted a future." Dell's eyes were unfocused, and it took me a second to realize she wasn't talking to me. She was looking straight at Cross.

Cara and Dell are not here tonight, but I didn't think they would be. I know how little Cara thinks of me, but I don't think she hated anyone as much as Adam. Everyone else who knows Adam's real identity is here though—me, Nik, Cross, and, unsurprisingly, Exlee—waiting at the bogs to send the firstborn son of the emperor into the dark for good. I suspect Viet knows as well, but he has so much work right now we wouldn't ask him to take time out, especially not to break his own rules.

Nik has wrapped Adam in a ceremonial cape I don't recognize, and I wonder if he had already made one for Adam just like he had one waiting for me, a light left on in case we ever found our way home. And Adam has found his way home, at last. He may have seemed like a monster or a serial killer in the city, but so does a croc when it gets loose downtown. Here, being put to rest alongside the body of a man like Nik Senior, he makes perfect sense. He belongs in this den of murderers.

And so do I.

Burial restrictions aren't the only rules being broken tonight, and Cross is wearing a tunic he isn't even supposed to own and reading from a book he's not supposed to touch. But no one could condemn him for giving Nik Nik the gift of seeing someone who understands grace speaking about his brother like he is a part of something bigger.

Cross draws a mark on Adam's forehead, then whispers in his ear. He reaches down and cuts a lock of hair from the black side of Adam's scalp, and then one from the white. Both locks go into a jar beside the body. He takes a handful of black bog sand from right beside the liquid pool and pours that into the jar too.

"Adranik Nazarian, I commend you into the earth, whom you loved, and whom you tried so hard to know. I return you to the denser reality of the creator of all. Don't be scared. Don't regret. Good or bad, the mark you made will remain. In your dark and your light, we will recall the shape of you always. Whatever time you had, it was enough. Whatever you accomplished, it was enough. We will remember your good deeds for the rest of our lives. We will forget your wrongdoings forever. Thank you, thank you, thank you, for spending your time in the dirt with us."

Cross nods, signaling the time for goodbyes has begun. Our last chance to speak to Adam, and to give him messages to take to other dead we believe he'll meet. Nik Nik speaks fiercely, almost angrily. I wonder if he's still speaking to Adam, or if he's letting our father know one more time exactly what he thinks of him. Exlee goes next; it's quick and elegant. I'm sure they have nothing to say to Adam, but we've only just buried Helene X, and maybe there was something they forgot to say. I walk up slowly, bending down.

"Hey, fucker," I say, so he'll know it's me. "Thanks. I don't think you were a good person and, I gotta say, you were a real shit brother. But you helped bring that wall down. You kept us safe. You were a villain. And a shithead. But we needed you, and there you were."

I take a breath, uncomfortable with talking, uncomfortable with the feelings pressing too big inside my chest.

"Tell Helene X how good I did? Tell her I brought the wall down, and tell her it was a little bit for her. We ripped the face off the place that wouldn't let her wear her own, and I want her to know that."

I gnaw at my bottom lip. "And tell, tell Cheeks . . . tell him he's a fucking hero. Tell him how they chanted his name in the streets. And the statue! Tell him how they're talking about making a statue of him to symbolize all the Ashtowners lost to Wiley violence. Tell him every eye in the desert's wet for him. Tell him there'll be at least a dozen kids named after him, and that even the Wiley teens are gonna get tattoos of his face. But, do me a favor? When you tell him . . . don't say it was me that said. Make sure he never has to hear my name ever again, okay? Okay."

I turn away sharp so I don't cry on my oldest brother's face. Adam wouldn't like it if my tears landed on him, making it look like he'd ever cried a day in his goddamn life.

Cross watches me go, and I pretend I don't see him seeing me cry. Eventually he leans forward.

"I take refuge in the dirt. I take refuge in the ash. I take refuge in the oil," he says.

We repeat the words back to him.

"I go to the dirt for refuge. I go to the ash for refuge. I go to the oil for refuge."

We repeat the words again.

Cross closes his eyes. "So let it be done."

He motions Nik and I to the body, and we each hold a side as we place him in the bog, where he sinks faster than any corpse I've seen. I know it's the weight of the mods, but it just feels like Adam's own impatience, irritated at all this sentimentality.

This was how he was supposed to die, originally. The stories condemned him to death by the emperor's hand in a bog just like this one. They weren't true then, but he is there now, in the way that all stories become true eventually.

Cross presents Nik with the mourning candle, a jar of wax containing Adam's hair and sand from the grave. The idea is you light the candle when you miss your dead, when you want to speak to them. By the time the candle's out, you're not supposed to need them anymore. Not sure I buy it, because my brother is shaking like he's been orphaned all over again.

I am fiercely grateful that no one else is here, because the way he takes Exlee's hand, like they are holding him up, is something I want to happen, and it couldn't if there was even one more pair of eyes in this circle of firelight.

And because I'm emperor's blood now, because I took the vow to be armed and alert every second just like Nik did, my brother is able to close his eyes and relax into the person he loves. I can't give my brother much, but I can promise this. I can keep my hands ready so his can be held by the one person in this desert who does know how to heal, how to give even the emperor peace.

Eventually, my brother dismisses me with a nod. I turn away from them, two of the most powerful rulers in the whole wide wastes, who love each other, but love their people enough to keep it secret. When I walk to my ride Cross is leaning against it, arms crossed, eyes trained on me. His stare is intense and unapologetic. My heart beats like a piston as I walk toward a body I used to only think of as being too pale and too tall. I'm so nervous I'm shaking with it. The fire at my back reflects in his eyes too bright, painting his skin a white-gold still flushed pink with heat. If he wanted to take pity on me, Cross would look down, or smile, or wave. Anything to add casualness to this encounter, however false.

But he isn't making it easier on me. The thing between us has grown unignorable. He's waited until my last obligation has passed to force a reckoning, but he's done letting me hide. Which is fine, because I'm done hiding, too. I won the war against the other world, so I'm happy to lose the battle against wanting to touch him, against letting myself be loved by someone who dares to talk to God, against remembering that even though I tell people the first word I thought when I saw him was *hate,* the truth was that first word I thought, all those years ago, when we were children misunderstanding each other outside of the House, was *want.*

I've said before that he's not humble, just quiet, and right now he's proving it. Because his crossed arms and the lilt in his mouth that rises a little with each step I take toward him are the most arrogant things I've ever seen. I stop moving when our feet are nearly touching, and our eyes are perfectly parallel because even now I'm not sure which of us is taller and I refuse to accept we are the exact same size. It doesn't matter, because the last thing I want to be with him is vertical anyway.

"Yeah?" he asks, when I keep staring.

"You as strong as you look, Michael?"

He uncrosses his arms. "Come try me, Devon."

Then my hands are in his hair, and his are in mine, and our mouths meet each other with decades of suppressed intensity.

And for the first time, the very first time, I know what it's like to get exactly the thing you wanted.

—

AFTER THE BATTLE OF ASHTOWN—WE CERTAINLY DIDN'T NAME IT—I CONTINUED MY TREATMENT FOR heavy metal poisoning until my nightmares went away completely. Then, slowly, I began to lose my memories of the other worlds and possible realities I had seen. Cara's marks have only gotten darker, and have never faded. I wonder if that means her memories don't either. We'll never know, because after that night she drifted away again, her legend a little more complex than the last time she became a story.

I may have forgotten what I have seen, but there are things I won't allow myself not to know. Like how I know that even though I will never be a person for whom there is only one other, the holy runner I've chosen will be the one who is with me through it all. That on the day I fear the most—the day my brother takes his place in the bogs, the day I stop being a sister forever—Cross will be holding my hand the way Exlee held Nik's when we sent Adam away.

And I know that the night we took down the wall, Esther found her way to the coordinates I had Cara give her, where one invader from the other world was able to slip through before the window closed. Because Adam was right, he would have brought muscle, but this one's body wasn't near the others, so he manifested outside the city, where Viet was preparing a martyr for burial. I know that she saw him across the moonlit desert, the way I used to see him when we went riding at midnight, but without tattoos, with no promises to the emperor. She saw a version of him that never made an oath, and I don't know what happens next.

I don't want to know, but I want to tell myself stories. Stories of a man who has only ever been called D'Angelo finding peace in serving someone completely who will never hurt him. Who follows gods with fervor and maybe never knows he once followed the emperor the same way. Who has kids if he still wants them, but whose kids will never call me *Aunty* like we talked about. Who finds a few extra slabs of metal, or pounds of rations, left on his door in tough times and who never knows where they come from, but swears he sees the outline of a tall woman in the distance.

He'll tell other people about her, but it will just be a story, one he will become bored with. One he will forget.

I don't mind. Some stories are too complicated to stay, too heavy to be carried on the wind, and when he forgets about me completely I bet it will feel just like being forgiven.

The thing I won't let myself forget—the thing that lingers even after I have forgotten the location of the cave, the feeling of enemy blood running down my chin, and everything else I swore would never leave me—is a memory that never happened. It's from a world where Ashtown and the Rurals merged, where my mother sent me back to my father when I was just a toddler. Which means it's from a world where something I'd only dreamed became possible.

Three children: a gangly Ruralite, a squat downtown boy so brave and so kind, and a girl with an edgy wildness who looks at the walls of the city like an old enemy. They play in the dunes laughing loud until a bright day forces them inside. The three stand at the window, watching in anticipation for the color to seep back into the world. The downtown boy puts one arm around each.

"Watch," he says, pulling them tight. "This is the best part."

ACKNOWLEDGMENTS

How does one write the acknowledgments for a book that was already written as a love letter? Truth be told, when I sold *The Space Between Worlds* it was a one-book contract, and I wrote those acknowledgments like I would never get the chance to write them again. Surprise! Much of what I said three years ago remains true. I still think my agent, Cameron McClure, is an angel (with teeth) who somehow puts up with my heinous schedule, and values me and my work highly enough to remind me not to accept less than my worth. I still think my editor, Sarah Peed, is the absolute best, (and not just because everyone deserves an editor who knows what a "service top" is), and that the team at Del Rey is made up of the most talented people I could ask to work with. I still count myself lucky to have been mentored generously under (and tolerated by) the likes of Jay Clayton and Pat Rosal. I still have love for the community of friends and writers I met along the way at UC Riverside, Rutgers-Camden, Vanderbilt, and in the wild.

But back then I only *thought* I knew what it meant to be grateful. In the years since the world has ended in so many big and small ways, it's permanently altered what appears in my mind when I even think the word "gratitude." I am still grateful to many of the people I was grateful to before, but now I have the absolute blessing of having felt their love and loyalty in the midst of the chaos and uncertainty of the last few years.

A special thanks to some of my oldest friends: Katheryn Root, for your constant care and concern, and for being one of the few who understands what it means to leave the desert that made us. And all my love to Joaquin Magos, for being the best of men, and Garrett Marak, for thinking of me even in your darkest times. As always I remain indebted to those amazing writers from Rutgers who welcomed me back when I returned to the Northeast: Nina St. Pierre, Deena ElGenaidi, Shelby Vittek, Melanie McNair, Juliana Roth, and Tim Lynch.

Three years ago, I thanked members of my cohort—specially Tori Hoover, Julianne "Gigi" Adams, and Wesley Boyko—for being welcoming. Now I want to echo that and so much more. I am so grateful to Tori, who, when the world first shut down and we were all distracted by our own survival, took the time to make bread and jam for others. And to her wife, Ian Round, who is also our dad, but not our Daddy, because that is a role filled by his dad. Gigi, who lends traits to a character in this book with some major differences, for putting her body on the line and deploying the privilege that could have kept her safe to help others. Wesley, who despite all appearances and theories does not appear in this book, because I always knew when I got arrested, you'd be arrested next to me, and you were. Every. Single. Time. Since I last wrote my acknowledgments there has been a tornado, a global pandemic, two wars, and an insurrection, but I am still writing these acknowledgments in the same way: sitting across from you at a café while you read some dead German man you're smarter than. And to everyone else who made Vanderbilt a home in my time there: Ethan Calof, for being curious and excited for something as small as high-watching terrible television or as big as a self-discovery trip into the desert; Webster Heath, for loving me like a cousin; Lucy SooMin Kim, for the times when our four-hour long phone calls were the only things keeping me sane.

To the members of the People's Plaza who lent their names or various traits to the runners in this book: Jama Mohamed (Mr. Splice), Emily Radigan (Mr. Em), Ruth Madeleine Reeves (General Ruthless), Adriantez "Kasai" Ellison (Mr. Sai), Jay Terry (Mr. Tear), Black Dragon, and Blaylock. And to all of the freedom fighters who were not only at the Plaza, but also active in building the community that followed.

The time before my book was released could not have prepared me for the incredible generosity of spirit I would find in authors whose works and careers are so much bigger than mine. Thank you so much to Mary Robinette Kowal, Alex White (and all the Smokies!), and Stina Leicht for making me feel like I belonged in a place I never imagined I would reach.

A huge thank you to Ophira Calof, and the sex providers who wish to remain anonymous, for lending your expertise, intelligence, and experience to ensure I presented disabilities and sex work in a way that did the least harm. Any mistakes made or offense caused is entirely my fault, and occurs despite, not because of, their generous critiques.

My biggest *thank you!* I reserve for the readers. Nothing made every dark night of the last three years bearable like the thought of you out there, arguing about your ships (have fun with this one lol) and drawing the kind of art I would like to tattoo on my face, because it makes me feel warm in a way I cannot describe. Thank you to the community of readers and fans at the B2Weirdos, Balticon, and every single book club that chose *The Space Between Worlds* to share with their friends.

And, as always and forever, to my sisters Trevia "Misty" Johnson and Vichelle Johnson. We are the sisters Johnson, and we can do anything . . . but agree. Until next time, (because I've finally learned that it's okay to believe in a next time).

—KYA

ABOUT THE AUTHOR

MICAIAH JOHNSON is the Compton Crook Award–winning author of *The Space Between Worlds*. Her debut novel was a *New York Times* Editors' Choice, and was named one of the best books of 2020 and one of the best science fiction books of the last decade by NPR. She was raised in California's Mojave Desert surrounded by trees named Joshua and women who told stories. She received her bachelor of arts in creative writing from the University of California, Riverside, and her master of fine arts in fiction from Rutgers-Camden. She now studies American literature at Vanderbilt University, where she focuses on critical race theory and automatons.